Garrett Haines

About the Author

KATHRYN MILLER HAINES is an actor,
mystery writer, award-winning playwright,
and the artistic director of a Pittsburgh-
based theater company. She is the author
of *The War Against Miss Winter*.

THE WINTER OF HER
Discontent

Also by Kathryn Miller Haines

Fiction
The War Against Miss Winter

THE WINTER OF HER

Discontent

KATHRYN MILLER HAINES

HARPER

NEW YORK • LONDON • TORONTO • SYDNEY

HARPER

HarperCollins books may be purchased for educational, business, or sales promotional use. For information please write: Special Markets Department, HarperCollins Publishers, 10 East 53rd Street, New York, NY 10022.

FIRST EDITION

Library of Congress Cataloging-in-Publication Data is available upon request.

ISBN 978-0-06-113980-2

08 09 10 11 12 ID/RRD 10 9 8 7 6 5 4 3 2 1

For Rebecca Margot and Christopher Claude.
Do great things. Be good people.
And for Garrett, who continues to read despite
the absence of dragons and trolls.

Acknowledgments

I CONTINUE TO BE OVERWHELMED by all the people who encourage me as I tell Rosie's tales. I'd like to thank my wonderful editor, Sarah Durand; her assistant, Emily Krump; and the rest of the talented staff at HarperCollins for all the work they do to make these books possible. I am also indebted to my agent, Paul Fedorko, for his advice and wisdom, and to Gregg Kulick, for his brilliant cover designs.

I couldn't write without the ruthless criticism, razor-sharp wit, and cheap wine offered by the talented members of SPEC, among them David Doorley (see? I said your name this time!), Beverly Pollock, F. J. Hartland, Judy Meiksin, Carol Mullen, Jeff Protzman, and Paula Martinac.

I am eternally grateful to Ralph Scherder and my first reader, David White, for their amazing critiques, good humor, and deft skill at getting me off the ledge.

For their generous support of all things Rosie, I am indebted to Mary Alice, Richard, and the entire staff at Mystery Lovers Bookshop. I'd also like to acknowledge The Six whose support, advice, and good humor keep me sane.

Families are unpredictable beasts, but I've been very fortunate to have one that shows me overwhelming love and support. For those who are related to me by blood, and those who might as well be, I offer my sincere thanks, especially to Loretta Miller, Stephen and Nancy Miller, Pamela and James Nicholson, Barb von der Haar, Larry Haines, and Wendy Gressman.

While I might write about backstabbing actors, monomaniacal

directors, and divas of all shapes and sizes, I have the good fortune not to perform with them. I am grateful to the immensely talented Randy "Bruno" Oliva, Steve Werber, Chris and Laura Bondi, Scot Rutledge, Randy Kirk, Carla "shiny object" Delaney, and Barbara Williams, for not just encouraging my nontheatrical pursuits, but for reminding me why I love theater and the people who do it.

I'd also like to acknowledge Dan Vancini. You know what you did and I thank you.

And always last, never least, I must express my gratitude to my four-legged assistants: Mr. Rizzo, Violet, and Chonka. You may not have thumbs or the ability to engage in commerce, but you support me all the same.

1 Just Around the Corner

March 1943

SOME GUYS BROUGHT YOU FLOWERS; Al brought meat.

"What the deuce is this?" I asked him. He was standing on the front steps of the George Bernard Shaw House, cradling two T-bones wrapped in blood-stained butcher paper as if they were puppies he'd just helped to whelp.

"I heard you've been low," he said. "I thought you could use a pick-me-up."

"And you thought meat would do the job?"

"Not meat, Rosie—steak, see?" He tossed me the package as if a closer acquaintance with the gory mass might up my enthusiasm.

I held the package at a safe distance from my coat. Blood leaked through the paper, creating a map of lands that didn't exist. "While I appreciate the gesture, I've got enough trouble in my life without bringing black market beef into the picture."

"It's on the up-and-up."

Al was a friend of my former boss, a gumshoe named Jim Mc-Cain. He was also an enforcer for Tony B., who in turn was one of mob boss Vince Mangano's lieutenants. If any of them was involved in something, it was illegal, immoral, or at least a direct violation of the Office of Price Administration.

Since rationing had started, the black market was thriving as those of us who were tired of making do without paid a little bit extra for the things we missed. *The Times* was full of tales of how the mob had taken to illegal trade like bobby-soxers to Bing Crosby, and if you sunk to their level and bought their goods you weren't just breaking the law, you were as good as joining the Nazi Party. In the past year, beef had become so rare that most of us had started to believe it was one of those things you talked about that never really existed. Like unicorns. And while I would've loved a big juicy steak all to myself, I was, in my heart, a good law-abiding gal.

Plus, my rooming house didn't have a public icebox.

"Besides, Al, what am I supposed to do with it? Cook it on my hot plate, or put it on the fire escape and pray the temperatures stay low and the cats stay away?"

He shrugged and raised his arms in surrender. The sun began setting into his head. Al was an enormous guy, with the height and bulk of your average skyscraper. "Toss 'em if you want," he said. "It's out of my hands."

I put my hand on his overgrown biceps. A mountain rippled beneath my touch. "Don't be that way. I like the gift, really I do, but for the record? I would've preferred stockings."

He shrugged again, and his tiny eyes bounced from one place to another: the building, the sidewalk, a hack cruising past us with its lights turned down low. He was determined to look at everything but me. "How you been?" he asked.

"I've seen better days."

He raised an eyebrow to invite me to go on, but I couldn't bring myself to say the words. It had happened: the war had finally hit home. No longer was it this sad distant thing like Carole Lombard's death that I read about and dismissed because it was too far away to really affect me. I hated the Nazis and the Japs. I hated news bulletins that interrupted our regular programs with tales of sunken ships, downed planes, and bombs ripping apart the London skyline. I hated how we had to sacrifice everything we'd once taken for granted, how we couldn't go an hour without being reminded that the things we wanted were being put to better use *over there.* But most of all, I hated that my boyfriend, Jack (okay, *ex*-boyfriend), was missing in action and I wouldn't get a chance to tell him that I had never stopped loving him.

No, I couldn't find the words. And even if I could, I couldn't bear to speak them. "What's new in your world?" I asked.

"Everything's jake." Al patted his soiled overcoat, searching for a deck of Luckies. His fingers, red from the cold, crawled across his coat like sand crabs hunting for their shells. "I hear it's going to snow."

Maybe if I'd been thinking less about myself I would've realized something was wrong. As it was, I could barely register that there was a world outside of my own head.

"Imagine that," I said, with all the sensitivity of the SS. "Snow in March."

He dropped the ciggy and ground it with the toe of his shoe. The sole flapped loose, revealing Al's tattered brown sock. "Enjoy the meat." His gift delivered and his sparse attempt at conversation complete, Al turned up the street and disappeared.

I pulled a copy of *Variety* out of my pocketbook and wrapped it around the steaks until a number of circled audition notices grew dark with blood. I lived at the George Bernard Shaw, a rooming house at West Tenth Street and Hudson in the Village for young women pursuing theatrical vocations. It had cheap rent, cheaper food, and enough drama to fill the hours when WNBC was off the air. I liked the place, but I liked complaining about it more. I found it comforting to kvetch about a situation I chose to remain in. It was one of the few constants in my life that I could depend on.

My meat and I entered the building and paused before the row of brass mailboxes. I said a silent prayer and fingered the small, filigreed door marked WINTER, ROSALIND as though by touching the box I could will the letter I wanted to magically appear. No such luck. I slammed the box closed and muttered a curse that was sure to get me what I wanted the following day.

In the lobby Norma Peate was at the piano mangling "For Me and My Gal." Ella Bart sat on the floor, her long Rockette legs stretched into a split while her torso contorted until she could read the script set in front of her. Both kept their eyes away from me as I crossed the room and climbed the stairs. On the landing, Minnie Moore and my longtime nemesis, Ruby Priest, paused their conversation. Their smiles couldn't have been more artificial if they were painted on plastic.

"Why the sourpuss, Rosie?" asked Ruby. It was a tone I wasn't used to from her—at once pitiful and sincere. Encountering Ruby without her usual venom was like seeing Abbott without Costello.

"I'm swell," I told her. "Never been better."

"Are you sure?" asked Minnie. She was a new girl and I didn't have a read on her yet. She seemed nice enough, but there's a lot to be said for the company you keep.

"Positive," I told her. "But thanks for your concern."

I rushed into my room as quickly as I could without looking like I was trying to escape. My roommate and best pal, Jayne Hamilton, was sitting on her bed varnishing her nails red while the radio accompanied her with "He Wears a Pair of Silver Wings." Our cat, Churchill, lay beside her, alternately wrinkling his nose and sneezing to express his displeasure at the stink of nail polish.

"How'd it go?" she asked as I secured the door behind me.

"Miserable. I'm officially notorious." The last show I'd been in had become fodder for the front page after the playwright was murdered. My one and only performance of the play occurred on the night the killer tried to commit murders number two and three, and the tale of his madness had spread almost as quickly as word about how much of a stinker the show was.

Normally, I was grateful for whatever publicity I got, but somehow people began to believe that my participation in their plays would spell not only a production's ruin but death to anyone associated with it.

Jayne wielded an emery board like a sword. "You did only one show! How does everyone know about it?"

"How do you think?" I was Ruby's understudy in that last, ill-fated show, and while she should've been satisfied that I'd done a fine job ruining my career on my own, I strongly suspected she was using every opportunity she could to remind people about what had happened and who had been involved.

"She wouldn't do that." Jayne's conviction was as pronounced as a pantomime's lisp. "You practically saved her life."

"By taking *her* part." I set the meat on the dresser and shrugged out of my coat. "She's not a rational person, Jayne. I did a good job and she knows it. If it hadn't been for the murder, I may well be doing a lot better than her right now. She can't take that chance."

Jayne plucked a cat hair from a wet nail. "She'll get tired of tormenting you eventually."

"Sure she will, but by then I'll be old, fat, and completely uncastable."

"Do you want me talk to her?" asked Jayne.

I turned down the Magnavox and slumped onto my bed. I'd deal with Ruby in my own way. There was no joy in letting others do your dirty work. "No, I want you to change the subject." I lay back on the bed and fluttered my arms like I was making snow angels in my quilt. Jayne kept her mouth closed, either unwilling to let the matter rest or incapable of coming up with a new topic. "What's with everyone around here? Nobody in the lobby would meet my eyes, and Ruby and Minnie acted like I'd just gotten a starred telegram."

Jayne resumed painting, her face moving closer to her hand in her attempt to block out my presence.

I smacked her bed. "You said something, didn't you?" No response. "You did!"

"They were worried."

"About what?"

Jayne met my eyes. "About you."

I kicked off my shoes and pulled a stack of pulps out from under my bed. The cover for the latest issue of *Astonishing Stories* had aliens flying homeward with beautiful, unconscious women in their arms. As strange as it may sound, I wished I were one of them. It seemed easier to be asleep and at the mercy of unknown creatures than to be sitting in my room living through this moment.

"Somehow I doubt that," I said. "Anyway, they shouldn't be worried. I'm fine."

"Rosie . . ." Jayne's voice slipped into a whine.

"I am."

Churchill leaped from Jayne's bed and walked a figure eight in the space between us. Each of his slow, deliberate steps was punctuated by the overextension of a leg as elegant as Margot Fonteyn's. You had to admire his beauty and grace, even if he was the devil incarnate.

"I take it there was still no letter?" asked Jayne.

"Nope."

"The mails are slow."

"A condition that is often made worse when no one writes you to begin with." I'd found out Jack was missing courtesy of a letter from a sailor named Corporal Harrington. I'd written him back asking for more information, and the wait between V-mail was killing me. It was agonizing how little we could do. Jack was one soldier of millions lost in a war being fought in more countries than I could point to on a globe. No matter how bound and determined I was to find him, I couldn't overcome the size of the problem.

A few weeks before, *The Times* ran a cartoon of a man walking around a series of corners, each time expecting to find the end of the war. At every turn was a pasteboard sign announcing good news that had occurred in the previous months: Rommel's retreat, Russian Victory, Russian Advance. But despite these optimistic reports, around each bend he found yet another corner and another until at last he encountered this month's bad news: Rommel was on the offensive. The message was clear—the end was nowhere in sight. It would go on forever; at every turn came the possibility of another catastrophe.

Jayne clapped her hands. "Off, Churchill. Now!"

The cat stood atop my dresser, his face inches from *Variety*'s headlines. I picked up a brown leather mule and threw it at him. He bounced from the dresser to the radiator and watched with glee as the meat and my clutter of cosmetics tumbled to the floor.

Jayne slowly approached the bloody mass. "What is that?"

"Al also got word that I've been down. That, my dear, is a freshly butchered pick-me-up."

"He brought you steaks? Who does that?"

"A man who doesn't know the first thing about women." I pulled my valise out from under the bed, dumped the meat in it, and fastened the latches. "You think they'll keep outside?"

"It's worth a try."

I dumped the suitcase out the window. It landed with a boom that echoed down the length of the fire escape and back up again. Night was rapidly descending, stars made visible by the blackout filling the sky in such a way that if you ignored the buildings, noise, and refuse you could almost pretend you were in the country.

"Maybe you should call Jack's family," said Jayne.

"I'm sure they got their own letter from Corporal Harrington." I plopped back on my belly and tried to concentrate on the pulp.

"Yeah, but maybe they heard something else, you know, officially." What she meant was maybe they'd gotten a starred telegram announcing Jack's fate, knowledge M. Harrington hadn't known yet or hadn't been willing to share.

"I'll give Corporal Harrington another week," I said. "Then I'll send out the cavalry."

"I could call them for you."

I rolled to my side and read in her face her desire to help me move forward. It wasn't simply a matter of learning what had happened to Jack. Right now I was in a state of blissful ignorance, able to convince myself that he was safe. And I needed that, because the day I found out he was missing, I also found out that he still cared about me. See, Jack hadn't written word one to me since he'd shipped out, and I'd just assumed I was never going to hear from him again. The letter from Corporal Harrington didn't just tell me that something might have happened to Jack. It made it clear that I was the person he wanted contacted if something did come to pass. As bizarre as it might sound, I was holding on to that fact as tightly as a life jacket. He still loved me and nobody—not anybody—was going to dilute that wonderful feeling by telling me he was dead or wounded so badly he wished it were so.

"I want to wait," I told Jayne. "If someone contacted me when he was missing, they'll contact me if there's any other news."

She turned her head away as though the wistful sound in my voice was too much to bear. I'm sure she would've argued with me further if Ruby hadn't knocked on our door just then and announced that Al had been arrested for murder.

2 The Prisoner

"AL'S IN THE HOOSEGOW?" I asked Ruby.

"The what?"

"The clink. The slammer. The Big House. The pen."

"If those are synonyms for jail, then yes, I suppose he is." Ruby was back to her usual self, her chin high and haughty, her voice clenched with irritation that she should be lowered to speak to me at all.

"Why didn't you get us?" asked Jayne.

Ruby twirled her dark hair around her finger and examined its ends with much more interest than she was giving to us. Her hair was rolled in the front and loose in the back—a style the slicks claimed was the new look but which could make even Ginger Rogers look homely. "I was about to use the phone, and he was more than happy to leave a message."

"He who?" I asked.

"*He* didn't say and *I* didn't ask."

Jayne jumped off her bed and pushed Ruby out of the doorway. I abandoned *Astonishing Stories* and followed her to the hall, where the public phone teetered atop a small marble-topped table. Jayne picked up the blower and asked the operator for Tony B's exchange.

"Are you sure you want to talk to him?" I asked.

Jayne shrugged. Tony wasn't just Al's boss; he was Jayne's boyfriend. A few weeks before he'd promised her he was going to go straight, or at least as straight as a lifelong gangster could go. It quickly became apparent, though, that he had no such intentions, and

Jayne had decided that the best way to tell him how she felt about his reneging on his promise was to give him the cold shoulder.

As soon as he came on the line, her voice grew hushed, her one-sided conversation impossible to penetrate. I paced the hall as they jawed, trying to remember if anything seemed odd about Al. Sure, he hadn't said much, but Al never did. He was his usual big, brooding self.

I rapped myself on the noodle. I'd missed an opportunity. I hadn't seen Al for weeks, and here he shows up, gift in hand, trying to tell me something I was too dense to pick up on. How did I miss it when the signs were so clear?

Jayne disconnected.

"What's the wire?" I asked.

"Tony says it's true. The coppers picked Al up twenty minutes ago and took him to the 19th Precinct."

"Who did he supposedly bump?"

Jayne took a deep breath. "His girlfriend."

"Al had a girlfriend?" When I'd first met Al, he'd just finished a three spot for writing bad checks. He'd turned to the sordid hobby as a way of getting money to keep some chippy in the lifestyle she'd become accustomed to. As far as any of us knew, when Al got three to five, she got lost. "Who was he seeing?"

"Beats me," said Jayne. "But whoever she is, she was found the night before last, beaten to death." I shivered at the thought of this nameless woman as bruised and bloody as the meat he'd brought me. Al couldn't have done that. He may have made his living roughing people up, but he wasn't a killer.

Was he?

As much as I liked Al, I didn't really know him. He was a nice guy who'd done me a good turn, and while that might qualify me as a character witness, it would hardly vindicate him.

"What can we do?" I asked.

Jayne's lips pursed; her forehead wrinkled. "Tony said we should stay out of it."

"You're kidding me, right? Is that supposed to mean he's guilty? Tony's helping him? What?"

Jayne shrugged. "I don't know—he just said jail's the best place for him right now."

"Unbelievable." Tony had implied before that he didn't hold Al in the highest esteem, but I couldn't believe he'd just let him rot in the pen. I marched back to our room and grabbed my coat.

"Where are you going?" asked Jayne.

"To see Al."

"What about Tony?"

"What about Tony? Look, Jayne, Al came here tonight for a reason. He needs my help and I'll be damned if I'm going to miss the opportunity to do him a turn a second time." I tied on my red wool snood and wrapped my scarf around my neck. "You coming?"

Jayne shifted her weight from one leg to the other. She had only recently started to stand up for herself, and you could constantly see her brain doing battle between what was easiest and what was right. "All right," she said, "just give me a minute to fix my hair."

Here's how it was: the month before, Jayne and I got in a little too deep trying to find out who killed my former boss—private detective Jim Mc-Cain—and the aforementioned playwright. Before he died, Jim had a feeling I was going to put my nose where it didn't belong, so he asked Al, who owed him a favor, to tail me just to make sure I stayed out of trouble. I didn't, not because I was trying to be difficult but because trouble has a way of following me. Rather than abandoning me as a lost cause, during those dangerous, difficult weeks, Al went without sleep, food, or a decent cigarette in order to see to it that Jayne and I were safe. I wasn't exactly appreciative of what he was doing for us; I resented his being assigned as our protector, and so I stupidly tried to lose him. Al played along, but at a crucial moment when it looked like Jayne and I were going to become red splotches on a white wall, he stepped in and saved us.

In other words, we owed him. Big time.

Jayne and I hoofed it to the Christopher Street subway station and caught a rattler uptown. Rush hour was over and the subway had a dim, sleepy quality to it that left the other passengers hunched and silent. Someone had abandoned that day's *Times* on a seat, so we huddled together and combed the pages for any mention of murder. There was plenty of it to choose from, though the deaths the paper spoke of were in North Africa, Europe, and the South Pacific. The new casualty numbers were out: 435 army, 71 navy. The list of names of the dead and wounded from New York snaked down the page, seven column inches of grief.

Jayne, sensing my focus, turned the page and adjusted herself so I could no longer read over her shoulder. I stared at the back of the paper. Even the "Amusement News" wasn't so amusing. Orson Welles had passed his army physical with flying colors. Metro-Goldwyn-Mayer was trying to get Mickey Rooney out of the draft.

"Anything?" I asked Jayne. She was dwarfed behind section A, looking like a child trying to play grown-up.

"War this, war that. Wait." She stabbed her index finger into the fold. "Actress Found Beaten to Death in Upper West Side Home." Jayne pulled the page closer to her face. "Her name was Paulette . . ." She squinted, trying to make out a surname lost in the previous reader's greasy fingerprint. "Monroe."

"No!" People seated near us turned to see what I was yammering about, and I smiled an apology their way before turning back to the paper. Prior to our arrival, Paulette Monroe had rented our room at the Shaw House until her big head and bigger career outgrew our humble abode. She'd done great things on Broadway before moving out to California and starting in the pictures. Her success at that point hadn't been terribly impressive, though she did have a heck of a lot more to brag about than I did.

"I thought she was in Hollywood," I whispered.

Jayne waved me away and continued reading the article. "She was just cast in Walter Friday's show. He's doing some new musical called *Goin' South*. She must've come back for that." Walter Friday used to be a producer whose name guaranteed success. You never cared what play he was doing or what actors were attached; knowing it was a Walter Friday production was enough to make you want to be involved. Unfortunately, he'd fallen on hard times lately, and a number of incidents involving booze, broads, and bad investments had taken him out of the spotlight. Last fall there'd been rumblings that he was about to make a comeback with a big show and some even bigger backers. Everyone was dying to be part of it.

Jayne pulled away from the paper long enough to look at me. Sure it was cold, but we were both thinking it: if Paulette was dead, Friday would be looking for another lead actress.

"Focus," I told her. "Al first, audition later."

We made it to 153 East Sixty-seventh Street and told the dame at the desk we were Al's sisters. She gave us the up and down—me tall and brunette, Jayne tiny and blond—and came to a silent conclusion that even if we were lying, we didn't look dangerous. She told us to wait in the chairs until an escort could be found to take us to a meeting room. Jayne and I slumped side by side into seats well worn by a thousand other keisters. We entertained ourselves by eyeballing that evening's parade of thugs, ladies of the evening, and the newest criminal type: the draft dodger. The papers were full of stories of men who claimed religious and moral reasons to sit out the war. Some of them were genuine, but many others turned out not to be part of the faith they thought excused them or took the government's money making weapons at munitions factories but didn't think such willing participation should extend to the battlefield. It was pointless to lock them up for lies and hypocrisy. Society had a way of taking care of men like that.

"I don't like this place," whispered Jayne. An unwashed gentleman handcuffed to a chain on the wall licked his lips at the sight of my pal. Her coat, which had been perfectly normal when we left the house, suddenly became too small to cover both her gams and her guns.

"Imagine how Al feels." I was still trying to wrap my noodle around the idea that Al could kill someone. He was an imposing guy, but that was the point—you sent him to remind people of the damage he could do, not to actually do the damage.

Al would clear this up. There had to be a simple explanation for all of this.

"This way, ladies," said a bull in a blue uniform. He checked our names against a clipboard and silently led us down a cement block corridor. We arrived at a small room that grew smaller with each passing second. The elbow directed us to sit on one side of a table and with a wagging finger announced the rule of the hour: under no circumstances were we to touch the suspect.

Al joined us five minutes later.

He still wore his street clothes, though now they seemed too big for him, an impossible feat given that the average parachute wouldn't have been large enough to cover him from head to toe. His hands were cuffed in front of him like some sort of flipper, and as he entered the room he waved to our escort in such a way that it was clear he'd already mastered the art of functioning in bracelets.

I was relieved to see him, and I expected him to be relieved to see us. I hadn't let him down. While I may not have been wise to what he wanted when he'd stopped by earlier that day, I was here now.

If gratitude were gasoline, Al was running on empty. He joined us at the table and half-whispered, half-growled, "What are youse doing here?"

"We're here to help." I matched his volume and pushed my chair forward. "I'm sorry I didn't catch on that something was wrong before, but I'm here to make it right. Just tell me what to do."

He shrugged in response. It wasn't the answer I was hoping for.

"It's a mistake, right?" I asked. "You're here because of some mix-up?"

He held my gaze just long enough to let me know that the only mistake I'd made was in coming to see him. He signaled to the guard at the door. The copper deposited a cigarette between Al's lips and touched the tip to a ready lighter.

At least he had a friend. That was good to know.

"Tony know you're here?" he asked, the cigarette clenched between his teeth.

"He seems to think it would be better if we didn't visit you—if no one visited you," I said. Al didn't react to the news. Either he agreed with Tony or he knew better than to disagree. "Know why that might be?"

He traced a series of initials engraved into the wooden tabletop. "When the meat's gone bad, you don't want to keep it in the icebox next to today's milk."

I smiled at that. It was a rare day when Al used metaphors. "Is there someone we can call for you?"

"Tony's taking care of all that."

"Can we get you cigarettes? Magazines? A deck of cards?"

"I got everything I need."

"Come on: there's got to be something—"

His eyebrow rose, chastising me for thinking I was capable of doing anything but regretting my actions after the fact. "What's done is done. I'm not your responsibility, see?"

"We're not here because we feel responsible."

"Then why are you?"

"We're your friends. You did for us and now we want to do for you."

He laughed, and his bound hands took hold of the cigarette and ashed it on the floor. "You don't owe me nothing. Our account is clear."

"Who was she?" asked Jayne.

The eyebrow remained raised, his eyes locked on hers. I'd often wondered if Al was sweet on Jayne, but seeing him now it was impossible to imagine him having affectionate feelings toward anyone. "She was nobody," he said.

"Nobody?" My stomach rolled with the word. If Al could so easily strip a murder victim of her identity, could he have also taken her life? "Did you do it?"

His eyes wouldn't meet mine. The silence I could take, but his refusal to look at me felt like a deception. What was he keeping from me? I reached across the table and took hold of his square chin.

"Hey!" said the guard.

"Did you do it?" I asked Al.

He lifted his head and stared at a spot just above me. It was an actor's trick. To an audience, seated at a distance, it would look like you were meeting their eyes. His tiny peepers were muddy, the life that should've been behind them strangely absent. A smile peeked out from the corners of his mouth, at once self-effacing and mocking. "I'm here, ain't I?"

The guard grabbed my arm and wrenched it away from Al. "I said no touching."

I grabbed air. "I got it."

"You enjoy my gift?" asked Al.

If he was going to lie to us, if he was going to make us feel like we weren't wanted, I was going to do the same to him. "Sorry, but I didn't see any point in keeping it. I'm not a big fan of ill-gotten gains. I chucked it the minute you turned the corner."

The copper kept hold of me and pulled me out of the chair and away from the table with a gruffness that wouldn't have been necessary if I were twice my size. "It's time for you to go."

Jayne's heels click-clacked behind me. I turned around in time to watch Al stare into the gasper's rising smoke, a sad smile quivering on his lips. "You two take care," he whispered as the guard pulled me out the door.

We didn't sleep that night, or rather I couldn't sleep, and I wasn't about to let Jayne do so without me. Instead, we sat across from each other in a red vinyl booth at Louie's—a hash house with long hours and low prices—and picked apart everything we'd just seen until it was too frayed to stand up on its own.

"I just don't get it," I told Jayne for the hundredth time. "That wasn't Al."

She sighed, her sleep-bleary blue eyes no longer able to focus on me. She stirred condensed milk into a mixture of coffee and chicory, as though she hoped that the act of moving spoon around in the cup might reinvigorate her. "We barely know the guy, Rosie. Sure, he helped us out, but that doesn't mean he's not capable of cutting someone down."

It was a terrifying statement that neither of us wished to explore for fear of what would happen if we held it up to the other relationships in our lives. If Al could be a killer, what dark secrets did Tony B. harbor?

"He went to prison for a woman," I said. "A guy who's willing to commit a crime and do time to keep a girl around can't be a killer."

Jayne held her breath and downed the java like it was castor oil. As soon as it was drained, she landed the cup on the saucer with a rattle. "Can't he? If he's willing to steal to keep her, he might be willing to put the curse on her to make sure she doesn't leave."

I couldn't answer that. The door to Louie's tinkled softly as a soldier came in with a garishly dressed date. She was in her early twenties—give or take—and her hair was dyed Rita Hayworth red. She wore a yellow dress that was so tight a mermaid would've found it snug and walked in such a way that every curve jutted out in a grotesque parody of woman. While the soldier had eyes only for her, she scanned the room looking for the next mark to land when this one was spent.

"And how does a guy like him get hooked up with Paulette Monroe?" I asked.

Jayne raised an eyebrow and leaned, unsteadily, toward me. "From what I heard tell she wasn't afraid to do whatever needed to be done to get to the top."

There was a word for a woman like that: employed.

"That's all well and good, but Al doesn't know the first thing about theater. How was he going to advance her career?"

Jayne wiped the table with her napkin, then carefully folded it and set it beside her cup. "Maybe Al has connections we don't know about or maybe he lied to her to get her interested."

I tried to imagine him using his relationship with us as an aphrodisiac. *An actress, huh? Two of my pals are actresses.* "He wouldn't do that. He's . . . Al."

Jayne tipped her head toward the ceiling as though by doing so she could summon the patience she needed to keep listening to me. "We should go," she said. Outside, the sun poked its head above the night's horizon and I suddenly felt like I could fall asleep on the table. Instead, Jayne and I linked arms, hit pavement, and made it into bed just as the sun finished its rise.

Paulette's picture was in a place of pride at the Shaw House. All of our 8 x 10s lined the foyer, but hers was the first mug you saw when you entered the front door. She was easily the prettiest among us, but she was the kind of pretty that reminded you of someone else. More than one person had paused at her photo and tried to recall where they knew her from. Was she in *Moon Over Miami*? No, that was Betty Grable. What about *Skyline Serenade*? No, that was June Haver. Even if you couldn't figure out who she was, one thing was clear: if this girl wasn't a star yet, she was destined to become one.

For someone who'd never met Paulette, I'd long held mixed emotions for her. Part of me considered her an idol, someone whose success I should aspire to. And part of me resented her and her smug smile for constantly reminding me that she had made it out of the Shaw House and into Hollywood. Many a drunken night I'd stumbled into the house and offered her photo a sneer for its silent reiteration of what I didn't want to face: she was on her way to making something of herself and I was a big fat nothing and likely to stay that way. Paulette's death didn't change that for me. In some ways it made it worse. If someone like Paulette couldn't have a happy ending, who's to say there was any hope for the rest of us?

The next morning Jayne and I were awoken by Ruby's squeals of joy. Normally, it was a sound I would've ignored, but she'd chosen to do it in our room while throwing our drapes open and letting the afternoon sun in.

"Wake up, sleepy heads—I have news." She rapped a folded newspaper against the iron footboard of my bed.

"And I have the urge to kill," I mumbled.

"It's one o'clock," said Ruby, her horror at our sleeping to such a late hour almost pushing the mirth from her voice. "And while you two were sleeping away the day, I've just been cast in Walter Friday's *Goin' South*!"

I shot Jayne a glance and we both silently acknowledged what had come to pass: while we were bemoaning Al's fate, Ruby had learned of Paulette Monroe's death and scooped up the part before the body was buried.

The move was cold, calculating, and void of empathy. And I couldn't believe she'd done it before I could.

"I thought you were doing the tour," said Jayne. She'd been in a show with Ruby for the past six weeks. It was the theatrical equivalent of ice cream on apple pie—a pro-American war piece that was overly sweet, awfully familiar, and left you feeling a little sick afterward. As the war worsened, attendance figures dropped faster than bombs during blitzkrieg, so the playwright decided that what the show really needed was to go on the road to all those small American towns that would appreciate its message. Ruby had been getting a lot more press than Jayne, and since my roommate was still speaking to Tony at the time, Jayne opted out.

"I decided against the tour," Ruby told us now. "The part was awfully small and, really, I couldn't stand the thought of performing for people who might not appreciate a truly professional production." She was dressed to the nines in a green wool suit. Churchill, sensing her apparel lacked a certain accessory, left the bed and rubbed his head against her pencil skirt.

"And what did Lawrence have to say about that?" I asked. Lawrence Bentley, the playwright and darling of Broadway, was Ruby's on-again, off-again beau. From the look on her face, it was clear he was off-again.

"Who cares? If I never see that self-absorbed hack again, it will be too soon."

I would've rolled my eyes, but I didn't have the strength. "Isn't that what you said the last time you broke up?"

"This time it's for keeps." She put her hands on her chest to signal that she was about to make an important announcement. "I've met someone new."

I pictured a fly caught in the silken tendrils of her web. "Surely Lawrence isn't going to let your absence go unpunished. Like it or not, he's got a lot of pull in this town."

"Yes, so much pull that he's been drafted." Ruby nudged Churchill with her shoe and the cat skulked away. "I doubt he'll have time to say anything about me. He knows it wouldn't make sense for me to languish on tour when I have so many other opportunities. Besides . . ."

"Yes?" I said on cue.

She squinted in a wholly unappealing way. I thought she might be constipated until a tear winked at me from the corner of her eye. I wasn't moved. Ruby could summon tears faster than General Mac-Arthur could hail a cab. "It's only fitting that a friend of Paulette's takes over for her. It's what I would want someone to do for me if I met some terrible fate."

"How very generous of you."

She dashed the tear away with a flick of her fingers. "Don't mock. I'm working for scale."

That *was* impressive. Ruby normally made more money than any other person in a production. Her willingness to work for scale meant either she really was trying to honor a dear friend's memory or she knew that working for Walter Friday could give her the boost she needed to write her ticket to Hollywood.

"I wasn't aware you knew Paulette," I said.

"We never met, but we have many friends in common. And I can't tell you the number of times people have compared me to her." I could see that. Like Paulette, Ruby was an up-and-comer who'd paid

her dues with a résumé as long as my arm. She'd make it big, if someone didn't kill her first.

Jayne threw her hands in the air. "Well . . . congratulations."

"Make sure you congratulate Minnie when you see her."

"Did she get cast too?" asked Jayne.

"In a small part," said Ruby. "But we need to celebrate our victo-
ries no matter what the size."

I snorted at that. "I'm sure she'll appreciate your heartfelt huz-
zahs. So what is this show anyway?"

"Something brand-new and very exciting. It's a musical about four
sisters who inherit a plantation house located near an army base in
South Carolina. The songs are very clever, and Friday intends to
revolutionize the musical."

"And how is he going to do that? Take away the music?"

"No." Ruby clucked her tongue at me. "He's adding a corps de
ballet to the show." She retrieved the newspaper from the crook of
her arm and turned the page to "News of the Rialto." "As a matter of
fact, there's an open call for dancers tomorrow at noon. Full scale for
rehearsals and performances." She tossed the newspaper on my bed.
"Of course, I'm sure neither of you is interested since it would be terribly beneath you." Were Ruby a normal mortal, sharing this sort of
information may have seemed generous and kind. But we knew her
better than that. She didn't expect us to go to the audition, but she
did hope that by telling us about it we'd spend the rest of the day
wondering if all we were good for were lousy chorus parts. You had
to admire the broad—it took a lot of moxie to make others feel so bad
about themselves without expending any effort.

"Thanks for the heads-up," I told her. "But we'd hate to over-
shadow you like that."

She responded with a sneer and wiggled out the door, her hem
coated with cat fur.

"How does she get these parts?" I asked Jayne.

She went to her dresser and with a sigh began untangling her
blond bird's nest. "You have to admit she's talented."

"I don't have to admit any such thing."

While Jayne got ready, I lolled about the room, unwilling to get up and start a day that was rapidly passing us by. I thought about Al in his eight by eight cell, his only contact with the outside world being a window the size of a dinner plate. He probably hovered in what little sunlight it provided the way Churchill did, greedily hoarding the warmth for the few hours he could feel it.

My eyes fell on the newspaper Ruby had left behind. There it was in black and white: "Walter Friday's *Goin' South* Loses Lead Actress."

"It could be fun," I said.

"What?"

"*Goin' South.*"

"It's a corps de ballet, Rosie."

I knew what she was saying. Dance choruses were one thing—almost every actress I knew could fake their way through one of those. But a corps de ballet? It wasn't just a regular old dance chorus dressed up with a fussy French name. It demanded legitimate dancers—the kind with years of ballet training.

I'd been in choruses, and while I wouldn't win any awards for my hoofing, I was passable. But my trying to be in a corps would be like Mickey Rooney trying to join the marines.

"I hear you," I told Jayne.

While I couldn't cut it in a corps, Jayne was one of those rare actresses who'd managed to transgress the invisible gulf between actor and hoofer. She was a damn fine dancer—often to her detriment. She was pretty enough to stop traffic and had plenty of natural talent, but she'd also been given a voice that was pitched so high that half the time only dogs could hear her. She was working on it, as best she could, and she was such a nice person that most directors were willing to overlook her vocal limits and give her a chance. On more than one occasion, though, she'd been bounced from a speaking part to a dancing role when the director got wind that her footwork had no such shortcomings.

"You're not doing anything right now," I said.

Jayne paused, hairbrush in hand. "Rosie . . ."

"What?"

She turned to me, a scowl slicing her pretty face in half. "I know what you're up to. You want me to audition for that show for one reason—Al."

"Actually two reasons: I also enjoy irritating Ruby."

The show Jayne had just left should have been the part of a lifetime, but it was made somehow less so when Ruby outshined her in a tiny role Lawrence Bentley added at the last minute. Rather than resenting Ruby for it, Jayne did what she always did—suffered in silence and convinced herself that she didn't deserve any better than what she got.

Despite this, the possibility of seeking revenge made her buoyant. "It would bug her, wouldn't it, knowing I was there, squealing about what she's really like?"

"One can hope. Plus, Walter Friday's involved, and it wouldn't hurt to meet the guy."

Jayne grinned mischievously. "I'll do it . . . on one condition."

"Fire away."

Her smile vanished. "You go with me."

"You know I wouldn't stand a chance. Why would I waste a day waiting in line for some cattle call?"

Jayne brushed her finger curls into smooth waves. "To keep me happy. If I'm going to do this for you, I need someone there to help me pass the time."

3 Best Foot Forward

WE WERE UP AND OUT by ten o'clock the next day, to give us plenty of time to grab chow, doll up, and arrive at the theater early enough for the proctors to still have fresh eyes, but late enough that it didn't look like we were desperate for work. The show was going to be at the Sarah Bernhardt, a huge Byzantine building nestled on Forty-fifth Street west of Broadway. It had been named for the celebrated French stage actress who had also had a career as a vaudeville performer and silent film star. In the lobby, above the stage doors, was a quote of hers engraved into the stone: "Life engenders life. Energy creates energy. It is by spending oneself that one becomes rich." She seemed like a stand-up kind of gal.

The relatively young space had become as well known for the art in its lobby as for the works on its stage, and it was the kind of theater every actor dreamed of one day performing in but few could afford to even set foot into to see a Sunday matinee. I'd been inside it once before, to see Shirley Booth in *My Sister Eileen*, and I was so overwhelmed by the feeling that this was real theater and everything I'd been doing was a sorry imitation that I missed half the show. Sure, size and location didn't instantly make every production I'd done irrelevant, but it was hard to get excited about a play when you had to come to each performance dressed in your costume because if you didn't you'd have to wait in line to change in the public restroom.

When we got to Forty-fifth Street, there was already a line of men and women weaving around the lobby, all testing the limits of their leotards and tights by stretching inhumanly long legs above their noggins while arching their backs until their heads almost brushed their buttocks. We took our places behind these contortionists, and I passed the time eyeballing bodies that were supposedly the same species as mine, but which were capable of very different feats than those of the tall, gawky package I trudged around the city in.

"What I wouldn't give to see one of them snap in half," I told Jayne. Her stomach growled in response. "Easy, tiger," I told her. "Job first, food later."

"Do you smell that?" she asked.

Someone had left one of the lobby doors propped open, filling the space with chilled winter air. Above the sensual mix of Evening in Paris and Eau de Sweaty Leotard came a scent that reminded me of my grandmother's kitchen. Never much of a cook, Granny could ruin the best cut of meat and the finest of fresh vegetables with her ancient iron stove, a device she insisted was an improvement on newer models. This was true if you liked your roast black and your potatoes hollow.

I diagnosed the source of the stench. "It's the deli across the street. And if that's today's special, I'm not having any." It should've been a crime, ruining meat when there was so little to begin with.

I turned my attention from my stomach to the crowd before us. Everything about these men and women spoke of strength and control; every movement they made seemed impulsive and effortless. Although she only reached most of the other dancers' shoulders, Jayne was clearly one of them. The minute we entered the lobby, her posture improved and her movements took on a deliberate, choreographed quality. I mimicked her stance as best I could, but no matter how hard I tried I couldn't echo the grace that entered her every move. One of these things was clearly not like the other.

Fortunately, nobody noticed that an interloper was in their midst. The casting directors entered the lobby at 1:05 and began renaming each dancer either yes or no so rapidly that a number of people had to stop them and ask them to repeat what they had just said. Jayne and I watched in growing anxiety as the men and women we assumed would be shoe-ins (tall, lithe, hair in perfect chignons) were given their walking papers while the less traditionally dancerly were asked to remain in line. I half wondered if the whole thing wasn't a cruel joke and the dancers they sent away were already being shepherded into stage two of the audition, while the unfortunately named yeses waited for the proctors to announce, "You do realize we were kidding?"

If there was a joke, nobody let us in on it. Before I could announce that I was there only for moral support, the casting directors breezed past Jayne and me, giving us each a yes that blurred the two words into one. There was no time to point out their error; as the directors left the lobby, an elfin man in green tights arrived, handed each of us a number we were to pin to our chests, and directed us to grab our things and join him in the rehearsal room on the second floor.

As the crowd started up the stairs, I pulled Jayne aside.

"What do I do?"

"What do you mean?" she asked.

"I just passed the first phase of an audition I didn't audition for. Don't you see a problem with that?"

"Not really. What else do you have to do today?"

She had a point.

Dance auditions were nothing like acting auditions. Aside from years of training or inherited skill, you couldn't prepare for a dance audition. That was kind of the point. The directors wanted to see not only what you could do but how quickly you could learn something new. You didn't walk in with some pre-rehearsed routine you knew as well as a monologue; instead, you and all the other poor schlubs watched a dance captain who moved at a rate you thought existed only on sped-up film perform a combination that he made look ridiculously easy but which magically changed into something much more complicated the minute you attempted it. And that was the easy part. The hard part was learning the combination in the first place, since it was rare that a captain demonstrated it more than twice. Some dancers had a kind of mental muscle memory that could instantly recall what they'd just seen, in what order, and duplicate it perfectly. I wasn't one of them.

Fortunately, Jayne was. We were instructed to spread out in four lines in the rehearsal hall, and I made sure to get behind my best pal so I could copy everything she did. I wasn't just thinking about myself. When I did mess up, being in my vicinity would make her look good.

The elfin man stood in front of us, his tiny back reflected on a wall-length mirror that also captured our mean, hungry faces. He lifted a short, ropy leg onto the bar and stretched, more, it seemed, to show off how flexible he was than to really prepare himself for whatever he was about to do. Once he was done preening, he nodded at the accompanist, an ancient, gray-haired doll who had long before mastered the art of simultaneously playing the piano and chain-smoking. Her gnarled fingers rose high into the air, before crashing onto the keys with a jarring intro. The elf leaped, whirled, reached, and froze in a series of movements that would've—outside of this space—gotten him a long stay at Bellevue.

"All right," he said, after clapping his miniature hands together, "now it's your turn." We mimicked his pose, waited for the accompanist to ash her Lucky Strike, and rushed into the opening bars of the song like parachuted infantry leaping out of a plane. Half the room remembered what they'd seen and did a fine job replicating it. After about the fifth step, the rest of us began making up whatever seemed close to the spirit of what the elf had demonstrated. Our efforts were rewarded with one sharp "No!" after another, each one doing nothing to fix our failing memories.

The piece came to an end. The elf put his fingertips to his lips as though he had to physically locate his next words before speaking them. "I'll do it again. Watch more carefully this time." He did and I did, though I can't say it counted for much. While the other dancers learned their lesson, I just didn't have the heart to care. Even if a miracle happened and I managed to nail this routine, I was still going to get axed further down the road. It was the natural order of things.

"You—tall girl," said the elf when the second humiliation had come to an end. Since the description fit half of the women in the room, we all looked around, trying to deduce which giantess he was referring to. "No, you," he said, pointing a finger my way. This was it; I was finally going to be given the gate. Thank God.

"I'll get my stuff." I bowed my head in my best imitation of shame.

"No, no," he said. "Let's try it with me calling out the steps."

I wasn't savvy to what the little man was doing—was he trying to torment me further as a way of getting back at all the tall Tinas who'd harmed him in the past, or had he seen something in my flaccid attempts at dancing that made him want to help me?

I abandoned my analysis of his motives as the rest of the dancers cleared the way, leaving me alone in the center of the room. I put my fear of humiliation in the same mental footlocker in which I stored the war and my worry over Jack and willed the audience to keep their laughter low enough that I couldn't hear it. "And a five, six, seven, eight." As the Lucky Strike bobbed along to the tempo, the elf shouted out the proper names in the combination. Red-faced, I performed each step as he asked, my memory finally kicking in long enough to remind me what was coming next. "Good, good," he said at the end. "We'll all take a break and announce the next cut in twenty minutes."

"What the deuce was that?" I asked Jayne as we sought out a drink and some privacy.

"I think the little man likes you," she said.

"Bully for me. Is this what my life has come to: flirting with men I couldn't care less about to get jobs I don't deserve?"

She shrugged. "Things could be worse."

We slumped against the wall in the hall outside the rehearsal room and passed a Coca-Cola back and forth until the sugar perked us up. The other dancers milled in and out of the room, pacing like wolves on the off chance the cut sheet had been posted without announcement. The movement abruptly stopped and the crowd split down the middle as the stairwell door opened. Ruby and her entourage had arrived.

"Oh look," I mumbled, "the real actors are here."

While we were suffering the indignities of auditioning, those fortunate enough to be cast in parts with names and lines had been
rehearsing in another room. Ruby led these blessed souls with her
head held at a haughty angle. Behind her lurked Minnie and three
other women.

From what I'd been able to piece together, *Goin' South* was about
four sisters—Stella, Sue, Ellen, and Kate—who inherit a former plantation house in South Carolina. On a whim, the girls abandon their
lives in the North and start over in what they imagine will be a
Southern paradise. The place is a run-down disaster and the girls
are soon given the boot when the army appropriates the house for
maneuvers. Naturally, one of the girls—Stella—falls in love with the
sergeant in charge and encourages him to move his men out sooner
rather than later. When the army departs, the sisters decide to turn
the house into a dance hall for soldiers and find themselves making
money hand over fist. Just when things seem rosy, a rival for the
sergeant's affections—the unfortunately named Myra Pentall—tells
him that the house isn't being used just as a dance hall; the girls
are also running a whorehouse. The sergeant makes a surprise visit
and catches the girls in what he wrongly interprets as compromis-
ing positions. He shuts the house down and breaks up with Stella.
Completely out of left field, Stella discovers that her dental fillings
are picking up radio signals from enemy aircraft. She reports what
she's heard, prevents an invasion, saves countless men, and, in the
last scene, marries the sergeant while her sisters and hordes of ador-
ing men look on.

The writer, from what I heard tell, was a raging alcoholic.

Paulette had been cast as Stella, and now Ruby had that honor.
I didn't know the other three women who were playing the sisters,
though Minnie had been cast as Myra, the sergeant's meddling ad-
mirer. Carl Lumboldt, an actor whose near-sightedness had kept him
out of the army, was playing the sergeant. In addition to performing
balletic interludes, the members of the corps de ballet would portray

soldiers, girls at the dance hall, and any other characters needed to populate the scenes.

Ruby snapped her fingers, and Minnie pushed her way to the front of the line and joined her mistress. Words we couldn't hear were delivered with a smile we didn't believe, which sent Minnie bustling in our direction. She fumbled in her pockets, pulled out a coin, dropped it into the Coca-Cola machine, then rushed back to Ruby with the icy dope in hand.

"She has a way with people, doesn't she?" said Jayne.

The elf interrupted any further observations. "Ladies and gentleman! If I don't call your number, you've been cut." With the speed of an auctioneer he read off digits that most of us forgot we'd been assigned. I read Jayne's chest and squealed as her number was called only to realize that my pal was frozen with fear, her eyes locked on my own number.

"You made it through," she whispered.

I pushed through the crowd and approached the cut list the elf had hurriedly taped to the wall. She was right: someone had made a horrible mistake.

The miniature man waved a stack of mimeographed scores and told us to form groups of eight. We'd have to sing and dance for the bigwigs next. They would make the final cut.

Jayne grabbed two girls and four guys and forcibly pulled me by the hand into a corner to rehearse with them. I half-heartedly practiced the steps we'd already done while singing a song called "My Tooth Tells the Truth Even as My Heart is Breaking" that I hoped was a joke. Long before we were ready, the elf beckoned "Tall Girl" and her group to join him in the rehearsal room.

A long table had been added to the front of the space. The elf took a seat at the end of it, at a safe distance from three new faces. One was Walter Friday, a jovial-looking middle-aged man with a perpetual tan, a bad rug, and a permanent squint. He nodded to himself as we entered, as though we were confirmation of something he'd been, up until that moment, arguing with himself about.

The man next to him was so large his thighs oozed off each side of his chair. Despite his size, he wore a well-fitted handmade suit that I bet cost more than the show's budget. His fastidious attention didn't just extend to his clothing—it was clear this was a man who lived for manicures, steam baths, and weekly visits to his barber. He had a cigar in his mouth—unlit—that was as much a part of him as his nose and his chin. His clasped, bejeweled hands rested before him, and I couldn't help but think of Al in the stir, forced to put his braceleted mitts on the table to make sure he didn't try anything.

The last man wasn't much larger than the elf, though his lack of muscle made him seem half his size. He wore heavy, black-rimmed specs and was pale—almost sickly so—and focused all of his attention on removing some object lodged in his left eye. It was so distracting I considered volunteering to come and do it for him just to get him to sit still.

Normally we would've done our thing and left, but before we could begin, Walter Friday asked us each to introduce ourselves and explain why we wanted to be part of the show. The other six dancers did as he asked, cooing compliments about Friday's artistic vision that the man couldn't have bought unless he was lit. Which I'm pretty sure he was. He leered at each one of them, a strange half-smile lingering on his puss.

Jayne went before me, and it wouldn't have mattered what she said, since all Friday was probably thinking was *nice rack*. His oversized companion leaned into Friday, cupped his hand to his ear, and whispered something that prompted Friday to make a note on the sheet in front of him.

"And you?" said Walter Friday.

There wasn't a pandering compliment that hadn't already been said. I could repeat them all, declaring myself champion of all apple-polishers, or I could accept the fact that my act would be seen through as quickly as Jayne's leotard. "My name is Rosie Winter and . . . er . . . to be frank I'm afraid someone's made a terrible mistake."

"And what mistake is that?" asked the fastidious fat man. He talked out of one side of his mouth like Humphrey Bogart. Or a stroke victim.

"I'm not a dancer. I can barely shuffle off to Buffalo. And to tell you the truth, I don't want to be in this show."

The fat man froze, uncertain that he'd heard me correctly. After sufficient time had passed to make me regret saying anything, he burst into laughter that shook the table and caused the sickly little man to poke himself in the eye. "I like you," he said. "You got more moxie than a kitten with a bag of hammers."

I assumed that was a compliment.

When auditioning as a group, you had two contradictory goals: to make it look like you could perform well with others, and to stand out enough that you'd be remembered apart from the seven other people you were auditioning with. I accomplished only the latter. As the others whirled, I wobbled. When they flounced, I flopped, until it had to look for all the world like I was a weed in a sea of poppies.

When we finished, Friday and the large man again bowed their heads in discussion. While we couldn't make out the words, it was obvious some sort of argument was afoot. Friday seemed to be winning, until the large man leaned back in his chair and gave him the kind of stare I'd seen nuns levy at ill-behaved children. You would always win when you had the fear of hell on your side.

Friday met his gaze and shrank into his chair, defeated. He mumbled something indecipherable and then, in a voice only slightly louder, said, "Thank you. Brock Smith, Gary Tilsdale, Jayne Hamilton, Rosalind Winter—congratulations. Rehearsals start on Monday. The rest of you are dismissed."

We froze, waiting for the punch line, but the elf was already ushering in the next group.

Jayne and I left the room and gathered our things, both of us shaking our heads in amazement.

"What's his grift?" I asked her.

"I guess Friday knows what he wants."

"Or at least his fat friend does. Maybe Friday lost a bet and this is his punishment."

Jayne pulled on her coat and hat and opened the stairwell door for me. "Do you have to analyze everything, Rosie?" Her tone was the same short, exasperated one she'd used on me the night we'd visited Al in jail. "Maybe they just liked you and wanted to give you a break. It does happen, you know."

She stomped down the stairs, her scarf flying behind her. Her back was rigid, her footfalls heavy. This wasn't just about me complaining—something else was amiss.

I rushed to catch up and finally reached her side as we pushed out the door and onto the street. "What's the matter?" I asked.

She slowed her pace and bit her lip. Her eyes left mine and found the ground. "I think I know him."

"Him who?"

She looked behind us and took my arm. We moved away from the theater and headed toward Fifty-second Street. "The big guy that's who. He's an . . . associate of Tony's. His name's Vinnie "the Butcher" Garvaggio. I met him at Ali Baba's one night."

"The Butcher?" I said. "I know I'm going to regret asking this, but why do they call him that?"

"It's a family name," Jayne snapped. "Why do you think?"

Nicknames were dangerous things. One of Capone's men, recently deceased, had been named Bugs Blacker. I thought it was a charming nickname until I found out that he got it because of his habit of throwing bedbugs into theaters run by men who didn't pay their monthly protection money. "I didn't think any of Tony's . . . acquaintances were involved in theater."

Jayne screwed up her mouth.

"Do you think he's the money?" I asked.

"What else could he be?"

I nodded at a passing taxi. "Interesting."

Jayne didn't like the way I said that, as though Garvaggio's association with Tony made him strictly section eight. She may not have liked Tony much at the moment, but she could be surprisingly protective of him. The way she saw it, most of the people he associated with were bad news, but they weren't bad news *because* he associated with them. "He's not the only one, you know," she said. "Tony says lots of guys back shows. It's an easy way to make money."

And to lose it. Broadway wasn't doing so well these days. As the Great White Way's lights had been extinguished as part of the war-mandated dim-out, so had its ticket sales and revenues. It was understandable. The war had taken our audience. Those who weren't fighting overseas were fighting gas and rubber rationing and the despair of living in a war culture. Who wanted to go to the theater when there was all of that to contend with?

Of course, getting people in to see the shows wasn't the only problem. The year before, the Drama Critics' Circle voted not to give a prize for best American play because they didn't feel there were any plays worth endorsing. Brooks Atkinson blamed this collective writers' block on the war for consuming the normal ebb and flow of life and drama, but even he thought this was a weak excuse. After all, while American theater was floundering, the Brits, despite enduring bombings and their own blackouts, were doing booming business and bringing forth new smash hits like *Blithe Spirit.*

"I'm surprised Garvaggio's being so obvious about it," I told Jayne. "Aren't these guys usually silent partners?"

"Maybe he likes a little more control than that. Or maybe he wanted the chance to ogle the dancers."

Or maybe he was brought in to keep the peace after Al allegedly knocked off one of Walter Friday's lead actresses.

4 Shadow and Substance

I let Jayne do the honors of telling Ruby we'd all be working together. I didn't stick around to see her reaction, though from what Jayne said there was much eye-rolling and pitiful cooing on our behalf. "I'm just thinking of your careers," Ruby told her. "This is such a step down for both of you."

I tried not to think about it myself. My mood had rapidly disintegrated since getting cast in the chorus. I hated feeling like I'd been given something I didn't deserve by virtue of the right person being part of the decision making. And I hated knowing I was doomed to stink at it. I could take being in bad parts in bad shows, but being a bad performer—that was going to be hard to swallow.

Of course, my ego wasn't enough of a reason to turn down the job. I was dying to get back into that theater and find out whatever I could about Paulette Monroe, especially in light of the mob's involvement in the show. From what Ruby told Jayne, the main cast had been signed several weeks before Paulette's death. Friday—or perhaps Garvaggio—had known whom he wanted in his show and made sure to secure them from the get-go.

The weekend before rehearsal started was agonizingly slow. I spent Saturday morning and most of the afternoon lying on my bed, trying not to think about Jack lost and Al locked up. How strange it was that a man I couldn't find I finally thought I understood and a man who had no way of leaving had become a total mystery to me. To distract myself, I alternated my focus between the newspaper and the radio. Secretary Wickard of the Department of Agriculture had commandeered the airways to discuss his proposal to stop the meat market from becoming the black market. I didn't get the gist of everything he said, but I gathered he wanted to license everything, from raising cattle to killing and selling them, to ensure that only authorized individuals had a stake in our steak. The Office of Price Administration didn't seem to appreciate these suggestions, if only because they didn't cover the only facet they cared about: price. The OPA and the USDA did agree on one thing: changes needed to be made and they needed to be in place by April 1.

Clearly we were going to have to become vegetarian. Or Canadian.

"You're awfully glum." Jayne lowered the volume on Secretary Wickard and set aside the copy of *True Detective Stories* she'd been pretending to read.

"What carnivore wouldn't be?" I shifted my attention to the newspaper. The Nazis had had a busy week. Always the humanitarians, they'd gassed 360 Polish prisoners held at Myslowice to "prevent the spread of typhus." They were also dropping a new bomb over London, one that weighed less and exploded much more easily. And they had warships poised to invade Norway.

Jayne picked up Churchill and put him in her lap, cooing the whole time about what a good, smart kitty he was. Fortunately for her, cats don't understand sarcasm. "What are you thinking about?"

"You know: stuff." Five truckers had been arrested in the city with seven thousand pounds of illegal meat. The army had increased their list of men who were missing in action by 111. I wondered when the navy would bother to do the same. Jack's name hadn't been in the papers yet, and I couldn't decide if this was a cruel oversight or proof that Corporal Harrington had gotten it all wrong. The very thought turned my heart into a timpani. If Jack were dead, would I feel it the way some couples claimed they could sense each other in jeopardy? If I didn't, what did that mean about how we felt about each other?

I wanted to tell all this to Jayne, but I couldn't. There was something humiliating about going months wondering if someone cared for you, only to find out he did, which made you wonder if he cared *enough*.

"I think sitting around here is a bad idea," said Jayne.

"I'll take that under advisement." I bumped the radio volume back up. Secretary Wickard had been replaced by Dorothy Sells of the Office of Defense Transportation, who had a bee in her bonnet about female defense workers who thought sex appeal and glamour belonged in the workplace. Tight sweaters and Veronica Lake locks were apparently inappropriate, no matter how many Office of War Information recruiting posters suggested the exact opposite.

"We haven't celebrated getting work," said Jayne. "That's a big deal."

"For you, sure. When you've been grossly miscast, I believe etiquette instructs us that the less said, the better."

She tossed a pillow at me. "Let's go to a picture."

"There's nothing I want to see."

"How about ice skating at the Garden?"

"No thanks."

"Why don't we see if they need ushers at the Henry Miller? I'm dying to see *Harriet*. I hear Helen Hayes got her voice back." The stage diva had been laid up with laryngitis and so had her production. Helen Hayes was too good for an understudy.

"Why? So we can be reminded of the parts we didn't get?"

Jayne lifted her chin heavenward while Churchill mimicked her stance. "I'm sorry Jack is missing, Rosie. I'm sorry you got cast in a show you weren't intending to audition for in the first place. I'm sorry Al killed someone and ended up in the bing. But you need to snap out of this. Moping never got anyone anything."

"No one's making you stay."

She closed her eyes for a beat, then sat up, removed Churchill to the floor, and looked at me. "You're right. I'm going to go have some fun."

She left and my moping developed into misery. I waited for her to return with a kind word and a full bottle, but after an hour passed I accepted that I'd scared her away. Churchill retreated into the space beneath the dresser, and I found myself dying to unleash my misery on someone. When no one volunteered for the job, I escaped to the lobby in hopes that I could find an unsuspecting victim to join me in my foul mood.

Minnie sat on the parlor sofa, flipping through the previous month's issue of *Picturegoer*. As Joan Crawford's head grinned from the cover, I plopped onto the wingback across from Minnie and tapped my hands in time to the Benny Goodman tune blaring from the radio. She momentarily left her page and acknowledged me with a tight smile that managed to simultaneously greet me and urge me to still my noisy mitts. Her message communicated, she returned to the slick, lifting its spine so that the pages protected her from any further attempt I might make at conversation.

Benny Goodman became the Andrews Sisters. My feet joined my hands in a riveting version of "Bei Mir Bist Du Schoen."

Minnie abandoned the magazine with a sigh. "I hear your boy-friend's missing."

I was so taken aback I jumped. "Um . . . yes. I mean, he's not really my . . ." My voice faded. I hated that my emotional turmoil was out there for everyone to watch and analyze. And I hated that I was em-barrassed about it. Wanting my privacy was one thing, but resenting everyone else's curiosity when I would've been just as interested in their personal tragedies seemed unfair. Maybe that was the point: I didn't want to be their entertainment, and I was ashamed that at one point I'd allowed them to be mine.

"I'm sorry," she said. "That must be hard."

I acknowledged the understatement of the year with a nod. Per-haps this girl was worth talking to. She could give me the coddling Jayne was unwilling to provide.

I smiled and eased forward in the chair. "It's a stage name, right?"

"What?"

"Minnie Moore."

My question surprised her. "Not according to my birth certificate."

"Then it looks like I've lost a bet." I was one of the few girls I knew who didn't use a stage name. I never understood the allure of changing something that distinguished you into something bland and simple. But then I liked my name. "It's nice to know I'm not the only one who held on to my moniker."

"Believe me—I've thought about changing it. I used to hate my name. It's not so bad now that I'm away from home."

"What made it so awful there?"

"They named my twin brother Mickey."

I let out a low whistle. "Mickey and Minnie Moore? Ouch. So someone in your family must love . . ."

She cut me off. She didn't make jokes and she wasn't about to allow someone else to. "It was a coincidence. That's all."

"Minnie Moore's a good name though," I said. "Very strong." She returned to the magazine with a nod. "How are you getting on?"

"What do you mean?"

"You know—living here, being in your first big show. It's a lot to take in at once."

"Oh, it's fine, I guess." She pushed a lank piece of hair out of her face. She was a plain girl and her habit of not wearing makeup wasn't doing her any favors.

"Ruby treating you well?"

"She's very nice." Plain *and* stupid.

"You must be high as a kite over getting cast as Myra. It's a great part."

She examined a hand full of broken and bitten nails. I resisted the urge to recommend a good manicurist. "It is. I was cast weeks ago, though, so the excitement's died down."

"Oh." I tried to remember if Ruby had told me that. "So you were cast at the same time as the . . . other woman. The one who died?"

She nodded solemnly.

"Were you close to her?"

"Paulette? Not really. I met her at the read-through a few weeks ago. She seemed nice enough, but she and her friends kept to themselves."

"Her friends?"

"The other leads: Olive, Zelda, and Izzie. Those four were thick as thieves."

I made a mental note to seek them out. "What was Paulette like?"

Minnie ran her hand over the cover of *Picturegoer*. "Like any other starlet, I guess."

I had no idea what that meant. "Was she good?"

Minnie didn't answer right away. She seemed to be fighting a quiet battle between dismissing Paulette as a pretty bit of fluff or giving her her due. I wasn't the only one who'd viewed her through the veneer of admiration and jealousy. "She could be. She committed, you know?" I nodded. Commitment was one of those rare skills in an actor—the ability to completely throw yourself into whatever you were doing. Most people held back a little, particularly when a role asked them to do or say something they wouldn't be comfortable doing or saying in real life. Commitment would've been crucial in a show as poorly cobbled together as *Goin' South*.

"It must have been such a shock, her being murdered."

Her face finally came to life. "Oh it was, it really was. I thought they might shut us down when they started questioning everyone."

"Did you know the guy they arrested?"

"Nope, never saw him before."

"But he was her boyfriend, right?"

"If he was," said Minnie, "he was one of many."

"So what did you end up doing?" I asked Jayne as she slinked back into the room. It was just after one a.m., and I was seconds from giving up on her and nodding off to sleep.

"Had supper with Tony, then we caught a picture at Radio City." She dumped her purse on her dresser and shrugged off her coat.

"So I take it you're not giving him the cold shoulder anymore?"

"I called a truce for tonight. It didn't seem right that I stop speaking to both of you." She sat on the end of my bed. "I'm sorry about before."

"It's all right."

She shook her head so hard her earrings tinkled. "No it's not. You're going through a lot, and instead of being a friend, I acted like you were choosing to be miserable."

"I think I am in some ways."

She put her hand on mine. "Even if you are, you're allowed to at a time like this. Next time I don't recognize that, give me a swift kick, okay?" She was tearing up a little, which made me do the same. "I have presents." She pulled a sack from inside her pocketbook and tossed it my way.

I dumped the contents onto the bed. "Chocolate bar. Nice. Stockings—even nicer. All legally obtained, of course."

Jayne winked. "Of course."

"And what's this?" I unwrapped a small rectangle that had been carefully shrouded in waxed paper. "Butter!" I held the stick to my nose and inhaled the sweet creamy scent of forbidden fats. "Would it be terrible if I bit off a hunk of this and ate it plain?"

"I won't tell if you won't."

I left my gifts on the bed and nudged a too curious Churchill away from my prizes. "You should avoid Tony more often." I rummaged through a bureau drawer and uncovered a box of saltines.

"So what did you do tonight?" asked Jayne.

"Made myself good and miserable. When that got boring, I decided to spread the joy and get to know our new housemate."

"Minnie?"

I nodded.

"What's the verdict?"

I located a knife and wiped it clean. "Nice, I guess. But it would require surgery to uncover her sense of humor." I slathered the butter on two crackers and passed one to Jayne. "None of that matters right now—Al does." I gave her the rundown on what I'd learned from Minnie.

"Paulette was seeing someone else?"

"At least one someone else, though Minnie thought it might've been more than that. I guess Paulette had a thing for military men, and Minnie's not too good at telling one man in uniform from another. Interesting, no?"

"Very." Jayne left the bed and retreated to her bureau. She plucked her baubles from her lobes and froze before returning them to the cigar box serving time as her jewelry box. "But it doesn't mean Al's off the hook."

I'd been afraid she'd say that. "Can't we pretend it does?"

The rhinestones landed with a ping in the Cuesta-Rey box. "It's still a motive, Rosie. If the woman you loved was seeing someone else on the side, murder seems like an excellent way to punish her."

"It goes both ways though, doesn't it? One of her other boyfriends could've bumped her off just as easily as Al for being unfaithful." I left my bed and freed our booze from its hiding place in the closet. This conversation demanded a cocktail. "So what picture did you see?"

"*They Got Me Covered.*"

"For someone who spent the evening with Bob Hope and Dorothy Lamour, you don't look too amused."

"We ended up leaving early. Tony had a meeting."

That was the problem with dating someone in the mob: undependable schedules. "And so the truce has already ended?"

Jayne's pixie face squeezed into a scowl. "I made it clear to him that I wanted what I wanted, and if he couldn't give it to me, I couldn't see him again."

"You have to do what you have to do." I was never thrilled by my best pal's choice of men, and not just because Tony was a criminal. He didn't call her, he forgot her birthday, and on one awful occasion he sent her home with a bruise he thought a ring would be big enough to make her forget. But I wasn't the kind of friend to tell her how to live her life. That was a decision she had to make on her own.

"Before I let him have it though, I asked him about Vinnie Garvaggio," said Jayne.

"What did he say?"

She spun toward me slowly, aware, no doubt, that telling me this information would make it hard to indict me for any future forays I might make into helping Al. "He said this was Garvaggio's first time investing in theater. Vinnie met Walter Friday last fall and was so charmed by him he decided to back Friday's big comeback. Apparently, there are a number of other big guns pooling the money for it too."

"Including Tony?"

Jayne sat on her bed and tossed her legs over the iron footboard. "Nope. He said he didn't like Friday and didn't trust that he'd see any return."

I'd never thought of Tony as a discriminating person, but then I suppose you'd have to be to continually toe the line between businessman and business end. "Interesting—why didn't Tony like him?"

"He wouldn't tell me, but given what you just said about Paulette Monroe, maybe he's more protective of Al than we thought."

5 Fallen Angels

WE AWOKE BRIGHT AND EARLY Monday morning and ankled over to the Sarah Bernhardt for our first official corps rehearsal. Upon arrival, we were ushered into the rehearsal hall we had used for auditions, where the same pianist (smoking the same cigarettes) entertained us with a piece from Liszt's *Faust* while we stretched and prepared ourselves for six grueling hours of dance instruction.

For the first time I was able to take in the ten men and eight women who, in addition to ourselves, would make up the corps. It was an unusual group. Most of the women were large for dancers—too tall, too wide, too thick. Jayne alone appeared properly proportioned, though in her tininess she stood out like a sore thumb. The men, on the other hand, were universally small. Not one of them was tall enough to meet me eye to eye, and I strongly suspected that if any of them attempted to lift me, their spines would collapse like a jack-in-a-box.

The elf wasn't the choreographer of the show. That honor was given to a middle-aged dame named Maureen O'Reilly, who, despite her Irish moniker, had a thick German accent that made her sound like she was on the verge of a coughing fit. "Back in my homeland de first zing a dancer learns is discipline. Today you vill dance like you are in Dublin." We waited for an explanation for the incongruity between her name and her accent, but none ever came. She was probably a victim of the war, forced to shed her national identity if she wanted to continue to work in peace. The land of the Liberty Cabbage welcomed everyone these days, except the Krauts.

She walked with a cane, though it wasn't immediately clear if she needed it or if it was an affectation. She was terrifying, not because of where she probably hailed from, but because of her way of sizing each of us up and spitting back a version of ourselves that was completely different from what we imagined. As twenty of us stood shoulder to shoulder, she walked the line and diagnosed the precise reason we shouldn't have been cast. "You are too fat," she told a zaftig dancer. "You have big bosoms," she told another. "You are short," she informed Jayne. "And you," she said to me, her tone making it clear I was the worst of the bunch, "are not a dancer at all." Having named our maladies, she threw her hands into the air and sighed. "Very vell. If zis is vat I am stuck vith, ve vill have to vork twice as hard and twice as long. He vill not humiliate me too."

I didn't know who *he* was, though it didn't take Einstein to figure out that our motley crew had been assembled to make Maureen's life more difficult. Out of retaliation, she had us begin the day by performing the same routine the elf had given us at the audition. We didn't get halfway through it before she pounded the cane on the floor and told us to stop. "It is clear you are not ready to dance. Today, ve vill focus on learning to valk." And *valk* we did. Not in the traditional sense, but as dancers, with our heads high, our limbs extended, and our backs effortlessly straight. For three hours we practiced like primates who'd just figured out what upright meant, and by the end of it every part of me hurt. I longed to slouch and stare at the floor as I shuffled home.

"That was awful," I told Jayne over lunch. We'd ducked into the deli across the street and hunched over twin servings of what they claimed was roast beef on rye but which tasted more like pork soaked in brown gravy. We managed to snag a corner booth just before the noon crowd packed the joint. It was curious to see a place that couldn't distinguish beef from pork enjoying a constant flow of business. It may have been the prices, which struck me as unusually low for wartime rationing. Or it could've been the sign on the counter that proudly proclaimed that the establishment would not be participating in the voluntary meatless Tuesday program that the city ration office was trying to encourage.

"How are we expected to dance without meat?" I told Jayne. "We'll be too weak."

"You still have Al's gift."

I'd tried to forget about the steaks. As scarce as meat may have been, I couldn't help but connect those thick slabs with Paulette's lifeless body. No matter how hungry I was, or how desperate for flesh, I couldn't see myself eating them anytime soon. "Wasn't it weird how Maureen was talking like we'd been assembled to make her life difficult?"

"It's an odd group," said Jayne. "Most of them seem like they can dance, but—" The restaurant door clanged open and Ruby and Minnie entered. While Ruby staked out a table, Minnie went to the counter and ordered for the two of them. Jayne and I slumped into our booth until all anyone could see of us were the tops of our heads.

"I bet she pays for her lunch," I told Jayne.

"Minnie?"

"Absolutely. Have you ever seen such undeserved fawning in your life?"

Minnie waved to Ruby from the counter, her face tight with apprehension. She was worried that she was taking too long for her royal highness. I scanned the room for any sign of Paulette's friends. I'd been hoping to find time to corner each one of them individually. If they were as close to Paulette as Minnie claimed, they might be able to clear up the mystery of Paulette's active love life.

"Where do you think the other actresses eat lunch?" I asked Jayne.

She picked apart her sandwich and examined its innards with the careful eye of a surgeon looking at a wound. "If they're smart, anywhere but here."

Ruby turned her head this way and that, trying to determine which table would empty next. After exchanging a few teasing smiles with suits seated near the window, her peepers landed on Jayne and me. The playful, seductive grin left. She raised a bemused eyebrow and glided to our side.

"Corps rehearsal today?" she cooed.

"Why yes," I said, pulling myself upright. "However did you know?"

"The tights and leotards gave it away. It's an interesting look for you." Neither Jayne nor I had bothered to change—instead we'd thrown skirts over our dance clothes and hoped we looked chic. "Walter says he's hoping to start working on the first number at the end of this week. I do hope you'll be ready by then."

That was good. If I didn't get a chance to talk to Paulette's friends before then, at least I knew we'd all be in the same room together soon.

"Don't worry about us," said Jayne. "We'll be ready."

Minnie appeared behind Ruby and cleared her throat. In her arms was a tray full of lunch for the two of them.

Ruby tossed a side glance at our table. I was only halfway through my sandwich, and I wasn't going anywhere. I turned and rested my legs on the bench beside me. "Enjoy your lunch," I told her with a smile. "The roast beef is particularly . . . delicious."

She wiped the grin off her own face. "Have fun at corps rehearsal." She and her minion retreated to the other side of the shop where a four top was getting ready to vacate a table near the kitchen.

"We could've asked them to join us," said Jayne.

"Don't go soft on me. You know how miserable that would've been. Besides, if she wants something, she needs to learn to ask for it. She can't spend her whole life expecting everyone else to do for her." As I devoured the rest of my sandwich, I spied Ruby and Minnie from the corner of my eye. Ruby dissected her sandwich, pointing out each layer of so-called food and demanding that Minnie verify that it had been prepared to her specifications. That task complete, Ruby divided her attention between eating and talking animatedly, no doubt forcing Minnie to relive every glorious moment she'd experienced at that morning's rehearsal. Minnie watched her with such rapt attention that if a bomb erupted in the room I doubt she would've looked away.

We finished our lunches and hustled back to the rehearsal room. Maureen's mood seemed to have improved since morning. Instead of instructing us to walk according to her strict standards, she told us we were now ready to attempt to dance. We took our positions at the front of the room and waited for her to shuffle us into whatever order she found the most aesthetically pleasing. I was paired with a miniature man named Delbert Rath and placed at the back of the line with the other towering dames. Mrs. Fentswallow, the chain-smoking accompanist, settled behind the piano and lit up in anticipation of her need to play. As she ashed between the ivories, Maureen instructed us to begin performing the steps we knew. I thought we were doing a grand job of impressing her, but as our partners spun us to the left, she slammed her cane onto the floor and screeched. *"Nein!"*

We froze in mid-step. It was amazing how much worse a reprimand sounded when it was delivered in German.

Maureen lifted the cane until it reached her forehead and tapped the tender skin there with its topper—a pewter griffin with red eyes. "Zat is not ze vay ve do it," she said. "You must connect each movement to the next one. Zis time ve vill do it faster!" She clapped her hands to mark the time. "Schnell, schnell, schnell! Zen you vill see." Maureen ordered Mrs. Fentswallow to quadruple the tempo and smiled at our fear-stricken faces. With a snap she ordered us back into the opening pose. *"Und fünf, sech, seiben, acht!"*

The music took on the rapid, looming quality of a bad dream after a Friday night drunk. Delbert and I tried to keep up, but the practicality of doing the same number of things in a quarter of the time struck that part of my brain that attempts to be logical as impossible. When everyone else was turning, we were still two steps behind, and our only hope of catching up was to eliminate everything that stood between them and us. We were approaching a leap, so I focused all my energy into reaching that movement at the same time as everyone else, at which point I'd do my darnedest to stay with them until the end of the routine. While the rest of the women jumped from a standing position, I was forced to do it from a crouch. I met them midair and was pleased as punch to find myself landing in time with them. Alas, I forgot to alert Delbert to my plan. Instead of landing in his arms, I hit the floor. My feet skated away from me, leaving it up to my knee to keep me from falling on my face.

My forehead met the floor, my mouth hung open, and as the others continued to twirl around me, I bounced on my knee, hoping for the momentum to be able to force myself into a standing position.

Most actors know how to fall. It's one of those handy skills you develop for the stage that becomes very convenient for everyday life. The problem wasn't that I'd fallen but that I'd fallen before. Two months earlier, after a night of champagne and self-pity, I'd fallen on an icy sidewalk and done a number on the same knee, destroying a dress of Ruby's in the process. And here I thought I didn't get a souvenir of that trip.

I took a deep breath to minimize the pain and found the sweet, familiar odor of butter filling my nostrils. Is that what happened right before death? Did you hallucinate all of your favorite things?

"Are you hurt?" Maureen asked when the song came to an end.

"Is Hitler German?"

"*Nein*. He is Austrian." *Oops.* "You vere a bar behind everyone else."

I lifted my head and silently let her know what I thought about her lack of concern.

"Can you valk?"

Delbert took hold of my arms and pulled me upright. As long as I didn't put weight on my injured leg, I was fine.

"I can hop."

She sighed and shook her head. I was being very inconsiderate. "You cannot dance injured," she said, though I suspect she was dying to complete the sentence before my injury was mentioned. "Go home. Ice your leg. Come back tomorrow. If it's not better . . ." Her voice trailed off. I got it. If it wasn't better, me and my bum leg were out.

She told the other dancers to take five, and Jayne and Delbert helped me out the door and down the stairs. I thanked Delbert for his assistance and sent him on his way while I hobbled out of the theater and onto the curb.

"Do you want me to wait for a cab with you?" asked Jayne.

"And face the wrath of Maureen? No, get upstairs. I'll be fine." I turned away from her and pretended to hunt for a hack. I blinked back tears that mixed with a light snow.

"Does it hurt?"

The pain was no worse than the thousands of other injuries I'd done to myself, but I couldn't get past the harm to my ego. "It's not so bad."

"You didn't even want to be in this show, Rosie."

"It's not a want; it's a need." If I didn't stay in the show, I wouldn't be able to talk to Paulette's friends, and if I couldn't talk to them, there was no chance I could find out what had really happened to Al.

Jayne rubbed my arm, to warm me up and reassure me. "It'll get better," she said. "Just stay off it for the rest of today."

I smiled at her tact. "I will. Now go. Seriously."

She went inside the theater, and I settled onto a bench shielded by the Bernhardt's marquee. There were no cabs in sight. I passed the time watching a brunette half a block away kiss her flame-haired soldier good-bye, then set my sights on a flyer plastered by the snow to the ground. The New York Wing of the First Fighter Command was desperately in need of women between the ages of eighteen and fifty to work in airplane interceptor centers. Don't Be Idle, the flyer warned. Our Pilots Need You.

"And I need them," said an unfamiliar voice. I looked up and found the brunette standing beside me. Now that I could see her up close, I recognized her as one of Ruby's costars and one of Paulette's friends. She was tall and thin, with the kind of grin that was made for Benson & Hedges ads.

"I don't think they'll pay you for that," I said.

"Don't be fooled; they won't pay you for spotting enemy planes either. And what I do is more fun." She pulled out a brass cigarette case decorated with two enamel hearts pierced by an arrow. "Smoke?"

"No thanks."

"Are you one of the hoofers?"

"I was until I managed to trip over my own feet."

She lit a Virginia Round and took a long drag. "Well, if it's any consolation, things are lousy in the other rehearsal room too."

"No injuries though, right?"

"Just a script that should be put out of its misery. I'm Zelda DeMarcos."

"Rosie Winter."

She shook my hand like we were sealing a deal and sat beside me. "Wait a second—Rosie Winter? I know that name . . . weren't you in *In the Dark*?"

I looked at the ground. "I see my reputation precedes me."

"I meant that as a good thing. You were fantastic."

"How do you know? I did only one show."

"Yeah, but it was the performance I saw. No offense, but it's criminal that you're in the dance chorus." I didn't correct her. She was right—it *was* criminal.

I grinned at my lap. "Aren't you supposed to be inside?"

"We're on a break so I went for a walk."

"And made a new friend?"

She winked at me. "Ran into an old one. Want me to hail you a cab?"

"At this point I'd take a lame horse and a rickety cart." She peered down the road. A hired hack passed us, and she waved at its red-headed blur of a passenger. "You were one of Paulette's friends, right?" I asked.

Her wry smile vanished. There was a glint of distrust in her eyes. "Sure. Everyone in the show was."

"But you and those other two women were particularly close to her, weren't you?"

She nodded.

I scrambled for an explanation for why I'd brought Paulette up. "I live at the rooming house she used to live in and she was always sort of an . . . idol of mine. I'm just sick over what happened."

That did it. The distrust left her. "You're at the Shaw House?"

"The one and only."

Zelda smiled. "She loved that place."

I hummed a response that was meant to imply that I did too. "At least they caught whoever did it. That must be a small consolation." She shrugged and I realized the stupidity of the comment. When someone you loved was taken away, there was no such thing as a consolation. "Did you know the guy who did it?"

A yellow came into view. Zelda rose to her feet and waved the cab to the curb. "Your chariot, madam."

"Thanks," I said. She took my arm and helped me hobble inside. "It was nice talking to you."

"You too." She watched as we pulled away, her face giving me no indication that she'd even heard my question.

The cab I couldn't afford landed in front of the Shaw House. I tossed the driver the last of my lettuce and watched irritably as he straightened the bill before sliding it into his pocket. His money stored, he cleared the meter and waited in silence for . . . something.

"This is the place, right lady?" His accent was standard Brooklynese, turning each of his *t*'s into *d*'s.

"I need a little help," I told him.

He threw his arms open wide and looked down at his chest. "Wish I could do something for you, but I got a bad back."

"Bet it would feel better if your wallet was a little lighter."

"Hard to say."

I threw my shoulder against the back door and forced it open with a groan. The light snow had turned into an early spring ice storm. My good leg tested the pavement before committing to standing on it.

"I ain't got all day," said the cabbie.

"That's what you think."

He pulled away in a squeal of tires. I saluted him with a Bronx cheer.

A million years later, I climbed the steps and entered the Shaw House. Paulette's picture watched me in silent judgment as I crossed the foyer and entered the lobby. I probably would've cut my losses and collapsed onto the sofa, except someone was already sitting there.

He was the kind of man I would've instantly thought of as handsome except for two things: his dress uniform and his somber expression. Since the war, I wasn't used to encountering men under fifty unless they were 4-F or fortunately associated. Sure, I saw enlisted men every day, but once they donned their uniforms and committed their lives, they became a mirage. The minute you approached them, you knew they would disappear bit by bit until the only thing left was a memory.

"Hiya," I said to this one, in case he proved to be real. He stopped playing with his hat long enough to return my greeting with a nod. I started to hobble across the lobby and toward the stairs but stopped before I was halfway there. I searched the lobby for signs of Belle, our housemother. Usually if there was a man within fifty feet of the house, she was standing at the ready to protect our collective virtue.

"Does Belle know you're here?"

He nodded at his lap. "She went to get something."

If I hadn't been hurt, I would've gone on my way without thinking any further about it. Maybe it was because I was already vulnerable, or because I was forced to move at a rate normally reserved for two-toed tree sloths—whatever the reason, my brain fixated on the man on the sofa and rather than accepting that he had his own reason for being there, I had to invent one for him.

The problem with any job that demanded creativity was that if you were good at what you did, you developed that odd muscle called imagination. While performing, I was called upon to picture myself in any number of absurd situations and convince myself they were real. It was a great skill to have onstage, but I couldn't turn it off during everyday life. And so my mind was constantly creating scenarios that bore nothing in common with truth, and my emotions, already stretched thin by the demands of feeling joy and sorrow when there was no reason for either, began to appear in response to my fictions. I could convince myself of anything except that what I pretended was real wasn't.

And so it was that as I crossed the lobby I began to mull why a man in a dress uniform would be at the Shaw House, and the only reason I could come up with was that he was there for me. If that were the case, then who was he? Only one identity made any sense and that was that this man was Corporal Harrington, the sailor who'd notified me that Jack was missing in action. And if he was here, and he was sad (and clearly he was), then the worst thing possible had happened.

I gasped and spun around, doing greater injury to my knee in the process. I took the soldier in again from top to tail and tried to remember what naval uniforms looked like and what insignia corporals wore. He had little wings on his collar. What was that—a seagull? Damn me for not knowing anything about the military! Why hadn't I gone to see *This Is the Army* with Jayne?

I begged myself to calm down. Whatever he came to say, I'd hear him out. I'd be strong and brave and invite him for a cup of coffee once his message was delivered. I'd let him tell me about Jack, and when he was done and gone, only then would I cry.

"Rosie." Belle entered the lobby from the kitchen. She wore one of several relics from her vaudeville days, a brightly colored, feather-trimmed, velvet dress that allowed for easy movement while rewarding visitors with a little too much sagging chest and expanding leg. "I'm glad you're here." I looked from her to Corporal Harrington and estimated how quickly I could run with a bum knee. If he never said what he'd come to say, then couldn't we claim it never happened? Belle gestured to the man and he stood. "This is . . ." *No,* my brain screamed. *Don't say it. I can't be strong. I can't be brave.* "Captain George Pomeroy."

"Captain George Pomeroy?" I repeated.

"Yes," said Belle. "Are you all right?"

I hopped on my good leg to put the color back in my face. "I had an accident at rehearsal. Nothing serious."

George stepped away from the sofa and gestured for me to take his place. He was polite, this soldier. No, not soldier. Pilot. Those wings on his collar were air force insignia.

"I'm all right," I said. "I was just headed up to my room."

"Do you mind if we come with you?" asked Belle.

I froze, unsteadily, with my leg raised like a flamingo's. Belle asking to bring a man to my room was like the Allies offering up England to Germany. It just wasn't done. "Did I hear you right?"

"His fiancée used to live here, and he wanted to see her room. I was just about to take him up there. She was in 2B."

That was my room. And Paulette's former room. "Sure," I said. "Right this way."

Belle charged ahead of us. As I hobbled up the stairs, Captain Pomeroy remained at a safe distance behind me. Despite his modesty, I knew that if I stumbled, he would reach out and steady me. He was the kind of guy who radiated consideration.

"Wait," I said to Belle. The pain in my leg had rendered me momentarily stupid. Belle couldn't come into my room. There was too much contraband, to say nothing of the cat.

"What's the matter?" asked Belle.

I leaned heavily against the railing. "The pain in my leg. It's really bad. Do you have any pain tablets?"

"Can't it wait?"

"It really can't."

Belle sighed and looked past me at the captain. I expected her to tell me to go climb my thumb, but George Pomeroy was a man in uniform, and that gave him a free pass for a lot of things these days, including going where no man had been welcome before. "I'll see what I can find." Belle waddled past us, and I ceased my demonstration of pain. The captain and I made it into the hallway, where I paused before my closed door.

"This is the joint," I said. "I should warn you—my roomie and I aren't known for our . . . cleanliness." He smiled at that. At least I think he did. He may have just momentarily relaxed his frown. I opened the door and ushered him in before hobbling over to Jayne's bed and landing rump first on her still sprawled pajamas.

Captain Pomeroy walked around the room examining the walls, ceiling, floor, and windows, but paying no mind to anything that belonged to us. Churchill crawled out from under the dresser and, sensing a new victim to entertain, approached the captain and rubbed his back against the captain's legs.

"I'd appreciate it if you kept the cat on the q.t. We're not allowed animals." I stood up long enough to nudge Churchill into the closet and close the door. I was feeling increasingly uncomfortable with my companion. It's not that I was threatened by him, but I longed for him to say something—anything—to break the awkward silence. "So what branch are you in?"

He was kind enough not to call me an idiot. "Air force."

I nodded. "When did your fiance live here?"

He looked out the window, taking in the neon hotel sign that served as our sun and moon. He had close-cropped red hair that turned pink in the thin afternoon light and a spray of freckles across the bridge of his nose that would always mark him as younger than he actually was. "About a year and a half ago. This place was very special to her. She talked about it all the time."

"What was her name?"

"Paulette Monroe." He read the recognition in my face. "Did you know her?"

"She was before my time, but I've heard of her. She was kind of a legend around here, what with going to Hollywood and everything. I was sorry to hear what happened."

He left his post at the window and came to my side. "May I sit?"

"Of course."

He landed heavily on my bed and stared at that object with such unfamiliarity that it was clear he hadn't slept for days. "Paulette promised me that the next time I came to New York she'd show me around, do it up right. She loved this place. Talked about it more than her mom and pop." Now that he was making a habit of this talking thing,

I picked up a slight Southern accent. His voice was soft and wistful, so close to feminine it was hard to imagine him shouting alongside other soldiers.

"How did you meet Paulette?"

He didn't answer me; he answered the wall. "At the Stage Door Canteen. We danced half the night and the next thing you know we were writing each other every day."

"And then you got engaged."

He looked down at red, wind-chapped hands and rubbed at a patch of peeling skin. "I did it on a V-Disc. You should've heard the other guys hooting and hollering as I recorded myself. Never thought I'd live that down. She wanted to get married right away, but I thought we should wait until my next leave—you know, so the families could be there. I never thought . . ." He didn't finish the sentence. He didn't have to.

I struggled to make sense of a woman with a gangster beau and an air force fiancé. Who was Paulette Monroe, and how did she end up with more men at once than I was likely to have in a lifetime?

"I hear they arrested someone," I said. He nodded. "Had Paulette ever mentioned the guy before?"

He rubbed at his thumb, an apparent habit of his. The skin was red and angry. "Never."

Of course she hadn't. Why would either man know about the other?

"Thanks for letting me see the room." George stood and straightened the creases on his heavily starched pants. "It's nice knowing what she saw when she was here. I feel like maybe, by being in the same places she was, it's a little like being with her, you know?"

I nodded and rose onto my unsteady feet. "Is the air force giving you some time off?"

"A couple of weeks."

"Are you spending it all here?"

"I'm only in New York till Saturday. There's going to be a service for her on Friday, so all her acting friends can be a part of it, then

I'm taking a train back home with her, for the real funeral." I thought about the long, hard ride he had ahead of him, probably the most time he and Paulette had ever spent together.

"Where are you staying?"

"At a hotel called the Endicott. It's on Columbus and Eightieth Street." I knew the joint. It was a step up from a flophouse and ran you two bits a night—less if you didn't want to pony up for a private bath. "Do you think I could have a moment alone in here?"

"Sure." I stepped out of the room and closed the door behind me. From the hallway I could hear the low rumble of his voice as he talked to the ghost he hoped was listening. I struggled to make sense of what he was saying, but the only phrase I could decipher was "I'm sorry. So, so sorry." I couldn't tell from his tone if it was her death alone that he regretted or if George Pomeroy had done something that needed a dead woman's forgiveness.

He opened the door and I jumped.

"Thanks for that," he said. "It's been swell meeting you."

"You too."

He turned back toward the window, and I imagined he was picturing Paulette looking at the same city view, wondering when the day would come that she could leave this dump and move on to something better. "Do you know there's a suitcase on your fire escape?"

"Yeah, but thanks for the reminder."

He shook my hand, took one final look around the room, and then, with a tip of his hat, disappeared.

6 A Woman of Impulse

RESTING UP SEEMED LIKE A foolish idea under the circumstances. As soon as I was sure Captain Pomeroy had left the building, I retrieved the valise from the fire escape, hopped back down to the lobby, and located Belle.

"What are you doing down here?" she asked. In one hand she held a tin of Surety Aspirin; in the other was *The New York Sun War Time Cook Book*, a culinary guide to such barely edibles as Victory Ham, liver and sausage loaf, and Norwegian prune pudding.

"I thought I'd save you a trip. I have a gift for you."

She handed over the aspirin and eyed the suitcase suspiciously. "Thanks, but I already have one."

"Not the case. Look inside."

She popped it open and flinched at the sight of the bloody meat, as though they weren't steaks but disembodied limbs. "Are you off your nut?"

"It's steak, Belle. A friend gave them to me and I figured you and your cousin might want them."

She lowered her gaze. "Why?"

"Why what?"

"Why would you give me something?"

This was the last time I was going to do something nice for anyone without a motive. "Because all in all you're a good egg and because it's not like I can boil meat in my teakettle. You either take it or I'm chucking it into the street."

"Are they on the up and up?"

I put my hand to my heart. "How could you ask that?"

"If you're buying from the black market, you're stealing from the mouths of soldiers."

"I've read the posters too. These are perfectly legit. I'd take it if I were you. Voluntary meatless Tuesday starts tomorrow and you know that doesn't bode well."

"All right, I'll take it. *This* time."

"What a gal."

She picked up the steaks and started toward the kitchen.

"Any chance you can get me a hot-water bottle while you're in there? My knee could use one right about now."

She gave me an irritated look that made it clear that despite any empathy she may have for my injured state, she didn't feel it was her duty to be my nursemaid. Still, she went into the kitchen and emerged a short time later with a red hot water bottle and a couple of dish towels to keep it from scorching me. I limped to the sofa and wrapped the bundle about my leg.

I wasn't sure how to approach the subject of Paulette Monroe, so I dove right in.

"Paulette must've been a pretty special dame for Captain Pomeroy to come all the way to New York. Did you know her very well when she lived here?"

Belle crossed her arms and cocked her head. The sour expression she usually wore clenched her features into a tight pout. "Well enough." Belle wasn't in the habit of making friends with the Shaw House women. It's not that she was cold, but I think our habit of viewing her as the maternal warden, and the likelihood that any one of us could be gone tomorrow, diminished the desire on both of our parts to get to know each other. Plus, as keeper of the rules, she had to remain at a distance lest she be accused of favoritism. If Belle was anything, she was fair.

"How long did she live here?" I asked.

"Three years, on and off. She did some touring shows, but she always came back here when she was done."

Three years was longer than most girls. The typical house stay was six months, just long enough for you to get on your feet or give up the ghost. I was at a year and a half myself and was beginning to wonder if I hadn't overstayed my welcome. It's not that I didn't love the place, but there was a big difference between choosing to leave and being forced to stay.

"And then she went to Hollywood?" I asked.

Belle turned away and focused on stacking newspapers that had been discarded on the sideboard. "She lived with some girlfriends for a while. Uptown. And then she went to Hollywood."

"So why'd she come back?"

"Walter Friday's pretty big, isn't he?"

"Five years ago, sure. But you couldn't drag me out of Hollywood to work with him now."

Belle shrugged. "Maybe she missed New York. She had a lot of friends here."

"Including male ones?"

She forced the corners of her stack into precise right angles. "What happens outside of the house isn't my business."

This was getting me nowhere. Belle signaled that we had reached the end of our conversation by attempting to haul the newspapers into the kitchen. The pile of twice dailies was more than she could handle and a few stray issues landed on the floor with a thump. Rather than attempting to pick them up, she gave the offending papers a kick and took what remained of her bundle into the kitchen.

I gathered up my hot water bottle and towels and decided to convalesce upstairs. As I hobbled past the papers Belle had dropped, two words from a headline caught my eye: *Broadway* and *slain*. I hopped closer and read the teaser: Johnny Levane, purported mob henchman, found slain in Broadway alley. The paper was dated March fourth, the day after Al went into prison. The article, in *The Times'* ongoing attempt not to glorify mob violence, had been relegated to the back page. There wasn't even a picture.

I picked up the paper and tucked it beneath my arm. I was probably whistling in the wind, but if the story involved the mob and the theater, I was going to hang on to it just in case.

Jayne woke me up at a quarter after five. I was sprawled face-first across my bed, drowning in a pile of my own drool. Churchill kept dry atop my pillow, swinging his tail in time to the ticking of my bedside clock.

"How you feeling?" asked Jayne.

I rolled over and flexed my offending pin. Hours of immobility and the now cold hot-water bottle had left me stiff. I wasn't in any pain, but I didn't think I was going to be capable of graceful motion anytime soon either. "Better, I guess. Did I miss much?"

"Nothing I can't catch you up on."

Somehow I doubted that.

"I brought you a present." She passed me a thin paper sack. Inside was the latest issue of *Harper's Bazaar* with a young model named Lauren Bacall on the cover. Miss Bacall stood in front of a Red Cross Blood Service Center, looking forlornly at the camera, her lips carefully painted a bright, patriotic red. I flipped through the magazine. It was the spring fashion issue. For those folks who had enough cash and coupons, the tropical look was going to be all the rage. How better to forget about your man risking his life in the South Pacific than by wearing high Cuban platform shoes and carved Catalin bracelets?

"Thanks," I told Jayne. "I needed some new reading."

"Did you sleep all afternoon?"

My nap-induced fog slowly lifted. "No. Actually, I had an interesting visitor a few hours ago." I filled Jayne in on my meeting with Captain Pomeroy.

"Poor guy. Widowed and cuckolded all in one week."

"Almost widowed," I said. "It's not like they were hitched. And remember: he doesn't know what Paulette was up to." I sat on the edge of the bed and tested my knee. "I really felt bad for the guy. You could tell he loved her."

"And maybe she really loved him."

"And Al. And who knows who else."

Jayne shrugged. "You can love more than one person, you know. Or maybe Pomeroy was her one true love and Al was . . ."

"A career move?"

"It's possible." It didn't seem fair that we assumed Al couldn't have been the love of her life. He was a good egg, wasn't he? And from what he'd told me in the past, he could be a devoted boyfriend.

Jayne peeled off her leotard and tights and tossed them onto the floor. She plucked her kimono from its hook on the wall and wrestled with it before finally wrapping it around her body. "What's this?" Her eyes had landed on the *Times* I'd dragged up from the lobby.

"Probably nothing, but I ran across that downstairs. You ever hear of him?"

"Johnny Levane? It doesn't ring any bells."

"Yeah, me neither, but I thought gangster, Broadway, murder . . ." My voice faded. I was looking for anything to exonerate Al and Jayne knew it.

She put the paper on the nightstand, where it would likely remain until the page was obliterated with coffee rings. "It won't hurt to hold on to it for a while. How's Ruby?"

I would've been less surprised if she asked me what I thought about Spam (for the record, I found it too salty but enjoyed it Aloha style with pineapple and avocado). There were certain topics Jayne never willingly broached. "Ruby? I would imagine surly and self-absorbed. You would know better than me."

"Didn't she come home?"

"I'm two steps behind you. I've been unconscious, remember? Why don't you give me the lay?"

Jayne sat beside me. She vibrated with excitement. "Sorry—you really did miss out on something then. Ruby got sick and had to leave rehearsal."

"How sick?"

"Mind you, I wasn't there, but apparently she went for her fitting and everyone in the costume shop got to admire what she had for breakfast and lunch."

This was too good. The only downside was that we'd missed it.

"Anyway, they sent her home and I just assumed that she would've been over here telling you how sick she was."

It was a good assumption. There was only one reason Ruby wouldn't come to visit me and rub in how much worse off she was than me—she was actually ill. And if that were the case, the last things she'd want were witnesses.

"Can you handle a walk across the hall?" asked Jayne.

"If I can't," I said, "I'll crawl."

7 Angel Face

WE KNOCKED ON RUBY'S DOOR for a good minute before her weak voice responded. I pushed it open and found her royal highness hidden beneath a pile of blankets, one pale white arm lying across her stomach.

The only thing missing was the violin music.

Ruby lived alone, which was fortunate since I doubt she could've crammed a roommate into her Shrine of All Things Ruby. While we made do with the furniture that had come with the house, Ruby had brought in her own sticks, including a canopy bed that rose to within an inch of the ceiling. Everything was pink and white, like an over-iced cupcake. Her walls were covered with photos and reviews, not push-pinned into place like most girls would do, but each tastefully framed and matted. And, of course, where there weren't photos, there were mirrors, since gazing at the real thing was always better than a reproduction.

"We heard you were ill," Jayne said. I had no idea how she managed to convey such an impressive depth of sincerity without drinking first. "We wanted to check on you."

Ruby adjusted her position until we could see first the tangled, damp mass of hair at the top of her head, then the red, swollen face dotted with hives.

"Wow," I said. "You look awful." I hadn't meant for it to come out like that, but when you're expecting mink and greeted with mange, you're compelled to react.

"Thanks a lot." Ruby burrowed beneath the quilt again. "Are they talking about me at the theater?"

I wanted to turn her malaise into misery, but Jayne shushed me with a wave of her hand and stepped forward. "Just out of concern. Everyone felt terrible that you were so sick."

Ruby's head again emerged from its cave, her expression a curious mixture of gratitude and suspicion. She knew Jayne was lying, but she needed the lie if she ever hoped to show her face at the Bernhardt again.

"Do you need anything?" asked Jayne. Before Ruby could respond, the door opened behind us. Minnie, pitcher and glass in hand, emerged from the hallway. She abruptly interrupted her mission to quench the infirm when she saw us standing in the room.

"Oh," she said. "I didn't realize you had visitors. I brought you some water." She deposited the glass at Ruby's bedside and filled it.

"Did they cancel rehearsal after I left?" Ruby asked.

Minnie turned away from her mistress and concentrated on folding Ruby's hastily shed clothing. "No. Walter was concerned about another delay, so we went forward with the day as planned."

"Oh." If Ruby's face turned any paler, we would have to search for her pulse. "Who stepped in for me?"

Minnie turned back to her, her abnormally large eyes growing even larger. "I did. It was awful, Ruby. I know every time I said one of your lines everyone was thinking about what a miserable replacement I was for you."

Ruby's cheeks pinked and she fought to hide a smile. "I'm sure it wasn't that bad."

"No it was, it really was. I don't know why I ever thought I could be an actress." Minnie looked down at her bitten fingernails and picked at a piece she hadn't yet devoured.

Ruby pulled herself up until she was propped by her pillows. "There's no reason for you to fret, Minnie. Your agony has ended. I'll be returning tomorrow."

Minnie ceased damaging her digits. "Are you sure that's a good idea?"

"Of course it is. I feel fine. I'm just having an allergic reaction to something."

"But shouldn't you see a doctor before you go back? You know, to make sure it's not contagious?"

Jayne and I silently took one step backward.

"Don't be ridiculous. If it were contagious, I would think after days of rehearsal, everyone would have it."

Minnie looked helplessly to Jayne and me for support.

I smiled at Ruby. That had to cue her that bad news was coming. "I think what Minnie's trying to say, far more tactfully than I'm going to, is that you'd really be doing everyone a favor if you didn't leave this room for a while. To be frank, Ruby, I don't think Walter Friday seeing you like this is going to do a thing to endear you to him."

"It's a just little swelling. It will be gone by tomorrow."

"And the war will be over, and butter will be plentiful, and I'll get a studio contract that will keep me fat and fancy for the next ten years." I freed a hand mirror from her bureau and brought it to her. "But just in case those things don't happen in the next twenty-four hours, I think you need to come up with a Plan B."

Ruby stared at her reflection, her thin, pale hands trembling just above the surface of her face. I wanted to enjoy the moment, but I found myself reluctant to find any pleasure in Ruby's situation. I was in a show where I had no talent, and she was in a mess where the one asset she could always depend on had been temporarily robbed from her. We were sisters in suffering.

"All right," she whispered. "Tell Walter I can't make it tomorrow and please ask Belle to call Dr. Archway."

8 Business Before Pleasure

As Jayne and I were getting ready to leave for rehearsal the next morning, Ruby's voice, strained with the effort to be nice, called out, "Rosie, I need you."

Jayne went to wait for the cab she'd generously offered to split with me. I cautiously approached the lair of the swollen. The night had not been kind to Ruby. The hives were bigger, the swelling increased, and her skin color hovered between fire engine and tomato soup. It took everything in me not to flinch.

"Hiya, Rube. What can I do for you?"

She left her bed and approached me, her natural poise and grace yanked down by the weight of her enormous, misshapen head. If St. Patrick's started sounding the hour, the similarity to Quasimoto would've been undeniable. "Are you going to rehearsal?"

"Absolutely." Truth be told, my knee needed another day of rest, but I knew Maureen wouldn't be willing to grant me one.

"Could you do me a favor?" Her hand reached toward mine. I reflexively backed away. "On your way there could you mail this for me?"

In her palm was a piece of V-mail directed to the AFPO address. I took it, taking care not to touch her skin, and slid it into my pocket. "Sure."

"You'll make sure it goes out p.d.q.?"

"As God is my witness."

She relaxed at that and slumped back to the bed.

•   •   •

We arrived at the Bernhardt early. While Jayne went into the rehearsal room to stretch, I went in search of Zelda. Since the odds
were good that Maureen would fire me after this rehearsal, I decided
that if I didn't talk to Zelda and her friends now, I wasn't likely to get
a chance again.

The actors were rehearsing a floor above us in a room dominated
by a table laden with coffee and Danishes. A mock-up of the set had
been arranged at one end of the room, and while the cast waited for
Walter Friday to arrive, they lounged on the makeshift tables and
chairs eating their breakfast and looking over their lines.

Paulette's friends sat together on a well-worn sofa, their legs
crossed right over left. Their staginess didn't end there. They all
wore belted wool dresses in complimentary shades of blue and styled
their hair—one blonde, one brunette, one redhead—with a part to the
left and a series of tight curls on the right. They mirrored one another in their bright red lips and nails, and the brown T-strap shoes
they'd polished to a shine. They'd even arranged themselves so that
the blonde—the smallest of them—was seated in the center while the
taller women flagged her on either side.

Everything about them said sophistication, and while I should've
found them utterly intimidating, Zelda caught my eye and offered me
a welcoming smile. *Hello again,* the grin said. *Don't be scared. We're just
like you only better dressed.*

I took a step in their direction and found my path blocked.

"Hi, Rosie." Minnie stood directly in front of me. I looked helplessly at Zelda. She had gone back to her conversation. "What are you
doing here?" The question was asked on the sly. I was an infiltrator,
not a guest.

"I . . . uh . . . need to talk to Walter Friday." I gazed about the
room as though Walter were hiding behind one of the folding chairs
Paulette's friends perched on.

"He's in his office. Phone call."

I glanced at my wristwatch. There was no hope of talking to Paulette's friends with Minnie here playing chaperone. And if I was late

to my rehearsal, I would only be giving Maureen another reason to give me the boot.

"Did you see Ruby this morning?" asked Minnie.

"I think so. It was hard to tell with all the swelling."

"Poor thing. I meant to stop by before I left, but I overslept. I feel awful—I told her I'd mail a letter for her and completely forgot to pick it up."

"No worries—she got me to do it."

Minnie looked surprised. Who could blame her? "That was nice of you."

"What can I say? Pity brings out the best in me."

"Do you want me to give Mr. Friday a message for you?"

"That's all right. I'll see him later." I began my careful limp back the way I came.

"There's a shortcut." She took two steps toward a door on the other side of the room and offered me a wide, off-kilter smile. I was overreacting. She wasn't making me feel unwelcome—I was.

"Thanks," I told her, then I exited through the door.

Minnie's shortcut put me in the hallway outside the administrative offices. It was separated from the rehearsal halls by a swinging door. I'd assumed we weren't welcome back there, but it was indeed a faster way to get from where I was to where I was going.

"What time will you be out of here tonight?" A low voice leaked into the corridor and planted me where I stood. The speaker had a slight lisp, as though he were being forced to talk while clenching a pencil between his teeth. It had to be Garvaggio and his omnipresent cigar.

"By five—six at the latest."

"I don't know if that's good enough, Walt." So he was talking to Friday. So much for the phone call. "My guys—they don't seem to trust you so much anymore. After the last time . . ."

"It was a mistake, Vinnie. It happens."

"Not in our business. When the space is ours, it's ours."

"Can't we talk about this later? I've got a rehearsal to get to."

"There won't be a show if you don't hear me out. Get it? I'm going to need the building on Thursday no later than five thirty."

"Impossible. We're bringing the dancers in. Things are supposed to run late."

"Then you're going to have to move your rehearsal, aren't you? If we want the space on Thursday at five, it's happening on Thursday at five."

Something in the office hit a hard metal surface, sending a hollow boom through the corridor. I couldn't tell if it was Walter Friday's head or his hand. "I can't keep this up, Vinnie. I can't be running a show with your people coming in and out of here."

"That's the deal we made."

"One of the girls is bound to see something. Your friends didn't do such a good job cleaning up last time."

"If you're that worried, Walt, maybe we should close down this show here and now."

"I can't do that!"

"But I can, get it? My job isn't to keep you happy—your job is."

Friday muttered something under his breath before slipping out the door. I flattened myself against a wall and prayed for invisibility. Fortunately, he was in such a tizzy that I could've hit him with a sledgehammer and he wouldn't have noticed. As soon as he was out of the corridor, Garvaggio started talking again. The conversation this time was one-sided. He was on the phone.

"How's our friend? Ain't that a shame. Did you let him know that as soon as he's out we'll be paying him a visit? Good. Good. Well, he should be scared. Go back tomorrow and make the point twice as hard."

The phone slammed into the base. I left the wall and limped toward my destination. I was almost past the swinging doors when a voice called after me.

"You lost, sweetheart?" Vinnie Garvaggio stood in all of his obese glory, the cigar still firmly clamped between his teeth. Despite the ring of smoke that surrounded him, he had a sweet, fresh smell. Never had I seen a dress shirt that was so white.

"I got a bum knee and was told there was a shortcut to the dance chorus rehearsal."

In his hand was a piece of bread so heavily buttered the middle of it had started to sink. He used it to point me in the right direction. "Through those doors." Then he winked at me, disappeared back into the office, and closed the door behind him.

Naturally, I was late to rehearsal. Instead of reprimanding me, Maureen greeted my return as an inconvenience she hadn't anticipated having to deal with. She'd assumed I was smart enough to stay away for good. "Leg all better?"

"Good as new," I said, which would've been true if *good* meant painful and inflexible.

"Und yet you are late." She clucked her tongue and rested both hands atop her walking stick. The other dancers were already assembled in their lines. There was no gap made to represent where I would be standing. Delbert had been grouped into a trio with another guy and gal and was doing his best not to make eye contact with me.

Maureen offered me the kind of smile she usually reserved for Hansel and Gretel when they visited her candy house. "Perhaps you should sit zings out to catch up." It wasn't a question; it was an order and one that I gladly took. The pianist began a piece I wasn't familiar with, which meant that after I'd left rehearsal the day before, the group had progressed enough to learn something new. It turned out Maureen had done me an immense kindness. While I rested in relative comfort on a folding chair, the dancers performed a militaristic combination of steps that I wouldn't have been able to duplicate if I'd had a hundred hours of rehearsal. They leaped, bent, whirled, and flew with the perfect grace and timing of a pack of starlings on the last day of fall. Despite this apparent flawlessness, when they finished, Maureen sighed and tapped her cane in time to her chant of *"Nein, nein, nein!"*

I would've been crushed, but the dancers accepted this reprimand and, on her command, repeated the piece, somehow making everything bigger, faster, tighter, and more cohesive. To this victory of movement Maureen sighed and announced, "Ve vill vork on it later. For now ve move on."

She reconfigured everybody for the next piece, sending half of the pairs to one side of the room, the other half to the other. When it was apparent she'd forgotten she still had me to contend with, I faked a cough to get her attention. "Oh, you," she said. "Go stand vith Delbert. In the back."

It was a rough morning. My knee didn't like being jarred, my ego didn't like being pummeled, and gravity insisted on raising her ugly head at every opportunity. Maureen, mercifully, directed little of her criticism my way, not because I was improving but because she was smart enough to know not to kick a gal when she was down. Where was the fun in that?

After lunch, we resumed our positions for the latest combination and with renewed vigor attempted to not disappoint Maureen. We were doing good—me included—until Luke Piccolo, a trollish man with a lazy eye, attempted to lift his partner above his head. Before his elbows reached his ears, he slipped, sending his partner, Lily, belly first onto the wooden floor. We all backed away in shock, waiting for a sign that she was still alive. A moan was our only confirmation.

"Can you stand?" Maureen asked for the second time in as many days. Lily pushed herself into a kneel and gratefully latched onto Maureen's arm for support. Slowly she rose, her face making it clear that every ounce of her was in pain. While Luke murmured excuses that ranged from Lily's weight to the poor construction of his ballet slippers, I stared at the floor, grateful it wasn't me that had fallen. A few feet from the scene of the crime was a particularly shiny patch of floor. I ran my ballet slipper through it to confirm what I suspected: the floor was slick enough to trip a rhino. And I was willing to bet that if I put my shoe to my nose, I'd be fighting the temptation to wipe what I found on a piece of toast.

With Lily out of commission, Maureen called it a day. Jayne offered to split another cab, but after six hours of movement my knee was so numb I could've hopscotched home. We caught the subway and exited at Christopher Street.

"Odd, isn't it?"

"What?" Jayne asked.

"Two accidents in two days? Yesterday when I fell I thought it was a fluke, but now I'm not so sure."

"Dancers fall all the time, Rosie."

What she meant was dancers like Luke and me, two people who clearly had no business being anywhere near a leotard. No, she wasn't thinking that. *I* was. I pushed it out of my mind. "When I fell yesterday I could've sworn I smelled butter, and today I noticed a particularly slick looking patch of ground near where Luke stumbled."

"So you think someone was trying to sabotage you?"

"Me, specifically? No. I'm good enough at doing that on my own. I do think, though, that someone was trying to create another problem for Maureen by making conditions unsafe for her dancers."

"It could be a coincidence," said Jayne. "Someone might've spilled something, and Maureen didn't realize it so it never got cleaned up."

"Perhaps." I was in a bad mood, and it was possible I was looking for problems.

"I'll mention the slick spots to Maureen tomorrow," said Jayne.

I was trying hard not to let my own misery seep her way, but she would've had to have been in an iron lung not to have felt a little of it. She'd had a good day, receiving some of the only praise Maureen would dole out for the year. It was natural that she'd be the person to tell Maureen about the floor. If I did it, I would get dismissed for trying to blame my lack of grace on invisible forces. But for some reason I read in Jayne's plan an arrogance that couldn't possibly exist.

"It'll get better, Rosie," she told me. It was a sweet lie, but it was still a lie.

"Is it better to quit or be fired?"

"They won't fire you."

"If I quit, I can still retain my dignity."

"What about Al?" It was cruel of her to use my own motives against me. Jayne was clever like that.

"If he's guilty, he's guilty. My suffering through another month of this isn't going to help anyone."

"You're not a quitter."

"I'm not a dancer either." I also wasn't someone who let insecurity eat away at me. At least not when it came to my career. I wasn't enjoying this new, whiny version of myself. Where was the girl who wowed the audience on the opening night of *In the Dark*? "Let's set this aside for a minute." I kept my voice low and told her about Walter and Vinnie's conversation. Not that it counted for much. All it proved was what we'd already suspected: Vinnie was backing the show in return for some favor that likely involved the theater being used as a mob drop point.

"For what?" asked Jayne.

"All I know is Vinnie doesn't want anyone around when his business is going down. And whatever that business is, he has to bring in a cleanup crew when he's done." We both shivered. It wasn't hard to imagine the basement of the Bernhardt being used as a holding spot for stiffs before they made their final journey into the Hudson.

Stiffs like Johnny Levane, the back alley body I'd read about in *The Times*.

"Let's not worry about the specifics of what they're doing right now," I said. "What this means is Friday managed to get himself into such a pickle that the only way he could get a show backed was to make a deal like this."

"Or he was forced to make a deal like this because of something he did."

"Isn't that what I just said?"

We rounded the corner to the Shaw House and paused in front of the building. "No," said Jayne. "Your way makes it sound like he was desperate to get the show produced and approached the only people who would give him dough. What I'm suggesting is he was strong-armed into the decision."

"They blackmailed him? I suppose that makes sense. I overheard Vinnie on the phone today talking about someone else. From what I could gather, he seems to be fond of using muscle as a persuasion technique." We went up the stairs and into the building.

Jayne absentmindedly spun the combination on her mailbox, and I did the same. "Of course," she said, "the show's had its backing for a while now, so none of this would have anything do with Paulette." She pulled a letter from the slot and glanced at the return address.

"No, but what if Paulette found out what the mob had on Friday and threatened to squeal? He could've done her in to keep her quiet." I reached inside my box and pulled out two letters.

"Rosie . . ."

"I know what you're going to say: How does Al fit into this? Maybe Friday framed him for the crime. Or maybe he wanted to make it look like a mob killing, and Vinnie set Al up to take a fall."

"Rosie . . ."

"I know it's far-fetched, but—" She stopped me with her hand, and I followed her gaze to the piece of V-mail I was holding, a letter carefully addressed by Corporal Harrington.

9 Lady of Letters

We made it upstairs in record time. While Jayne clicked on the radio and opened a tin of food for Churchill, I attempted to unfurl the letter without tearing it. The handwriting I'd learned well enough to forge zigzagged across the page. Unfortunately, so did something else.

"Son of a gun."

"What?"

"War censor." The thick, black lines of the censor's pen inked out the majority of what Corporal Harrington had written me. I held it to the light, hoping to make out shadows of the words that had once been there, but the censor had been careful in his work. This was a letter lost.

"Well, what do the uncensored parts say?"

"Dear Miss Winter. Thanks for your letter. I wish I had better news for you at this point, but so far nothing else has been discovered. I know it must be hard, waiting for word, but please don't lose hope. It's all we have anymore. I think you should know that right before Jack disappeared. . ."

Jayne waved the cat food tin at me. "Right before he disappeared what?"

"That's where the letter stops and the censor starts. The only other bit of text is his signature at the end."

She took the letter from me and duplicated my attempt to hold it up to the light. "You've got to be kidding me. This is just cruel."

Cruel wasn't the half of it. Now when I wasn't agonizing over where

Jack was and what was happening to him, I could obsess over what he did right before he disappeared. Ate chicken? Declared his undying love for me? Stumbled upon a German camp and unwittingly learned secrets of the Third Reich?

Jayne attempted to hand back the letter, but I pushed it away. "Keep it away from me. Please."

"Maybe you should write him and let him know what the censor did. Tell him to send it again."

"And how is a second letter going to get through when the first one didn't?"

She snapped her fingers. "You could tell him to write it in code so the censors wouldn't know what he's talking about."

"Great idea except then I wouldn't know what he was talking about either."

"Oh." She shrunk onto her bed. "It was just a suggestion."

The radio encouraged me to "Ac-cent-tchu-ate the Positive." I gave Jayne a weak smile. "It was a good suggestion. Just not a very useful one." I was prepared to dissolve into sobs of frustration when Ruby knocked on the door. This would've normally been the point where I vented my anger at the world by telling her to scram, but one look at her bloated, distorted face and all I could muster was a tiny squeal of despair.

Jayne fared better. "How are you?"

"Better." Ruby delicately tucked her hair behind her ears. "Don't I look better?"

We both muttered something we hoped sounded like "yes, of course" but which was probably "just like a horse."

"Dr. Archway verified that it's an allergic reaction."

"To what?" I asked. In the hallway the phone began to ring.

She shrugged. "The only thing I'm allergic to is mustard, and Lord knows I avoid that. He said it's possible—in some rare instances—for people to suddenly develop allergies for foods they've always eaten or things they've always encountered." She said this as though it was something to be proud of. Ruby was so extraordinary she had developed rare allergies. Top that! "Anyway, he gave me a shot of something and said I should be as good as new in another day or two."

I had no idea how that was possible but decided it would be kinder to accept her interpretation of his prognosis.

She lifted her hand to stroke her hair but seemed to remember that what it framed wasn't the porcelain beauty that used to be there. She flinched at the memory of what she'd become and brought both arms stiffly to her sides. "Did you mail my letter?"

From across the room I could see it poking up from the top of my purse. "Of course I did."

Ruby's tough exterior peeled even further away, until I was certain that in a matter of minutes we'd be looking at her skeleton.

Norma Peate hollered from the hallway that Jayne had a call. She flounced away, leaving me with the visitor of gloom and the letter of doom. It was shaping up to be a fine evening.

"Get mail?" asked Ruby. Before I could answer she palmed the V-mail and took a gander at the postmark. In most girls' eyes, the farther a letter traveled, the greater value the correspondent possessed.

"Yep."

"You don't look too happy about it." The minute the words left her mouth I knew she regretted it. I was impressed; Ruby was normally as perceptive as a blind man at a silent movie. "Is it about John?"

"Jack."

"Right. Bad news?"

I flipped the letter over so she could see the strong black lines. "Hard to say. The censor thought it was interesting enough to keep from me."

"What a rotten thing to do." She sighed heavily. "It must be so hard for you. Not knowing." Before I had time to register her empathy, she changed the subject. "I worry about my boyfriend all the time. He's an air force pilot."

I'd forgotten about Ruby's new beau. Perhaps this was why she was suddenly less repellent to be around. Love had tamed her. "Is that who your letter was for?"

She nodded.

"Where'd you meet him?"

"At the Stage Door Canteen. Izzie, Olive, and Zelda volunteer there and they asked me to join them one night."

"They were Paulette's friends, right?"

"And mine. I've known them for ages, and when they got wind that Lawrence and I were through, they suggested I join them one night. Olive said the fellows get a kick out of meeting actresses. Besides, I thought it was time I do something noble for the war."

I bit my tongue to keep from telling her that donating blood or knitting socks might have been more effective.

"His name's Donald J. Montgomery, the third, and he's going to be in town on leave this weekend."

"When did you meet him?" I asked.

"I don't know—maybe a month and a half ago."

"So Paulette wasn't home yet?"

"No. This is before they knew she was returning. In fact, I thought I was going to be moving in with them until she took Walter's show." There was a slight bitterness in Ruby's voice. Paulette had ruined her escape from the Shaw House. If it hadn't been for her, Ruby's life might be going very differently right now.

"You still could," I said. "Of course, you'd break Minnie's heart if you left her here by herself."

"She'd get over it. Eventually." A wisp of a smile lingered on her lips. She knew that Minnie worshipped her, and she liked it. As quick as the smile arrived, it vanished. A scowl weighted down her features. "Incidentally, I didn't appreciate what you told Walter."

"Come again?"

"He called me today in hysterics over what he described as my 'devastating disfigurement.'"

"Much as I'd like to claim responsibility for that little bit of hyperbole, I didn't say word one to Walter Friday today." And if it wasn't me, and it certainly wasn't Jayne, only one other person could've told him. "Did you ask Minnie? Maybe she's the one who squealed."

"She's the one who told me you did it. Anyway, I calmed him down, but I'm clearly going to have to go rehearsal tomorrow."

In a world where looks didn't matter, it was a wise move. In Ruby's case, it was career suicide.

"Ruby, know that I mean this with the best possible intentions: if you want to prove to Friday that you're much better off than he's been led to believe, you can't go to rehearsal. Not like that."

"I'm better!"

"Sure you are, and Frankenstein found a bride, but they were both still monsters. Trust me on this: given the kind of guy Walter is, he won't be able to stomach so much as a blemish on you."

"But if I miss a whole week . . ."

"You'll catch up. Learn your lines and wow him come Monday."

Her eyes briefly glazed over with cynicism before the reality of her situation took hold. Her shoulders slumped and her head tipped forward until I couldn't see her face at all. "I'll think about it."

Sure she would. And she'd probably seek Minnie's opinion, which, no doubt, would echo my own. After all, an actress who stood to gain something from another actress's absence would hardly encourage her to show up to rehearsal.

10 The Best of Friends

Just as I suspected, Ruby opted to sit the rest of the week out. I stumbled through the next two days of rehearsal, waiting for Maureen to state the obvious and cut me free. Instead, she ignored me like a loose tooth you're hoping will right itself. I began testing the limits of her patience, deliberately screwing up the few things I knew how to do, but despite the fact that I was the only thing about the corps that wasn't improving, she never said a word to me. In fact, I suspected she'd figured out a way to block me out entirely.

"You're doing it wrong. Watch me do it." During our union-mandated breaks, Jayne encouraged me to rehearse with her, which was the last thing I wanted to do. Every time she gracefully glided through the steps I'd screwed up moments before, my brain interpreted her attempts at help as a slap in the face. *You'll never be as good as me,* each of her perfect pliés said. *You don't belong here.*

"I'm hopeless, Jayne. Accept it—I have."

"You're not hopeless. You just need to practice more."

"No, what I need is a drink and a partner who doesn't think being assigned to work with me is a form of punishment."

"They're bringing in the cast in two hours." It was Thursday, the day of reckoning. Despite Garvaggio's threats, Friday hadn't moved rehearsal.

"So?" I said.

"Friday will be there." What Jayne was implying was that if I didn't cut it tonight, Walter Friday might cut me by tomorrow. Fear tactics were no longer working on me. I was starting to believe I'd developed some kind of immunity to losing my job. If Friday did let me loose, I think I would've died of shock. "I know you can do this, Rosie. You're just not trying."

"Close your head. I've got blisters on my blisters from trying."

"Try harder." She had her hands on her hips, her head tilted back until she could meet my eyes.

"You sound like Delbert. What's the point? I'm never going to be any good at this. I wasn't even supposed to be cast in this lousy show. I came to support you, remember?"

"So you're just going to give up?"

"Maureen doesn't mind, so why do you?" I said.

"I can't believe you! How is that going to make the rest of us look?"

"Pretty good, I imagine."

Jayne stuttered before finally landing on the sentence she wanted. "How can you be so selfish?"

I showed her my palms. "I'm an actress, not a dancer, remember? Two months ago I was a lead. How can you expect me to care about this stupid dance chorus?"

"Because *I* do." Jayne started to leave. She paused with her back to me. "And you weren't a lead. You were an understudy who got a lucky break. Remember what that felt like?"

"Jayne . . ."

She kept walking. I wasn't in the mood to follow after her and beg her forgiveness. I was the one who was suffering—why should I have to apologize for it?

Maureen called us into the auditorium and announced that we would continue where we had left off. I took my place at the back of the line beside Delbert and prayed that the floor would open up and swallow me whole.

By the time we took our dinner break at six, Jayne's words were ringing in my ears. I was the thing holding the whole corps back. I was their Achilles' heel. I had no appetite, so I spent the hour in the theater where the stage manager was preparing the stage for our first joint rehearsal. When I tired of watching him sweep, I crept back upstairs and went over the dance steps on my own. It was a futile effort. What would happen if I just didn't show up for rehearsal? Would anyone notice? And if they did, would Jayne look for me or would she be grateful that I'd given up the ghost?

In the end, I didn't find out. Instead, I showed up for rehearsal at seven on the dot, took my place, and went through the first dance number, a kind of ballet cityscape designed to show the hustle and bustle of the big city that the sisters would eventually be abandoning for life on the plantation. Garvaggio had joined Friday, upping our collective anxiety. Our worry was futile. Walter and Vinnie filled the time between scenes with frantic whispering I strongly suspected wasn't about the show. A herd of elephants could've stomped across the stage and they wouldn't have noticed.

Since Jayne was refusing to meet my eye, I passed the time between dances watching what the real actors were up to. With Ruby still absent, Minnie was given the chance to play Stella while the stage manager read the part of Myra. Minnie was surprisingly competent. She may not have looked the part, but she had a strong, clear singing voice and did a fine job of pretending to be a beautiful woman. I searched for a sign that she was relishing the chance to step into Ruby's shoes, but between scenes she remained off to the side, too tentative to even attempt to interact with the other stars. If she wanted this opportunity, she was doing a good job hiding it.

Paulette's friends had the kind of powerful stage presence that I wished I could harness for electricity. Between scenes, they congregated in the front row of the house and laughed and talked among themselves. I envied them. I wanted to be part of the safe little klatch that arrived at rehearsals together and followed them up with a drink at a nearby bar. I wanted to be with women who said kind things and didn't try to tear their best friends down.

We took a break at nine, and I drifted away from the stage in hopes of finding Jayne. Instead, I ended up face to face with Minnie.

"You did a nice job," I said.

"Thanks." She struggled with her next words. "So did you."

"Didn't your mother teach you not to lie?"

She shrugged. She knew there was no point in denying that the corps' efforts had been this side of disaster.

"Speaking of which . . ." I had already ticked off my best friend; why not antagonize someone else? "Why did you tell Ruby that I told Walter about her face?"

"Didn't you?"

I put my hands on my hips. "No."

"Oh." She scraped at her thumbnail. "I just assumed, since you were looking for him, and since she heard from him, that you were the one who told."

It was a fair assumption. But I wasn't in a fair mood. "Well, I didn't. How about checking your facts first? The last thing I need is Ruby thinking I'm telling tales behind her back." I started to leave.

"I'm sorry, Rosie. Truly. I didn't mean to get you into trouble. Ruby was upset and wanted to know who would say something like that. I really thought it was you." She looked near tears. Minnie was a person who couldn't stand to be disliked.

I, on the other hand, was making a career of it. "It's okay."

"I'll tell Ruby if you like." It was hard to be around earnestness when you weren't used to it. I wanted to think that Minnie was being manipulative, but there was nothing in her demeanor to support that.

"Don't worry about it. At this point, Ruby thinking one more bad thing about me won't tip the scales. And I would've thought the same thing if I were you."

"So you're not mad?"

"Of course not."

She bent her head like she was about to pray.

"Have you seen Jayne?" I asked.

She tipped her ear toward the lobby doors. "She left the building a few minutes ago."

"Oh."

Her eyes darted nervously around the theater. "I could look for her with you."

Without Ruby around, Minnie was clearly desperate for companionship. If Jayne and I were on better terms, I might've taken her up on it, but as it was I wasn't a good candidate for company.

"Thanks, but I better do this on my own."

"All right." She turned to leave and bumped into another of the leads standing behind her.

"Minnie," the woman said. Her voice was crisp and cold. It wasn't a greeting so much as a dismissal.

"Sorry," said Minnie. "I wasn't looking where I was going." She lowered her head and continued away from us. Rather than leaving the theater, when she reached the doors, she lingered. I had the oddest feeling she wanted to protect me from this woman, and after witnessing her chilly greeting, I could understand why.

"I'm Izzie," said the woman.

"Rosie."

"How's Ruby doing?" She was a tiny blonde—near kin to Jayne—with a smile that had twice the number of requisite teeth. This should have made her curious to look at, maybe even abnormal, but the effect was dazzling. Even her smile was better than the average bear's.

"Swollen," I said. "They think it's an allergic reaction."

"Will she be back soon?" She had a low, husky voice that she'd cultivated through years of drinking and smoking. You had to admire that kind of dedication to your craft.

"Monday's the plan."

"Oh, thank God." She lowered her voice. "I don't know how much more I can take of that one." She rolled her eyes toward Minnie. "Give Ruby my best, would you?"

"Absolutely."

Izzie turned and started to walk away. It was weird to think that Ruby had friends, weirder still to think she had befriended Minnie when it was clear none of the other actresses wanted anything to do with her. Had we misjudged Ruby all this time, or was the antagonism she directed at Jayne and me really directed only at us?

Izzie stopped and turned back to me. "You want to join me and the other girls for a smoke?"

Our break would be over soon. Even if I found Jayne, I wouldn't have time to talk to her. Besides, there was no time like the present to find out what I could about Paulette. "Sure, that would be great."

The other women were sprawled about the lobby, commanding the space like they didn't just own the place but provided the nails that held the walls together. Zelda greeted me with a smile while Izzie introduced me to the third member of their trio—Olive Wright.

Even in repose you couldn't stop looking at the three of them. They weren't just pretty—their every gesture held an air of confidence and precision, as though they'd accepted at some point that everything they did from here on out was for public consumption.

"I don't know how you do it," said Olive. She was a redhead whose pale skin was dotted with the ghosts of freckles she'd tried to disguise with any number of creams and cosmetics. "I could never be in a corps de ballet."

"You've got that right," said Zelda. She threw her long, thin legs over the arm of the chair and blew a perfect ring of smoke into the air. "I've got two left feet." The disfigured dogs in question were clad in a pair of lizard skin pumps that looked like they belonged in a shoe museum. I attempted to hide my own scuffed ballet slippers behind a chair.

"You're an actress, Rosie, right? Not a dancer?" asked Izzie.

"Is it that obvious?"

She swatted at my arm as though we were old friends. "Shut your mouth. I just meant you manage to pull it off, and this is probably the last thing you're trained to be doing."

"The jury's still out on whether I'm pulling it off."

"Actually, Rosie was in *In the Dark*," said Zelda.

"Get out!" Olive opened up Zelda's cigarette case and helped herself to a smoke. "I loved that show. It's a pity they closed it so fast."

"You know how it is with murder," I said.

"You were heartbreaking," said Olive. "In fact, the whole cast was pretty amazing. Which was remarkable considering what a stinker the script was."

You had to feel good being complimented by women who clearly didn't dish out kind words indiscriminately.

"Speaking of bad scripts," said Izzie, "it must be killing you being in this show."

"You know how it is," I said. "You got to go where the work goes."

"Ain't that the truth?" said Zelda.

I liked these women, and not just because they made me feel better about myself. Olive's hand glittered with a small gold band.

"You married?" I asked.

She looked surprised to find the slight piece of jewelry on her hand. "Yep. Two weeks tomorrow. He promises that we'll get a better ring on his next leave. I told him as long as it doesn't turn my finger green, I'm fine."

"What branch is he?"

"Air corps. Air force—whatever they're calling it now," said Olive. "He's a pilot, stationed in Germany."

"Ouch," I said.

Olive sighed and held her ring up to the light. "Tell me about it."

"I understand you're responsible for Ruby's latest love," I said.

"Don Montgomery?" asked Izzie. "Is she still seeing him?"

"According to our conversation yesterday, they're practically engaged."

"Good for her," said Olive. "He's a right gee."

"Loads better than Lawrence Bentley anyway," said Zelda. They quietly passed a look between the three of them that I couldn't read.

I decided to change the subject. Who knew if these women would ever talk to me again? "I hear there's going to be a service for Paulette tomorrow."

"Ah yes: big black hats and insincerity from Broadway's finest," said Izzie. "I can't wait. Did you know her?"

"I was friends with . . ." I stopped myself short of telling them I knew her accused killer.

"Rosie lives at the Shaw House," said Zelda. "Everyone knows everyone there."

I nodded. "Paulette was already in Hollywood by the time I moved in, but everyone still talks about her. In fact, I met her fiancé the other day. George Pomeroy."

"How was George?" asked Izzie.

"Sad. Devastated. Take your pick."

"He's in good company. It's a hard thing to wrap your head around. She was a good egg," said Olive.

"A great egg," said Izzie.

"How long have you guys known her?"

"Forever," said Olive.

"It just seems that way," said Izzie.

Olive ashed her cigarette into a silver stand and leaned toward me. "Izzie, Paulette, and I did a tour of *Private Ryan's Wife* about five years ago. We'd been bosom friends ever since." I knew the show. It had run for eighteen months. You couldn't do a tour for that long without ending up related to someone.

"Those were the days," said Olive. "No shortages, no gas rationing. You were put up in decent hotels."

"And the men were still around," said Izzie. "Don't forget that."

I grinned at my lap as they recounted the good old days of theater before the war. It had been a different time. When the war came, theater budgets were slashed, touring shows were cut, even summer stock—that little bit of Gomorrah in upstate New York—had started to vanish, since no one had the gas to travel to see the shows anymore. Sure there was still work in the city, but that had begun to lose its luster. Shows couldn't get financing, politics was taking over the stage, and actors were heading west to Hollywood. Even the repeated attempts to add streetlights in front of the theaters to make up for the diminished limelight had been turned down. It used to be that dark was a way to describe the night a theater was closed. Thanks to the blackout, it had become a way to describe the constant state of Broadway.

But none of that meant much when faced with a death. I imagined Paulette's friends would've gladly given up the theater if it meant they could have their pal back.

"How did you meet Paulette?" I asked Zelda.

"I started rooming with Olive and Izzie when Paulette went west and didn't meet the woman herself until she returned a month ago."

I was surprised by that. I'd assumed all three woman had known Paulette—and one another—for a long time.

Zelda tapped her cigarette into the silver ashtray. "I thought for sure she'd want to kick me out when she returned to New York, but she was so gracious about my living there. She's the one who got me the audition with Walter. I don't think he would've looked at me twice if it wasn't for her."

"You must all miss her terribly," I said. "And to have to start rehearsal with someone new so soon after . . ."

"That's show biz," said Izzie.

"No, that's Walter Friday," said Olive. "He can't afford to shut down for a day, you know that. His mother could die front row center and we'd keep rehearsing around the corpse just to make sure we opened on time."

They mused on that for a moment, until the black humor left their faces and tight, grim smiles moved in. "It's easier this way," said Izzie. "We've barely had time to think about what's happened."

"And Ruby helps," said Olive. "The way she walks in here like she's the queen of England demanding our attention. She's a pistol. I knew she'd be a good fit. Thank God Walter took my advice." So Ruby had had an in on the job. I hadn't realized that.

"But she's no Paulette," said Izzie.

"No one could be," said Olive.

They slipped back into silence, the ghost of their dead friend hovering between them.

"I'm sorry," I said.

Izzie put her hand on mine. "Don't be, Rosie. We have to talk about her at some point. Ignoring what happened doesn't make it go away. One of these days we're all going to have to wake up and admit that she's not back in Hollywood ignoring our phone calls because she's too busy going to fabulous parties. She's gone."

A whistle blew somewhere in the building, and the stage manager's voice rose to a glass-breaking pitch and announced, "Two minutes."

The women stabbed out their cigarettes in the lobby ashtray, and I followed them, silently, back into the theater.

11 They Walk Alone

AFTER REHEARSAL JAYNE LEFT THE theater so quickly that she was gone before I even remembered she wasn't speaking to me. She wasn't at the Shaw House when I got there; nor was there any sign that she'd come and gone, so I kicked off my rehearsal clothes and took a shower. As the water washed away my aches and pains, I thought about Paulette's pals and the grief they were carrying with them. How would I have felt if Jayne were killed? That was one loss I'd never had to imagine, but now that I tried to picture it, it seemed incomprehensible. How much worse it would be if it happened now, when I'd never gotten a chance to apologize to her.

I already knew what it was like to regret how I'd treated someone. I didn't want to feel that way again.

I rehearsed what I'd say to Jayne. A "sorry" wasn't sufficient. What I'd said wasn't a one-time transgression she'd forget and move on from. It was one in a series of missteps I'd made as of late, and I owed it to her (and myself) to figure out what was the matter with me.

Back in the room, Churchill lay sprawled across my dirty clothes, his tail dancing in the air like a charmed snake he was attempting to hypnotize me with. I resisted his voodoo and sat on the edge of my bed.

"Problem one," I told him. "Jack." I was in limbo as far as he was concerned: first, because I didn't know the status of our relationship, and second, because I didn't know where—or even if—he was. Did I give up and grieve, or did I hope and pray? Right now I was doing both, and neither was accomplishing anything.

Churchill's tail danced in rhythm to my contemplation, his sleepy amber eyes on the brink of closing. What could I do? Write Corporal Harrington and once again face the censor's black lines? Or . . .

I rose from the bed and put on my robe. I located Corporal Harrington's censored letter and took it across the hall. A radio sizzled in the background, its signal wavering as it fought to convey news from across the ocean.

I knocked once. "Harriet? It's Rosie."

Harriet poked her head out the door and smiled. "Long time no see. Come on in."

Harriet Rosenfeld was the go-to girl for anything war-related at the Shaw House. A talented actress with an appetite for things on the far left, she'd become less and less interested in theater the longer the war dragged on. Part of that was because she was Jewish and growing increasingly anxious about what was going on abroad. The other part was due to her fiancé, Harold Levanthal, a soldier who also wrote for *Stars & Stripes*. I suspected he was sharing with her a side of the war the rest of us weren't privy to, and the enormity of what was really going on was too tremendous for her to pass her days pretending to care about other things.

Harriet closed the door quickly behind me, and I took in the room. What had once been a space full of news clippings, books, and other war-related material was now bare. Harriet's belongings were confined to two boxes and a trunk neatly stacked beneath the window.

It used to be that when a girl left the Shaw House it was because she was either giving up or getting married (often both). Nowadays the sudden appearance of a suitcase followed the unwelcome arrival of a telegram or phone call, notifying the recipient that her brother, father, or lover wasn't coming back after all.

Harriet had gotten engaged the previous December, and the thought that her sweet-faced Harold was gone made me gasp.

"Rosie. What's the matter?"

Death was getting too close. It could happen to anyone.

"Sit down," she told me. "You look pale." She led me to the bed and pushed me forward until my head was between my legs. "Deep breaths."

"I'm okay," I said. I struggled to sit upright. "The question is, how are you?"

Her eyes scanned the sky looking for the trick in the question. "I'm fine. Why?"

I nodded at the luggage.

"Oh, I'm not . . . Harold's not . . . I got a traveling gig, that's all. Belle said she would put my things in storage, but she needed the room."

It took me a minute to find my voice. "Congratulations. Those jobs are few and far between."

"Thanks." She noticed the letter in my hand, and I could see her absorbing the thick, black lines. "War censor?"

"What else." I handed her the page and she scanned the few un-altered words. In addition to being more informed than Edward R. Murrow, Harriet was very skilled at figuring out what the war censor deleted. A number of the girls in the house regularly relied on her to decipher their mail.

"Whoever did this was thorough." She held the page to the light and shook her head. "I'm sorry, Rosie, but there's no hope of getting anything out of this one. It's about your MIA boyfriend, right?" I nodded. I hadn't told Harriet about Jack, but then I hadn't told Ruby or Minnie either.

"I didn't expect you'd be able to figure it out, but I was wondering if you had any ideas about how I could get around the censor. I need to know what he said."

"There are a couple of options, but they all take some planning. They easiest one is to devise a code. That's what Harold and I do."

And what Jayne had suggested. Sort of. "But he wouldn't know it."

"Not necessarily. Most of the outgoing mail isn't read—it's what's coming into the States that the government's worried about. What I would do is write him a letter that looks as innocuous as possible—in-troduce yourself like you're a new pen pal. So much of that stuff's going overseas that I doubt anyone would take a good hard look at it, assuming they opened it to begin with. Then, in the letter, tell him the problem and suggest a solution."

"You think that would work?"

"Absolutely. Worst case scenario, he doesn't get your letter and you're back to square one." My mind rumbled with possibilities for espionage. Use numbers instead of letters? Communicate the real information using the first word of each sentence?

"So what's the gig?" I asked.

"USO camp shows."

"Really? Like with Bob Hope?"

"I should be so lucky." She rolled a pair of trousers into a tight ball and stuffed them into a small valise on her bed.

"I'm surprised you're going," I said. "You don't strike me as the touring show type."

"I just feel like I need to be doing something to help. I don't have the stomach to nurse or the patience to join the WAACs—I figured this was the next best thing." This was her official line, prepared for when casual acquaintances asked her what she was up to. She lowered her voice and stepped closer to me. "We're still working on our USO story." She had started doing research on a story for Harold some months before. "I decided I needed to go into the field."

"Well . . . good luck I guess."

"Thanks." She wore cat's-eye specs and her brown eyes danced behind their thick lenses. "You might be disappointed, Rosie."

"About what?"

"If I've learned nothing else from this war, it's that the military isn't in the habit of sharing information. Even if you figure out what the letter says, it doesn't mean you'll find out what happened to Jack."

"I don't really have any choice though, do I? This is the only connection I have to him right now."

"If it were me . . ." She cut herself off, recognizing that indicting someone for not behaving as you would during a time of crisis wasn't exactly appropriate.

"Say whatever you were going to say."

She looked down her glasses at me. "If the only thing keeping you from finding him is distance, then maybe what you should be concentrating on is how to eliminate *that* problem."

The thing was, it wasn't the only thing keeping me from finding Jack. If I could hop on a plane tomorrow and talk to Corporal Harrington face-to-face, I still wouldn't know where Jack was. After all, the navy couldn't figure it out, and they were the military.

"I think I'll stick to the mail for now."

She shrugged. "If you need anything else, you can always write me. I know how hard it is." The picture of Harold was the last thing she had to pack. She placed him facedown, on the cushioning provided by a pink satin evening gown, and closed the suitcase. "And if you ever feel like getting out of here and going on the road, I hear the USO shows are a kick."

"Thanks," I told her. "I'll keep that in mind."

I worked on the letter to Corporal Harrington for two hours. The code was as simple as possible, just in case I couldn't remember what I'd asked him to do. The first letter in each word would be part of a larger sentence of what he was trying to tell me. I asked him not use to Jack's name, just in case. And to send the new letter immediately.

Having come up with a solution to at least one of my problems, I felt marginally better. The others, however, still hovered. I had hurt Jayne. I knew even less about what was going on with Walter Friday and Vinnie Garvaggio, and what I did know wouldn't do anything to get Al off. If my life were a baseball game, I'd be very close to out.

Churchill stopped grooming himself and cocked his head toward the door. We both watched the turning knob as though we were captives eagerly awaiting the return of our jailer.

"Hiya," said Jayne. She'd been crying—that much was apparent. Spider-webs of mascara rippled beneath her eyes. "I thought you'd be asleep."

"You mean you were hoping."

She shrugged in confession and pulled the rest of her body into the room.

"Where have you been?"

"Tony's. Where else have I got to go?" It was the sad truth of our existence. Without each other we really had nothing.

"I was a big jerk before. I forgot that while this show might mean nothing to me, it's everything to you."

She flinched.

"And I'm apparently still putting my foot in my mouth."

"It's just that you're making me feel like I'm a fool for putting any stock in it. How can I possibly think this show will amount to anything when you think it's a disaster?"

"It's not a disaster. I am." I'd said it—the thing that had been eluding me since I first got cast in the corps de ballet. "I hate failing, Jayne. I failed Jack. I'm failing Al. And now I'm trapped in a role I don't deserve and dragging the whole chorus down, and even though everyone knows it, no one will do anything about it." Since I'd started performing, I'd pictured myself as some star in the making and those around me—Jayne, Ruby, whoever—never quite reaching the heights I would. It was egotistical and awful. But just as terrible things weren't supposed to happen to me, in the movie of my life my friends were the supporting cast and I was the leading lady. Friday's show had turned that whole thing topsy-turvy, and now I had to consider the very real possibility that I was destined to a life of disappointment and mediocrity.

"You're hardly the only one who doesn't belong in that chorus, Rosie. The whole thing's higgledy-piggledy."

"Thanks, I guess."

"What I mean is, you're not a dancer. We both know that. At least not the kind of dancer they need for this show. That doesn't mean you're a failure. I'm never going to get cast as Lady Macbeth or get the chance to play Hedda Gabler. It's just the way our talents go. It's nice in a way. I like that we're not both good at the same things. Could you imagine having to compete with each other for every part?"

"No." I took a deep breath and squeezed her tiny hand in mine. "Do you think I should quit?"

She tucked a stray lock of hair behind my ear. "It's up to you. But if someone is setting this show up to fail, I think it's only fair that you figure out why."

I nodded at the floor. Al was important, not my ego. Churchill tiptoed across our laps, then circled behind us, where he settled with his rump next to Jayne's.

12 A Superfluous Husband

PAULETTE'S MEMORIAL SERVICE WAS SCHEDULED for the next morning. In a rare show of humanity, Walter Friday moved rehearsal to the early evening to give everyone time to pay their respects and to attend the Theater Wing's Memorial at the Winter Garden. Plenty of grief to choose from. No waiting.

Jayne and I dressed in our best show of mourning and arrived ten minutes late to the service at St. Mark's in-the-Bowery at Second Avenue and Tenth Street. It was the perfect place for an actress's funeral. Over the years the church had hosted performances by Isadora Duncan and Martha Graham, lectures by Ben Hecht and Edna St. Vincent Millay, and even served as a stage for Harry Houdini. The arts weren't its only concern, however. It had been named one of New York's branches for Bundles for Britain. Throughout the vestibule were boxes and crates marked with hand-scrawled labels indicating which donated item should go in which bin. Larger signs tacked to the walls distributed orders and reprimands: WE NEED SHOES AND BABY'S CLOTHING. THESE ITEMS ARE INTENDED FOR OUR ENGLISH FRIENDS. IF YOU ARE IN NEED OF CHARITY, ASK DON'T TAKE. As Jayne and I passed by these collection stations, I took in the meager offerings that waited in the bottom of the nearly empty containers. Had the war gone on so long that people were already running out of things to donate, or was it difficult to consider sending your belongings overseas when you knew there were people around you who needed them just as badly?

We entered the church and eyeballed the jam-packed pews. As a testament to Paulette's successful career, the place was filled. The crowd was a weird hodgepodge of family, performers, and the people who ran our industry from behind the scenes. We ended up standing at the rear of the congregation with the other latecomers.

The service was much, much longer than we'd expected.

I don't mean to begrudge my people, but there were moments when I wished actors could shed their need to be the center of attention and just exist. Alas, that's precisely what we were trained not to do, and so those occasions that demanded someone else be the focus of attention—say a bride or a body—typically became mortifying spectacles that those of us who could control ourselves referred to as "inappropriate." So it was with Paulette's funeral. Surrounded by a hundred of her closest friends and two hundred acquaintances who wanted to claim a brush with fame and infamy, Paulette was remembered with three hours' worth of monologues, songs, poetry, and one rather risqué interpretative dance. I'm not sure who organized the affair or who thought the funeral was the perfect place for such a tribute, but it quickly became apparent that those who chose to honor the deceased were hoping not only to move the crowd but to further their own careers. Paulette, it seemed, had befriended a number of directors and two well known agents.

Jayne and I took in the event the way we took in all bad theater: with our arms crossed, our eyes on the exit, and our elbows at the ready if something should strike us as amusing. Jayne had just finished bruising the lower half of my ribcage, thanks to a lisping portrayal of Juliet's death, when I spied Paulette's fiancé, Captain George Pomeroy, sitting at the front of the church. Beside him sat Olive, Zelda, and Izzie, each in a tasteful black dress. Behind them was Ruby—in a hat so heavily veiled she could've used it for beekeeping. While everyone else feigned interest in the performers, Paulette's friends and her grieving fiancé looked on in disbelief at the sleek white casket covered in a spray of roses and ivy.

I nudged Jayne and directed her to the bereaved. Our enjoyment quickly vanished, and for the rest of the service we watched them as they grimly said farewell in the midst of this grotesque carnival.

When the circus came to an end, we attempted to fight our way to the front of the church. The crowd blocked our progress. I flattened myself against the wall while Jayne was carried away by a wave of humanity. As I searched the crowd for her low platinum head, a woman with a figure like the *Hindenburg* bumped into me.

"Sorry," she said with an embarrassed laugh. Her hair was a strange color, closer to pink than blond. It hurt to look at it. "I should've waited things out in my seat. I had no idea it would be so crowded."

"I guess Paulette had a lot of friends." We were trapped as the crowd around us struggled to move, so we did what any two people forced into physical intimacy did: we bumped gums.

"How did you know her?" the woman asked me.

A mob thug I thought was my friend killed her. And you? "I'm an actress. We're all one big community. How did you know her?"

"I was her sister-in-law."

I looked for a trace of George Pomeroy in her. Perhaps her hair wasn't pink. "I'm so sorry. This must be so hard for you. And your brother . . ." I searched the crowd again for Jayne.

"Yes, it's been very difficult. I met Paulette only once, but it was clear they were very happy. I guess it's a small consolation, knowing they've been reunited."

I frowned, uncertain if I'd heard her correctly. "Come again?"

"I like to believe that in the afterlife Paulette and Michael are together again."

"Your last name isn't Pomeroy, is it?" I said.

The woman creased her fleshy face and shook her head. "Of course not. I'm Phyllis Dewey."

"And your brother was Michael Dewey. Paulette's husband."

"Yes." She widened her eyes, uncertain if I was slow or merely one of those people who liked to repeat information. "Is something wrong?"

"Not at all. I hadn't seen Paulette in quite a while, and I guess I somehow missed the news that she'd been widowed. When did your brother die?"

"Last March. He was a bomber pilot."

I thumped myself on the noodle. "That's right. It's all coming back to me. It was such a tragic loss. We didn't think Paulette would ever recover from it."

She titled her noggin to the left. "I thought you said you didn't know?"

"How could I forget a thing like that?" Jayne appeared on the other side of the aisle, and with a quick jerk of my neck I begged her to rescue me.

She fought her way to my side and put a firm hand on my arm. "There you are! I've been looking for you everywhere."

I looked at my wristwatch. "Why did you wander away? You know we have to be at the theater at one."

Like a ballroom dancer, Jayne carefully followed my lead. "My watch stopped," she said. "I didn't realize how late it was."

"If you'll excuse us," I told Phyllis Dewey. She bid me farewell with a tight smile. I matched her grin and pulled Jayne out the church's door.

"You're not going to believe this," said Jayne as we turned down Second Avenue. "I got stuck having my ear talked off by Paulette's mother-in-law."

"Let me guess: a Mrs. Dewey?"

"No. Her name was Boatwright. Her son, Edward, was shot down six months ago in North Africa. Paulette and he had been married only a few weeks when it happened." Jayne lifted an eyebrow. "Who's Mrs. Dewey?"

"Mother to the big broad with the bad dye job. She was Paulette's sister-in-law and her brother, Michael, was apparently also Paulette's husband at the time of his death."

Jayne scrunched up her nose like I'd just offered her a bad piece of fish. "So Paulette was—"

"Extremely popular and very unlucky. I don't get it: two husbands, a fiancé, and a boyfriend? Was she going for a world's record?"

"What do we do with this?" asked Jayne.

I searched the street before us for the answer. It was a gray day, the sky hammered out of new steel, the ground littered with dirty pools of water. "We go see Al."

13 The Guilty Man

THE DAME AT THE DESK at the 19th Precinct gave us the same instructions as before. We waited only five minutes before being ushered into the little room at the end of the hall.

Al was waiting for us. His street clothes had been replaced with striped pajamas.

"New rags?" I asked by way of greeting.

He scowled as we walked in. It was getting harder and harder to remember a time when he ever liked us. "What do you want? I thought I told youse not to come back here."

"And yet here we are."

The guard lingered in the back of the room, his attention divided between the sports page and us. The paper was abuzz with that night's upcoming fight at the Garden. Heavyweight Tami Mauriello was hoping to best Jimmy Bivins before he departed for basic training.

"We've been digging into your former girlfriend's past," I said. "We have some questions."

"Ask someone else," he said. "I don't have time for this."

"Seems to me all you've got is time."

His shoulders rolled forward the way a bull-mastiff rippled its muscles to intimidate predators. "I told you two to leave me alone. What's done is done." He turned his attention to Jayne, knowing that if I didn't shrink away from him, she might. "Tony know you're here?"

"It's not Tony's business," she squeaked.

"I bet he'd think otherwise. I bet he wouldn't be too happy knowing you were spending your time here." It was clearly intended to be a threat, but Jayne was past the point of being afraid of Tony.

"Is that how you felt when Paulette was seeing other guys?" I asked.

"Who?" His expression was blank. If this was a put-on, he was doing a fabulous job hiding his tells.

Jayne tapped a red painted nail on the table. "Paulette Monroe. The girl you killed."

"That's between me and her."

"And her two dead husbands and her devastated fiancé," I said. The guard stopped pretending to read the paper. Murder and bigamy were much more interesting than heavyweight fighting. "She was a popular girl, Al. You couldn't have been too happy about that. Assuming you knew."

"Of course I knew."

I raised an eyebrow. "She was straight with you?"

He put his hands together and pointed his fingers at me. "Like an arrow."

"And it didn't bother you that she was stepping out?"

He leaned back in his chair and his shoulders lost their bulk. He was trying to look defeated. "Sure it bothered me, but Pauline's business was Pauline's business."

"Her name was Paulette."

He straightened up again, perhaps recognizing the futility of continuing his act. "What do youse want from me? Why are you here?"

"Because there are two things I hate: bad theater and bad acting, and you, my friend, are guilty of both."

"Says you. You want to see my confession? How about the crime scene photos?" He lowered his chin and set his gaze to seething. "I did her real good, Rosie. Smashed her head in with a lamp. The guys downstairs had to identify her by her teeth."

The hair on the back of my neck rose. It wasn't real; it couldn't be. "I don't believe you, Al. You can dig up her body and kill her again and I'm still not going to believe you."

"I don't care. Jimmy!" The guard at the door snapped to attention. "Get 'em out of here. And don't let them in again. Get it?"

"Whatever you say, Al." Jimmy rose to his feet and approached us. It wasn't what I imagined the prisoner-guard relationship to be like, but then nothing was what I imagined it to be anymore.

"Easy, Jimmy," I told him. "We're big girls. We can see ourselves out." I shook my head at Al one final time and made it to the door. Jayne lingered behind me.

"I'm disappointed in you," she said.

"Yeah?" said Al. "You and me both."

We stopped off at the house to change, then shared a plate of Spanish spaghetti at Schrafft's on Christopher Street. From our window booth we watched a line of women snaking out of a cobbler shop. The tightening shoe ration had inspired every skirt in the West Village to take in her best pumps for a little repair work.

"Penny for your thoughts," said Jayne.

The war had even changed pennies. We were being encouraged to keep the copper coins in circulation so the government could replace them with another, less useful sort of metal. "They've taken our shoes; they've taken our stockings. What are they going to ration next?" I asked Jayne. "Brassieres?"

She didn't answer. Neither of us was very hungry. Al's feigned confession loomed above the plate, turning the red sauce from appetizing to appalling. Had there been much blood? Was Paulette alive for most of the attack? Or had she mercifully fallen unconscious when the first blow struck, never even knowing who it was that hit her?

I shook the questions from my head. "I'll bet Paulette's friends know what's going on."

"Al doesn't want our help," said Jayne.

"You think I don't know that?" I downed a swallow of hot tea with lemon. "I can't give up on him, Jayne. He can tell me to breeze off a dozen times, but it doesn't change the fact that he came to me that day looking for something." My worst fear was that the window of opportunity had passed and Al knew it was fruitless to seek my assistance any longer. I couldn't bear to think that the chance for me to help him had been lost.

"What if he's guilty?"

"What if he's not?" I scratched at my chin to let Jayne know she had a little bit of sauce on hers.

"What if he is? Tony wouldn't let him rot in jail if he didn't deserve to be there. You know that."

I sighed and fished my tea bag out of my cup. It had steeped too long, turning the liquid completely opaque. "Then I'll accept that I'm wrong and that this was all a waste. I'm not there yet. I need more time." I sank the lemon with the spoon. "What do you make of Paulette's past?"

"Odd, but not unheard of."

"So you think she's just really unlucky in love?"

Jayne picked through the sauce with her fork, looking for meat. "What's the alternative? That she's marrying these guys and arranging for their planes to crash?"

"I guess that's unlikely, huh?"

She didn't respond. I knew I was being silly, but desperation does that to a girl. Besides, something told me George Pomeroy was a very lucky man. Paulette's first husband's death would've felt like some random tragedy, but her second husband's must've seemed like confirmation that Paulette was destined to a life alone. Maybe she ran out and got engaged to George to see if she could break her unfortunate streak. If they married and he lived, then Michael's and Edward's deaths were an unfortunate coincidence. And if he didn't . . .

Jayne pushed her plate away and folded her napkin. "Do you really want to go to this thing at the Winter Garden?"

"You don't have to go with me."

"It just seems like it'll be so . . . depressing."

"So's half of Shakespeare and yet you sit through that." I put on my coat and pulled on my gloves. "I won't mind if you skip it."

"No, I'll go. But the minute I hear crying, we're out of there."

We headed to the Winter Garden, for a little festival of fun the American Theater Wing War Service had dubbed "The Theater People's Dedication to a Cause." The event was a kind of entertainment world powwow designed to recognize the people in our industry whom we'd lost to the war. It was the last place I wanted to be, but I felt obligated to go. It was my way of keeping vigil for Jack.

About three hundred of us showed up at three o'clock for a somber afternoon of poetry and music. Lawrence Tibbetts sang the Lord's Prayer, Lynn Fontane read "Shakespeare Bids Adieu to the Stage," and the Fred Waring Choral Group roused us with "The Battle Hymn of the Republic." In between the performances, the head of Actors' Equity lectured us on the actor's part in the war. We were already doing a lot, it turned out, but we needed to be doing more.

As he spoke, we rifled through programs listing the names of those who were already lost. Actors, writers, directors, dancers, designers, and technicians—both men and women—had left the New York theater for the European one and found that their brand of drama didn't end the same way ours did. More would be lost, our speaker reminded us. We needed to do whatever we could to bring this war to a swift end.

Not everyone had been lost in battle. The month before, Pan Am's *Yankee Clipper* crashed in Lisbon and took a number of entertainers traveling with the USO with it. I recognized some of the names in the program, but the majority of the dead had been unknown to me. Somehow this made me sadder than if I'd known every one of them. I used to joke that the number of actors in New York was infinite, but seeing so many of them lost, it became frightfully clear that the number was much smaller than I'd assumed, and shrinking every day.

From the Winter Garden we headed to the Sarah Bernhardt, anticipating replacing our day of grief with an equally trying evening with Maureen.

We weren't so lucky.

The theater was silent when we arrived, the usual chatter of arriving actors and set construction absent. I checked my wristwatch and Jayne's to verify we were neither early nor late, then quizzed her to make sure we hadn't misremembered the call time.

"Six," she said. "I swear on my mother's life."

We journeyed upstairs to the rehearsal halls and found our usual room empty, save for a cigarette smoldering in an ashtray on top of the piano.

"This is weird," said Jayne.

The hairs on the back of my neck agreed. I'd read a tale like this in *Amazing Stories*, where our eager hero discovers the rest of the world has gone missing during the brief length of his afternoon nap. What if all the directors, dancers, and actors had disappeared? Would that mean I'd finally get a decent part?

"Let's check Friday's office," I said.

Jayne followed me through the actor's rehearsal room, out the door Minnie had shown me, and into the corridor to the administrative offices. Friday's door was closed, but a light leaked out from under it. Two voices took turns in conversation. One was Friday's baritone; the other was also male but high-pitched and nervous.

"Who's the jobbie?" I asked Jayne.

She bent down to the doorknob and peered through the keyhole. After a beat she returned to her feet and pulled me to the side. "The nervous guy from the audition. You know, the one with the thing in his eye?"

I'd forgotten about him. "What's he doing here?"

Jayne put a finger to her lips and again lowered herself to the doorknob. I did the same, balancing my head atop hers until we looked like a totem pole.

"I'm sorry, Mr. Friday. But there isn't money for that."

"There's never any money, for crying out loud! For someone being squeezed for so much juice, I sure am left thirsty."

"The show's been expensive, sir. You know that."

"You think I haven't cut corners? And what do I get? One disaster after another. And now the press has wind of it." A newspaper rattled. "Did Vinnie see today's papers? They're already predicting the show's going to fold and they don't even know about Olive yet."

"Mr. Garvaggio said he'd take care of it."

"Yeah, I know how he's going to take care of it. No thanks. We should just shut down the show now. Cut our losses."

"You would still have to pay . . ."

"I know that, you idiot. We've been through this, a thousand times we've been through this." There was a rustle of movement and then a sound like a muted moan. "Beat it," said Friday. "I don't want to see your mug again today."

Jayne and I scurried to the edge of the corridor and pressed ourselves against the wall. Seconds later, the nervous man with the giant specs departed Friday's office with a ledger book clasped to his chest and a frown so pronounced we could've used it for an umbrella.

"Accountant?" I said to Jayne.

"What else?"

We looked at each other for instruction on what to do next. She took a deep breath, inflating her bosom to comical proportions, and approached the door.

"Mr. Friday?"

His voice was still muffled. "What is it?"

Jayne turned the knob, unwilling to await invitation, and we both went inside. Friday sat at his desk, a half-empty liter of Black & White scotch resting in front of him. He hadn't bothered to use a glass. It wasn't necessary when you were planning on finishing the bottle. "It's Jayne Hamilton and Rosie Winter, sir. We were told rehearsal was at six, but it doesn't look like anyone's here."

"You didn't get a call?"

"We've been out all day," said Jayne.

"Rehearsal's canceled until further notice. Go home, girls." He set his red eyes back on the bottle and gripped the drink with a swollen hand. His tongue darted in front of his teeth and he made a sucking sound.

We shared a look of confusion and turned on our heels.

"Wait." The bottle danced unsteadily on the desktop. He pointed a shaking finger my way. "What's your dress size?"

I did my best to cover my upper body with my arms. "Who wants to know?"

He rose unsteadily from the desk and swayed. "Don't take it wrong. Can you wear an eight?"

That was the nice thing about being poor: I never had enough money to overeat. "Sure. Why?"

"Can you act?"

I put my hands on my hips and stared down at him. "What do you think I'm doing right now?"

He moved close enough that I could trace the red veins threading his eyes. "We know you're a lousy dancer. How's your voice?"

"Do you want sixteen bars or will you take my word for it?"

I hadn't realized when we entered what a mess he was. His suit was rumpled, his shirt untucked, and his pants had clearly been stolen from a much larger man. "It could work," he said. "It could definitely work."

"Do you want to clue us in on what's going on?" asked Jayne.

"Olive Wright is in the hospital."

So that's what he'd been talking about. "We saw her this morning," I said. "At Paulette's funeral."

"Yeah, well shortly thereafter she got mowed down by a car. She broke both legs, her pelvis, and her collarbone."

"Wow." I stepped backward and sank into a chair. My legs began to ache in sympathy. "Poor Olive."

"Poor Olive? Poor me! This was the final blow to this production. Until you girls walked in here, I thought we were closing down for good."

"And we changed that how?" asked Jayne.

"I need a new Sue Kane. Rosie here is the right size, so I figure we'll give it a whirl." To illustrate his point, he took my hand, pulled me out of the chair, and spun me around. As I orbited him, I caught a whiff of his afternoon cocktail.

I freed myself from his hold and backed away from the stink. "No offense, Mr. Friday, but I'm getting cast because I fit in the costume? Why not just hold another audition?"

"He'll never let me. I know him. And he won't give me the scratch to have new costumes made. No, you're perfect, and as an added bonus, the dance Frau will be thrilled to get rid of you." His pan was pink with drink and glee. "Be a pal, won't you? Most girls would love to be part of one of my shows, and you're not just getting a role—you're getting a lead."

There was nothing to consider. Of course I'd do it—the part would guarantee me more access to Paulette's friends. Plus, I could free myself from the humiliation of the corps de ballet.

"You're right," I told Friday. "This is an opportunity I can't afford to pass up."

14 Lady, Be Good

FRIDAY GAVE ME A SCRIPT, a call time, and a drunken kiss just south of my nose. With nothing more to do, Jayne and I hoofed it out of the theater and into Horn and Hardart, where we emptied our pockets until we had enough coin for two cups of joe. Once we had a table, we turned our attention to the nagging question of the day: What was going on at the Sarah Bernhardt?

"Clearly Friday's desperate," said Jayne.

I poured condensed milk into my java, then passed the creamer to Jayne. "While I know you're right, for the sake of my ego can we pretend like this was a savvy move on his part?"

"I don't mean about casting you. I mean about keeping the production going."

"Too true."

"Think about what's happened in the last week." Jayne counted off the calamities on her cutlery. "His lead actress is murdered, leaving him short an actress and in the papers."

"Check."

She slid her knife forward. "His dance corps is cast, but it's clearly not the group of dancers he thought it was going to be."

"You're in it, aren't you? You're hardly chopped liver." Jayne raised an eyebrow, and I finally understood why someone would cast a bunch of chumps and one good hoofer. Jayne was there to make the rest of us look bad. Even the least discerning audience member would have to realize she was head and shoulders above everyone else. "Maureen did make it sound like someone was setting her up. Who would do that, though?"

"Who do you think?" Jayne leaned toward me and lowered her voice. "Garvaggio."

"But why? He's got himself a great deal going: a space to use however he pleases, and a desperate producer putting money in his pocket."

Jayne outlined my errors on her placemat. "He can't get his money back unless the production makes money. Maybe he finally read the script and realized it was hopeless."

"He's had plenty of time to figure that out. This sabotage is recent. Something else had to have happened to motivate him."

We left the automat and headed down Seventh Avenue, toward Times Square. It was going on seven thirty, and in front of the Paramount a long line of kids hummed with excitement. Lobby cards told us that there were two reasons for their anticipation: Babe Ruth was making a personal appearance to try to inspire kids to help out with the war effort and there was an evening showing of an MGM Technicolor cartoon called *Who Killed Who?* Judging from the poster, Babe Ruth had better hope he was the opening act; the cartoon featured a talking dog *and* Santa Claus.

Jayne's eyes drifted across the street. "Don't we know her?"

I searched the darkening night for the woman in question. "Her who?"

She pointed at a tall brunette with her arm wrapped around a man in dress blues. It was Zelda. I waved at her, and she returned the greeting. Her head bobbed right and left, and when she was sure it was safe, she dragged the soldier across the road and greeted us in person.

"You're Jayne, aren't you?" asked Zelda. My pal nodded and Zelda introduced herself and thrust a black-gloved hand her way. The ensemble she'd donned at the funeral had been topped by a calf-length black mink coat and a funny little hat that indiscriminately sprouted netting, ribbons, and flowers. "You're doing a fantastic job in the corps. It's a shame you don't have a solo."

"Thanks," said Jayne. She was trying not to look impressed by Zelda, but I could tell it was a losing battle. "That's some coat."

"This old thing?" Zelda winked and directed a graceful arm toward her companion. "By the way, this is Captain . . ."

"George Pomeroy," I finished for her. Paulette's fiancé stood at attention, his face much less sullen than it had been that morning.

"That's right." Zelda's forehead crinkled. "Do you know each other?"

"We met at Paulette's rooming house," said the captain.

"Of course. I forgot all about that. I've been showing George around the city. We're headed to Longchamps for a bite." The familiarity she'd shown when they were across the road was gone. Putting her arm in his seemed like the last thing she wanted to do. "Did you hear about Olive?"

I nodded. "We just came from the theater and got the news from Walter. Have you seen her?"

Zelda stepped closer and lowered her voice. "I was with her when she got hit."

"What happened?" I asked.

Zelda brushed a spray of netting out of her eyes. George watched the gesture with an odd kind of longing. Did he remember Paulette doing the same thing, or was he wishing he could be that gaudy little hat? "It was the strangest thing. We'd left the church after the service and started walking uptown to find a cab. We had a walk signal and were crossing Third Avenue, when this car came out of nowhere and slammed into her."

"You're lucky you weren't hit," I said.

"Tell me about it. I have these shoes to thank for that." She thrust a black Ferragamo pump at me. The T-strap wasn't fastened. A part or parts were missing. "The buckle broke right before we crossed, so I bent down to fix it. Had I been beside her, who knows what would've happened."

"Those are shoes worth holding on to," said Jayne.

Her foot retreated into line with her other shoe. "So you say. And to think: moments before I was livid that I'd spent fifty bucks on broken shoes."

I think I gasped at the price. For fifty bucks I could've gotten five pairs of shoes and still had enough money to get lit.

Jayne covered for my faux pas. "So did the car stop?" she asked.

"Heavens no. Whoever it was kept on driving. Thank goodness George came along. He was the only one who had the peace of mind to get her out of the road and call an ambulance."

George shifted his attention to the pavement. He didn't like being singled out for bravery. Pity he joined the military.

"Is Olive going to be all right?" asked Jayne.

"Eventually. But she's going to be laid up for six weeks or more. She's out at New York City Hospital."

"On Welfare Island?" I asked. That was a hike. I was surprised she wasn't someplace closer by.

"Her pop works out there, and he insisted she convalesce somewhere where he could keep an eye on her." So that explained Olive's immaculate appearance—she had a fat family. Maybe she spread the wealth around and helped out her friends a little too. "I don't know what Walter's going to do. Rumor has it that he might bump Minnie into her part and recast Myra."

Jayne elbowed me. When I didn't respond to her prompt, she cleared her throat and smiled up at Zelda. "Actually it looks like Rosie's going to step in for Olive."

"For real?" Zelda's voice was high and squeaky, much like the throng of children we'd just passed. "That's swell, really truly swell. I know Olive will be thrilled you're the one taking her spot."

"It's got to be better than the corps," I said.

We went back to the Shaw House to plan out how we wanted to spend what would undoubtedly be one of our last free evenings. I was leaning toward staying in. Jayne was pushing for bowling at the Radio City Lanes. Since the games cost more than a quarter a piece, my suggestion was winning.

"Do you think she was on the make?" I asked Jayne.

"Who?"

"Zelda. She and Captain Pomeroy looked awfully chummy. And when she stuck out her leg and showed us her broken shoe, I swear to God his eyes almost popped out of his head. "

Jayne unzipped her black dress and eased it past her girdle. "What's it matter if she was? If I'd been engaged to someone who was seeing so many other people on the side, I'd probably leap at the first chance I got for a date too."

"I'm not questioning his morality; I'm questioning hers."

Jayne grimaced and unfastened her girdle. "Any woman who can pay fifty bucks for shoes doesn't play by the same rules as you and me."

"Fair enough." I spread out the newspaper on my bed and steeled myself for my daily game of what awful thing has happened now. The new navy casualty numbers were out: 24,271 dead since Pearl Harbor. The city was buying livestock to provide meat for public institutions. We'd knocked out fourteen Japanese planes that had tried to bomb New Guinea. And New York's immigration authorities were holding a dozen French sailors accused of deserting the French navy.

I flipped forward to the theater news. Another war drama, *Men in Shadow*, had opened at the Morosco. There was going to be a special benefit matinee of *The Skin of Our Teeth* for the Stage Relief Fund. And here was the thorn in Walter Friday's side: an article cataloging the latest problems plaguing his production called, "Murder and Mayhem: Should *Goin' South* Be Renamed *Goin' to Open?*"

"What do you think Garvaggio's using the Bernhardt for?" I asked Jayne.

She replaced her dress with her kimono and examined the condition of the polish on her fingernails. "The only thing that makes sense is storage."

"How do you figure?" That was the thing about Jayne. When you got past the voice and the body, she was smart as a whip.

"It's a huge building," she said. "You don't want access to a building that size and in that location unless you have something you want to put in it."

I'd entertained the idea that the basement of the Bernhardt had been transformed into a gentleman's club and casino, not that either venture was illegal, but it was much more exciting than picturing rooms full of boxes of stolen merchandise.

"So what's he storing?" I asked. "It has to be something particular, something he couldn't store anywhere else. That means it demands either a space the size of the Bernhardt or the location of the building."

Jayne shrugged. "Beats me."

"I bet Tony knows."

She didn't respond. She'd turned her attention to removing unwieldy bits of hair from Churchill's back.

"Do you think he'd tell you?"

"Doubtful." Clearly, wads of feline fur were the most fascinating thing she had ever encountered. It was the only explanation for how she was acting.

"Is it too hush hush?"

"No, but Vinnie Garvaggio is." She stopped grooming Churchill and attempted to flick away the hair that remained on her fingers. "I'm not supposed to say his name in front of Tony again."

I felt like I'd walked in halfway through a movie. In German. Without subtitles. "Since when?"

"Since the night we went to see *They Got Me Covered*."

No wonder she'd been in such a bad mood. She hadn't been the only person handing out ultimatums.

"That doesn't seem very fair. I mean, you're in the guy's show. Surely Tony doesn't expect you not to talk about that."

Churchill became her focus again. If this kept up, I was going to shave him. "You know Tony," she said.

"Not really. No." Tony B.—big, imposing, and illegally connected—had never been one of my favorite people. But when your best friend's in love, you don't question her choice in men, not unless you want to hand over a free ticket for her to do the same to you. "What am I missing here, Jayne?"

She dropped her head and addressed Churchill's rump. "He doesn't know I'm in the show."

"But you said you asked him about Garvaggio."

She lifted her head and reluctantly met my eyes. "He talked, I listened. He told me Garvaggio was bad news and that I couldn't take the job. He wanted me as far away from him as humanly possible."

"So then why did you take the job?"

Jayne's mouth dropped open in astonishment. "He doesn't own me, and he doesn't have the right to tell me what to do!"

I raised my hands in surrender. "Easy. Nobody's saying he does. But if you believe that, then why did you lie to him and tell him you're not in the show?" She didn't need to tell me her reasoning. It was obvious. Jayne wanted to assert herself, but she didn't want to suffer the consequences of her actions, especially if one of those consequences was losing Tony for good. It was one thing for her to dump him, quite another for him to give her the gate.

"He's going to find out," I said.

Jayne left the bed and went to her bureau. "I'll use a stage name."

"Isn't he going to be a little suspicious when all of your weekends are suddenly occupied?"

"I'll tell him before that happens."

"Really?"

She gave the mirror a tight smile in response. If she didn't answer me, I had nothing to hold her to.

"It's your life," I told her.

The next morning I left for rehearsal before Jayne so I could have some quiet time to get my head together. The other actresses were already assembled in the theater, though Friday hadn't shown up yet. Zelda was performing vocal warm-ups off in a corner. Izzie sat in the house knitting.

She looked up at me and waved. I grinned her way and plopped myself in the seat beside her. "Zelda told me you're the new Olive," she said.

"Until Friday wises up, that seems to be the case." I struggled for a segue to Paulette. "That funeral was something else yesterday."

Izzie's knitting needles moved with remarkable speed, turning a bundle of navy blue yarn into a narrow cylinder. "Wasn't it? I felt so close to Paulette all morning. I really felt like she was there."

"It's amazing how many friends she had."

"I know. I told Zelda that if I kicked tomorrow, I'd be lucky if a dozen people showed up to see me off." Onstage Zelda's voice rose and fell to "Do Re Me."

I chose my next words carefully. "I didn't realize Paulette had been married twice. And widowed. That must've been awful for her."

Izzie's needles stopped. "She didn't like to talk about it. Paulette didn't handle grief very well."

Who did? I nodded solemnly. "Is that why she came back to New York?"

Zelda had stopped singing and started racing through a tongue twister: Peter Piper Picked a Peck of Pickled Peppers. A Peck of Pickled Peppers Peter Piper Picked. "Paulette needed to be surrounded by people who cared about her. She felt so . . . alone after it all happened. I think she was starting to think she was cursed."

So I had been right. What would've happened if George had died instead of her? Would she have sworn off men or continued to test fate until she'd driven herself mad?

What would I do if Jack were declared dead? Would I ever recover, or would I assume that any future relationships I entered would be equally doomed?

"Are you all right, Rosie?"

I shook myself back into reality. "Sorry. My mind drifted. I was just thinking about how hard it must've been for her to move on after each death."

"You have to, though, don't you? If someone loved you—if they *really* loved you—they wouldn't want you to spend the rest of your days miserable."

It was an interesting point. I'd always assumed the dead would demand fidelity the same way the absent insisted on it. "What are you making?"

Izzie's needles came back to life. "Socks."

"For a friend?"

"For whoever wants them. I knit a couple of pairs a week and send them overseas."

"Wow. I can't imagine being able to make one sock a year."

"I'm a fast knitter. I figure it's the least I can do. My pop got trench foot in the Great War. He always said it would've made a world of difference if he'd had an extra pair of clean, dry socks."

I didn't know what trench foot was, but it was clearly something to avoid.

"Last Christmas the four of us made three dozen pairs. After that I swore I'd never knit again, but it seems like such a small thing to do, you know?"

I knew all right. If I learned nothing else from the memorial service at the Winter Garden, I did realize I was doing absolutely nothing useful.

"What else do you do?" I said. "To help, I mean."

"Not nearly enough, I'll tell you. All of us donate blood of course. And we each have pen pals. I'm planning to start a Victory Garden when the weather warms up. I was helping with the Theater Wing food drive for a while, but now that I'm doing this show I don't have much time for it."

"Ruby says you go to the Stage Door Canteen too?"

She fought a yawn. Bloodshot eyes attested to her late night of dancing. "I can't call that work. We may cook a few meals, but we're there for the fun."

Years before I'd sworn that when I finally made a name for myself I would focus on becoming a good person to balance out the inherent self-centeredness of my profession. I would volunteer for Stage Relief, donate money, and lend my name and face to causes that deserved to benefit from it. That was all far away, though—hypothetical promises I'd never have to collect on if I never became any more than what I already was. It was easy to make a promise when there was no guarantee you'd have to fulfill it.

Izzie, Zelda, and Olive didn't have to make empty promises. They were already living the lives I should've been living—that all of us should've been living. They entertained soldiers at the Stage Door Canteen. They knit them socks. They wrote to pen pals and gave blood. And what did I do? I complained about censored letters and a lousy dancing job and an imprisoned man who was probably getting exactly what he deserved. I was a long, long way from sainthood.

"Rosie?" Izzie stopped knitting and rested her hand on my shoulder. "Are you all right?"

"I want to help," I said. "What can I do?"

Izzie's response to my plea for something to do to help the war effort was to give me her ball of yarn and ask me to hold it taut. This was hardly what I had in mind, but I figured I had to start somewhere. Sainthood wasn't reached in a day.

The sock had grown by three inches when Walter Friday finally emerged. Dark gray smudges beneath his eyes tattled that he'd either taken to playing football or he'd given up sleeping. He was wearing the same suit I'd seen him in the day before, and despite his tucking in his shirt and straightening his tie, it had to be apparent to everyone that he'd taken to passing out in whatever he happened to be wearing at the moment of collapse.

"Good morning, ladies." His speech was slurred. I wondered how much whiskey he'd gotten in his morning coffee and if I might be able to get some. "I'm sure you have all heard by now that Rachelle will be stepping in for Olive."

I looked around for this mysterious Rachelle who'd usurped my part and found Friday starting at me.

"Rosie," I whispered. "My name is Rosie."

"Isn't that what I just said?"

I shook my head to tell him it wasn't. Zelda stifled a laugh. Izzie looked heavenward. And Minnie, whom I hadn't seen until that moment, started like someone had goosed her.

Despite my less-than-ideal introduction, rehearsal went remarkably well. While I by no means stepped seamlessly into Olive's part, Zelda and Izzie were such giving actresses that when I was uncertain about what to do next, they literally took me by the hand and guided me. Minnie showed me no such courtesy. She wasn't bad, as I'd noted before, but she acted in a bubble, her lines never quite reaching the person they were intended for.

I'd heard that at his height Friday was a monomaniacal director, the kind of man who sat in his office with a miniature mock-up of the stage and moved chess pieces that stood in for his actors until he had precisely the blocking he'd wanted. I'd even heard he was prone to getting up onstage and manhandling his performers until they'd done exactly as he wished. Today he was slouched in his seat while we worked, a pair of cheaters protecting his eyes from the stage lights. It was impossible to know if he was happy with what any of us were doing, or if he was using the opportunity to catch up on much-needed sleep.

"Is he always like this?" I asked Izzie. The three of us were spending our lunch break across the street, eating what the deli claimed was pepper steak but which tasted suspiciously like chicken.

"Nope," said Izzie. "This whole Olive thing has been a terrible blow."

"Which he doesn't think the show will recover from?" I said.

"Don't take it personally, Rosie," said Zelda. "You're doing a great job. It's just in two weeks' time he's gone from working with his dream cast to losing three actresses. He was the same way when Ruby first joined us." I'd so willingly bought into Ruby's claim that she was a legend in her own right that I was shocked to hear Friday was anything but thrilled when she stepped in.

"What do you think about all this?" I asked them. "Have you ever been in a show with so many . . . problems?"

"That's the euphemism of the year," said Zelda. She lit a cigarette and stared at the end of it like she was surprised to find it on fire. "When Paulette was killed, it just seemed like rotten luck, but with Ruby getting sick and Olive getting hurt . . ."

"There's also been problems in the dance corps," I said. "Both myself and another dancer slipped on something the other day, and in case you haven't noticed, we weren't the most impressive group of hoofers to begin with."

Izzie's and Zelda's eyes met and they shared a smile. Of course they'd noticed. People two counties away had noticed.

"Do you think the show is being sabotaged?" I asked.

Zelda finally took a puff on the gasper. She closed her eyes as she inhaled, enjoying every noxious bit of smoke. "Sure it's possible, but why would someone do that?"

I shared Jayne's and my theory with them and gave them the lay where Vinnie Garvaggio was concerned. Neither was surprised that mob money was backing the production. Not only was Garvaggio the most obvious gangster either of them had ever encountered, but both had done enough Broadway shows to know that the money came from whoever was willing to provide it, no matter how dirty their hands were.

"Let's say you're right and Garvaggio's trying to shut down the show," said Izzie. "What does that have to do with Paulette?"

"I'm not sure." Killing someone wasn't sabotage. It was a last resort. Perhaps Paulette's death wasn't the first thing Garvaggio did to undermine the show but rather the catalyst for his decision to pull out of it?

I opened my sandwich and searched its contents for a sign of what it consisted of. There was too much mayonnaise to tell me. "What do you guys know about this fellow who killed Paulette?"

"The papers said he was a thug," said Zelda. "Probably a mobster like Garvaggio." My stomach clenched. I didn't like Al being reduced to a stereotype, no matter how true it was.

"What do you mean the papers said? Didn't you ever meet him?"

Izzie shook her head. "First time we heard his name was after Paulette was dead."

"So Paulette never mentioned him?"

"Of course not," said Zelda. "Why would she?"

At least I had confirmation that Al was a big fat liar. "I heard she'd been dating him. That this was a relationship gone bad."

"Where on earth did you hear that?" asked Izzie.

I decided it would be a bad idea to mention that I'd gotten it directly from the horse's mouth. "I can't remember, but at the time I thought it was credible."

"Paulette was engaged," said Zelda. "She wasn't the kind of girl to hook up with a trouble boy."

I swallowed that insult. "What happened the night she was killed?"

"We had plans to go to the Stage Door Canteen and she bowed out at the last minute," said Izzie.

"How come?"

"George was in town," said Zelda.

Had I known that? I'd been under the impression that George didn't come to the city until after he found out about Paulette's death, but maybe that was an assumption on my part.

"That's right," said Izzie. "Anyway, Olive was dog-tired and I had a headache something awful so Zelda told us to head home and that she'd take care of kitchen cleanup. What time was it, Zel?"

"I think you two left the Canteen around ten."

"Olive and I came home and shared a bottle of something. We got to talking, and the next thing we know we hear Zelda come home. Anyway, we were all heading upstairs when Olive noticed that the light was still on in the parlor. She called out to see if Paulette was in there. When she didn't answer, Zelda went in there to turn out the lights."

"And that's when you found her?" I asked.

Zelda nodded, her eyes locked on her sandwich. "We had these lamps in there, with big porcelain bases, and one was shattered and its pieces were scattered around her body. It was obvious he'd hit her with it. She was all bruised and bloodied. I guess he knocked her out, then had a go at her. I could barely recognize her."

"The police said she'd been there for at least three hours. The whole time Olive and I were in the kitchen, Paulette had been lying dead in the parlor," said Izzie.

"You didn't know." Zelda took Izzie's hand and squeezed it. "For all you knew, she was with George."

"And what about him?" I asked. "What time did he leave?"

"I'm not sure," said Zelda.

"Didn't you ask him?"

Zelda twisted her napkin until it began to tear. "He was so upset. We all were. There was no way he was involved in this. I didn't want to treat him like a suspect."

"But the police did, right?"

They were silent for a beat. Izzie pushed her plate away and rested her crumpled napkin atop it. "The police never questioned him."

"Why not?"

"There are rules at the Canteen," said Zelda. "There's supposed to be no outside fraternizing. A girl can get her ticket revoked if she's seen with a soldier she danced with at the Canteen outside of the club."

"Paulette's dead. It's hardly going to bother her if word gets out that she was dating someone she met at the Canteen."

Neither of them responded, and I read the reasoning in their faces. It wouldn't bother Paulette, but it would bother them. If people found out Paulette was violating the rules, they might assume her friends were too, and if that were the case they might also lose their own Canteen privileges.

"So how did they connect Paulette to the guy they arrested?" I asked.

"He confessed," said Izzie. "He showed up at the police station two days later and said he was the one who did it."

The story was so different from what I'd imagined that I wasn't sure how to respond. I'd assumed Al had been picked up shortly after I'd seen him, not that I was his last stop on the way to him turning himself in. And that broken lamp. Why would he hit her with that? He was more than capable of overpowering her without knocking her out first.

"Were there fingerprints, anything that connected him to the crime?"

"He wore gloves," said Zelda. "It was cold that night, so he must've never taken them off."

I'd known Al for three months, all three in one of the coldest winters we'd ever had. In all that time I'd never once seen him wear a pair of gloves.

15 An Ideal Husband

REHEARSAL ENDED AT FIVE. ZELDA and Izzie invited me to join them for dinner, but I was desperate to talk to Jayne and told them I'd take them up on their offer another time.

Jayne was already home when I arrived, nursing her feet in a bowl of hot water and Epsom salts. WMCA was on, rattling the headlines. The Germans had entered Kharkiv. The French were being encouraged to do whatever was necessary to prevent the Nazis from mobilizing workers for Reich factories. The State Department had unconfirmed reports that Hitler had suffered a complete nervous breakdown.

If only we could be so lucky.

"Did Maureen miss me?" I asked.

Jayne stretched her legs and momentarily lifted her blistered feet out of the water. "Believe it or not, I think she does. Your replacement made her realize that she should've been happy with what she had."

"I already have a replacement?" I dumped my script on the bed and unpinned my hat.

"Yep. Her name's Gloria Abatrillo. And from what she told me during the break, this is her first time onstage."

"Ouch. Where did Friday find her?"

"He didn't. Her boyfriend, Vinnie Garvaggio, thought now was the time for her to strut her stuff." Churchill approached the bowl and bent as though he was going to drink from it. The salty foot stew was unappealing, and he sneezed and skulked away.

"Gesundheit. Poor Maureen." At least that explained why Friday had been willing to cast me in Olive's part. If he hadn't, who knows who Garvaggio might've stuck in the role.

"Poor me." Jayne's voice walked the line between amusement and hysteria, teetering more toward the latter. "I've seen Great War vets with one leg who had more grace than she does. Maureen decided that the only way Gloria was going to learn is if we all took responsibility for her mistakes, so every time Gloria messed something up, the rest of us had to show her how it was supposed to be done. Only Gloria's not the sharpest tool in the shed, so she didn't pick things up after watching us do it once. Nope, we had to do it seven or eight times before she got it through her baby blues that we weren't just putting on a show for her entertainment."

I stifled a chuckle. I knew when Jayne was willing to laugh at her predicament. This wasn't one of those times. "Need a drink?"

"Do you have to ask?"

I freed our contraband from the depths of the closet and set to mixing us martinis. "Why would Garvaggio do that?"

"Do what?"

"Get his girlfriend's hopes up by putting her in a show he wants to shut down?"

"Rosie." Jayne tilted her head and smiled at me like I was the most precious idiot she'd ever had the good fortune to know. "Why does a man do anything? Garvaggio's married and he wants to make sure Gloria stays happy, or at least happy enough not to tell his wife what he's really doing every night from ten to twelve. I'm sure he offered her the part to sweeten the pot. And believe me: she's not going to put two and two together if he does manage to get it shut down."

I passed her a drink and gave her the rundown on my lunchtime conversation with Zelda and Izzie. As I came to the end of my story, she slid her feet out of the bowl and on to an awaiting towel.

"That doesn't make sense," she said. "Why would Al confess?"

"Beats me, though I certainly intend on asking him."

Jayne rubbed her feet dry and slipped on a pair of socks. "I know you want to believe this makes him innocent, Rosie, but you have to know that when a man owns up to a crime, especially a man who's been in the joint before, there's got to be a good reason for it."

I plucked my olive from the glass. "Like he did it?"

"That would be one, sure."

"I hear you." I ate the olive and chased it with a little firewater. "But you've got to admit, George Pomeroy's behavior seems odd. He made it sound like he hadn't seen Paulette since the night they got engaged."

"Grief makes people do funny things. You know that."

I sat cross-legged on my bed. "And what about the way Tony's acting? He and his friends have all kinds of connections. They could've helped Al beat this by coming up with an alibi for him. There were no fingerprints and Paulette's friends had no idea who he was. Why confess? He could've gotten away with it free and clear."

"Guilt?" asked Jayne.

"It seems to me that if your sense of guilt is that profound, you don't kill someone to begin with." I sighed and burrowed my fingers into Churchill's back. He froze, uncertain whether to allow himself to enjoy this rare pleasure or to protect himself from what was surely going to turn into an attempt on his life. "I wonder if this Gloria might be of some use to us."

"Sure, as long as we don't ask her to dance."

Churchill relaxed and pushed against my hand. "You know stuff about Tony's business. Maybe she knows what Garvaggio is really up to."

Jayne rolled her eyes. "I doubt she even knows there's a war on."

Jayne had a way of assuming a dim bulb persona whenever it served her best, well aware that a big chest, short skirt, and coy smile went far toward getting a woman what she wanted. It was possible Gloria was the same way. "Still," I said. "We should talk to her. If Vinnie thinks she's as dumb as you do, chances are he's not too careful about his business around her."

Jayne sighed dramatically to let me know how very taxing this request was going to be. The idea of trying to make nice with someone you wouldn't talk to unless you wanted something instantly put me in mind of another dame I'd rather avoid.

"Have you seen Ruby?" I asked.

"Nope. I don't know if anyone has."

An image flashed in my mind of Ruby lying incapacitated in her room, her past behavior making it unlikely that anyone—even Minnie—was checking on her. The vision should've cheered me, but I felt strangely responsible for her. I deposited my empty glass on the nightstand and disentangled myself from the cat. It was a sad day when I preferred Ruby's company to his. He was used to being the lesser of two evils. "I'm going to check on her. You want to come?"

Jayne stared at her swollen feet and silently debated the merits of walking on them between now and the next rehearsal. "Do you mind if I soak and sulk instead?"

"Not in the least."

I left our room and knocked on Ruby's door. As I waited for her response, I prepared myself for whatever ghastly state her appearance had reached. No matter how bad it was, I wouldn't scream. Not until she'd turned away from me.

"Come in," she said.

I opened the door and found myself unable to follow my pledge to conceal my emotions. I gasped and backed into the hallway.

Ruby stood directly in front of me in a mid-calf-length navy blue dress covered in fringe that was designed to come alive whenever the wearer stepped onto the dance floor. Her hair was in an elaborate updo that framed her face in a series of undulating curls so skillfully made that not a single hairpin showed. And her face—that face—was back to its previous grandeur, better in fact since she'd spent an hour applying Elizabeth Arden's latest line with a careful, studied hand.

"You look great," I managed at last.

"Thanks." For once, it didn't sound like arrogance. While she must've realized what a thorough job she'd done healing, I was the first person who was brave enough to bear witness to her transformation and confirm its success. "The medicine did its job and here I am: as good as new."

"Are you coming back to rehearsal?"

"Of course. I haven't told Walter yet, or Minnie for that matter. I decided I'd make a grand entrance on Monday and shock them both."

"I'm surprised Minnie hasn't been by to witness the miracle for herself."

She opened a golden glass apple and removed a bottle of Apple Blossom perfume from inside of it. "She tried to come by, but I sent her away."

"Why?"

She dabbed the scent behind each of her ears. "I got tired of her hovering."

That was cold, even for Ruby. "I thought you two were bosom friends."

More perfume scented her décolletage. "I felt sorry for her when she first moved in, but let's face it—she and I have nothing in common."

I was eight beats behind and struggling to catch up to the music. "You mean aside from the fact that you're both actresses starring in the same show?"

She replaced the bottle in the apple. "I would hardly call her part a lead."

So that's how it was: now that Ruby had a big part in a big show populated with people more like herself, she no longer needed Minnie.

I was having a hard time remembering why I had ever felt sorry for her.

"Where are you off to?" I asked.

She turned her back toward her dressing table mirror and surveyed the fringe at the rear of her dress. "I have a date with Captain Montgomery, no thanks to you people."

"Come again?"

"Donald called here every day for the last week, and each time someone told him I was out. Fortunately, I was able to get to the phone before anyone else yesterday; otherwise who knows when I would've heard from him again."

"Has it occurred to you that whoever answered actually thought you weren't home?"

"Please, Rosie. Everyone knew I was sick."

That was true. The martyr wouldn't have dared let that knowledge slip past anyone at the house. "So where are you two lovebirds going?"

"He's taking me out for dinner and dancing."

"Good for you." I stepped farther into the room and perched on the edge of her pink-clad bed. "Did you hear about Olive?"

Of course she hadn't. Without Minnie stopping by, she had no way of knowing what had transpired the last few days. I filled her in on what had happened. To her credit, she seemed genuinely dismayed, not enough to muss her makeup or hair, but at least she momentarily turned her painted-on grin into a frown.

"So you've taken over for her?" she asked. I couldn't read her tone but decided she hadn't intended to imply that she was anything but thrilled that I'd be working with her.

"That's right. Anyway, I'm curious about something. An awful lot of accidents seem to be striking this production, and we can't discount that your illness might be among them. Do you have any idea why someone might want to shut this show down?"

"Not in the least." Her patience was waning. I no longer rated a smile with teeth. "Do you need anything else, Rosie?"

"Nope," I said. "Have a great date."

Jayne was asleep when I returned to the room, her besocked feet elevated on a pillow, her mouth open and emitting a sound usually associated with drunken sailors. The radio had been switched to WEAF, where Saturday night dinner music was filling the airwaves. Her chest rose and fell to the rhythm of Dinah Shore singing "Blues in the Night."

I didn't want to rouse her from her nap, so I refilled my drink, picked up a copy of *Detective Fiction Weekly*, and retreated to the radiator by the window, where the waning daylight was being supplemented by the neon blue hotel sign across the street. In this pale, aqua hue I attempted to read, but my ability to concentrate was interrupted by activity taking place on the street below me. People meandered down the walk, vendors hawked tantalizing foods, and children pushed strollers and wagons teetering with books they'd been collecting for the Victory Book Drive. The gas ration had recently been eased, and a few vehicles made their way past the building, but for the most part traffic on the street was reduced to the hoofing variety. Well, that and the odd horse-drawn carriage that remained as a holdover from earlier times, when the only gas rationing people knew of was when the master of the house attempted to limit his wind at the dinner table.

The story I was trying to read was typical detective fiction fare: dame in distress isn't what she appears to be and the detective finds out—in the nick of time—that she's been playing him from the get-go. Because this was a pulp, the dame in question was gorgeous, with eyes like limpid pools (whatever that meant) and hair like corn silk (ditto). The moral was to always look beneath the surface. Or appearances aren't what they seem. Or don't trust good-looking women in tight red dresses. Maybe there was no moral, which was its own sort of moral.

A yellow pulled up to the curb in front of the Shaw House. The rear door creaked open and produced a man in air force dress blues. My breath caught momentarily in my throat, as it always did when I was confronted with someone in the military. They were striking, these men who so willingly went off to battle. Even when you knew them, the armed forces seemed to change them into another creature entirely. They were no longer boyfriends, fathers, or brothers; now they were soldiers.

This particular soldier (or pilot or whatever the various divisions preferred to be called) ducked his head back into the cab and gave the driver some sort of instruction. He emerged with a bouquet of flowers, slammed the back door closed, lifted his hat, smoothed his hair, and didn't so much walk into the Shaw House as skip up the stairs. It was charming and playful and would've made me melt if

Jimmy Stewart was doing it. As it was, I couldn't help but feel sad for the poor guy. This may be the last joy he ever felt. And not just because he was Ruby's date.

I couldn't help myself. I slid on my saddle shoes, dashed out the door, and arrived in the lobby just as he was entering it. Nobody else was down there, and so upon my arrival he had no choice but to speak to me.

"Good evening, ma'am." He removed his hat and bowed his head in greeting. I'd been correct in my upstairs assessment. He was a handsome man.

"Good evening. Are you looking for Ruby?"

The bouquet of yellow roses hung awkwardly from his hand. He had no idea what do with them. "How did you know?"

"Lucky guess."

"Yes, I am. I'm early, I'm afraid." He'd learn not to do that again. Ruby loved making an entrance, which meant that no matter what time you showed up, she showed up fifteen minutes later.

"I'll get her for you." I turned tail and started up the stairs. Before I'd made it to the first landing, he stopped me.

"Miss?"

I hummed a response and turned around.

"Is she still pretty?"

I wasn't sure I understood the question. I'd never mailed her letter, so he couldn't know how bad off she'd been (assuming she'd written to tell him). Perhaps he'd begun to fear that the woman he'd met late one night in a darkened club wasn't as striking as he hoped. "Yes, she's very pretty."

He pantomimed wiping sweat off his brow. It came off as surprisingly cute, as though he recognized how inappropriate it was to fret over a woman's looks when it was her personality that had roped him. "It's been a month. The mind can play a lot of tricks in thirty days."

"You passed a picture of her on the way in here." I pointed toward the foyer, where Ruby smiled to the right of Paulette. "I won't tell her if you peek."

"It's all right," he said. "I'm willing to let my imagination do what it wants now. Did she like the dress?"

"Navy blue with fringe?"

He nodded.

"She's wearing it tonight."

"I hoped she might." He took a deep breath and sat on the couch. "All right. I think I'm ready to see her now."

I left him to his thoughts and climbed the remaining distance upstairs. I gave Ruby a courtesy knock to let her know her man awaited her, then disappeared back into my room.

Ten minutes later I watched from the window as the queen and her prince emerged from the Shaw House and chattered en route to the cab. It was clear he was enchanted with Ruby, which meant they'd at least have something in common. He opened the cab door for her and helped her sweep her coat clear of it. Then he joined her and they drove away, their two heads remaining as far apart as the backseat would allow.

Something about Ruby's date gnawed at me. He'd been sincere, nervous, and very sweet—the kind of guy the cynic in me wanted to label as too good to be true. There was an epidemic of these kind of men lately. Men like George Pomeroy.

That was it. While Zelda, Izzie, and Olive seemed certain that George had nothing to do with Paulette's death, I had no reason to share their confidence. After all, I knew the police had the wrong man and they didn't. Even if he wasn't the one who killed Paulette, George might still have seen something that could verify if Al was involved.

I left the room and went into the upstairs hall. Thirty seconds later I was listening to the line buzz as the operator tried to connect me to the Endicott Hotel.

"Good evening," said a chipper female voice. "How may I direct your call?"

"I'm trying to reach a guest—a Captain George Pomeroy."

"One moment please." The line went silent for the better part of a minute. I was starting to think the operator had forgotten about me when she finally returned. "I'm sorry, Captain Pomeroy has checked out."

That was right. He'd said he was staying in New York only until Paulette's memorial service. "Can you tell me when?"

Papers shuffled across the telephone line. She must've been flipping through the guest registry. "Monday, March eighth."

"Thanks. Did he leave a forwarding address?"

"No."

So he'd checked out on the day I'd first met him. He stayed in the city for at least a week after that. The question was, where?

16 The Return of Eve

WE OFFERED TO ACCOMPANY RUBY to the theater for her first rehearsal on Monday, but apparently our escorting her would've diminished the desired shock she wished to create. "Go without me," she advised. "And don't breathe a word to anyone." Jayne's feet were in better shape after a day off, so we took the subway uptown and walked the remaining distance to the Bernhardt. We parted with a promise that we'd find each other during lunch and attempt to talk to Vinnie Garvaggio's girlfriend, Gloria.

Walter Friday was already in the theater when I arrived, his sickly pallor and wrinkled suit both absent and replaced by something more optimistic. He greeted me upon arrival, remembering my name this time, and instructed me to join the other women onstage, where we would take the show from the top.

As we each sought our mark for the opening of the show, the theater doors opened and Ruby rushed in as if this were the final reel and she had to stop the wrongly accused from meeting his end via the electric chair. "I'm back!" she announced, her arms stretched out like she was going to sing the news. "Did you miss me?"

Zelda and Izzie wiped off their solemn expressions and greeted her with a grin. Minnie smiled weakly and exchanged her script for the one the stage manager had been using. She'd been demoted both onstage and in Ruby's heart.

"Are you healed?" asked Friday.

"Completely." Ruby removed a fur-trimmed wool cape from she shoulders and gracefully slung it around the back of a theater seat.

"And I used my time wisely and learned the script. It will be like I never left."

"I could kiss you," said Friday. Ruby may have been jubilant, but she wasn't stupid. She stepped out of his range and stiffened. "Let's get cracking then. Places everyone."

Personal feelings aside, it was good to have Ruby there. While Minnie had been passable in her part, the qualities that made Ruby unlikable in person made her magnetic onstage. Her return also coaxed something new out of Zelda and Izzie. No doubt they were as convinced as I was that the production was doomed, and now with Ruby once more in good health, they felt renewed hope that the show might survive.

We went through the first act, then took a ten-minute break. Minnie disappeared while the four of us retreated to the lobby. I thought I'd feel out of place with Ruby back, but rather than excluding me from their conversation (as I assumed she would), Ruby made an effort to involve me. I wasn't sure if this was because I'd helped her when she was sick, or she didn't want Zelda and Izzie to know how she really was. Either way, I was thrilled with the change.

"So how is he?" asked Zelda. She had her brass cigarette case at the ready and seemed dismayed to discover it held only one cigarette.

"How's who?" asked Izzie.

"Donald Montgomery," said Zelda. "Remember? A little bird"—she cocked her head toward me—"told us he's on leave and back in town."

Ruby waited until their chatter had ended and offered them a coy smile. "He's just fine, thank you."

"You have to give us more than that," said Izzie.

Ruby pantomimed locking her lips and throwing away the key.

"I can tell you that he's not afraid to keep the meter running," I said.

Izzie put her hands on her knees and leaned toward me. "You met him?"

"On Saturday. I'm the one who greeted him in the lobby."

Zelda showed Ruby her back. "What did you think of him?"

"Very tall. Nice posture. And greatly relieved when I told him he'd correctly remembered that Ruby was what some men considered attractive."

Ruby's brows tipped downward. The little bird was on perilous ground. "What a thing to say."

"I'm just repeating the facts. He was worried he'd misremembered you. He was also very pleased to hear that you were wearing the dress he'd bought you."

"He bought you a dress?" asked Zelda.

"Not just any dress, but one pictured in the March *Vogue*." I'd found it that morning while flipping through Jayne's copy during breakfast.

"So he bought me a dress and some perfume. So what?"

Izzie clucked her tongue. "Sounds serious."

They were teasing her and she knew it, but rather than responding with the hostility she'd directed at me, she smiled and playfully swatted at Izzie.

"It's not serious. Yet. We did have two lovely evenings though. He's very nice. A true gentleman. And very intelligent. He has a Ph.D., you know."

"In what?" asked Izzie.

Ruby fought a yawn. "Some science thing. It's not important. Anyway, we're going out again tonight."

A familiar sickness bubbled up in my stomach that I immediately recognized as envy. I was used to being jealous of Ruby. She got more work, had better clothes, and managed to evade stink even when she was the only one rolling around in the pigpen. But I'd never envied her relationships before. Her ex-boyfriend, Lawrence Bentley, was the kind of man you'd wish on Ruby, someone so self-absorbed that you could fail to show up on a date and he wouldn't even notice. Already I could tell her soldier was different.

Izzie patted Ruby on the back. "Good for you, Ruby. I had a feeling this would work out for you."

"I guess we should set Rosie up next," said Zelda.

"Rosie has a boyfriend," said Ruby. She snarled the word *boyfriend* as though it had another meaning entirely, like harelip or typhoid.

"No I don't," I said. Ruby's shocked face loomed before me. What was the matter with me? I wasn't ready to abandon Jack to whatever his fate was, but I was equally unprepared to let Ruby decide my future for me. "What I mean is, he's not really my boyfriend anymore," I said. "Technically, we split up before he shipped out."

"So you'd be interested in meeting someone?" asked Izzie.

I smiled sweetly Ruby's way. "Possibly. I mean, if you can introduce me to someone like Don Montgomery, I could hardly say no."

I waited for lightning to strike me dead. I was a terrible person, but who could blame me? Irritating Ruby was just that much fun. And besides, meeting someone and dating them were two very different things.

We continued rehearsal until shortly after twelve, then we all dispersed in search of lunch. Izzie had invited me to join her, but I declined the invite and went looking for Jayne. She was waiting for me in the lower lobby, her face pulled long by the irritation that had been her own morning's rehearsal.

"Bad day?" I asked.

"Bad would've been an improvement. I didn't think today could be worse than Saturday, but I'm here to tell you miracles happen."

"Shall we get some chow?"

Jayne nodded toward the ladies' room. "I invited Gloria to join us. She's freshening up."

On cue, a woman emerged from the restroom. "Here I am," she said. Gloria was downright Amazonian, making me feel petite in comparison. Her ginger-colored hair was done up in ringlets that framed her wide face like she was a fun-house version of Shirley Temple.

"You changed," Jayne said. Gloria was wearing a satin pantsuit that had become all the rage the previous fall, the kind of getup you wore for cocktails at Delmonico's, not cold cuts at the local deli. Jayne didn't bother to hide her dismay at the ensemble. It was clear that Gloria was less perceptive than a bag full of kittens at the bottom of the Hudson.

"Who's your friend?" asked Gloria.

"I'm Rosie Winter. I'm Jayne's roommate."

"Charmed." She offered me her hand. As I took it, I became entranced by a rock the size of Topeka.

"Nice ring."

Gloria let go of me and held the slice of ice as far from her face as her arm would allow. I'm sure this was because the stone was so big that she couldn't take it all in unless she held it at a distance. "Thanks. Vinnie said it matched the color of my eyes."

I wasn't sure which of them was color-blind, but the gem in question was clearly a diamond and Gloria's eyes were blue.

"Shall we?" said Jayne.

We crossed the street to Mancuso's Deli and took turns putting in our orders at the counter. Jayne got the egg salad and I settled for the roast beef that wasn't really roast beef, while Gloria debated the merits of both of our choices for more time than it took for Hitler to occupy France. At last she decided to also have the beef, and we retreated to a booth and flagged down a waitress to request some coffee.

"So how do you like the show, Gloria?" I asked.

She flashed a smile, showing me teeth smeared with Orange Flame lipstick. "Oh, it's too much. I never knew Broadway could be so exciting." She had a lisp when she talked, though I couldn't decide if it was genuine or some affectation she'd picked up to complete the childlike effect.

"Have you been dancing long?"

"Only since I was this big." She illustrated her former height with a hand dropped to the booth seat. "Of course, I never thought I'd get to be a professional dancer, but Vinnie says I'm made for the stage. And the pictures."

Sure, I thought. The silent ones.

"How'd you meet Vinnie?"

"My pop introduced me. Vinnie sometimes works for him." So Gloria came from a made family, and a high up one at that.

"How long ago was that?"

She looked at her fingers and ticked off a calculation. "I guess it's been three years now."

"It must be pretty serious," I said.

"Oh, you know."

I did know. Nothing was serious when your boyfriend already had a wife.

"That's great that he's backing this show," I said. "I'll bet Walter Friday was thrilled to find a partner who was so enthusiastic about theater."

Jayne watched me, open-mouthed, from across the table.

"Oh, Vinnie loves the arts. He also puts in the for the amateur ice show at the Garden each year."

"Can't bring a guy a lot of money though, can it?" I said. "I mean, I know Walter's been struggling and, let's face it, theater hardly brings in the big bucks these days."

Gloria's face dropped. I had just told her Santa Claus didn't exist. "Really?"

Jayne cleared her throat and joined the interrogation. "What Rosie means is, most people don't just invest in theater. They have other things they do too."

Jayne spoke her language. Gloria's face softened again. "Oh, well, Vinnie does all sorts of stuff. But theater is his love, you know? I guess you got to have the other stuff to keep it going."

The jobbie at the counter called our order number, and for a few minutes we were distracted by the demands of condiments and cutlery. "Sounds like Vinnie's a smart man," I said.

"How do you figure?" asked Jayne.

"He doesn't put all his eggs in one basket. We should think about doing something like that. Maybe we could invest the money we're getting from this show into something."

"Like stock?" asked Jayne.

"Naw. Remember what happened in '29." I did a fine job of wrinkling my brow the way my pap always did when he talked about money. "What other stuff does Vinnie do to earn his cush?"

Gloria spoke through a mouthful of beef that wasn't beef. "He's in sales."

I knew evasive; it was a skill I was well practiced in. Gloria wasn't being evasive when she described Vinnie's other vocation. This was what she truly believed he did.

"What kind of sales?" asked Jayne.

Gloria smiled at her sandwich. It didn't grin back. "He doesn't really talk about his business with me. I think he sells hard-to-find stuff. All I know is anytime I want something, he makes sure I get it." She snapped her fingers. "Like that."

There'd been a cartoon in Sunday's paper of a bull labeled "black market" terrorizing people on the streets. Uncle Sam was screaming at the bottom of the panel, "Is there a bullfighter in the house?" When I was being a good patriot, I knew it was wrong to sneak a cookie when you'd just been told by your mother that she was saving those for company. I also knew what a huge surcharge Vinnie and the like were levying at us poor saps who couldn't go another day without a bar of chocolate and a deck of Luckies. Make no bones about it: we were lining organized crime's pockets. While for many the war was an exercise in anguish, for others it had become an incredibly profitable venture. I was sickened by that thought.

At the same time, though, we were living in a world where sliced bread was no longer available at the corner bakery (that metal had to be put to better use) and where the luscious banana filling of my Hostess Twinkies had been eradicated along with any sign of that glorious yellow fruit. We were constantly being told to use it up, wear it out, fix it up, or do without, and yet we had seen almost no benefit from our efforts. We'd already done all that in the thirties—did we really have to do it again? Sacrifice without reward was a terrible state to be in. We needed something to keep us going.

When the war was over, I'd probably look back at the sacrifices I made and see them for how small they really were, but right now, in the fray, every one of us needed something forbidden, not because we were greedy pigs who didn't care about our boys abroad but because we needed to be reminded of how normal life once was and that what we were fighting for was the return to a way of life where butter was commonplace, sliced bread the norm, and the man by your side as natural a thing as the air you breathed.

"That's got to be handy," I told Gloria. "What I wouldn't give for some silk stockings and a pound of butter." I turned to Jayne. "How's the egg salad?"

"Fair. How's the roast beef?"

"Disgusting."

"Ham again?" asked Jayne.

"Oh, to be so lucky. No, this is something else. It's not beef; it might not even be meat. How's yours taste?" I asked Gloria. She was already halfway through her sandwich, her gusto being evidence enough that only one of us lost the lunchmeat lottery.

"Dee-lish. I never get tired of roast beef. Or steak. Vinnie says I could eat a whole cow if you gave me a chance."

I pushed my plate away. "I can't finish this."

"That's what you said the last time," said Jayne. "Why do you keep ordering it?"

"Because hope is all I have left. Besides, if we stop ordering meat on the days they still have it, they might think we won't notice it if they initiate meatless Wednesdays and Thursdays." Sunday's paper had warned us of the problems the anticipated meat, butter, cheese, and fat ration was going to create when it started on April 1. In addition to worrying about the unsanitary conditions of any black market beef we were tempted to buy, the OPA was urging people not to start hoarding meat now in anticipation of what would be available later on.

"So you're saying it's going to be my fault?" said Jayne.

I shrugged. "You're the one who ordered the egg salad."

Jayne finished off her sandwich, save her crusts, which she left in the center of her plate. "I'd rather not have meat at all than order it and be disappointed by it."

I tossed my crumpled napkin at her. "Close your head."

"No, really. I'm tired of Spam, Wham, and deviled ham. When I have meat, I want it to be a steak. A good steak."

"You should talk to Vinnie," said Gloria. "He could get you whatever you wanted."

"Including steak?" I asked.

"Sure," said Gloria. "He supplies half the restaurants in Manhattan."

17 A Message from Mars

"AT LEAST NOW WE KNOW why he's called the Butcher," I said. It was just after six, and Jayne and I were on our way to the subway after a grueling afternoon at our respective rehearsals. "It's kind of a relief to know that it's only meat he's been slicing."

"We don't know that for sure," said Jayne. "After all, she thought the roast beef at Mancuso's was fabulous."

We boarded the train and wedged ourselves into what little standing room remained. A vet with a pin for a leg offered to give us his seat, but we waved him down with a smile and a nod of thanks. I reached up for a strap to help me keep my balance, and Jayne grabbed on to a metal support within her grasping range.

I kept my voice low and continued our conversation. "So Gloria doesn't have a refined palate—so what." The woman to the left of me reeked of Shalimar. The smell was so overpowering that I had to breathe through my mouth. "We've got the missing piece of the puzzle. Garvaggio is probably using the Bernhardt to unload his meat." It was the perfect location for such a venture. Downtown, near all the good restaurants. "And I'll bet Al's gift was a sign."

"The steaks?" asked Jayne. "How do you figure that?"

"He probably couldn't come right out and tell me that Garvaggio was the one who iced Paulette, so he gave me something that would lead back to him."

Jayne shook her head at her feet. "You're reaching, Rosie. Sometimes a gift is just a gift."

"But you agree with me about what Garvaggio is using the building for?"

Jayne adjusted her grip. "It's a good theory, but we need to prove it."

"No problem—we'll take a look at the basement of the Bernhardt."

Jayne's blond head bobbed in rhythm with the train. "So let's say we do that, survive the experience, and verify what he's doing; that doesn't answer all of our questions. If Garvaggio is using the Bernhardt for meat, why would he want to shut down the show? And why would he hurt Paulette? Or Olive?"

I hadn't the faintest idea. The train careened to a stop. I grabbed Jayne's arm and pulled her toward the doors.

"Where are we going?"

"Welfare Island. We're going to pay Olive a visit."

We switched trains and headed toward East Seventy-eighth Street. There we boarded a ferry that took us to the one-mile-long island that had become home to a number of New York's hospitals including the Cancer Institute, Central Neurological Hospital, and the new Welfare Hospital for Chronic Diseases. It was also home to the city's many dependents, the aged, blind, and indigent. They lived out their days in their own mini-city that covered twenty acres.

It seemed like an ingenious idea to group all these centers of health care together, until you realized how isolated they were and how disheartening that had to be for their patients. Back when it was known as Blackwell's Island, Welfare Island used to be home to a number of the city's penitentiaries. I couldn't shake the feeling that the sick and old were being handled much as the criminals had been, literally being shipped off and forgotten about.

We stopped off at a vendor outside New York City Hospital and combined what money we had for a bouquet of red carnations, blue bachelor buttons, and baby's breath. The gal at the desk in the lobby told us which room number Olive was in and directed us to the elevator a corridor away. It was dinnertime on her floor, and all around us nurses in crisp white uniforms were delivering trays laden with soup bowls bearing steaming liquid that smelled like dirty socks. None-theless, the mere sight of food made my stomach growl.

Olive was in the woman's ward in a large room that probably bore much in common with the field hospitals the wounded were experiencing abroad. We'd been given a bed number that we hunted out as we walked the wide aisle that separated the ill from the injured.

"Olive?" We paused before bed 39. Behind a curtain the mummy was attempting to spoon red gelatin into her mouth.

"Rosie? How nice of you to come by!" Olive was covered from head to toe in wide white bandages. One of her legs was suspended from the ceiling; an arm rested in a sling in front of her chest.

"This is Jayne Hamilton," I said. "She's one of the dancers in the show."

"Of course," said Olive. "It's so nice to meet you."

Jayne returned the greeting, then busied herself by putting the flowers in a spare water glass at Olive's side.

"How are you?" I asked.

"I look worse than I feel. They wanted to make sure I didn't get an infection so anything that was scraped, bumped, or bruised was wrapped in gauze."

"I'll bet your pop had a hand in that."

"He certainly encouraged the idea."

I nodded at her tray of virtually untouched food. "How's the chow?"

"Inedible, I think. Either that or the accident did something awful to my taste buds."

"Any idea when you'll be out of here?"

She shrugged, and her face instantly reflected regret at the motion. Any movement was painful. "Zelda and Izzie told me you're taking over for me."

"Clearly, Friday was desperate."

"No," said Olive. "You'll do a great job. These things happen for a reason."

"Did they tell you anything else? Like how strange I find it that so many accidents keep happening to people involved in the show?"

"They mentioned it." A squeaking noise came from the other side of the drape. A man in blue overalls peeked his head around the curtain and waved at Olive. "Come in," she said. "Meet my friends."

He disappeared back into the corridor and the squeaking grew closer. A custodian's cart came into view, followed by the man we'd just seen.

"Rosie, Jayne—this is my pop, Kenneth Wright."

He shook our hands and offered us each a radiant, toothless smile. His once-handsome face was marred by wrinkles; his skin was the same ash gray as his hair.

"Pleasure, ladies. S'always always nice to meet friends of Olive's." He tipped his cap at us, gave Olive a kiss on the cheek, then both he and his cart left.

So much for assumptions. Olive's family didn't have the bees to keep her in nice clothes and expensive shoes. She was lucky she still had teeth.

"Do you have any idea who hit you?" asked Jayne.

"None. It all happened so fast."

Someone dropped a tray two beds away. "Do you know what color the car was?" I asked.

"Zelda said it was black and the windows were dark."

"Tinted?"

"Right." She sighed and looked at the toes of the leg in traction. They wiggled at her in sympathy. "Anyway, one minute I was crossing the street, and the next minute the sound of an ambulance was bringing me round."

"So that's it?" I asked. "You started crossing and the car slammed into you?"

The bandages at her forehead moved. "Not exactly. Zelda's shoe broke—for the second time that day—and I spun around to say something to her. I'd been teasing her about those ridiculous shoes since she bought them. I think I might've even taken a step toward her, and that's when the car hit me. It's funny how grateful I am for those dumb shoes now. Not only did they save Zelda, but from what the doctors say, they might've saved me."

"How so?" asked Jayne.

"I guess it had something to do with the way the car threw me. If I'd been one step farther into the intersection, I would've been hit by oncoming traffic."

"Whoever it was, wanted to kill her," I said. Jayne and I were a block from the Shaw House, toting home a box of takeout Chinese. "That wasn't an accident designed to put her out of the show. They wanted to do away with her for good."

"It could be a coincidence."

"That a woman was murdered and one of her best friends almost killed within a week of each other? I'm not buying it. They've got to be connected. And I think we can rest assured that whatever that connection is, it isn't Al."

We entered the building and paused before the mailboxes. I emptied my mind of all thoughts. I wouldn't wish for a letter. I wouldn't will it here. It had to come of its own volition.

The brass door swung open and a beautiful sight awaited me: V-mail!

"He's written back," I told Jayne.

"Corporal Harrington?"

I examined the return address. "The one and only. Shall we?"

We went upstairs and I delayed the inevitable reading of the letter by changing into a pair of lounging pajamas, mixing us drinks, and refilling Churchill's food and water bowls.

"Enough already," said Jayne.

We settled side by side on her bed, and while she created a picnic of rice, pork, and vegetables, I opened the letter with the handle of my comb.

"No black lines," I said. I read slowly, savoring the text like it was a chocolate bar. A moldy chocolate bar peppered with worm holes.

This couldn't be right. I had to be misreading.

"He's dead."

Jayne gasped and lifted her hand to her mouth. "Jack?"

"Corporal Harrington." The letter was brief and to the point. My only contact with Jack's unit had been killed two days before I received his last letter. Another man at the field hospital had taken it upon himself to reply to me when my letter arrived. I read the last paragraph aloud: "I now nothing you seek obviously. Officially naive. We injoy lengthy letters. Correspond anytime. Like Ladies. Paul."

I rubbed my eyes to make sure I wasn't hallucinating. "Far be it for me to criticize someone who's fighting for our freedom, but is it just me or does this guy write like Tarzan?" I skimmed the letter a second time. "He spells like one too. Apparently, the navy doesn't teach you to spell *know* with a *k* or *enjoy* with an *e*."

Jayne took the letter from me and reread it. "What kind of guy uses a condolence letter to pitch woo? For all he knows you were Corporal Harrington's girl and are stinging from the news that he's dead."

I'd seen countless movies and read untold numbers of books that depicted a woman bursting into tears. On film she would be fine one moment and burying her head in her arms the next, the sounds of sobs instantly drawing the attention of those around her. I always thought that was a lousy bit of theatricality—everyone knows when they're going to cry. It's a gradual process that starts with tears stinging your eyes and the muscles about your mouth twitching whether you want them to or not. It wasn't pretty and it wasn't instantaneous. Or so I thought. Something in me snapped right then. I'd like to say it was grief over the loss of this unknown soldier, and maybe a little of it was, but more than anything I was overwhelmed with how absolutely helpless I'd become.

"Shhh, Rosie. It's all right." Jayne tried to quell my sobs with soothing words and gentle touches. They didn't work. Her kindness only made me cry harder. "Jack's not dead."

"We don't know that," I whispered.

"Come on now. It's all going to work out. He'll come home."

There it was again, those awful words I'd uttered myself when I first received word that Jack was missing. It had become our national refrain: He'll come home. Did we really believe that, or would we realize that there were many women who hoped that to be the case, only to learn that he wouldn't, not alive anyway?

Had Corporal Harrington's wife thought that? Was she cursing her naïveté?

"Talk to me, Rosie. Tell me what's the matter."

I shook my head. "Everything. Just . . . everything."

Churchill joined us on my bed, drawn by the pork and the emotion. Jayne pushed him out of the path of the food, and the cat resentfully settled on his haunches and began to nibble on the edge of the letter. Let him eat it, I thought. Let him devour the news until he was as sick to his stomach as I was.

"Wait a minute." Jayne grabbed a corner of the letter and delicately tried to remove it from Churchill's mouth. The cat was having none of it. She pulled with more force, and the corner he held on to ripped off, freeing the rest of the page. "Didn't you say you suggested a code to Corporal Harrington?"

I mopped at my eyes with the sleeve of my blouse. Why was she reminding me of this? To show me how ineffective I was? "Yeah. So?"

"So maybe we should look at that last paragraph again. For a man who knew his way around a word when the letter began, he sure does shift into Tarzan speak."

I sat perfectly still, letting her words tumble about in my brain. Maybe all wasn't lost. "Read it to me again." I fumbled under my bed for my box of stationery and a pen. As Jayne slowly reread the last paragraph to me, I jotted down the first letter of each word: INNY-SOONWILLCALL. "You're a genius!"

"I'll remind you you said that."

I smiled through the few tears that remained. They fell onto my scribblings, blurring the ink. "I mean it. I never would've noticed that. He's not illiterate. He's just really bad at constructing sentences out of code." So Paul was coming here and wanted to see me. Why? "Should I write him back?"

"I would. You want to make sure he knows that you know that he's savvy to what's going on."

While Jayne dished out our dinner, I blew my nose, picked up my pen, and started writing on a fresh piece of V-mail. "Dear Paul, Condolences are nice. Thanks. Weeping almost instantly terminated. Rosie."

18 A Room in Red and White

I should've been relieved that my contact with Jack's shipmates hadn't been completely severed, but the rational part of my mind reminded me of how terribly selfish it was to make a man's death all about me. Corporal Harrington was gone, and while I'd never met him—or even known his first name—he showed me a great kindness in alerting me to Jack's condition. Right now there was inevitably a mother or wife or sister who was crying herself to sleep over his absence, still not believing the news that he wouldn't ever return home again. Had they heard from him lately? Or had he used his brief free time to write to me instead?

I tossed and turned all night, unable to comfort myself enough to let my mind rest. By the time the sun rose, it was clear I wouldn't be sleeping that night so I tried to retreat into an old issue of *Photoplay* to keep my mind from the war. The slick featured an interview with Bette Davis, who was running at the mouth about male/female relationships. She was excited that men and women were becoming equals in society, but she worried that they weren't protecting their reputations in the process. "Good sports are dated every night of the week—prudes are saved for special dates. Good sports get plenty of rings on the telephone, but prudes get them on their fingers." It was obvious she'd said these things before we'd entered the war. There was no such thing as a prude now, just women who regretted valuing their reputation over the happiness of the people they loved.

Jayne remained asleep beside me, her mouth open so she could greet the morning with a zither squeal. For the first time in months

I could hear birds squawking outside, not blue jays and robins but street-toughened pigeons who hibernated like bears until the weather warmed up. Spring was coming. For some reason I thought it might pass us by this year.

I put on my robe and slippers and toted a copy of *Weird Tales* I'd exchanged for *Photoplay* downstairs to the lobby. It was against house rules to walk around semi-dressed, but I figured it was early enough that Belle wouldn't care. To my surprise, there was coffee percolating in the dining room. I poured myself a cup and nestled with it and my pulp in front of the fireplace.

"Couldn't sleep?"

The voice came from the parlor sofa. Minnie was sitting there, also still in her nightclothes. She was wearing glasses and had her fingers jammed into a copy of *Forever Amber*.

"I got some bad news about a friend," I told her. "I decided sleeping wasn't worth the effort."

"I'm sorry to hear that."

"Thanks." Ruby's yellow roses were in a vase in the middle of the coffee table. The smell was overwhelmingly sweet. "What about you?"

Minnie frowned and pushed her glasses up her nose. "Ruby hasn't come home yet. I guess I was too worried to sleep."

I felt terrible for her. Here Ruby was giving her the brush-off and she either hadn't realized it or didn't want to accept it. "Didn't she have a date?"

"Sure. At eight o'clock last night."

"I'll bet guys like to stay out to all hours when they're on leave. Trying to cram as much fun as they can into a short period. I wouldn't worry about it. Ruby can take care of herself."

Minnie looked unconvinced. "She barely knows him."

"You can pack a lot of conversation into nine hours. Besides, Zelda and Izzie thought he was a right gee."

She looked like she was going to dispute that claim, but she stopped herself. "What was your bad news?" she asked.

"A friend was killed in action."

"Your boyfriend?"

I stiffened. "No. Someone else."

I was worried she'd ask me for details—ones that I couldn't provide, but she seemed satisfied with the information I'd given her. She nodded and her eyes drifted back to her book. I took that as a sign that our conversation was over and turned back to *Weird Tales*. Exhaustion was finally returning. I would stay for five pages, then try to go back to sleep.

"I lost my brother last year."

I wasn't even halfway through the first page when she spoke.

"I'm so sorry, Minnie."

"He was shot down over France."

Someday someone would create a manual of things to say to those grieving war losses, and when they did, I would be the first to buy it. As it was, I could only apologize as though I'd been personally responsible for the death. "I'm so sorry. This was your twin brother? Mickey?"

She talked to a pillow emblazoned with needlepoint of the American flag. "The one and only." She shook her head as though she was trying to free her thoughts from whatever bonds held them. "Anyway, I wanted you to know that I understand what you're going through. If you ever need to talk, just let me know."

"Thanks. That's very sweet of you." I wanted to say more—that I didn't think it was fair the way Ruby was treating her, that I hated how isolated she was in our show—but I had no idea how to broach either subject.

"Congratulations, by the way," she said. "It's great that you got Olive's part."

I'd forgotten that there'd been discussion of her being a contender for the role. "Thanks. Friday was desperate and I was there."

"Oh, I'm sure that's not true. After all, if he was desperate, he always could've cast me."

We shared an awkward grin, neither of us certain of where to take the conversation from there. Gradually, I returned to *Weird Tales*, though I can't say I read one word on the page. Something was sticking in my craw.

Until we had proof otherwise, we were assuming that Garvaggio was trying to sabotage *Goin' South* and that those actions were separate from Paulette's murder and Olive's accident. But what about Ruby's getting sick? Was her illness another example of someone attempting to queer the production, or did her allergy attack just happen to occur at the same time as everything else? Could it have been something even more menacing, not an attempt to make her sick but another attempted murder?

I stole a look at Minnie. She was the one who would've benefited the most from Ruby's being put out of commission. And given Ruby's treatment of her, she certainly would've had a motive for seeking revenge on her. But was she capable of doing something like that?

I didn't have time to figure it out. Scratching noises outside warned us that someone was unlocking the front door. It swung open with a thump, though neither of us could see who our guest was. We could hear her, though, as she drunkenly informed her escort that she "had to go." This was followed by a sound similar to the one Churchill made when he was cleaning himself. Minnie and I looked at each other, her face red with embarrassment, mine frozen with amusement. The slobbering outside continued, and I wondered if I should remind the participants to come up for air. It turned out that my advice was unnecessary. Ruby finally untangled herself from her suitor, bid him farewell once again, closed the front door, and glided into the lobby singing "My Devotion" loudly and surprisingly off-key for someone starring in a musical. Vaughn Monroe had nothing to worry about.

"Good morning," Minnie and I told her in unison.

She stopped mid-waltz, looked at both of us, and burst out laughing. I had no idea what she found so amusing, and I don't think she did either, since as soon as she was able to catch her breath, she quieted her laugh and frowned at us. "What are you two doing up?"

"I couldn't sleep," I said. "And Minnie was worried about you."

Ruby attempted to hide her drunkenness by straightening her posture and removing her navy blue gloves. It wasn't working. "I'm fine as you can see."

"Good date?" I asked.

Maybe it was the booze or the early hour or her genuine affection for this particular soldier, but instead of telling me to go chase my thumb she smiled a dopey grin and wrapped her arms about her chest. "Wonderful date. He took me to dinner and dancing and was a perfect gentleman." She sighed dramatically and stared at a point just past my head. "He said I reminded him of Gene Tierney. Have you ever heard a more lovely compliment?"

Of course I had, but now wasn't the time to mention it. Her lipstick had put up a noble fight but had lost the battle to remain where she applied it. The Victory Red cream darkened the skin around her mouth so that it looked like her rash had returned. I had a feeling her soldier was facing the same malady.

Ruby closed her eyes and swayed from side to side. Was she drunk, goofy, or finally experiencing genuine affection for someone? It was hard to believe Ruby could love anyone but herself, but then so were half the things the papers told us these days. We were living in the age of the impossible.

"I take it you're going to see him again?" I asked.

She sang her answer to a tune I didn't recognize. "Oh yes. He's on a week pass and I intend to be with him every moment I can." She unpinned her hat and ran a hand through her hair. "I suppose I should get some beauty sleep." She turned toward the stairs and paused. "I'd recommend the same for both of you. Staying up to this late hour has made you both look downright . . . haggard."

It wasn't the worst insult she could've levied at me, but it was bad enough. Ruby Priest was back.

I eventually returned to bed and racked up three uncomfortable hours of sleep before Jayne roused me and reminded me that I had rehearsal.

"I'm never going to make it." I threw on a pair of gray wool trousers, a white silk blouse, and a cardigan. None of the items were fashionable, and it was doubtful that they were even clean, but their handiness made all of that irrelevant.

"Take a cab," said Jayne.

"Sure, let me just rip out one of my solid gold teeth to pay for it." I ran a brush through my hair and shoved everything I might possibly need into my pocketbook. "Toodles," I told Jayne, and then I rushed out the door.

Izzie, Zelda, and Ruby were sprawled about the stage, recapping Ruby's date in minute detail. While they obsessed over what she'd eaten (braised ox tongue in raisin sauce) and what they'd danced to (Ruby swore she couldn't remember any of the songs—the moment he touched her all she could hear was the beating of her own heart), Minnie sat in the house, looking over her script with furious concentration. I was about to go to her when Zelda called out my name.

"Rosie! There you are. We were starting to think you weren't going to show." I dumped my things in an auditorium seat and pulled myself onto the stage.

"I overslept and forgot that the only person who's getting anywhere on time today is J. P. Morgan." The surly financier's funeral was that morning, and judging from the traffic, everyone in the city wanted to bid him farewell. I waited for Ruby's inevitable biting comment, but it didn't come. She seemed wary of me, as though she'd forgotten precisely what she'd said in the wee morning hours and was hoping I wasn't going to recount it for her. As I took my seat beside her, she rose from hers and excused herself. "Where's Walter?" I asked.

Izzie shrugged. "Beats us. Zelda and I got here an hour ago and there's been no sign of him.

"By the way," said Zelda. "I've got a present for you." She tossed me a small booklet. *The Stage Door Canteen Volunteer Handbook* landed on my lap with a *thwap*.

"Thanks, but I didn't get you anything."

"Izzie and I are going the day after tomorrow. We thought you could join us. They're always thrilled to have another set of hands."

I put my thumb against the edge of the book's pages and watched the contents fly by. "I'm not sure if Thursday night is so good."

"Why not?" asked Izzie.

I couldn't bear to admit that Ruby had been right: I didn't want to meet another man. I wanted the safe return of the old one. "I might have stuff to do."

Izzie and Zelda exchanged another one of their patented looks. It wasn't hard to read this one. It was full of scorn.

"Well, if it's something more important," said Zelda.

"What could be more important?" asked Izzie.

Zelda nudged Izzie with her knee. "Hush, Izzie."

Izzie stood up. "No, I mean it. I want to know what's more important than spending an evening entertaining a bunch of men who may well be dying tomorrow. I'm sorry, but I'm sick to death of all these girls beating their chests about how they want to do something good, and when they're offered the chance, suddenly they're not interested because it's inconvenient. War's inconvenient, and I bet every man at the Canteen wishes he could be somewhere else. They don't have that choice and I don't think we should either. It's the least we can do."

It was a rousing, angry speech that instantly managed to diminish me. Of course I'd go. They weren't asking me to do anything more than what I should've been willing to do since Pearl Harbor. "You're right," I whispered. "My evening just opened up."

Izzie responded with a radiant smile.

After we'd talked through the details and determined what I should wear (something appropriate for both dancing and washing dishes) we still had fifteen minutes before Walter Friday appeared. He rushed into the auditorium like he was propelled by a hot foot, and once he'd caught his breath, he addressed the crowd with a solemn shake

of the head. It didn't take Einstein to figure out that something else
had gone wrong.

"Sorry for the delay, ladies. There was a problem in the scene
shop." That problem, it turned out, was a water leak that had destroyed a large portion of the flats that had been painted for the set.
How this "accident" occurred was another story: the scenery had
been nowhere near the water pipes. "It's criminal," he said under his
breath. "They should've made provisions for something like this."

We went through rehearsal like tentative children who fear at
any moment Pop is going to call them out for something. When
we broke for lunch, the other gals headed out while I decided to
hang back and catch up with Jayne. I waited outside her rehearsal
room, where Maureen was continuing to torment them by making
them go through whatever they had been working on one final
time before being dismissed for lunch. I tried to watch them from
the small glass window set into the door, but the spectacle of seeing Gloria simultaneously trip over her own feet while toppling her
partner was too much to bear. I may have been glad to no longer
be part of the corps, but that didn't mean I wanted to see the others suffer.

I moved away from the door and filled my time by looking at the
handbook Zelda had given me.

"What's that?" Jayne appeared at my side, her face flushed from
dancing.

"*The Stage Door Canteen Handbook.*"

"Let me guess: men and women must remain four inches apart
and skirts must be two inches below the knee."

"More like no one's faithful in a foxhole and you can't spell virtue
without *T R U* and *E*." I tipped my head toward the rehearsal hall.
"Did it get any better?"

"I've got only a half hour for lunch. What do you think?"

We opened the door to the stairwell. Ruby's voice filtered up from
two flights below. "I'm just surprised you asked her is all. Rosie isn't
very reliable, and she's a mess on the dance floor—to say nothing

about how she's treated that ex-boyfriend of hers. Did you know she didn't write him once after he shipped out?"

I clenched my jaw until I tasted blood. I was in no mood to face her comments about how inappropriate my decision to go to the Canteen was, and I certainly couldn't stomach her opinions about my past behavior. I grabbed Jayne's arm and steered her toward the other corridor, the one that housed Walter Friday's office. We'd cut through the other rehearsal room and hit the stairs just as Ruby was leaving them.

We opened the doors and stepped into the empty corridor. The musty, manly odor of cigar smoke lingered, telling us Garvaggio had recently been there. The smell wasn't the only thing he'd left behind. The door that led to the basement stairwell was also open, and as far as we could tell, the path was clear.

"This seems remarkably fortuitous," I said. "Shall we see where they go?"

"What if Garvaggio comes back?" asked Jayne.

"I don't think the question is 'what if' so much as 'when.' Maybe one of us should stay up here as a lookout."

A clamor came from down the hall. Jayne and I flattened ourselves against the outside wall so anyone who appeared wouldn't see us. Our subterfuge was unnecessary. The noise turned into a sound like a seal barking.

"Gloria," Jayne whispered.

"You sure?"

"Believe me: I'd know that laugh anywhere."

We remained frozen as Gloria's voice filled the hallway with its yelping cackle. It faded and she lisped, "Oh, Vinnie—don't you want to see me dance? I've gotten real good."

Garvaggio grunted something we couldn't decipher, but which I was pretty certain was a prelude to something we should be grateful we couldn't see. "Sounds like Vinnie decided to eat in," I said. "Shall we go down?"

"I'm staying up here," said Jayne. "If he's a fast eater, you're going to need me to help clear the way for your return."

I took off my shoes and soundlessly made my way down the stairs and into the bowels of the building. The boilers groaned and belched, filling the space with far more heat than ever reached the theater. The scent I thought came from the deli was stronger down here: a burnt pungent smell that simultaneously disgusted me and left my stomach begging for food. Bare bulbs hung from the ceiling, providing me with just enough light to keep me from walking into things. A large room off to my left was filled with paintbrushes and cans. Next to this room was a space full of tools, most of which I couldn't identify. A half-assembled flat leaned against the wall, waiting for the legs that would allow it to stand on its own. Drawings prepared by the show's designer were tacked onto a bulletin board, each dissected by penciled lines indicating how high and wide something would need to be in relation to something else. From here I entered the cross-under, a long hallway that passed beneath the stage floor so that during scenes when there was no scrim or drape to hide behind, actors could exit one side of the stage and enter on the other without the audience seeing them.

It was a lonely, scary place, the cross-under. Here discarded furniture and props awaited new purpose, though the deeper I got into the tunnel, the less likely it seemed that any of those items would ever be given a new life. They'd been buried here and forgotten. I emerged into the other side of the basement, where rooms fanned off the catacombs to store supplies and materials. The biggest one was taken up by the costume shop, a space filled with the entire history of man's existence rendered in clothing. Roman tunics hung beside Elizabethan gowns, which made acquaintance with a flapper's flirty, tasseled dress. Hundreds of pairs of pants were arranged by color and size, as were enough white shirts to outfit an army. There were also shoes, hats, corsets, wigs, and bins filled with all kinds of costume jewelry reduced to the categories of rings, bracelets, necklaces, and crowns.

Beside this room was one filled with lighting instruments. Dozens of ash cans hung from a pole, waiting for someone to put them to use.

Cables were wound into neat packages and heaped into a tremendous pile that looked, in the dim light, like a nest of sleeping vipers.

Everything was as it was supposed to be. The Bernhardt was a well-stocked, well-outfitted theater.

Except for our set, that is. The dozen flats destroyed by the mysterious leak leaned against the passageway wall, their canvas covers rippled and warped by the sudden downpour. Scenes of a realistic southern landscape had been transformed into a Salvador Dalí painting. Pools of water still rested beneath the flats, the liquid turned oily and multicolored in the fluorescent light. I searched for the source of the water and couldn't find one. This was the work of someone who had to extend some effort, connect and drag a hose, fill a few buckets.

The catacombs continued on, and I went with them. While the other rooms had been left wide open, these doors were closed with no indication as to what they hid. I tried one handle and found it locked. I tried a second knob and found it equally immovable. A mechanical humming sounded behind this door, constant and familiar. I moved toward a third closed door and stumbled. The floor was slick. There was an antiseptic smell to the place. Bleach, maybe? Somebody had been cleaning something, and if Walter Friday was to be believed, they hadn't done a very good job of it. I followed the wetness to the last door and put my hand on it, expecting to find it unyielding. It turned on the first try, and I stared into the darkness trying to figure out what it contained. There was a smell in there I knew too well, the same smell I'd gagged on the day I found my former boss's body. I fumbled for a light switch in the dark. My hand made contact with one that felt cold and wet, but when I flipped it on nothing happened. I stepped back into the hallway and tried to decide what to do. Was there a flashlight somewhere? A candle? My hand fell into my line of sight. It was tinged red with blood.

19 The Lady Killer

I GASPED AT THE SIGHT of red on my hand and stumbled backward. I tested each of my fingers and searched for the source of the blood. It wasn't coming from me. Before I could enter the room a second time, a noise like a car door slamming grabbed my attention. It was coming from the load-in doors, an oversized entrance just to the right of me. A man's voice barked incomprehensible instructions. The lever used to keep the doors in place began to shake. Keys jangled outside.

I ducked back into the cross-under and ran to the other side of the basement. The men were in the building now, but unless they were coming my way, I was safe. I slipped off my shoes and took the stairs two at a time. The door came into sight, and so did the small window set in its center; only instead of glowing with the dim light of an empty corridor, a shadow was blocking my view. I slowed my pace and snuck up on the window so I could see out, but no one on the other side could see me. Garvaggio was back, twice as big as I remembered him.

I squatted like a hen about to lay an egg and tried to think of a perfectly good reason for why I was coming up those stairs. Lost? Unlikely, unless I was a boob. Jayne might be able to pull off the wide eyes and big chest game, but I would be unconvincing. Could I have been sent there by someone to retrieve something? That could work, though who and what better make sense and not be easily verifiable.

"It's amazing," said a voice. It was Jayne. "I never knew how much work went into making a single cigar." I stood back up and carefully looked out the window. Garvaggio had his back to me and was illustrating something with his stogie. I caught Jayne's eye and with a flutter of hand movements begged her to get Garvaggio out of the way. She nodded at him—and me—and smiled that brilliantly coquett-ish smile of hers, the one that could mince meat and butter bread.

"I've always wanted to try one," she said. "Do you think it's wrong for a woman to smoke a cigar?"

"Nothing wrong at all, doll." I couldn't see Garvaggio's face, but the tone of his voice made it clear: the idea of seeing Jayne smoke a cigar was as exciting as seeing Salomé do the Dance of the Seven Veils. "You want a puff of this one?"

"That's yours. I couldn't take it."

"Suit yourself." He returned the cigar to his mouth.

"Though if you had another one, I might be willing."

Garvaggio turned until I could see his face in profile. He put a bejeweled hand into his lapel pocket and pulled out a cigar still wrapped in cellophane. He was smiling a wry little grin as though he believed Jayne was doing exactly what he wanted her to do when, in fact, he was the one being manipulated. "As a matter of fact, I got one right here." He stripped it of its wrapping and held it beneath his nose. "Now this ain't no ten-cent smoke. This is the finest Cuban tobacco. You ain't going to have a better cigar than this." He held it out to Jayne like he was offering a scepter to the queen. She picked it up and looked at it. His hand disappeared back into his coat and emerged with a sterling silver lighter. "Need a light?"

"Absolutely." Jayne's eyes drifted to the window, and she shrugged. This was it? He was going to bend over to light her cigar and I was supposed to open a squeaky door, stomp through the corridor, and disappear without his knowing I was there? I shook my head to let her know her plan was unsatisfactory. I wasn't moving an inch until Garvaggio was dust.

He struck the flint and leaned toward her with the lighter cupped in his hand. She put the cigar in her mouth and matched his lean. Right before the flame met the tip, she backed up and removed the Cuban. "Maybe this isn't such a good idea."

"What's the matter?" he asked in that strange sideways way of his.

Jayne spoke too quickly; her voice crackled with nerves. "What if Mr. Friday comes through here and sees me smoking? I doubt he'd be too happy about that." It was a weak excuse and Jayne knew it. Walter Friday wasn't the kind of man who wanted his women to refrain from anything.

"Don't you worry about Walter."

She wagged the cigar in front of Garvaggio's face. The gesture tantalized him as thoroughly as the sight of a bare thigh. "Still, I'd feel better with a little privacy. Isn't there someplace we can go?"

He gave her a knowing smile. "How about my office? It's as private as private can be."

Jayne agreed with a nod and tossed a terrified look my way before following him down the hall. I waited until their footsteps died and the door closed before slipping out of the stairwell and entering the corridor. I tiptoed toward the rehearsal room, banged open the door, and walked back into the private corridor as though I'd just entered it.

"Jayne? Are you up here?" I called. "You told me you'd meet me downstairs at one." I whistled for her and called to her in a variety of exasperated tones. When that didn't grant her release, I went door by door, knocking and calling Jayne's name to at least give the impression that I had no idea where she was.

Garvaggio's office was silent, though the odor coming from it made it clear someone was smoking in there. Rather than knocking and giving him the chance not to respond, I turned the knob and stepped inside.

"Oh, sorry," I said.

Jayne was sitting on his desk, or rather she was cowering on it. Garvaggio's mitts sat on each side of her and the man himself leaned forward until Jayne, with nowhere else to go, was practically lying on the desktop. The cigars sat smoldering in a crystal ashtray, forgotten the minute Garvaggio realized there was something tastier on the menu.

"What's the problem, sweetheart?" Garvaggio straightened up and returned the cigar to his mouth.

"I'm awfully sorry to interrupt you, sir, but I was looking for Jayne."

"No kidding?"

Jayne straightened up and tried to replace what had to be terror with irritation. "Well, you found me. What do you need?"

I looked at the floor, hoping a good explanation would rise out of the worn oak boards. Instead, I saw my hand, still stained red with someone else's blood. I lifted the arm and held it limp at the wrist. "I cut myself and I was wondering if you had something to wrap it in."

Vinnie took a step backward lest I decide to use his suit as a canvas. Jayne leaped off the desk much more quickly than the injury—had it been real—would have merited and took my wounded hand in hers. "Oh, you poor thing. Sure. We'll get you taken care of." She smiled sweetly at Vinnie. "Thanks for the cigar. I'm sorry I can't stay."

"That just means you've got to come back again." He winked at her. "You know where to find me."

As Vinnie set about creating a cloud of smoke, Jayne and I escaped into the corridor and into the rehearsal hall. Just in case he was still within earshot, Jayne pulled me down the public stairwell and we disappeared into the ladies' room off the lobby.

"Thanks," I said when the coast was clear. "I'm eternally grateful for whatever you just had to endure."

She turned on the faucet and gargled with a handful of water for a good thirty seconds before spitting it into the sink. "I feel like I've been licking a fireplace grate."

"I hope that was the only thing near your mouth."

Jayne mopped at her face with a towel. "I gave him one kiss. It was either that or keep smoking."

"I think you made the wise choice. So he's not faithful?"

"I thought we already established that with the wife and the mistress."

"You know what I mean: if he's willing to share cigars with you, who knows how many other women he's done favors for."

Jayne retrieved a tube of lipstick from her pocket and repaired her face. "You mean like Paulette?"

"Why not? We know she was a popular girl without too much regard for commitment. And we know she was willing to do whatever was required to get ahead. Maybe Garvaggio pulled her aside for a private smoking session, and she was less than pleased with his manners."

"Anything's possible."

I turned on the water and put my bloodied hand beneath.

"What did you do to yourself?" asked Jayne.

"It's not what I did; it's what someone else did and forgot to clean up." I told her about the dark room on the east side of the basement, the one that had been carefully scrubbed except for whatever someone had left coating the wall.

"Creepy."

"You're telling me. I was actually grateful I couldn't turn the lights on. So I guess we can rule out black market storage."

Jayne grimaced. "Does that mean we have to reconsider the idea that he's using the Bernhardt as a place to murder and dispose of people?"

I waved my still-red hand at her. "It seems like a reasonable assumption."

Outside, the bell at St. Mary the Virgin's chimed that it was one o'clock. It was time to go back to rehearsal. With empty stomachs. Not that touching a bloody wall had increased my appetite.

"Be careful," said Jayne.

"Don't worry about me. But if I were you, I'd steer clear of Gloria."

"Why?"

"She strikes me as the kind of gal who isn't too forgiving when another skirt shows up smelling like her boyfriend's cigar."

Rehearsal zoomed by that afternoon. It was the last time it would be just the actors. Starting the next day, the dance corps would join us full time, and our cozy little family would be extended and changed. Then, in two brief weeks, the production would open.

While everyone concentrated on using their rehearsal time wisely, I was imagining what was in that room in the basement. Like Lady Macbeth, I couldn't get the image of the blood on my hand out of my mind. Who had died down there and who were the men who were entering the basement just as I was leaving? Were they there to finish cleaning up?

It didn't make sense. Garvaggio was a pro, the kind of guy who killed someone at four and showed up for dinner at five without even having to change his shirt. Whatever had happened in that room must have been a scene of tremendous violence, a death so ill-planned or so grotesquely carried out that even after a careful scrub, there was still gore left behind. Either that, or the person who committed the crime hadn't been mindful about the mess he had made.

No. There had to be more. Literally more. One person hadn't died down there. Several had. That was the only explanation for the state the room was left in. If several people were killed, it was inevitable there was mess. Maybe one of them had attempted an escape while the other one was meeting his end.

I closed my eyes against the image and opened them in time to rejoin rehearsal and make my entrance. I wasn't at the point yet where I knew my lines, so I had to concentrate on everything around me to pull the pages from the places they currently occupied in my brain. I stumbled over a word here and a song melody there, and while Friday was accepting of the fact that the new girl was a step behind, Ruby was anything but.

"You do know we open in two weeks, don't you?" she hissed at me under her breath.

"You do know I've had the script for two days," I replied. I resented her tone, not just because it was unfair to expect me to already be on par with everyone else but because her attitude toward me had changed so drastically since the week she was sick.

Focus, I told myself. Act circles around her. Show her that you can do more with two days of rehearsal than she could with two months. I tried, but instead of being the world's greatest actress, I became the world's hammiest, overacting each line until the words could've

sprouted feet and been given their own equity cards. I may have suc-
ceeded in humiliating myself, but at least my ineptness got Walter
Friday's undivided attention.

"Let's rein it in, Rosie," he said, which set off a twitter of giggles
behind me. Zelda and Izzie had to be regretting any kindness they'd
shown me, to say nothing of how my lack of talent must've made Minnie feel. "Do like you were doing yesterday. That was perfect."

We started back at the top of the scene, and I tried to think about
the words I was saying and nothing else. I was feeling much better
when a clatter downstairs made it impossible to continue.

"Oh, for crying out loud," said Friday. "They know they're not
supposed to use the loading dock during rehearsal. I can't hear myself think in here." He looked at his watch and sighed. "All right—let's
call it a day. Tomorrow afternoon we start the circus. All songs, all
choreography. Be on time."

We gathered our things, and I bolted before Ruby could offer
any further words of wisdom on my abilities. I set up camp outside
Jayne's rehearsal hall and read the *Canteen Handbook* while Maureen
tormented the dancers.

"Any questions?" Zelda entered the hallway and paused before me.

"I think it's pretty straightforward." In my anxiety over the trip
to the basement and my embarrassment over rehearsal, I'd forgotten
about Izzie's lecture that morning. It came rushing over me now. "I
want to explain about before. About why I tried to back out of the
Canteen. I'm not like those other women Izzie mentioned. At least I
hope I'm not. I'm feeling a bit . . . conflicted."

"About what?"

I closed the manual. "The boyfriend Ruby mentioned. My ex-
boyfriend? He's missing in action."

"I'm sorry."

"I wasn't sure where he and I left things before he shipped out
and now . . . even though there's a good chance that he's not coming
back, I feel like it's wrong for me to . . . " I couldn't find the right
words so I let the sentence die on its own.

Zelda crouched down and joined me on the floor. "It's all right, Rosie. Moving on is difficult. It has to be so much worse when you don't know for certain what's happened." She put her hand on mine and gently squeezed. "Don't think of it like a betrayal. You're just going to the Canteen to help out for a night. Izzie's right—those guys need us. And if it helps, think about how you'd like this ex of yours—"

"Jack."

"Think about how you'd like someone to treat Jack if he were far from home with nothing to look forward to."

"Thanks."

She struggled back to her feet. "See you tomorrow."

Jayne was set free a half hour later. She and I walked toward the subway station at Forty-sixth and Broadway, and I caught her up to speed on my thoughts about what could've been occurring in the room downstairs.

"You think it's like a murder room?" she asked.

"Why not?" I said. "If Garvaggio gets to use the space for whatever he wants off-hours, I don't see why murder should be excluded." To our left a sign told us that codfish cakes at Longchamps were only eight-five cents.

"But why?" asked Jayne. "What's the use of killing someone here?"

"Less likely to be found, maybe. Closer to wherever the mob hides the bodies." It was starting to sound like a bad real estate ad: "Efficiency in Theater District. Close to Hudson River. Perfect for members of Mangano crime family."

"Yeah, but more likely to have witnesses. Think about how many people come and go through this building each day."

We passed a magazine stand that had given up half of its kiosk to selling war bonds. A phonograph had been rigged up on the counter, and from it Bugs Bunny's voice asked us, "Any Bonds Today?" The stand was plastered with ominous commands: STAMP OUT THE AXIS, AMERICA WAKE UP, YOU MUST HELP. The most upsetting sign of all read BUY MORE WAR STAMPS, only beneath the word *war* you could still make out where it used to say "defense." The good old days: when the only thing we thought we'd have to do was defend ourselves.

"I don't think Garvaggio's people do what they do during the daytime," I said. "Somebody was opening the loading dock when we were rehearsing, and it made a terrible clatter. There's no way they could regularly be doing that while rehearsals are going on in the theater." Something Jayne had just said was echoing in my mind. Witnesses. "What if that's what happened to Paulette?"

Jayne pulled on a pair of gray wool mittens. "She was killed at home."

"No, I mean why she was killed. What if she walked in on what was going on downstairs and Garvaggio decided it would be better to get rid of her than run the risk that she might tell the cops?"

"Then why not do to her what they're doing to everyone else down there? Why kill her in her own home?"

"She was Friday's star and too well known to just disappear. That would've brought more questions than Garvaggio would've wanted to deal with, so they kill her at home and make it look like an intruder got to her." My mind continued racing through all the possibilities. "Garvaggio's worried that she might've squealed to someone before he bumped her off, so he decides the best thing to do is to pull out of the theater before the authorities get wind of what's going on."

"Where does that leave Al?" asked Jayne.

"He could've found out what was really going on downstairs, so they decided to frame him for Paulette's murder. That way, no one would believe anything if he did squeal."

Jayne let that roll around in her head for half a block. "That's not how those guys play, Rosie. If Al saw something he wasn't supposed to, he'd be gone. They wouldn't take that kind of chance."

Hearing her say it, I realized she was right. Al was nobody to Garvaggio, and even less to the coppers. If he disappeared tomorrow, the only people likely to care were Jayne, me, and Tony, and it looked like at least one of us had already given up on him.

"I think we need to consider another possibility," said Jayne.

"What's that?"

"Paulette, like you said, saw something she shouldn't have, so Garvaggio sent someone to take care of her. That someone did, but he didn't do a very good job covering his tracks and ended up in the bin."

"So you're saying not only is Al a murderer, but he was stepping out on Tony too?"

"It makes sense," said Jayne. "I can't think of another reason why Tony would turn his back on him."

20 Two on an Island

I SPENT THE NIGHT WORKING on my lines to make sure I'd be ready to wow everyone the next day. When my brain had had enough, I went down to the parlor and rifled through a weeks' worth of newspapers Belle had left sitting by the fireplace. I was looking for missing persons and found bodies, the kind of news relegated to the back pages since neither the missing nor the found were people of import. There was a name here and there—a missing child, a confused elderly man, a thug last seen in Hell's Kitchen—but none of them jumped out at me as the kind of victim that would end up in the basement of the Bernhardt paying for whatever crime they'd committed against the mob. They could've been out-of-towners, brought to New York to make it less likely that they'd be traced to where they'd come from. Maybe the Chicago mob was calling in a favor from their brothers out east. Did different syndicates do that kind of thing?

I turned the page and caught up with the news I'd managed to miss. The USDA and the OPA had finally reached an agreement regarding livestock price ceilings. When those went into effect on April 1, so would two new rules to curb the black market: all livestock dealers would have to obtain permits to continue their businesses and all slaughterers would be issued permit numbers and would have to stamp that number on each cut of meat.

Between the meat ration and the USDA rules, beef was going to be harder to get than a waiver from the draft board.

I flipped over the paper and landed on the social announcements. Smiling couples posed for the camera while brief blocks of text declared their intentions to wed. Every man depicted was military; every woman beside him desperate to take his name before the war took his life.

I tossed the paper into the fire someone (most likely Belle) had laid.

Jayne's explanation for what was happening at the Bernhardt kept drifting into my mind with the same insistence that lines I thought I knew kept coming back to me. I had to admit that it was the first theory that actually made sense. Al was desperate for dough—he always was—and so he must've cut a deal with Garvaggio. He works for him on the side, and if something goes wrong, Al agrees to take the fall. Why, though? Was Garvaggio offering him so much coin that he was willing to take responsibility if he got caught? And what had gone wrong with Paulette's murder? As far as we knew, there were no witnesses, and no one close to Paulette had any idea who he was. Unless his own conscience was the culprit, there was no reason why he couldn't have gotten away scot-free. Unless . . .

If a witness wasn't causing problems for Al, maybe Tony was. If he'd gotten wind of what Al was doing and let Al know that he didn't appreciate him stepping out, Al may have been forced into confessing to Paulette's murder in order to keep Tony happy. But that didn't make any sense. Why would Tony care if Al owned up to a clip job when they were both devoted to a life of crime? Al was out of commission now and Tony was out a man, a good man who'd saved his girl. Surely that couldn't be the reason.

When Al had been watching me for Jim McCain, he was terrified Tony was going to find out. He told me, "When you work for Tony B., you work for Tony B." The unspoken consequence of violating this rule was that there was some kind of retribution. Loyalty was everything to Tony, and it may well have been that when he found out Al was working for Vinnie Garvaggio's gang, he decided he'd rather have a dead friend than a live traitor. And Al, knowing that, did the only thing he could to save his own life. He confessed to murdering Paulette and went to jail to make sure that he was safe from Tony.

•   •   •

Our rehearsal wasn't set until two that afternoon, so I decided to forgo whatever sleep I could've gotten and visit Al instead.

"Do you want me to come?" asked Jayne.

I couldn't be positive if Tony was the one who put Al in the pen, and until I was, I wasn't about to share my theory with Jayne. "I think I want to go alone this time. Every time we've gone together he's clammed up. Maybe seeing me one-on-one will make him more willing to spill."

I made it to the 19th Precinct by ten a.m. and went through the same motions I had in the past to see Al. This time, though, the dame at the desk told me the visit was a no go.

"Why?" I asked.

"He's gone, sweetheart."

We were living in a time when *gone* was the kindest euphemism for death. A dozen soldiers I knew were gone, and Jack was halfway to getting there himself. "How?"

"They take them there by bus."

I shook my head clear. "I mean, where did they take him?"

"Rikers Island. This isn't a hotel, you know. They don't stay here indefinitely."

"Can I visit him there?"

"Sure. And you can stick your hand in boiling water too. Doesn't mean you should." She sighed and shuffled through a stack of papers on her desk. "You're going to need a visitor's pass to get on the ferry and to the island. When do you want to go?"

"Today."

"I'll call ahead and get the paperwork taken care of. If I were you, I'd keep my coat on and buttoned. Nothing gets a prisoner more riled than a pair of pins sticking out of a short skirt."

I thanked her for her advice, such as it was, and stepped outside the station to hail a cab. As I named my destination, the driver started to laugh, an asthmatic chuckle that sounded less like merriment and

more like one of Zelda's vocal exercises. Still, he took me, guffawing
all the way about how a girl like me should be able to get herself a decent fellow who hasn't done time. The soldiers will be coming home
soon, he assured me, as though desperation for romance had led me
astray. Why date a criminal when you can date a hero? Was there a
difference? I wanted to ask him. Could Garvaggio's basement crimes
really be that different from what was taking place on the battlefield?
I kept my mouth closed, though. I needed this guy to come and collect me later on.

We arrived at East 134th Street in the Bronx, and I approached
the guard at the ferry and told him who I was. The lady at the 19th
Precinct had, as she'd promised, paved the way for my voyage, and I
boarded the ferry and took a gray, foggy journey across the East River
to the island that now housed the state-of-the-art penitentiary.

Rikers Island was pretty impressive to the naked eye. It spanned
some four hundred acres, many of them made by dirt from subway excavations and other refuse. For years fires burned beneath
the ground and people claimed that the only thing that lived on
the island were rats. Most of the rodents were gone now, though
it seemed fitting that a place that once burned and smoldered and
served as a residence for vermin was now the hell on earth known as
our penitentiary.

For a miniature Hades, the place was deceptively attractive. Dozens of acres were given over to a pig farm that produced a healthy
portion of the state's pork supply (pity it wasn't beef). The grounds
were landscaped with the kind of care usually given over to royal
gardens. The buildings were new and modern, designed to house a
unique vocational, educational, and recreational system for the prisoners. It was, in many ways, a better place to live than Manhattan.

It also wasn't the kind of place that one planned on staying in
long term. Most of the men at Rikers were serving two to three years.
I hadn't heard of anyone being sent there while awaiting their trial,
though it was always possible this was common practice and I simply
wasn't aware of it, my prison knowledge being what it was. Part of me

was happy to know that this was where Al was staying. It was a much more optimistic place than the 19th Precinct.

I went through another security check upon my arrival and told a formidable-looking guard stationed at the main doors who I was and whom I wanted to see. He didn't ask me my relationship to Al, only if I was bringing the prisoner anything. I assured him my presence was my present, and he directed me to another room where I would again announce myself to a guard and wait until the prisoner was ready to see me.

This room was more physician's waiting room than penitentiary purgatory. A radio buzzed in the corner, relaying the scores for the Rangers' game. A handful of people sat on comfortable-looking couches while reading that day's newspapers and outdated magazines. I gave the bull at the desk my name, and he crossed off some sort of prepared list he had waiting in front of him.

"Al's a popular guy today. There's someone in there with him now. They'll probably be another few minutes. Take a seat and I'll let you know when you can go in."

I figured Al's visitor was probably his long-suffering mother, a woman I'd never met, but whom I pictured as tiny and furrowed, with the sort of perpetually weepy eyes that made you feel guilty for things you hadn't done yet. I busied myself with a copy of *Life* magazine that had a photo of WAVES at the navy training center in Oklahoma on the cover. Inside the magazine was an extensive photo essay detailing the contributions of the WAVES and the WAACS, those brave young women who were willing to don uniforms and fight the war for themselves. They looked so happy as they posed while training. Their uniforms were tailored and feminine as though they needed to be further distinguished from their male counterparts.

"Rosie Winter. Long time no see."

I closed the magazine with a start. A man in a chalk-striped suit stood in front of me, blocking my view of the guard at the door.

"Hiya, Tony. You're looking well." I stood up as though he were the queen and found myself uncertain about what I should do with my hands. He embraced me and planted a kiss on my cheek that sent me off balance. "What are you doing here?" I asked. It wasn't a completely stupid question. Given Tony's line of business, the odds were good that he knew more than one inmate staying at Rikers.

"I came to see how our boy was getting on in his new accommodations. You?"

"The same," I said.

He nodded at this news. I felt very small. He could crush me between his thumb and forefinger. "Jayne with you?" he asked.

"No. No. She didn't want to come. Seemed to think it was a bad idea."

"That's my girl." Tony was a big guy. Not Al big, and certainly not the size of Vinnie Garvaggio, but large enough to make you plan out your path when you were trying to walk by him. In the past, he never intimidated me, even though I knew that given his job and his connections he was someone to fear. The people Tony may have killed (and I wasn't positive he had) were Jimmy Durante caricatures in my mind—comic-book gangsters drawn to die and completely deserving of whatever fate served them. Now with the idea of why Al was really in jail ringing in my head, I no longer saw Tony as some innocuous tough guy. He could do real harm to real people. Including me.

"How come you didn't see things the same way?" he asked.

"Al's my friend, Tony. I owe him big for what he did for Jayne and me."

I expected him to hold me by the collar of my blouse and whisper a threat in my ear about why I might want to stay away from Al from this moment forward. His body language would be subtle enough that the others in the room would assume it was just two old friends embracing. He didn't do that, though. Instead he leaned toward me and in a low voice said, "Tell him to do the right thing."

"Excuse me?"

"When you see him. Tell him to do what's best."

"What does that mean?"

"He knows." He put on an overcoat that had been draped over

his arm and applied a gray fedora. "You, me, and Jayne should get together some time."

"Sure. That'd be swell."

Tony left, and the guard called my name and said I could see my prisoner now. *My prisoner,* as though I had any claim to Al. The bull led me into a big open space that was dotted with tables and chairs. Men in striped jumpsuits emblazoned with the numbers they used instead of names sat scattered about the room, some smoking, some engaged in quiet conversations with well-dressed mouthpieces or conservatively attired women.

The guard directed me to a table marked 21. "Al will be with you in a minute," he told me with a wink. "He needed a potty break."

I sat on a wooden bench and felt like I'd just been put into the meat case at the butcher. Men glanced my way, not with suspicion or any desire to do me harm but with a strange longing. Maybe I resembled their wives or girlfriends, or just embodied something they hadn't seen since they started serving their sentences. Whatever it was, they gazed at me, then forced themselves to look away as though I was too painful a reminder of something they might never see again.

"Rosie."

Al stood opposite me. The tone of his voice made it clear that he hadn't been expecting to see me and wasn't thrilled by the surprise. Still, he was stuck until the guard came back to retrieve him.

"Hiya, Al." I stood up too quickly, and the bench banged against the floor. Al gestured for me to sit down, and we both did so at the same time. "You look good." He did too. The exhaustion that had marked his face at the 19th Precinct was gone. "How's this place treating you?"

"I've been in worse."

"I didn't realize they held people here until their trial."

He clasped his hands together and set them on the table. "There ain't going to be a trial, Rosie. It's all done."

"But . . ." I stopped myself from protesting. Had Tony done this?

Had he delivered Al's sentence behind the scenes and then come to gloat that that's what he got for messing around behind his back? If he did, then why had he told me to urge Al to do the right thing?

"I saw Tony in the visitor's lobby," I said. "I guess he'd just gotten through with seeing you." Al nodded, and I realized I hadn't given him much of an opening to say anything more. "Does he come to see you a lot?"

"When he can. No one likes to visit this place, especially if they've been on the other side of this table before."

I'd never heard tell of Tony serving time. It made sense—most of his associates had records—but it still unsettled me. It was the first hard proof I had of his having done anything wrong in the past, and that meant the odds were good that he could do wrong in the present. "He told me to tell you to do the right thing. Any idea what that means?"

"Not a one," he said.

"He treating you right?"

"He was here, wasn't he?"

But to do what? I wondered. Remind him to keep his mouth shut? Demand he seek vengeance on Vinnie to prove his loyalty?

"Why are you here, Rosie? I thought I told you not to visit no more."

"That was at the 19th Precinct. I figured the rules changed when you got shipped out here." I bit my lip and decided that as long as I was there, I might as well make the most of my visit. This would probably be the last time Al agreed to see me. "If you didn't want me to come, you could've told the gatekeeper I was persona non grata."

"It does good for a man's reputation to have a dame visit him."

"Then I guess you owe me one, and I'm here to make you pay up. I want to know why you confessed to Paulette's murder."

"We're back there?"

"We never left. Seems to me someone like you could've gotten away scot-free with the crime, or could've called in enough favors to wipe away any trail you'd left. Paulette's roommates had no idea who you were until the day the cops called and said they'd caught her killer. So why did you go to the police before they ever bothered to come to you?"

"You do something bad enough, it weighs on you."

"You've done lots of bad things before, Al. You can't be in your line of work and be ruled by your conscience."

"Maybe I've changed. Maybe I went too far this time."

"Who could blame you, with Vinnie Garvaggio pulling the strings."

Something changed in his face. He leaned toward me and lowered his voice. "What are you going on about now?"

"Garvaggio." Al pushed at the air with his hand, begging me to lower my voice. I obeyed. "Everyone knows you were working for him."

"I wouldn't throw the guy a glass of water if he was drowning."

"That's not what I heard."

"Then get the potatoes out of your ears." His noodle swiveled right and left. "And don't go rattling that name in here."

"All right already." I decided to change my tactics. If appealing to his desire to exonerate himself didn't work, maybe guilt would. "How does your ma feel about all this? Can't be thrilled knowing you're in here again."

He looked down at his hands; they were worn and red. Chemical burns. He was probably assigned to work in the prison laundry. "She don't know I'm in here, and I'd like to keep it that way."

I thought about using that as my leverage, but even I wouldn't go so low as to threaten to tell a man's mother that he was in the bing.

"I don't know the woman, Al. I'm not going to blow your cover. Isn't she going to be curious when you stop showing up for holidays, though?"

"She thinks I'm out of town. If my visit is extended, so be it."

Poking him wasn't working and neither was guilting him. I decided to play it straight.

"I think you're a liar, Al. Not about your ma, but about this whole messed-up business. I don't think you killed Paulette, but I do think you're willing to take the fall for someone else to save your head. You don't have to answer me, I wouldn't in your shoes either, but I want you to know that I'm on to you. Maybe I'm an idiot—Jayne thinks so anyways—but the pieces don't add up. I don't think you're capable of this, and until someone shows me a picture of you with the body in one hand and a weapon in the other, I'm not going to buy it."

"Is that why you came by yourself? Jayne don't agree with your theory?" It was the first hint of remorse I'd heard in his voice since this whole awful thing began. He didn't mind serving time or lying to his ma, but he couldn't stand the thought that Jayne had bought his story.

"She says you're a louse who belongs behind bars. Of course, Tony's been feeding her some of that. You haven't ruined her opinion all by yourself."

He pushed back from the table and rose to her feet. "Yeah, well maybe you should listen to her. Sounds like Jayne's the only one with a lick of sense in her head. You're not welcome here. Get it? If you show up here again, I'm not coming out."

Tears stung my eyes. I'd lost Jack and now I was losing Al too. "Don't you worry," I said. "The only part of me you're going to see is my back."

21 The Guilty Man

I MADE IT OUT TO the waiting area and crossed my name off the pad I'd signed in on. I was about to grab my coat and dust when a hand took hold of my elbow.

"How'd it go in there?" It was Tony. He was still there. Waiting for me.

"I think this is going to be my last visit for a while. Al wasn't too happy to see me."

Tony released my elbow and slid on his gloves. "You got a way back to the city?"

"Just a ferry and a cab."

"How's about I give you a ride? The parade starts at one and ain't no one getting nowhere after that."

It was St. Patrick's Day, a day made for depending on the kindness of gangsters with private cars. I couldn't have Tony drop me off at the theater. If Jayne wasn't supposed to be performing in Garvaggio's show, I wouldn't win any favor by admitting I was either. "If you could get me to Times Square, that would be great. I'm supposed to meet a girlfriend for a late lunch."

We met Tony's driver at the ferry landing, and I piled inside the heap with him. I sat by my door and Tony sat by his. A cloud of cigar smoke connected his side of the car to mine.

"Did he say anything?" he asked.

"Nothing useful. It wasn't so much a conversation as me trying to get him to talk, you know? I rattled on about what Jayne and I were up to, and he sat there and sulked until I couldn't take it anymore."

Tony closed his right hand and popped his knuckles. "That sounds like Al all right."

"So he's like that with you?"

Tony lowered his window enough to ash his cigar. "Absoyoootley." He rolled the window back up and examined the tip of the Cuban. "So this is how he's going to play it."

"Play what?"

Tony nodded, continuing a silent conversation I wasn't going to be asked to join.

"I can't believe he waived a trial," I said. "Did anyone try to talk him out of it?"

Tony's eyes were naturally large and distended, almost comically so, yet he disguised his oversized peepers by keeping his lids at half-mast. It gave him a seductive, mysterious look and often made it hard for me to know exactly what he was looking at. "It's his choice. If he wants freedom, he knows what to do. When a man's made up his mind, only he can unmake it."

I'm a sucker for a philosophic mobster.

Tony dropped me off near Times Square, and once he was safely out of sight, I started hoofing it to Forty-fifth Street. I could hear "The Wearing of the Green" in the distance, being played by a band of bag-pipers for the holiday. I used to love the parade, but this year the sound of marching bands struck me as more militaristic than merry. The pip-ers might as well have been the Nazis' procession arriving in Paris.

I'd played it all wrong with Al and blown my last chance. If he was innocent, he clearly didn't want my help, probably because he rec-ognized how futile it was. And if Tony was the reason Al was locked up, my mentioning that I'd just run into him didn't do anything but cement in Al's mind that I was in cahoots with his enemy. I'd failed us both. Again.

I sulked my way through the first half of rehearsal. If anyone noticed my sour mood, nobody said anything. Scowls and frowns were the order of the day. The dancers had joined us, but as Jayne had warned me, they weren't ready to dance with music, much less perform alongside the rest of the cast. Walter Friday watched them with a bemused look on his face. Vinnie Garvaggio sat beside him, chomping his way through his cigar in time to the music. When the action paused, he called out to Gloria, complimenting her on her hoofing. This did nothing to help her performance.

When Garvaggio wasn't reinforcing Gloria's self-delusions, he was leering at Jayne. My best pal responded to the constant winks and suggestive nods by trying to avoid making eye contact with him, but the attention was unnerving her so much that she was forgetting steps, losing time, and wobbling on landings she used to nail. Even Maureen noticed her inability to focus and shouted out reprimands to her star pupil. "You can't perform vith two people in the audience? Vhat vill it be like vith more, eh? Und here I zought you vere my saving grace."

As for the rest of us, Zelda, Izzie, Ruby, Minnie, and myself went effortlessly through our scenes, trying our best to blend into the dance sequences seamlessly enough that Friday would have no reason to stop the action. Despite my awful morning at Rikers, I managed to remember most of my lines and even figured out where they went. Having overcome that barrier, Ruby now took me to task for what she described as my "tone-deaf singing."

"I know you don't have any solos, Rosie, but that's no excuse for making the audience cover their ears with their hands."

At the break I looked for Jayne and found Garvaggio had pulled her aside for a private conversation. She kept her arms wrapped around her upper body and countered each attempt he made to move close to her by moving two steps backward. I thought about rescuing her, but I caught Gloria's eye from across the room. She was watching them as intently as I was.

"Tomorrow night's the night." I spun around and found Zelda and Izzie standing behind me. As much as I liked them, they had a nasty habit of sneaking up on me. I considered asking them to wear bells around their necks just so I could keep from being startled.

"Tomorrow's the night for what?" I asked. *"Amos 'n' Andy?"*

"The Stage Door Canteen," said Izzie. "Remember?"

I hadn't. With everything else going on, my promise to join them at the Canteen was the furthest thing from my mind. "Any chance we can make it next week?"

"Oh no," said Zelda. "A promise is a promise. Don't be scared. It'll be loads of fun, I promise."

"I'm not known for my kitchen skills."

"None of us are," said Izzie. "And the men couldn't care less. They're there for a cute skirt, not a good meal."

This cute skirt wasn't in the mood to provide them with either.

Rehearsal didn't end until well after eight that night. By the time Jayne and I started home, we were both yawning so much as to make conversation practically impossible. I finally forced her to jaw on the subway, since I was afraid both of us would doze off and miss our stop.

"Al made it pretty clear to me that I'm not to visit him again," I told her.

"Why are you surprised? He made it pretty clear the last time you saw him too." The train stopped and a handful of St. Patrick's Day revelers climbed aboard. With them came the sickening stench of cigarette smoke and whiskey.

"Tony was there," I said.

That perked Jayne up. "Really? You didn't say anything . . ."

"About the show? Of course not. As a matter of fact, you earned a gold medal from him for having the sense to stay off Rikers."

Jayne rested her head against the window. "Did you learn anything from Al?"

"Not really, no. He still insists he's guilty, though he seemed more than a little bothered that you agreed with him. Part of me thinks we should've sent you instead of me. I'm starting to think he doesn't care what I think."

"Rosie . . ."

"It's true. The way he was acting today, it was like I was public enemy number one." An idea slipped loose from my exhausted brain. "This might be important, though: he hates Garvaggio."

"I know the feeling."

I scooted closer to her to keep the eavesdropping Irish at bay. "No, he really hates him. When I accused him of working for the guy, he acted like I'd slapped his mother. Used a mixed metaphor and everything."

"Wouldn't you? I mean, Al may be in prison because of the guy."

"But why tell me that he can't stand him. Why would I care?" Across the aisle was a poster depicting a Chinese man. THIS MAN IS YOUR FRIEND, the text declared. *HE FIGHTS FOR FREEDOM.* If only everyone on our side were so clearly defined.

Jayne struggled to swallow a yawn. "Maybe Al's afraid it'll get back to Tony that he was working for Garvaggio."

"If Al's in jail and Tony's been to see him, don't you think it's likely he already knows the how and why?"

Jayne rubbed her eyes and mulled this over. "True. . . . He wants me to have a drink with him after rehearsal tomorrow."

"Tony?"

She cocked her head to the left. "Not Tony, you dumdora. Vinnie."

"I hope you did the right thing."

She lifted her head proudly. "I was firm but polite."

"You turned him down?"

"Of course I turned him down! Can you imagine what Tony would do if he found out? Vinnie Garvaggio is as kosher as a two-dollar ham."

I beckoned her to lower her voice. "This isn't about your love life. Don't you think an evening alone with Vinnie would be the perfect opportunity to find out more about him?"

"Like what? How cold his hands are?" I gave her a look to let her know the dumb act was wearing thin. She surrendered with her palms to the sky. "He barely told Gloria anything—why would he tell me any more?"

"Because you're not Gloria. Because you've got something she doesn't."

"Obviously you haven't seen her in a leotard."

I gently rapped her arm. "I mean you're a good conversationalist.

You know how to play the game. I'll bet dollars to doughnuts Vinnie will be singing after ten minutes in your company."

"What if Tony finds out?"

I thought back to my earlier theory, the one that said Al was where he was because he'd crossed Tony, not because he'd actually murdered somebody. Did Jayne run the same risk if she was found in Vinnie Garvaggio's company? I didn't want to think so, but if you're operating under the belief that someone is dangerous, it's best to assume that's the case under all circumstances.

Still . . . he was Tony. And even if their relationship was in flux, he cared about Jayne. Besides, it was terribly inconvenient to have to worry about him right now.

"Don't worry about Tony. If he doesn't know you're doing this show, he certainly isn't going to know if you dip the bill with Garvaggio."

Jayne sighed and knocked her head against the back of the seat. "All right. I'll go out with him. For one drink. In a public place."

"You'll get no disagreement from me."

"Want to tag along?" Her exhausted eyes were widened to their full capacity.

"Jayne, I'm hardly batting a thousand when it comes to getting information out of people. The only thing Garvaggio would spill if I were there would be my drink. He wants to be alone. With you."

She worked the hem of her coat around her finger, winding the thick, checked wool so tightly her nail turned blue.

"Besides, I've got plans. Tomorrow night I'm volunteering at the Canteen. I can't let the men in blue down."

"Yeah, but you feel no such loyalty for a blonde in ballet slippers."

I patted her hand. "It'll be fine. I'll meet up with you after. We'll set a time and I'll show up wherever you two are and break up the festivities. How's that sound?"

She exhaled, and her breath fogged up the window, erasing everything outside the subway car. "Like you're going to owe me a big favor after tomorrow night."

22 Tonight's the Night

THURSDAY'S REHEARSAL BARRELED PAST US, broken up now and again by breaks that lasted half as long as they should've. I was a nervous wreck all day, using what little downtime I had to fret and worry. Given that Jayne was the one with the undeniably unpleasant evening in front of her, I couldn't quite pinpoint where my own sense of dread was coming from. I'd like to think I was such a kind and intuitive friend that I was merely suffering her anxiety with her, but as rehearsal ended and Jayne went off to powder her nose and bolster her courage, a voice reminded me that I had plenty to fear on my own.

"Ready, Rosie?" asked Izzie.

"For what?"

"You're coming out with us. Remember?"

Ruby appeared to Izzie's left just as I was working up the courage to invent a reason why I couldn't join them.

"I hope you don't mind," said Izzie. "But Ruby wants to tag along too. I thought it might be fun, all of us girls hanging out together."

Ruby offered me a smile, the first one she'd given me that day. It wasn't a welcoming grin, but a tooth-filled reminder that she could make my life miserable if she wanted to.

"I thought you had a date tonight," I said. "With your pilot what's-his-name?"

"*Captain* Montgomery and I aren't meeting up until later tonight. He had a family engagement." Ruby's eyes bored into my head, silently ordering me to back out of my plans and leave her in peace.

Any desire I'd had to put a kibosh on the evening evaporated. If Ruby didn't want me there, then I was definitely going.

"I'm ready if you are," I told them. We headed toward the doors as Jayne emerged from the ladies' room. She mouthed the words *ten o'clock* to me to remind me that I had to rescue her from our predetermined location. Jayne was going to insist Vinnie take her to the Tap Room, a supper club that was as far away from Tony's usual stomping grounds as the moon was from the sun. Not only that, but the joint was well lit, since the owner believed dim lighting encouraged pickpockets and other flimflammers.

As we passed through the door and onto the street, I noticed Minnie hoofing it in the opposite direction from us. Her head was tilted toward the pavement and her pace suggested that while she was moving, she didn't have a particular destination in mind.

"Do you think we should ask Minnie along?" I asked.

"She wouldn't come," said Zelda. "I've asked her to do things a thousand times and she never takes me up on it."

"I feel bad for her. She seems like she's in her own little world during rehearsal."

"It's her choice," said Izzie. "We've invited her out, attempted conversation, and each time we did she gave us that sour puss and a lame excuse. Life's too short to beg for friendship."

"I bet she'd come if you asked her," I told Ruby.

"I'm sure she would, but I have no desire to ask her."

"Because she was good enough to be your nurse, but she's not good enough to be your friend?"

Ruby glowered at me. She didn't want to be reminded that there was a time when her head was swollen by any means other than her ego. "No, because she's no fun."

"You've got that right," said Izzie. "That one's uppity. And a bit of a prude." I found that hard to believe. After all, Minnie had been reading *Forever Amber,* one of the raciest books on the market. "I offered to hook her up with a pen pal and she acted like I'd just suggested we watch a stag film. I don't think she wants to associate with women like us."

We passed by a group of women trolling for the Women's Action Committee for Victory and Lasting Peace. We each took one of the flyers they offered and shoved them into our pockets. "And what kind of women are you?" I asked.

"We're not V-girls, if that's what you're worried about," said Izzie.

"I would be if I knew what that was." The war had given new prominence to the letter V, tacking it on to any number of things to link them with the Allies' goal for victory.

"You don't know what a V-girl is?" asked Zelda. I shook my head. "Think whore without the money."

Izzie gave her a gentle push. "Zel!"

"Well, it's true. V-girls are young girls trolling for soldiers. They'll put out for anyone in a uniform."

"I doubt Minnie thinks any of you are like that," I said. I had a feeling Minnie was like me, mourning one man so deeply that she couldn't consider meeting another. Could anyone blame her if she didn't jump at the chance to write to a stranger looking for romance? "I've talked to her a little," I told them. "She had a brother who died recently. If I were her, I'm not sure I'd want to spend my nights at the Canteen either."

"And yet here you are," mumbled Ruby.

"We all know someone who's died," said Izzie. "That's no excuse. Every one of those men at the Canteen has lost someone they cared about, and it seems to me that her time would be better spent sympathizing with them rather than sulking. I mean, look at you: your boyfriend's missing in action, and rather than making yourself miserable over it, you're doing something worthwhile."

Was I? It was hard to say anymore.

"So what do we do when we get there?" I asked.

"You like to dance?" asked Izzie.

"When a German masquerading as Irish isn't yelling steps at me, sure."

"After we're done with the food prep, we go out and dance with the servicemen. They've always got great bands and far too many men for us to handle. You'll love it—it's like being the prettiest girl at the ball."

The Stage Door Canteen was a joint effort of the USO and the American Theater Wing. Part dance hall, part supper club, it had become *the* stop for servicemen visiting our fair city. The best local restaurants donated food for the soldiers to eat, and the prettiest actresses on Broadway volunteered their time to serve them dinner and trip the light fantastic. Even big-named stars got involved, no doubt aware of how carving up ham for our boys in blue was the perfect PR opportunity. There were shows, too, put on by headliners like Tommy Dorsey and Glenn Miller, and "showlets" that gave the latest Broadway productions a chance to do a scene or two to lure servicemen to come see the real thing. Every week thousands of men—and women—in the armed forces flooded the joint, and its popularity was only going to grow. RCA was filming a movie about the Canteen and Bette Davis had opened a similar spot in Hollywood.

We arrived at the infamous blue door, where hundreds of servicemen were already lined up, anxiously awaiting five o'clock when the Canteen opened. A sign posted outside greeted them with the words AN ALL-AMERICAN PLACE FOR THE ALL-AMERICAN BOY. Of course, it wasn't just American men who were welcome; foreign serviceman had been invited as well. As we passed them, they hooted and hollered at us in accents that told of hometowns in England, Australia, and even France. Zelda, Izzie, and Ruby took it all in, replying with promises to dance with each man, followed by blown kisses the soldiers eagerly caught in their hands. On New York's stages they may have been up-and-comers, but at the Canteen they were already superstars.

The Canteen was located in the basement of the 44th Street Theatre, west of Broadway, where *Rosalinda* (a revival of *Die Fledermaus*) was taking up the main stage. A burly doorman greeted Izzie with a grin and listened as she introduced me. He let us pass, and we entered the building and followed the narrow stairs down to a surprisingly small space crammed full of cocktail tables that ringed a miniature dance floor. Our sky was a slanted pipe and beam ceiling. Our stage barely contained a motley crew of musicians who struggled to set up and tune their instruments. Young women with heavily made-up faces and enviable figures wore white aprons atop bias-cut dresses they'd chosen for the way the skirts fanned out when they danced. They carried platters of donated food and put bottles of Coca-Cola on ice. Alcohol wasn't served at the Canteen, but it didn't seem like anyone cared. The men didn't come to drink away their sorrows—they intended to dance them into oblivion.

The Canteen was a hold-over from World War I and had an impressive pedigree: Lee Schubert had donated the space (a former speakeasy) and paid for the heat; Irving Berlin had made a gift of the piano. And all about the space were signs of other people's generosity, including vibrant painted scenes contributed by Broadway's best designers, furniture cobbled together by stage carpenters, and lighting as theatrical as anything you might see on the 44th Street main stage, which had been rigged up by the electricians' union free of charge. It was an amazing monument to cooperation in an industry whose members weren't known to try to promote anything but themselves.

Of course, doing their bit wasn't the only reason women like us came to a place like this. In addition to the actresses staffing the kitchen and the buffet, there were a slew of other Broadway types donating their time and services to the Canteen. Agents, producers, directors, and reviewers worked with the rest of us poor schlubs, picking up plates, refilling drinks, scooping out chow, and stirring the punch.

Zelda went up to an older woman with jowls like a bulldog and explained whom she had with her and that we'd be happy to help out wherever we were needed. The gal's name was Elaine DeVincent, her rank Canteen Hostess. She was the ultimate arbiter of who got into the Canteen and who was sent packing. "It's good to see you again, Ruby," Elaine said. Ruby gushed an insincere response. "I'm all out of handbooks—does the new girl know the rules?" Zelda replied that she'd given me her copy and with a wink let me know she'd give me the real scoop in a minute. We were sent into the kitchen and each given an apron to wear. There we worked elbow to elbow with a dozen other men and women, washing and drying dishes, slicing ham, brewing coffee, plating doughnuts, slicing cakes, making sandwiches, folding napkins, and exchanging gossip about who was supposed to be there that night (Dinah Shore and Charles Coburn had been sighted moments before).

"Here's how it is." Zelda moved close to where I stood, spreading mayonnaise on bread, and lowered her voice. "You can dance with whoever you want, but it's better not to turn anyone down. They encourage us to pay extra attention to the black fellows—Elaine wants to make sure everyone feels welcome, no matter what their color."

"Gotcha."

"Don't share personal information. Don't ask a soldier where he's been or where he's going. And under no circumstances are you to date anyone you might meet here."

I couldn't believe I'd been worried. I didn't need to fear that I was trying to replace Jack. I couldn't date someone I met there even if I wanted to.

As though she heard my thoughts, Izzie elbowed me in the back and joined our conversation. "That last bit is a whole lot of hogwash. Everyone here dates; they just don't get caught. Isn't that right, Ruby?"

Ruby didn't respond. Instead, she turned the same shade as the ham and began sawing at it like it was a tree she was hoping to fell.

"What Izzie means," says Zelda, "is discretion is everything. If you want to meet up with someone outside of the Canteen, you better make it far from here, where there's no chance of any of the other girls seeing you. They're a real nosy bunch, and if they even suspect you're doing something you shouldn't, they'll report you to the hostess. After that, your ticket's revoked and the only way you're getting back into the Canteen is if you join up yourself."

"So then why do it?" I asked.

"For the men, of course," said Izzie. "Everything we do, every risk we take, is to make them happy."

A horrible rumbling sounded from outside the kitchen. I wasn't sure if I should run or duck for cover. Zelda pointed to a clock suspended above the stove. "Five o' clock on the dot. Let the fun begin, ladies."

Once we were finished preparing the food, Zelda and I hauled the heavy stacks of dishes into the main room and deposited them on the buffet table. With our task done, we hovered near the wooden rail that separated the tables from the dance floor. For the next hour and a half the packed club was entertained by cast members from *New Faces of 1943*, followed by three numbers from the Dorothy Fields–Cole Porter show, *Let's Face It!*, both of which were rumored to be closing soon.

I was transfixed by both of the performances. They weren't anything extraordinary, but the men's reactions to them were. They watched with open mouths, laughing harder at the jokes than they deserved and clapping until their hands were red.

"It's something, isn't it?" whispered Zelda.

"Absolutely. I'm glad I got a chance to see it." I turned to her and found tears welling up in her eyes. "Are you all right?"

Zelda wiped her face with the back of her hand. "This place gets to me sometimes. I have a brother in the navy, and tonight every sailor I see is wearing his face."

"I know the feeling."

Zelda smiled. "I'll bet you do." She rummaged through her pockets until she found a handkerchief. "I'm sorry Izzie was so hard on you the other day."

"Don't be. Sometimes that's the only thing I respond to."

"You don't have to do anything you don't want to. Izzie and Olive can be very persistent, but if you're uncomfortable with something, you're not obligated to listen to them." One of the performers stepped into the spotlight, and the music swelled. Zelda's lips kept moving, but I could no longer hear her. She elbowed me in the ribs and shouted, "Come on—bathroom duty."

Our job didn't end with food prep. We also had to monitor the restrooms for cleanliness. Zelda approached the men's room door and knocked. When no one replied, she sent me inside. "I'll do the ladies. Just lock the door, make sure there's paper, and wipe down the sink. If it takes more than two minutes, you're working too hard."

I did as she said. Although the evening was only an hour in, the place was already tattered. I picked up the garbage, mopped up the vanity, and neatened the various pamphlets and flyers left for the serviceman to peruse. Most described opportunities for soldiers in the New York area, including discounts they should be taking advantage of during their leave. An illustrated red pamphlet with a come-hither blonde on the cover enticed the reader with the title *Sex and This War*. It wasn't the steamy read I thought it would be. "Don't drink too much," it warned. "Beware loose women. It would be a shame to miss out on Victory because of VD."

Apparently the war wasn't the only thing soldiers had to fear.

"Learn anything?" asked Zelda when I was done.

"Men have bad aim and syphilis is more dangerous than the Solomon Islands."

Zelda threw her head back and laughed. "Ah yes, the army's latest concern is the evil that women do."

"And what is it we're supposedly doing?"

"Oh, you know." I didn't get a chance to find out what I supposedly knew. The crowd erupted onto its feet and gave the performers a standing ovation.

"So now what?" I asked.

"Now the work ends and the fun begins."

As the performers took their bows and left the stage, the musicians took their places and with no introduction struck up "I Left My Heart at the Stage Door Canteen," the Irving Berlin song that had become the club's anthem. A mass of humanity rushed the dance floor, and I watched in amazement as people who hadn't known each other seconds before held each other close enough that they could feel the beating of each other's hearts. The soldiers were a mix of officers who wore their ranks upon their shoulders and the newly enlisted who had their hearts upon their sleeves. Despite the differences in experience, they all had a similar wide-eyed stare that took in the humble surroundings with a kind of awe that made it clear they were trying to remember it for posterity. This girl, this song, this moment, would go into a foxhole, onto a plane, below a ship's hull, and help them make it through some dark and terrible night.

"When the song ends, get ready for a flood of men to come your way," said Zelda.

"So I just dance?"

"And talk. Honestly, most of the fellows in here are more interested in conversation than fancy footwork."

There were many things I felt equipped to do in life, but talking to strange men wasn't one of them. "What do I talk about?"

"Whatever they want." She put her chin to her chest. "You have talked to a man before, haven't you?"

"Ha. Ha. I just meant what sorts of things should I talk about?"

"Family. Pets. The latest Glenn Miller platter. Whatever hits you."

As she described, as soon as the band played the last note, these once-intimate couples parted ways and began searching for new partners. I'm sure there must've been some who stayed with whomever they'd just been dancing with, but to my perspective it seemed like everyone was searching for someone better than the one they'd just held. Either that, or they were trying to cram an entire lifetime's worth of romantic experience into a single night.

"Would you care to dance?" A man in a navy blue sailor suit paused before Zelda and me. I assumed he was talking to her, until Zelda's elbow told me otherwise.

"Me?" I asked.

He nodded and offered me his hand. For a split second I thought about refusing him and holding out for someone from a branch of the military that didn't also house my ex. I didn't want to start the night off with a black mark against me, though, so I followed him onto the dance floor and we began a cautious foxtrot to "Somebody Else Is Taking My Place."

"You're a good dancer," he said.

"Could I quote you on that? There's a certain choreographer who'd be shocked to hear it." The air turned hot and humid. Cigarette smoke dimmed what lighting there was until it seemed as though we were dancing through a haze.

"You got a name?" he asked.

I don't know why I lied. Maybe I believed that if I used a name other than my own I wouldn't be betraying Jack. "Delores."

"Delores what?"

"That's enough for now," I said. "We have rules about surnames. What do I call you?"

"My friends call me Peaches."

"You're kidding, right?" I was a tall woman, but Peaches towered above me. He wasn't wiry but so solidly built he almost seemed like another species.

"Why would I kid about a thing like that?" he asked.

"'Cause you don't strike me as the kind of man who fits that kind of nickname."

"We all give one another nicknames based on where we're from. I'm from Georgia." He had a nice Southern lilt. It didn't soften his voice the way the accent usually did but made everything he said feel more rounded and substantial.

"So you ended up with Peaches because Georgia was already taken?"

"No, but it didn't seem advisable to let the men call me by a woman's name."

"You're right—Peaches is much more manly."

His hoofing became more confident. He'd spent a lot of time on the dance floor, probably far more time than I had.

"I haven't seen you here before," he said.

"That's because it's my first time."

"Lucky me." He was handsome in a plain sort of way, a man who would be beautiful to his wife but would never cause hearts to pitter-patter from the big screen. Not that I was going to win any prizes myself. "So what brings you here?" he asked.

"A couple of girlfriends with a regular appointment."

"So you came unwillingly?"

"I wouldn't say that." Just like that I lost the gift of gab. I thought about the topics of conversation Zelda had proposed to me, but the idea of bringing up any of them seemed horrible. Instead, I eased my hold on Peaches and rested my head on his shoulder. We danced for a few measures like this and for one wonderful moment I closed my eyes and imagined I was at Nick's on Seventh Avenue and Grove Street, a club Jack and I used to go to that had the best swing music in town.

"I'm navy," he said.

My head snapped up. "I know. Was I supposed to ask that?"

"Most girls usually do."

Strike one for me. I didn't even ask the right questions. "And what do you do for the navy?"

"Bomber pilot mostly." He winked at me. "It's terribly dangerous."

A bomber pilot named Peaches. Swell. "So I'm supposed to be impressed?"

"Most girls are."

Despite what appeared to be derision that I wasn't asking the right questions or viewing his answers with the requisite amount of awe, I got the impression that Peaches was pleased I wasn't behaving like *most* girls. This intrigued me. And worried me.

"I was shot down a month ago," he said.

"Then how is it you're dancing here with me?" I asked.

"I'm lucky, I guess. The crash banged me up enough that they gave me two weeks of liberty Stateside, but not so much that I can't cut a rug."

"Two whole weeks. What does it take to get a month?"

"You don't want to know," he said. "What do you do?"

"When I'm not tripping the light fantastic with strange men named after fruit, I'm an actress."

"Movies?"

"Why does everyone always ask that?"

"Was that the wrong response?"

"No. Yes." I was feeling more like myself. "It's just that I'm a stage actress and that's all I've ever wanted to be, yet everyone acts like performing in the movies is a loftier goal and those of us on Broadway are just biding time until Hollywood comes knocking."

He shook his head and clucked his tongue. "It's the same with being a navy pilot. Everyone wonders why I didn't go out for the air force."

"Really?"

He broke out a brilliant smile. "No, I just wanted to make you feel better."

I swatted him playfully.

"Are you in anything now?" he asked.

"Only the greatest disaster in Broadway history."

"Wow, then you *must* be good. I'd love to take you out to dinner sometime."

His failure to segue into the invitation threw me for a loop. My confidence left me as fast as it had come. "That might be hard. I hear you fellows are pretty wrapped up with that war thing. Unless you're suggesting I wait until it's over."

"Would you?"

I looked around the room for Zelda and Izzie. Each of them was occupied with a soldier, fighting their own battles over what to say. "I'm a very impatient woman."

"In that case: I meant now."

"Don't think bad of me, Peaches, but this is my first night here and I don't want to get tossed from the joint for violating the rules out of the gate."

"So you've got a guy?"

It would've been the easiest thing in the world to say yes, but I couldn't. Not because it was a lie, or even because there was a chance Peaches and Jack had encountered each other, but because I believed I'd renounced my claim to Jack the day I decided not to write to him. "No, I just have a strong sense of what's right and what's wrong."

He swung me around and dipped me. "Rules are meant to be broken."

I became upright again. "And so are hearts, but that doesn't mean I'm ready to sacrifice one to the cause."

"Don't you want to do your part for the red, white, and blue?"

"I thought I was."

He pulled me close to him, and his hand brushed the bare skin at the top of my back. "One dance is hardly going to push us toward victory."

"But a full meal will?"

"It's like the posters say, 'Food will help us win the war.' "

"You're a persuasive man."

"That's why I'm an officer. If you won't eat with me, why don't you tell me when you'll be here again? At least then I can eat in your presence and get another spin on the dance floor."

It was hard to say no to a man in uniform. It's not like I was wooed by his fancy dress duds, but like Zelda said, the thought that he was about to go back to whatever godforsaken place he was stationed in and might never set foot on American soil again was a compelling reason to give him whatever he wanted. I couldn't go my whole life withholding the things that gave other people pleasure.

"I hadn't planned that far ahead," I said. "Why don't you pick a night and I'll make sure I'm here?"

"Saturday," he said with a grin.

I danced once more with Peaches, this time to "The Boys Will See Us Through." I might've gone for a third spin if Elaine hadn't tapped me on the shoulder and told me there were dishes that needed to be washed. I excused myself and spent the next half hour elbow deep in sudsy water. I was about to return to the dance floor for another whirl when the clock above the stove caught my eye. It was a quarter to ten. If I didn't meet Jayne as agreed, she'd have an ing bing. I left the kitchen, caught Zelda's eye from across the room, and cocked my head in the international sign for *I need to get out of here. Now.*

"I was wondering where you were hiding, Delores." Peaches was back.

"More dishes than hands, I'm afraid."

"You seem to be the only one in here actually working."

"Come now: Hedy Lamarr is carving ham, and I think I saw Leslie Howard spiking the punch."

He offered me his hand. "Got time for another dance?"

"I'm afraid not. I promised I'd get a friend out of a fix at ten. It was swell meeting you."

"You make it sound like it's the last time. Don't forget about Saturday night." He differentiated the days of the week on an invisible calendar hanging in the air before him. "That's this Saturday night, the day after tomorrow."

"Saturday's the day before Sunday, right?" I tapped myself on the head. "Don't worry—once it's in here, I never forget."

"And don't plan on leaving early. My heart can't take that."

"Agreed." I gave him a firm handshake and a quick salute, then joined Zelda at the coat rack. "I've got to blow," I told her. "I promised Jayne I'd meet her for drinks at ten."

"You can't leave without telling me how you made out."

Across the room Peaches was talking up another girl, a blonde in a skin-tight pink sweater who didn't look a day past eighteen. "I danced. We talked. It wasn't so terrible."

"Are you going to see him again?"

"If I say yes, I'm breaking a rule."

"So no then?"

I winked at her before dashing up the stairs and onto the street.

23 Nothing But the Truth

Unfortunately the Tap Room's bright light policy had ended at about the same time as the dim-out began. In its place were heavily shaded wall sconces and candles that provided just enough light for a waitress to make it to your table without spilling your drink, but not quite enough for her to be able write down your order. I arrived ten minutes late and stood at the entrance to the restaurant and scanned the crowd. Every man in New York had taken out a woman who looked exactly like Jayne. I eliminated them one by one until I found Garvaggio crammed into a corner booth with his back to the wall. Jayne was at a safe distance from him, and their table was littered with empty glasses and half-filled ashtrays.

I'd tracked her down, but I needed a plan. Pretending to casually bump into her was way too amateurish—even in times of war a woman didn't go to a supper club by herself. Claiming I'd been sent to retrieve her after getting word that her mother was sick seemed too obvious and would only invite further inquiries that might create problems for Jayne later on. I decided to go with devastated best friend searching for a beloved shoulder to cry on.

I ducked into the ladies' room and locked myself into the stall. I thought about Greta Garbo's death scene in *Camille* and managed to squeeze out a tear that vanished as soon as it appeared. Next I summoned the last days of Pip, a rat terrier I'd loved as a child and who'd met an unfortunate end beneath the wheels of an ice truck one hot summer's day. Poor Pip didn't do the trick though—there was too much distance between my memory and my emotion. It was time to bring out the big guns. I closed my eyes and replayed Jack's last words to me as he boarded the bus to the navy yard, his final stop before he climbed aboard a frigate and hit the ocean. He'd been cold and cruel that day, out of retaliation, no doubt, for my own frosty response to the news of his departure. As the bus pulled away, I realized how ridiculous it was to hold a grudge against him for enlisting. It was too late, though. He was gone.

That did the trick. I was crying. Then I berated myself for using such an awful memory to pull this cheap stunt, especially after I'd spent the evening in the arms of another man. This made me sob even harder. I was a terrible person. I couldn't even give my memories the respect they deserved.

Maybe this was the evil Zelda was alluding to.

Before I lost my nerve, I left the bathroom and cut back toward the main entrance to the restaurant. Desperate for a prop, I pulled Ruby's unmailed letter out of my pocketbook and smashed it into my hand. With mounting hysteria, I approached Jayne's table and caught her eye.

"Rosie? What are you doing here?"

"He's done it," I said. I squeezed the letter into a ball. "I just got a Dear Jane. He couldn't even wait until his leave to break up with me."

"No!" She left her seat and wrapped her arms around me. I upped my sobs, and she whispered beneath the din, "It's about time. I was about to fake a fever."

I continued my display of woe. "I'm so sorry to bother you. I didn't know what else to do. I was afraid if I stayed home by myself I'd . . . I'd . . ." More tears. I was getting good at this.

"It's all right. Shhhhh . . ." She pried the V-mail from my hand and held it out of my reach.

"Those are his last words to me!"

"And that was the last time you're ever going to read them. He's not worth this."

"I thought we'd be together forever! I don't know how I can go on without him." I pounded my chest. I wailed. I was Medea clutching the corpses of my children. "Now I've ruined your evening. You must hate me."

"We don't. Do we, Vinnie?" Jayne elbowed Garvaggio in the ribs, though how she made contact with him through all those protective layers of blubber was anyone's guess.

"No problem, doll," he said by way of consolation. Apparently his acting ability only extended to pretending that Gloria had talent. "Why don't you join us?" He attempted to make more room in the booth, but all he really achieved was bumping his belly into the table. The empty glasses danced before settling back into stillness.

"Oh, I couldn't join you. I'm miserable company." Translation: I didn't want to. I wanted to grab Jayne, hit pavement, and find out what he had told her before I arrived.

"I insist," said Garvaggio. "One drink. It'll take the edge off."

The thing about men like Garvaggio was that they're impossible to say no to. It's not that they're particularly persuasive, but everything they said and did carried with it the air of a threat. It was a phenomenon I'd noticed with Tony before and, to a lesser degree, Al. A made man could be as soft as a bunny, but because he was what he was, you always felt like you had to do what he said, just in case.

My ma was like that, too, and she wasn't even Italian.

"How about a smell from barrel?" he asked.

I assumed he was offering me a drink. "All right." I slid into the booth next to Jayne and found her hand. "I'll take a martini. Dry."

One way to determine a man's power was how quickly he could get service workers to respond to him. Tony could raise an arm and a waitress would be at his side within seconds. All Garvaggio had to do was wiggle a finger.

He ordered my drink, and the three of us sat in silence. Although my tears had stopped, the heavy emotion that had brought them on hadn't. Jack's departure weighed on my mind. I fumbled for conversation to distract me.

"What do you think of the show?" I asked. "Are you happy with how it's going?"

Vinnie smiled. One of his bicuspids was malformed, and it gave him an inadvertently terrifying quality, like an otherwise friendly dog burdened with fangs. This was the spot where he normally rested his cigar, since there was not only room there but the malformed tooth easily locked onto the stogie and held it in place.

"I think it's going great," he said out of the side of his mouth. "Couldn't be happier."

"Is this the first show you've been a part of?"

"Nah. I've backed lots of stuff." He swirled a rocks glass full of whiskey.

"Anything I would've heard of?"

"Doubtful. Most of 'em were a while ago." His hand slid toward Jayne's and made tentative contact with it. I could feel her stiffening beside me, and so I did the only thing I could possibly do to help her: I started crying again. This time there were no real tears, just loud, fake sobs. I wasn't going to continue mining my memories of Jack for a man who thought our current production was going great.

"Rosie." Jayne freed herself from his touch and put both hands on me, safely out of his reach.

"Here I go again." I blew my nose onto a cocktail napkin. "I just can't bear to see you two . . . knowing I'm alone . . . it's just so . . ." I buried my head in my hands and made a general spectacle of myself.

"We should go," said Jayne. "Thanks for the drinks, Vinnie. And the conversation."

He tried to stand, but he was wedged in too tightly to move. "You want a ride? I got a car out front."

"Thanks, but I think Rosie's going to need some fresh air to get this out of her system. See you tomorrow."

Jayne kept her arm wrapped in mine, and I feigned misery until we reached the subway platform. There, like two toddlers whose inconsolable sorrow was zapped by the promise of a lollipop, we snapped our heads up and shared a grin.

"For a man who tops three hundred pounds and is missing a tooth, he's surprisingly charming," I said.

"And fast. If I ever get stuck alone with him again, I'm wearing pants."

We boarded the train and made it past the derelicts, factory workers, and good-time girls who made up the subway's population at this hour.

"Brilliant performance by the way," said Jayne. "I actually felt bad for you when you first showed up."

"It was either that or tell him your mother had just died."

She searched the subway car and knocked on what she thought was wood.

"Did you learn anything?" I asked.

"A little. I mentioned Paulette. Asked him what he thought of her. It was weird. He knew who she was, of course, but I didn't get the feeling she'd ever stood out to him. Certainly not like a dame he'd been seeing after hours."

I found us two seats and pointed them out to Jayne. "Maybe he's put enough distance between him and her to make it seem that way."

"Maybe. I said I was kind of scared to join the show after what had happened to her. He assured me I was safe, says there's lots of security going on behind the scenes that I don't even know about."

Someone had abandoned a newspaper on the seat. I picked it up and attempted to fold it. "That's a funny thing to say."

"How so?"

"Paulette's supposed murderer is in jail, a fact he certainly knows. Don't you think he'd tell you there was nothing to worry about since the bum was locked up?"

Jayne frowned. "Maybe he was more interested in using my fear to get close to me, you know, like 'Don't you worry, this big strong man will protect you.'"

The column on top of the folded newspaper was the "News of the Stage." The writer had gotten wind of Olive's exit and my entrance and pithily captured the event with the headline: MUSICAL COMEDY THREATENED WITH TOO MUCH DRAMA: WITHOUT WRIGHT WHAT ELSE WILL GO WRONG? I flipped the page and eyeballed an article on a

U-boat battle in the North Atlantic. The navy was reporting casual-
ties. Great. "Did Garvaggio say anything else interesting?" I asked.

She examined her nails. She'd painted them Jungle Red for her
night out with Vinnie, though in either her haste or her anxiety she'd
smeared them before they'd completely dried. "Not really. I asked him
what he does with himself when he's not at the Bernhardt. He says
he's got a number of other businesses demanding his attention."

"But he didn't tell you what they were?"

"Nope." She cleaned the color from her cuticle. "I might be easier
to talk to than Gloria, but he had no intention of sharing anything
with me. What is this anyway?" Jayne shifted in her seat, setting off
a chorus of crinkling paper. She put her hand in her skirt pocket and
pulled out Ruby's V-mail.

"A letter Ruby asked me to mail."

"And which you promptly forgot to."

"It's her own fault: she knows I'm unreliable." I folded the sealed
letter in half and put it in my coat pocket.

"How was your evening?"

I stretched my legs. After a day of rehearsal and an evening of
dancing, every part of me hurt. "I spent the last five hours at the
Stage Door Canteen washing dishes and dancing with a navy pilot
named Peaches."

"Cute?"

Was he? It was getting hard for me to remember. "Persistent. He
expects me to be there on Saturday."

"And judging from your tone, you won't be."

I hadn't been planning on standing him up, but now that there was
distance between him and me, it was easy to imagine doing exactly
that. "Would it be terrible of me if I didn't show?"

"It wouldn't be the greatest thing you've ever done. What's the
harm of going there and dancing with him again?"

I traced an engraving on the back of the seat in front of us. Someone had drawn a heart with the initials E.F. in the center. "I don't
want to give him the wrong impression."

"Don't worry, I don't think he'll ever think you're a good dancer."

I tapped her knee with mine. "Very funny. You know what I mean."

She was silent for a moment. "If you're really not interested in him, you should let him know. If you're not interested because of Jack, I think he deserves to know that too. There's enough lying going around right now."

Pity she hadn't told me that before I gave him a phony name.

"Would you go with me?" I asked.

Jayne's head dropped to her chest. "Rosie . . ."

"I rescued you tonight, remember?"

"You were fifteen minutes late."

"But I came, didn't I? I came, I rescued, and I cried like a baby."

She lifted her head and rolled her eyes at the ceiling. "All right, I'll go. I've always wanted to see what the Canteen was like."

"And while you're at it," I said, "could you be sure to call me Delores?"

24 All the King's Horses

HERE'S SOMETHING I WOULD NEVER understand about society: we are led to believe women are morally superior to men. Even the Office of War Information supported this idea by distributing propaganda aimed at convincing Nazi women of the error of their ways. I suppose it made sense: we women are the child bearers and the primary force on the home front. We are supposed to be the nurturers. But what this theory didn't point out was that women are also capable of great cruelties. They can shun their children, humiliate their lovers, and dismantle their friends more easily than men can, perhaps because everyone assumes it isn't in their nature. Especially at a time when our nation was at war, we wanted to believe that women could hold us together, keep the home fires burning, and all that nonsense. We didn't want to know that they are capable of spreading social diseases, committing theft, or using their misplaced jealousies to discourage others from doing good.

Such was the case with Ruby Priest.

"Have a good time last night?" Ruby cornered me on the stairwell the next morning as I was getting ready to leave for rehearsal.

"I've had worse," I said.

"You spent an awful lot of time with that one man."

"What can I tell you—he said I danced like an angel and it would break his heart to have to take a spin with anyone else." I tried to move past her and down the stairs, but she checked me like a linebacker.

"Somehow I doubt that. I hope you're not planning on seeing him again."

I wished I could find a way to bottle her contrariness so I could take a whiff of the stuff whenever I needed to change my mind. "I hadn't decided yet."

She crossed her arms, and her enormous shoulder pads completed the football player effect. "It's against the rules, you know."

"Only if it's outside of the Canteen." If I couldn't move past her, maybe I could move past the subject. "How was your date by the way?"

Though her face was made up and her clothes immaculate, Ruby looked tired. Dark circles showed through the pale makeup she'd applied to hide them. Her eyes were red, not from crying but from a late night in a smoke-filled room. Despite this apparent exhaustion, she grinned at my question and pointed out these souvenirs of a late evening like they were badges she was proud to wear. "It was wonderful. Thank you for asking." Her hand settled on a necklace I hadn't seen before. It was a small gold flower with a diamond at its center on a delicate, filigreed chain.

I tried to walk around her again, but she countered each of my steps until we were waltzing.

"I wouldn't bother if I were you," she said.

"Wouldn't bother with what?"

"Meeting him again. Believe me, I know how these men operate. They're interested in only one thing."

"And apparently you've been giving it out."

She ignored me. "He'll insist you meet up with him outside the club, and the next thing you know he'll stop writing you and you'll be getting kicked out of the Canteen for violating the rules."

"Is that the worst thing? You know what a terrible correspondent I am, and I'm not sure I want to spend my every waking evening washing dishes and chipping ham."

"The theater community is small, Rosie. You saw all the muckety-mucks who were there last night. And that's a small percentage of the people who regularly work there. These aren't normal times and people take the Canteen very seriously. If a girl were to get kicked out, I wouldn't be a bit surprised if it affected her career."

Her rationale had so many holes I could've used it to drain spaghetti. "And apparently this rule doesn't apply to you?"

"Donald doesn't come to the Canteen anymore, and as far as anyone knows, he was never there to begin with. Everyone, however, saw you dancing with your navy captain last night, and if you meet him at the club again, you'll only further cement the idea that you two are fraternizing."

"A fact that I'm sure you would be happy to remind them of." My head spun. I'd given up any thought that Ruby and I were friends or that ill Ruby had been the true Ruby and this nasty person standing before me was a character she donned for self-preservation. Ruby wasn't a nice person; I could accept that. And yet I couldn't fathom why she would choose this issue of all things to make such a stink over.

"What am I missing here?" I asked.

"Whatever do you mean?"

"Since when do you care about my reputation? I would think you'd be thrilled if I managed to get myself kicked out of the Canteen and blacklisted at every theater in town. After all, you didn't want me to go there to begin with."

"I have no idea why you think so badly of me. I do . . . care about you." She gagged on the words like they were drenched in ipecac syrup. "In fact, after the kindness you showed me when I was sick, I feel this is the least I can do for you in return." Sure she did.

And then it hit me. She couldn't've cared less if I sold myself to the highest bidder and became this season's biggest scandal. What she couldn't stomach was the fact that I was friends with her friends and that by working at the Canteen and dating a man they encouraged me to see, I was further endearing myself to them. It was bad enough she had to treat me like an equal on stage, but socially? That was inexcusable!

"I appreciate your concern, Ruby. It's wonderful to know someone is looking out for my reputation, but I think you'll agree that during wartime, we must sacrifice. I'm willing to be misperceived as a harlot if it will help just one soldier get through his day."

•   •   •

Garvaggio was back at rehearsal, watching Jayne the way a cat followed a fish in a bowl. She did everything she could to avoid making
eye contact with him, but I imagine it felt like she was a magnet and
he was north and no matter how hard she tried, he was the thing she
was being led to. If Gloria noticed her boyfriend straying, she didn't
show it. She greeted Vinnie with the same good humor she'd used
the day before and fell into her dance moves with the same ill-placed
gusto she'd previously demonstrated. Despite her lack of skill, the
show was finally coming together. We all knew our lines, nobody
slipped and fell, and the cast seemed, on the whole, quite healthy.
Naturally, this made me suspicious. This was just the kind of calm
one would expect before another major catastrophe.

During our morning break, Vinnie pulled Walter Friday aside
and asked to speak to him out in the lobby. Most of the cast stayed
in the theater, but I feigned a sudden need to use the bathroom and
lingered just inside the women's room with the door slightly ajar.

"What time will you have everyone out of here?" Garvaggio asked
him.

"It can't be before eight. We have too much work to do. The corps
is a disaster."

"We'll be back at seven and I don't want there to be another soul
here."

Friday's voice went up an octave. "I thought you weren't doing
another delivery until next week."

"The schedule's been moved up."

"I got union carpenters who need to start on the new set."

Garvaggio talked through a plastic smile. "So let 'em start somewhere else."

"Where?"

"That's your problem, not mine." Garvaggio started to walk away,
ashing his cigar in his wake.

"Vinnie . . ." Friday's voice was pure desperation, his face bad melodrama. He was in a pinch he knew he couldn't get out of. He couldn't make Garvaggio see his point of view; he couldn't make his show miraculously improve. In fact, the only thing he could do was make things worse. "I'm begging you here. You can't keep shutting rehearsals down like this. We've got less than two weeks."

Vinnie walked back toward him, and though his pace was as slow as his body was large, he still seemed menacing. He kept his voice low and planted what should've seemed like a congenial hand on Friday's shoulder. The pain in Friday's face said otherwise. "You knew the deal, Walt. I held up my end of the bargain." A man appeared at the theater's doors and poked his head inside. Vinnie nodded at him and pulled on his enormous overcoat. "The truck's here. Seven. Don't disappoint me."

Friday didn't. At six thirty on the dot he ended rehearsal and dismissed us for the night.

"Ready?" Jayne limped to my side and momentarily shifted her weight against the stage's edge.

"What's with the bum pin?"

"You didn't see?" I shook my head. I'd found it easier to ignore those moments of rehearsal that didn't directly affect me. "Gloria's shoe flew off during the last number and sent us all tumbling like a row of dominoes."

"Ouch."

Jayne shrugged. She was beyond the point of caring what happened to her. "I'll ice it and it'll be fine by morning." She glared toward the lobby, where we could hear Gloria's seal-like cackle. "I have no guarantee, however, that she'll live to see the next rehearsal. Mind if we take a cab?"

The stage manager turned off the house lights and clicked on the ghost light, a single bulb that would illuminate the stage overnight. "Why don't you go ahead without me," I said.

She raised an eyebrow. "Why?"

"I think now would be an excellent time to get to the bottom of what's going on downstairs."

"In the murder room?!" she said. I shushed her with my hand. "I'm going with you."

"Don't be silly, hop-along—there're too many stairs to conquer. The only thing you could do is slow me down. Trust me: there's nothing dangerous about this. Garvaggio is due here at seven. I'll hide out until then. I'll be in and out—one hour tops."

"And then you'll come home?"

I drew an *X* on my chest. "Cross my heart and hope to die."

Jayne's face made it clear that she didn't appreciate my choice of words.

While the stage manager finished locking down the building, I hid in the ladies' room. When I was satisfied everyone was gone, I made my way to the private stairwell and quietly descended into the basement. As before, I passed through the cross-under and arrived beneath the other side of the stage, where I'd found the bloodied room and locked doors. No one was there yet, so I rearranged some spare furniture until I had a comfortable little hut that masked me from view but gave me a clear view of anyone who might be coming in the load-in doors. To the casual observer I would look like just another pile of theater junk awaiting new purpose.

Forty-five minutes passed before anyone joined me.

I was about to abandon my hut and head home when the load-in doors began to rattle. A motor humned in the alleyway behind the building. The engine died and a number of voices replaced it, all unfamiliar to me. Garvaggio's men had arrived.

I shifted in my hiding place to make sure I had the best view possible of the entrance. Chains began to rattle and groan as the oversized metal doors lifted clear of the floor. The truck sputtered back to life, and a cloud of exhaust drifted into the corridor. They were backing the vehicle up so they could unload its contents as close to the theater as possible. This would make it impossible for anyone who might be in the alley to see what it was they were up to.

The truck died for a second time, and the men left the cab and entered the building. There were four of them, all large, dirty, and clearly disenchanted with their work. They were tough and working class, their grammar loose and inconsistent. None of them used one another's names.

A man with a mustache and a voice like a scratchy 78 was the leader of the group. He barked orders and stomped about the basement unlocking doors with a ring of keys hanging from his belt. "Let's take care of 'em one at a time. We don't need no repeat of last time."

"We'll be here all night," whined a kid with a scar that ran from his temple to his chin. The boss ignored him. He had no time for malcontents. One of the other men unlocked the back of the truck. Mustache tossed him a shotgun and directed him to go inside the murder room. My legs started to shake so badly I was certain I was going to knock over my hiding place.

Mustache moved into my line of sight, preventing me from seeing the truck. I heard the doors open, heard the shuffling and whines of the hidden cargo, but I couldn't see the victim's face. Whoever it was, his steps were heavy, his voice mute. At last the man moved and gave me a clear view. I gasped as the prisoner appeared. A horse stood in the middle of the basement.

He was a pathetic specimen. His back was bowed; bald patches dotted his fur; his weight was half of what it should've been. The man with the keys led him by the reins. The restraint was unnecessary—the horse was too dazed to do anything but obey.

I couldn't reconcile what I was seeing. Why was there a horse here, and why did it appear there were a dozen more in the back of the truck? Sure, I knew the mob ran horses, but somehow I pictured that happening at Belmont Park, not in the basement of a Broadway theater. And I certainly expected more healthy-looking animals, not these spent beasts who could barely walk without assistance.

"I think I bet on this one once," said one of the men. "Son of a bitch lost me a pair of c's."

"Then maybe you should do the honors," said the boss.

"Gladly."

My mouth dropped open and stayed there as the horse made its promenade into the room with the blood-smeared walls. They'd fixed the lights since my last visit, and from my angle on the floor I could just make out a number of implements I recognized from my corner butcher shop. So that was it. These horses . . . they were . . . and then they were going to . . .

I was breathing too rapidly and starting to feel lightheaded.

Did Vinnie know about this? Was it possible his men didn't realize those were horses, not cows? I'll grant you as a city girl myself I wasn't up on the distinguishing characteristics of the bovine, but surely these guys had at least seen one in a movie before.

No, you dumdora. Of course they knew. That was the point.

The guy with the gat entered the room they had taken the horse into. The door closed and a sharp crack echoed throughout the basement. A loud thump followed. From the truck came a chorus of sympathetic whinnies. They may not have been able to fight their fates, but the other horses certainly weren't happy about it.

I knew I should've been relieved their cargo was horse, not human, and yet the lingering stench of death filling my nose and my head seemed incapable of discerning between the two. Garvaggio was in the murder business no matter how you sliced it.

Try as I might to rationalize that this was part of the natural order of things, I couldn't help but transfer this cold-blooded execution into human terms. Was this what prisoners of war suffered through? Did the men on the Bataan Death March have the same vacant expressions on their faces when they were about to meet their ends? And what of the German soldiers? Suffering was suffering no matter who you were doing it for.

The longer I sat there, the more dark places I began to probe until I worried I wasn't going to be able to ever leave that basement again. I had to, though. I couldn't sit through a dozen crackles of a shotgun followed by the lifeless thump of a body hitting the floor. And I certainly couldn't sit through the emotionless dismembering of the animals, as they were transformed from once strong, graceful creatures into steaks, chops, and ground meat.

I was going to throw up if I didn't get out of there soon.

As the men prepared to lead the next horse into the room, I carefully made my way out of my shelter. I had positioned the opening of my hiding place toward the cross-under and now, while the men were distracted, it was easy to slip out unnoticed and creep toward the darkened tunnel. As I stepped into it, the second horse struggled and the men's voices rose and fell in a series of instructions of how to tame it. I began to run. I didn't want to be around for the second gunshot. If I didn't hear it, maybe it would never happen, and if it never happened, maybe I wasn't guilty of sitting back and doing nothing while two helpless animals died.

I left the theater and entered the street. I rushed away from the building until there was no way I could possibly hear what was going on in the basement. I paused beside a trash can and inhaled a deep breath of cold night air mixed with the sweet stench of rotting food. I was all right. It wasn't my fault. There was nothing I could've done.

I stepped backward into the privacy provided by the door to a haberdasher and focused on slowing my breathing.

Even though the lights had been dimmed for almost a year, I'd never gotten used to seeing Broadway dark. It wasn't completely pitch-black—dimmed lights from the lobbies leaked onto the street and provided the smallest bit of illumination under the marquees—but there was barely enough light to navigate by. In the dark, the theaters became hulking dinosaurs, the lampposts barren trees. And the people became much quieter, aware of the dark's peculiar ability to amplify every word and footfall. No one could talk loudly in the dark. It seemed like a kind of sacrilege.

"Any change, Miss?"

Startled, I turned and found I wasn't alone in my hiding place. Beside me a man extended a can hoping for a little bit of tin. It used to be that he'd make his request silently, knowing the power of the can to tell his story, but now that night prevented us from making out all but the faintest hint of a human being, his approach had become more brazen, his shame masked by the same shadows that beckoned us to be more cautious.

I gave him a nickel. I needed to do something good no matter how small the gesture.

I continued on, weaving a path down streets I normally avoided. I didn't want to go home yet. I needed to clear my head.

I passed a post office with windows plastered with pleas to buy war bonds. Beside it a butcher shop demanded that passersby "Share the Meat as a Wartime Necessity" and in smaller print explained the government-mandated allotments for beef based on your age. A five-and-ten hawked pastel-colored Easter baskets and candy eggs. Not chocolate ones—those were extinct—but dyed sugar confections that looked much better than they tasted. Last year at this time Bugs Bunny had offered Hitler a grenade in lieu of an egg. I wondered what he would offer him this year.

"Excuse me. Don't I know you?"

For the second time I jumped at the sound of a voice and backed into the shop window. When no one attacked, I turned and found a vaguely familiar face staring out from beneath an air force–issue hat. It was Ruby's pilot, the very tall fellow with the nice smile.

"You do know me," I said. "I'm Rosie Winter. A friend of Ruby's." I hoped he didn't realize what an exaggeration that claim was.

"That's right. It's awfully nice to see you again. I'm Donald Montgomery." He gave me his hand, and my fingers took a swift journey up and down. "Are you okay? You look like you're about to be sick."

"I'm fine." I forced a smile. There was no way I could share the horrors of witnessing an equine execution with this man. "What are you doing out here?"

"Doing a little sightseeing before I meet Ruby. I haven't gotten a chance to see much of the city and decided there was no time like the present. Are you headed home?"

I nodded.

"Mind if I ride with you?"

"Not at all." We started walking together toward the Times Square station. He had a loose, leisurely stride that made it seem—even when he had a purpose—that he wasn't in a rush to get where he was going.

I needed a distraction, some innocent diversion to keep my mind out of the basement. "So where are you taking Ruby tonight?" I asked.

"I'm not sure yet. I want it to be someplace pretty special, you know? You got any ideas?"

I searched my mind for places that would sound fabulous to him but horrible to her. "How special?"

"Can you keep a secret?"

"It's what I'm known for."

He patted his overcoat and located some unseen item. "I'm proposing tonight."

"Proposing what?"

"Marriage, of course." His hand disappeared into his pocket and emerged with a tiny oval, iced with a much tinier diamond.

I took the ring from him and pretended to ooh and ah over it. It was nice, if small. I certainly couldn't see Ruby proudly dangling it in front of our faces. She demanded ostentation.

"It was my grandma's," he said. "I thought about buying Ruby a big new one, but I figured this would mean more, being an heirloom. She always tells me how much family means to her."

I bit my lip to keep from laughing. Ruby hadn't talked to her family in over a year. "It's very nice," I said. The longer I looked at it, the better it seemed. I don't mean the stone looked bigger or the ring more expensive, but I suddenly wanted to cram it on to my finger and close my hand so he couldn't take it back. "Don't you think it's a little soon? I mean you and Ruby just met."

"We've been writing each other."

"For what? A month?"

"Five weeks. Long letters. I think I knew just about everything about her before I saw her the second time."

Somehow I doubted that. If he had, surely he wouldn't be proposing marriage.

He put the ring back into his pocket. "So you can see why I want to go someplace nice tonight."

"Absolutely." The irritation I'd felt at Ruby the last few days returned and multiplied. Who was she to tell me that I had no right seeing someone when she was toying with this pilot's heart? Sure, she might've waxed philosophic about meeting the man of her dreams, but it was clearly just talk. The minute he tried to turn the relationship into something more, he'd get a chance to meet the real Ruby, the one who was convinced she deserved the sun and moon and who wouldn't let anyone stand in the way of her receiving either.

We reached the station and boarded our train. I gave him the names of a couple of nice joints—places with good food and great atmosphere. At least, if Ruby turned him down, he'd get a nice meal out of the deal.

For the duration of our ride he praised his queen, telling me things about her I knew weren't true, things he cataloged as being among the many reasons he loved her. I listened stoically, curiously aware that it wasn't my place to tell him the truth no matter how badly I wanted to. His description of Ruby gradually changed into a prediction of their future together. The war would end and they would come home and start their life together in Goshen, a little town an hour and a half north of the city. He wanted children right away—a whole houseful. They were, he thought, the reason for living.

I stifled a snort. "That'll be a challenge with Ruby's performing schedule. At the very least you might want to keep an apartment here."

He cocked his head to the side and looked at me. "Come again?"

"Ruby's still going to act, isn't she?"

"I don't know about that. I suppose there's always community theater. Of course, I can't see her doing anything like that until the children are bigger."

Most actors are driven to do what they do the same way artists have to paint and composers have to write music. Theater wasn't a temporary placeholder until something more stable came into our lives—it was what we lived and breathed for, and anything else we did had to complement that effort. I knew women who'd left the stage, gotten hitched, and settled down with a brood, but I can guarantee every one of them felt the familiar pang of hunger whenever they encountered an actress they once knew on the radio or in the lingerie ads in the *Brooklyn Daily Times*. I'd almost quit the stage a half dozen times, but even I knew it would be like losing a limb. Sure, I could learn to function, but who wants to go through life with only one arm when they don't have to?

I couldn't tell him that, though. "I'm sure you'll work it out," I said. "Love overcomes everything."

At last we pulled into the Christopher Street station and the evening performance of *One Hundred Reasons Why Ruby Priest Is the Perfect Woman* came to an end. I let out a sigh of relief that continued as we climbed out of the station and into the Village. I was home. I was safe. I hadn't been shot in the head and divvied up for dinner.

25 Proof Through the Night

"Do you have any idea how worried I've been?" Jayne launched herself across our room and slammed into me. I almost toppled beneath her weight, but I steadied myself and gave into the half-hug, half-strangle she greeted me with. "Don't ever do that to me again."

"I won't."

"I'm serious. You've been gone two hours, Rosie. I thought you were dead or worse."

I didn't ask what worse was. I didn't have to.

"What happened?" she asked.

"Things took longer is all."

Jayne scowled. She clearly wasn't buying what I was selling. "I do hope you're going to tell me more than that."

"I know your foot is bad, but can we go somewhere? I don't think I want to tell you what I have to tell you here."

"Why not?"

I didn't have an answer for her. I wanted to keep our home sacred, free of the taint of everything I'd just witnessed. If we didn't talk about it there, maybe the Shaw House could remain a refuge from the awful things that men did.

We hoofed it to Rothco's All-Night Pharmacy, where we huddled side by side at the red laminated counter and ordered milkshakes. I needed something sweet to counteract the story I was about to tell.

"I know what Garvaggio's up to," I said at last.

"What's it going to take for you to spill?" asked Jayne. "I'm dying over here."

"Believe it or not, his men were unloading retired race horses into the basement of the building."

"He's running horses? Out of the Bernhardt?"

"Not exactly." I took a long sip of soda, then pushed the glass away. "He's in the black market meat trade."

She wasn't getting it. That was clear. "So the blood you found downstairs was from meat?"

"Sort of." I willed her to pick up on what I was saying without making me spell it out. "I think he's using the Bernhardt as a temporary butcher shop. His guy kills the animals and slices them up in the hall of horrors, then gets rid of whatever he doesn't need by burning it in the boilers. The evidence goes up in smoke. He has people pick up their orders the same day or soon after."

"And nobody notices?"

"It's a theater. Of course it's going to have a lot of traffic going in and out. Who's going to think that it's people going in there to pick up meat?"

"No wonder the place always smells like steak."

"It's not steak you're smelling."

Jayne emptied her black cow before asking the obvious. "What do you mean?"

"I said they were retired race horses."

Her eyebrows met her hairline. "No!"

"I saw them with my own eyes." I told her about the slaughter I'd witnessed the hour before.

She pushed her glass away. "That's disgusting."

"Tell me about it."

"Those poor horses. How does he get away with it?"

"It's the black market, Jayne. There's a reason they call it that. There's no regulation. There are no rules. Ten to one the markets and restaurants he's selling to know the score but pretend ignorance. All that's important to them is the meat comes cheap and comes often. They jack up the prices and the customers buy it, accepting it is what it is because it would never occur to them to think otherwise." And I was willing to bet a week's pay that one of those places was Mancuso's Deli.

"I think I'd know if I were eating horse."

"People can convince themselves of anything. Believe me. Especially when the last time you had real meat was before Pearl Harbor."

Jayne's pale face turned a lovely shade of green. "But wouldn't you get sick?"

"From horse meat? It's doubtful. The cow just lost the lottery on what animal we eat. I think the bigger issue is Garvaggio's butchering and storage methods. While his personal hygiene is beyond reproach, I doubt he applies such standards to his meat."

Jayne spun from side to side on her stool. "So why would Garvaggio want to shut down the show?"

I searched the counter for the answer. My eyes lighted on a copy of *The Times* left by a previous customer. The news had been all aflutter about meat being sold through the black market. There had to be a connection "Well, if it's meat Garvaggio's dealing, it's illegal for one."

"What isn't?"

"No, the government really has a bee in its bonnet about beef." After two years of being at war, I was finally figuring out how the government worked. If they were telling us something, it was only because they'd been aware of it for quite some time and had decided it was safe to share it with the public at large. "The feds are introducing all these measures to curb the black market, including staging raids at places suspected of being part of the trade. Garvaggio isn't just selling meat illegally; he's selling the wrong kind of meat, so he might be nervous enough that he wants to change locations to keep them off his tail. If that's the case, he has no reason to want to continue financing *Goin' South*."

Jayne nodded at the counter. "I could buy that. But what does this have to do with Paulette and Al?"

That question again. "I'm not sure. Logic tells me one of them figured out what I just put together and threatened to squeal to the authorities."

"So you think Paulette saw the horses and Garvaggio took her out?"

Perhaps Paulette had the courage to do what I couldn't: she'd tried to stop what was happening and paid for it with her life. "It would make sense, wouldn't it?"

"But then why would Al be in jail?"

"I'm not there yet." Maybe I was wrong before when I thought Al had confessed to keep himself safe from Tony. Maybe it was Garvaggio he was hoping to protect himself from.

"What do we do about all of this?" asked Jayne.

"I don't know about you, but I'm not eating beef for a while."

"Rosie . . ."

I finished my malt and searched my pocketbook for enough tin for a tip. "I need to think about this some more. I can't stand the thought of what's happening to the horses, but you know as well as I do that messing with the mob never ends well." What we needed was for the government to get wind of Garvaggio's operation and shut it down, but we couldn't do that without running the risk of Garvaggio finding out we were the ones behind it and demanding retribution. While I felt bad for the horses, I wasn't willing to put us in jeopardy. Yet. "As for Al, the only thing we can do is try to talk to him again."

We wrapped ourselves in our coats and exited into the street. As we walked, my mind kept drifting back to the basement of the Bernhardt where a dozen horses were meeting their ends.

"Don't think about it." Jayne squeezed my hand and then looped her arm in mine.

"I'm trying not to." Our steps fell into the rhythm of my thoughts: Don't think about the horses. Don't think about the horses. Don't think about the horses. I shook my head, but the thought remained firmly planted. "I forgot to tell you about my escort home. I ended up traveling with Ruby's new beau."

"She's going to be thrilled to hear that."

"She has nothing to worry about. Our young man is quite enamored with Miss Priest. He's planning on proposing to her tonight."

Jayne stopped walking. "They just met!"

"A fact I pointed out to him. Several times. He's not as smart as I assumed, though, because he's planning on moving forward with it.

Oh, and he expects her to end her acting career, at least temporarily, so she can take care of the children."

"Children? Ruby? I always thought she'd eat her young."

"Didn't we all."

"She'll never say yes," said Jayne.

"You and I know that, but he doesn't."

"Boy I wish I could be a fly on the wall during that proposal." I did too. It would be an infinitely more pleasant way to spend the evening than lamenting all the deaths I should've prevented.

I couldn't sleep that night, not that I tried too hard. I wasn't sure I wanted to doze for fear of what I might end up dreaming about. Once again I went downstairs determined to feed my insomnia something other than all the unpleasantness I had bottled up in my head.

Just like the time before, Minnie was sprawled on the sofa, flipping through a copy of *Time* magazine with Harry S. Truman on the cover.

"Hiya," I said. She looked up and smiled, as unsurprised to see I'd returned as I was to see her. "Ruby not home yet?"

"Nope."

It was only going on one, an early hour to end an evening by anyone's standards. I sat on the wingback by the fire and stared into the flames. The whole house smelled of burning meat. "I think you might be waiting a while," I told her.

"Why?"

I spread a red, white, and blue afghan on my lap. "Her pilot had big plans for her tonight, and I don't think they'll be done until sunrise."

"Isn't he tired of her yet?"

I was surprised by her reaction. Sure, I could imply Ruby's date was counting the minutes until he didn't have to see her again, but Minnie doing that was unthinkable. Perhaps she was finally catching on to the real Ruby. "Actually, I think he's the exact opposite of tired of her. One might even call him addicted."

She raised an eyebrow to beckon me to continue.

"This is between you and me, but I have it on good authority that he's going to propose to her tonight."

Minnie inhaled sharply. "Did Ruby tell you that?"

I snorted. "Definitely not. I said it was a good source."

Minnie's eyes dropped to her lap and remained there.

"Why do you care, Minnie?"

"They just met . . . and Ruby . . . she's . . ."

I couldn't stand to watch her struggle to find words. "Your only friend?" Minnie nodded. I would talk to Jayne. If Ruby didn't have time for Minnie anymore, maybe she and I could. "Don't worry: as well-intentioned as he may be, Ruby would never go through with it."

Minnie lifted her head. "Why not?"

"Look, I don't want to tell tales out of school, but you should know Ruby's favorite thing in the world is Ruby, and I don't believe for a moment that she would willingly change from a me to an us. Especially when she gets wind that her husband-to-be expects her to drop the theater so she can drop some babies."

Minnie smiled and her plainness momentarily evaporated. She could be a pretty girl. Who knew?

"How was the Canteen the other night?" she asked.

"Oh, that." I swatted at the air as if a fly was buzzing about me and I wanted to silence it for good. "It was fine."

"Did you meet anyone?"

I was too tired to object to the topic of conversation. Besides, it was infinitely more pleasant than reliving the horses' deaths. "I danced with one fellow a few times. I'm supposed to meet him there again tomorrow night."

"Aren't you going to go?"

This girl was perceptive. "I'm going to agonize over whether or not I should."

"Why the agony?"

I shifted my position until my legs were bent beneath me. "I get the sense he expects this to turn into a romance, and I don't think I'm ready for that."

She nodded knowingly. "Because of your missing boyfriend."

"Because of many things, including I, unlike Ruby, believe a relationship consists of more than a few love notes and a handful of face-to-face meetings." I had the floor and decided to run with it. "I just find the situation the war put us in so desperate. I mean, look at all the war brides. Some of them, I'll grant you, married their long-time sweethearts, but most of them barely know the guys they're getting hitched to. Why should we let the war rush us into decisions we wouldn't otherwise make? What's going to happen when all these men come home and find strangers in their beds? Because that's what they are. It seems like a recipe for disaster to me."

Minnie stared into the fire. "You're assuming they're coming home."

"I have to, don't I?"

"You might, but that doesn't mean their wives do."

"That's an optimistic outlook. Why would someone get married if they didn't believe they were going to survive long enough to be reunited?"

Minnie shrugged. "Why does anybody do anything?" She thumbed through the pages of *Time*. "You're right, though. About not going to the Canteen. I'm not sure I would either in your shoes."

The conversation died a natural death as the fire died into embers. I left Minnie and went back to bed, where the horses were replaced with the question she'd given me. Why would someone make a commitment to someone who might be dead tomorrow? Perhaps it was for the same reason I knew I'd show up at the Canteen the next night—to give a soldier a little bit of happiness to carry him through whatever awful thing he had to face. Maybe I was too cynical to accept that love could come fast and furious and didn't need the long-term nurturing I assumed it required. It was very likely that everything I thought I knew about love—the stuff I learned from my relationship with Jack—wasn't true at all but merely the data I received from an experiment that wasn't performed correctly to begin with.

26 Marriage of a Star

When we arrived at rehearsal the next morning, the entire cast was onstage, their voices a cacophony of excited conversation. I looked for a sign of what could've caused the commotion. Had Friday been killed? Had there been another fire? Had someone discovered what was going on in the basement?

Izzie broke off from the group and rushed toward us. "Ruby's engaged! Isn't it wonderful?"

I combed the room for Minnie but didn't see her. Jayne and I climbed onstage and masked our lack of sincerity with practiced smiles that only Ruby would know disguised our real feelings. "Congratulations," we said in unison. Ruby thrust her hand at us to show off the tiny white gold and diamond ring she wore.

"It's temporary," she said. "A placeholder until we have time to get a more appropriate ring."

The other girls continued their chatter, begging Ruby to recount the trajectory of their romance and the precise way her intended had proposed (on the dance floor at the Rainbow Room, while "I'll Be Seeing You" was playing). Ruby gladly gave into their requests, but rather than wearing the blush of the newly engaged who can't believe their good fortune, her accounting of how she had swiftly traveled from Canteen volunteer to wife-to-be sounded more like a Horatio Alger story. Becoming engaged was an accomplishment to brag about, not a milestone in a relationship she cherished.

I shared this observation with Jayne as we disappeared into the back of the crowd.

"She's probably still stunned," she said. "I certainly would be."

It was a fair comment—for Ruby anyway—but I wasn't buying it. I still couldn't get past how ill-suited Donald Montgomery seemed for her. Lawrence Bentley, for all his arrogance, had been someone who shared in Ruby's second greatest love: the theater. While I believed Ruby had snagged a man who cared about her, it was obvious to me the train didn't travel in both directions.

"Places everyone!" Walter Friday entered the auditorium from whatever dark corner he'd been hiding in. We all took our spots backstage and readied ourselves for a run-through. I finally located Minnie. She sat in a folding chair intended for whoever would be operating the drapes. Her face was long and heavy, her eyes smudged from recent tears.

I went to her side and offered her my handkerchief. "I guess I was wrong."

"It looks like it."

"Don't worry. It won't last. She's already demanding a new ring; it won't be long before she insists on a different man. Ruby won't be going anywhere."

"Oh, I'm not upset about that." Her face told me otherwise.

"She isn't worth this, Minnie. She hasn't been much of a friend to you lately. Don't waste your energy on her."

Her only response was to blow her nose.

"How 'bout you join Jayne and me for lunch?"

"Thanks, but I don't think I'm going to have much of an appetite today."

I had to admit defeat—it would be impossible to cheer Minnie up. And I wasn't sure why I cared to begin with. I guess I felt a strange kinship with her. We were the late-night parlor dwellers, women who lost sleep worrying about things we couldn't change.

The run-through began, and I temporarily lost myself in the show. Things were still rocky onstage, but they had markedly improved. If nothing else, we couldn't be called a complete disaster.

Or at least I thought that was the case until the dancers made their first entrance. All of the work from the previous day had gone out the window. Gloria seemed to be performing her own routine, one that looked an awful lot like a drunk weaving down the street. I couldn't stand to watch it, so I ducked backstage and found myself side by side with Ruby.

"You're not seriously going to go through with this, are you?" I said.

"Whatever do you mean?"

I picked up her hand and flashed the ring in her face. "Who are you—Gloria Vanderbilt? You barely know the guy."

She freed herself from me. "One needn't know someone long to know they should be together."

I thrust my nose into the air and mimicked her tone. "Oh, *needn't* one? You do know he wants to start a family right away and has every intention of your leaving the stage and joining him in the thriving metropolis of Goshen, New York?"

"How do you know that?"

"He told me."

She sighed and I knew he was going to get an earful about sharing such intimacies with the riffraff. "First of all, it's none of your business. Second of all, the war isn't over and may not be for some time. By the time he returns, I'm sure I'll be happy to settle down."

I should've been thrilled. Ruby getting married could only mean more opportunities for the rest of us, but I was bothered by her attitude. Most women I knew would be dying for the war to end and their lives to begin, but Ruby was acting like it was a blissful intermission she hoped to extend so she wouldn't have to watch the second half of a picture that was boring her silly. If that was love, I wanted none of it.

At a quarter to five Jayne and I were in the Canteen kitchen emptying containers of food onto serving trays. The place was short of help that night, and Elaine was glad to see me with a new face in tow. While we scooped, the dapper Artie Shaw was setting up on the platform in the main room, punctuating our clatter with the moan of a trombone.

When we were done transferring food to plates, I led Jayne out to the main room and settled with her in the darkest corner I could find. The men had already been permitted inside and were kicking off the evening dancing to "Begin the Beguine."

"Isn't it something?" I asked.

"I'll say. I can't believe they don't charge us for being here." Although I wouldn't have thought it possible, the place was even more packed than it had been on my last visit. How could anyone ever have claimed that Saturday night was the loneliest night of the week?

A sailor caught her eye and Jayne spun toward me and flashed me her pearly whites. "Any lipstick on my teeth?"

"Not a smidge."

"How's my hair?"

"Blond and resplendent. Go get 'em, tiger."

She left my side and met the sailor halfway. I couldn't hear them above the din of the crowd, but I knew the conversation that was transpiring as they awkwardly bumped gums before agreeing to share the dance floor. The poor kid didn't know what he was in for. Jayne wasn't capable of holding back and pretending she was just a normal girl who knew a little fancy footwork. From the moment she stepped on the floor, she was a dancer with a capital *D* and he was fighting to keep pace with her. I only hoped, for his sake, that he hadn't bragged about his abilities before going out there.

Someone tapped me on the shoulder. "See, now I've lost money."

I turned and found Peaches beside me. At least I think it was Peaches. I hadn't remembered him being quite so handsome.

"And why are you out the cabbage?" I asked.

"I made a buddy a bet that you wouldn't show up tonight. He was trying to make me feel good and told me he'd put a ten spot on your being here with bells on."

I lifted my hands and wiggled my fingers. "No bells."

"He didn't say where the bells would be." He offered me his hand. "Shall we?"

We went out onto the dance floor, and for five dizzying minutes I let myself forget all the doubts I had about seeing him again. I'd been overreacting. Spending an innocent evening dancing with a guy at the Canteen was hardly the first step toward marriage. And who said Peaches would want to marry me anyway? It was pretty arrogant not to want to see a guy because I assumed he'd fall madly in love with me and insist on something more than a casual foxtrot.

"Penny for your thoughts?" he asked.

"Careful," I said. "Someone might hear you and demand you put fifteen percent of that penny in war bonds."

"I'm willing to take that chance."

I chewed on my lip. "I was just thinking that this wasn't so awful."

"I hadn't realized it might be. There are some women who believe I'm easy on the eyes and a dream on the dance floor."

"I thought we established the other night that I'm not some women. And I didn't mean it like the insult it came out as. I just . . ." Why not risk honesty for once? As Jayne said, it was only fair to be upfront with the guy. "I was worried you might be wanting a lot more out of this meeting than I was willing to give."

"There are girls I can pay for things like that."

"You know what I mean—emotionally."

"But you've decided I'm here for only a quick dance."

"Aren't you?"

His eyes grew soft, his smile weakened, and I knew that much of what I'd seen of him up until this point had been a facade. "I'm here for whatever you're willing to give me."

We danced twice more before I begged for a break and a beverage. Peaches left me to get us some punch while I searched out a vacant table.

"So you did have plans to see him again." Zelda drummed her red nails on my tabletop and smiled down at me. "Why didn't you tell me you were coming tonight?"

"I figured the less fanfare the better."

"Did I see Jayne out on the dance floor?"

"The one and only. What about you: Are you solo tonight or is Izzie out there making a soldier's dream come true?"

"Just me. Izzie was beat after today, so I came stag to help with the dinner rush. I'm sure Elaine was thrilled to have you two help out. Saturdays are the busiest nights." Zelda looked at her watch. "I'm actually hoping to sneak out of here. I'm bushed from today."

"You and me both. If I were you, I'd make a run for it now, before this song ends."

"You sound like an old pro. See you tomorrow, and tell Jayne I said hi."

She rushed away as the band played the closing bars of "Deep Purple."

"Was that Zelda?" Jayne arrived and perched in the chair across from me. Her face was bright red, her hair a blond tornado.

"The one and only. She just made her escape."

"Where's Peaches?"

"Fetching punch. Be proud of me: I made it clear I wasn't looking for anything more than a good time."

"Bravo. Did you tell him your real name too?"

"I'm working on it. What about you—how was your sailor?"

"Which one? I've danced with four, and it looks like the rest of the fleet expects a twirl."

"If Tony could see you now."

"Wouldn't that be a pip?" She looked down at the table and, with her finger, drew a circle in its top. "They're really sweet. I forgot what it was like to be around boys like them."

"They're gentlemen too," I said. "I don't think there's a guy in here who would think of raising his hand to you."

She drew a second figure inside of the first one. "One of them asked me to write him."

"You should."

"I'm thinking about it." She lifted her head and frowned. "Why does that guy look familiar?"

I followed her gaze. "Who?"

"The redhead by the doors. I swear I've seen him before."

I shifted to get a better slant on the man in question. "You have seen him before. That's George Pomeroy."

27 The Uninvited Guest

PAULETTE'S FIANCÉ DISAPPEARED INTO THE men's room. I struggled to push my way through the crowd and toward the doors when Peaches—glasses of punch in hand—stepped in front of me.

"Where's the fire, Delores?"

"I saw an old friend."

"Kind of rude to leave when you're still entertaining a new one." He offered me the glass of punch. It was overly sweet and lukewarm.

"Trust me—he's not that kind of friend." Jayne arrived at my elbow and tugged at my dress. "This is my roommate, Jayne."

Peaches shook her hand. "Hello, roommate Jayne."

She smiled up at him. "Hello yourself."

The men's room door opened and George Pomeroy reappeared. He turned left toward the coat check girl.

"Say, Jayne."

"Yes, Delores?" She said my new name slowly, like she was uncertain how to pronounce it.

"Could you please make sure our pal George doesn't leave without my talking to him? I'll only be a minute."

"Sure thing."

She disappeared into the crowd and had just about reached the coat check counter when George, clad in a leather bomber jacket, pushed through the front door.

I gave Peaches back my glass of punch. "I really enjoyed seeing you again."

"Why don't I like where this is going?"

"I need to scram. Believe me: this isn't the brush-off. There's just something I need to attend to that's slightly more important than standing here right now."

He set the glasses on the railing and offered me his hand. "So I guess this is good-bye."

"Easy now—what about tomorrow night?"

Just like on the dance floor, the humor was gone from his eyes. "This is my last night in New York, Delores. I'm spending the rest of my liberty at home."

"Oh." I'd forgotten his time was finite, that I wouldn't be able to bump into him whenever I decided I wanted to see him. *If* I wanted to see him.

"You actually look a little sad about that."

I was shocked to find tears blurring my vision. "That's because I am."

"I ship out from here in about a week. I could come back a day early. Could I see you then?"

"Does a cat meow?"

"Let's set it then: a week from Monday. Five o'clock here at the Canteen. Will you promise me you'll be here?"

There was something in the way he said it that made it clear he didn't believe I'd return. I burned with embarrassment. It was one thing for me to wrestle with whether or not to show, but I didn't want him to think I was anything less than excited to see him.

"Wild horses couldn't keep me away," I said. We shook hands to seal the deal. Before I knew what I was doing, I leaned toward him and gave him a light kiss on the cheek. "Good night, Peaches."

"Good night, Delores." I pushed through the crowd and claimed my coat. Jayne was no longer in the building. I found her outside, anxiously pacing as she awaited my arrival.

"He went uptown. He's got at least a block on us."

"Don't worry—we'll catch up." We ran after him and soon spied his red head bobbing half a block away. He waved down a cab and disappeared inside.

"Nuts!" I said. Jayne fumbled with her purse and came up with a handful of crumbled bills. Seconds later we piled into our own cab and told a very amused driver to follow the yellow in front of him.

Two minutes and twenty cents later, our driver let us off at West Fifty-seventh Street where, moments before, George had exited his cab and disappeared inside a building.

We were in front of a refurbished brownstone, the kind of place where a room could be had for a little bit of coin in my neighborhood but cost an arm and a leg in this part of town. I searched the landing for door buzzers and mailboxes but found only one. Whoever George was visiting lived alone. With an uptown address.

"Now what?" asked Jayne.

"We buzz," I said. "I'm not leaving here until I know what he's up to."

We rang the bell and tried our best to undo what the brief run had done to our appearances. Heels click-clacked down an unseen foyer. A blond head popped up behind the frosted-glass door panels. After a rattle and two clinks, the door opened.

"Rosie!" Izzie stood before me still dressed in the clothes she'd worn to rehearsal. "What a nice surprise. What are you doing in our neck of the woods?"

I gestured toward Jayne and brought her into the conversation. "We were at the Stage Door Canteen tonight."

"So Zelda told me."

"We could've sworn we saw Paulette's fiancé there. I've been wanting to talk to him, so we tried to catch up with him and the next thing you know we saw him go into your house."

Her expression didn't change. If George was up to no good, she didn't know it yet. "Why don't you come in and I'll get him for you?"

As we entered the foyer, a phonograph greeted us, singing "Angels of Mercy."

"Zel? Guess who's here?"

To our left was a parlor crammed with overstuffed, brightly colored furniture, each piece uglier than the next. On top of the various tables, fireplace mantels, and other available spaces was a weird hodgepodge of war mementos: vases shaped like *V*'s; postcards of Polynesian dancers; a statue of a dog peeing on Hitler; a red, white, and blue radio; and something that looked like a skull. In the middle of it all sat Zelda, flipping through a stack of phonograph records.

"Well, come in already," she said to me, as though it were her house.

As Izzie disappeared up the stairs, we entered the room and surrendered our coats. To the right of the parlor was a lavish dining room decked out with a mahogany table and chair set that seemed to have been plundered from Henry the Eighth's fire sale. Paintings dotted the walls vying for the award for "Most Horrifying Depiction of a Historical Scene." The walls themselves were papered in ornate patterns that pinched a nerve just behind my eyes. The drapes were floral, each held away from the window with a gold-colored tassel.

"Sit, sit," said Zelda. "What's your poison?"

"Rum and Coca-Cola," said Jayne.

"A martini, if you can make one," I said.

"Did you hear that?" Zelda said to Jayne. "She's challenging my bartending skills. I'll be back in two shakes of a lamb's tail." She left the room, and Jayne and I fought for space on a mohair love seat overtaken by gold-fringed throw pillows with needlepointed poems in their centers. These ditties had titles like "To a Friend" and "My Wife" and brief texts that waxed philosophic about loyalty and love.

Jayne let out a low whistle. "Isn't this something?"

"Have you ever seen anything tackier?"

"Tacky? Do you have any idea what this stuff costs?"

I searched the room for price tags. "More than it's worth?"

Jayne ignored me. "How on earth can they afford a place like this?"

Before I could answer, Izzie rejoined us, her face flushed from her journey. "George will be down in a sec. You caught him at bath time."

"And why is George bathing in your house?" I asked.

Izzie located her own half-drained drink and wet her whistle. "He's our guest. He had a reservation at an awful hotel on the Upper West Side and we thought that with all this space it was foolish for him not to stay here. It's what Paulette would've wanted."

Jayne wriggled on the sofa until her back met its back. Her shoes dangled two feet above the floor. "This is some place you've got."

"How do you guys swing a joint like this?" I asked. "I can't even afford a newspaper in this part of town."

Zelda entered with our drinks in hand. We each took a dainty Austrian crystal glass and held our breath lest it should shatter. "It's Olive's. It came with her husband."

"Her *dead* husband," said Izzie.

"Oh." I took a sip of my drink to keep my tongue from wagging. "I'm sorry."

"Don't be," said Zelda. "You didn't know."

A past conversation wiggled through my brain. Didn't Olive say she was married when I first met her? Had she remarried, or did she still consider herself hitched even though the former mister was six feet under?

"Did the war mementos come with the house?" I asked.

Zelda laughed. "No, those were gifts."

"That's the bad thing about pen pals," said Izzie. "They always want to send you stuff."

I took a quick spin around the room, admiring their collection of souvenirs. It *was* a skull. I was definitely going to need another drink.

"So what is it you wanted to see George about?" asked Izzie.

Was it time to come clean? I looked toward Jayne for the answer.

"It's about what happened to Paulette," said Jayne. "Rosie and I just can't stop thinking about it. We wanted to find out if George could shed any further light on what happened that night."

"Why?" asked Izzie.

I hadn't expected the question. I took a deep breath. Was it the worst thing if they found out I was a friend of Al's? "I know the guy in jail."

The ice in Izzie's glass rattled like dice in a cup. "You know Paulette's killer?"

"No. I mean yes—he's a friend. Of both of ours. But I think he's innocent." I looked longingly at my still-filled drink. I should've drained it before the conversation began.

"He confessed," said Zelda.

"I know. Believe me I know, but there's a reason for that. . . . I just haven't figured out what it is yet. I thought George might know more about what happened. Maybe he could answer some questions that have been bothering me."

Izzie crossed to the fireplace. On the mantelpiece were a number of photographs, all of them of men in uniform. "Wouldn't that be better left to the police?"

Of course it would.

"Rosie used to work for a detective," said Jayne. "She was the one who unraveled what was going on at the People's Theater."

"Really?" asked Zelda. She was impressed, or at least as impressed as Zelda ever got. Even Izzie eased her scowl.

"Really," I said. "And if I learned nothing else from that experience, I did figure out that the police aren't as on the ball as you might think." And the press rarely gives you credit for the things you do.

"What could it hurt?" said Zelda.

Izzie met her eyes, then looked away. "I suppose it's ultimately up to George."

George arrived two drinks and ten minutes later, his hair still wet from the shower he'd taken. He was wearing pajamas under a thick terry-cloth robe. Both garments were too big for him, swallowing his hands and feet. They'd probably belonged to one of Paulette's husbands, or perhaps to Olive's.

I reintroduced us and cut to the chase. "I understand you were with Paulette the night she died."

He looked from Izzie to Zelda, searching for which one of them had made this preposterous claim. "Who told you that?"

"Weren't you?" asked Izzie.

"Of course I wasn't." He sank into the chair closest to her. "Why would you think that?"

"Paulette told us she had plans with you," said Zelda. "That's why she didn't go to the Canteen that night. Naturally Izzie assumed that meant you had seen her."

"I had a message at my hotel," said George. "She couldn't see me after all. I tried to call her back, but there was no answer."

"And you're positive the message was from Paulette?" I asked.

George shrugged. "I had no reason not to think so. The girl at the desk just told me someone had called and wanted me to know Paulette couldn't meet with me after all."

"So it could've been a man or a woman," said Jayne.

"I guess," said George.

I returned to my spot on the sofa. "Didn't you think it was strange that she would cancel on you? She hadn't seen you in months."

George ran a hand through his wet hair. "Of course I thought it was strange."

"So why didn't you come over here to see if something was the matter?"

"I thought she was worried about the Canteen finding out about us. She'd mentioned to me that she'd felt like she was being watched, and I assumed she was scared that one of the other girls had gotten wind that she was seeing someone."

"So what?" I said. "If you're in love, if you're planning on being married, who cares about the Stage Door Canteen?"

"It was important to her," he said. "She'd put in so much time there." He looked at Izzie and Zelda. "All the girls had. It kept her busy, made her feel like she had a purpose."

"What did you do that night if you didn't come here?" asked Jayne.

"Stayed at my hotel. Read a book. Went to sleep. There wasn't any point in doing anything without Paulette."

I mulled this over for a moment. "The day we met, you made it sound like you hadn't come into town until after Paulette died. Why?"

He shook his head and worked his hands into knots. "I don't know. I guess I wasn't thinking too clearly. She was dead. That was all I could think about."

Jayne was right—grief did make people behave strangely. But something else was bothering me. "Why are you still in town? I thought you were going home with her for the funeral."

He looked at Zelda, then at the floor. "I couldn't. I tried. I went to the train station and everything, but when it came time to board I didn't have the courage. Her memorial service was hard enough, but to be at her funeral . . . the finality of it all was too overwhelming."

Somehow I doubted that.

"Have you considered that we're barking up the wrong tree?" asked Jayne. We were back home, counteracting Zelda's inferior bartending with our own efforts. Our gin was cheap, our glasses sturdy, just the way it should be.

"In the last hour, that's all I've been thinking about. There's something very fishy about George Pomeroy's story. And the thing is, he knows it. I can see it in his face, but it's like he can't tell us the truth."

"I don't trust him." Jayne went to her dresser and smeared cold cream on her face. "And not just him. I don't trust the lot of them."

"Izzie and Zelda?"

"And Olive. Just because she's hurt doesn't get her off the hook. Who's to say one of them didn't kill Paulette? Didn't you tell me they didn't find the body for three hours? That would've certainly given them ample opportunity."

"Olive and Izzie, sure. But Zelda was still at the Canteen when they went home." I struggled to open a new jar of olives. "What's the motive, though?"

Jayne lay back on her bed and carefully sipped her drink to keep the cold cream from her glass. "Jealousy? Paulette's career was going a lot better than everyone else's."

"How does killing her change that?"

She wiped a dab of cream from the glass's edge. "Maybe Olive and Izzie were up for the same parts?"

"They're different types. Besides, Paulette's been a star for a while." If we were trying to pin Paulette's death on a jealous actress, Ruby made a lot more sense. Or even Minnie. "Why kill her now?"

"Maybe it was a different kind of jealousy. Obviously Paulette had a way with men."

"Most of whom died." I got the olive jar opened and floated the fruit in each of our glasses. "Besides, Olive was married and Izzie is hardly hurting for dance partners. It seems to me that each of those girls had a ring for every finger."

"Maybe one of them wanted someone Paulette had reeled in."

"Who? George Pomeroy?"

Jayne drained the drink and devoured her olive. "You said yourself George and Zelda were looking awfully cozy." Plus, George was staying in their house, wearing someone else's pajamas.

"I just can't see girls that close doing something like that, especially over a guy like George."

Jayne threw her hands in the air. Fortunately, her glass was empty. "I give up. They're innocent. All of them."

"I'm not saying that. I'm just saying we don't have a clear motive. At least not for the girls. George, on the other hand—"

Jayne snapped her fingers. "Could've wanted to kill her for the same reason we thought Al might want to."

"Bingo. Maybe he found out she was stepping out on him and he couldn't stand the thought of putting up with it anymore."

"But if we've considered that possibility, why haven't Izzie and Zelda?"

"They didn't have to," I said. "As far as they knew, the killer was locked up two days after Paulette was found."

28 The Blackmailers of New York

WALTER GAVE EVERYONE SUNDAY OFF. On Monday, Jayne and I did our best to treat Izzie and Zelda as though everything were fine at rehearsal. That was the best acting that was going on at the Bernhardt. The rest of the performances were forced, unprofessional, and frightfully unpolished.

"Is it me, or is it getting worse?" I asked Zelda. Rehearsal was over and we were all packing up our things and looking for ways to commiserate.

"It certainly isn't getting any better."

"We're thinking about heading over to the Canteen. Want to join us?" Jayne and I were hoping that if we got Zelda and Izzie out we might get a chance to ask them more questions about George.

"Sure. Why don't we ask Ruby too?"

I had a million reasons why, but I kept my mouth shut.

The five of us met in the lobby and hit the pavement. We hadn't made it two feet when a voice stopped us.

"I've been looking for you, Jayne."

My pal and I turned toward the sound and found Tony's black Packard parked curbside. Tony was standing outside of it, leaning against the rear door while smoking a stogie. His driver waited impatiently at the wheel.

Jayne's glee at this surprise visit quickly turned to worry. "Tony. What are you doing here?"

"One of my boys told me he'd seen you the other night at the Tap Room with Vinnie Garvaggio."

Izzie picked up on the uncomfortable direction the conversation was heading and quietly told me they'd see us at the Canteen. I bid them farewell with a pained smile and remained glued to Jayne's side.

Tony dropped the cigar to the ground. It was only half-smoked, and I bit back a reprimand for his wastefulness. "You in this show, Jayne?"

Had the question been directed at me, I would've lied. Jayne had scruples, though, and believed omitting information was one thing, deliberately changing it quite another. She dropped her gaze to the ground, and her right foot made a semicircle on the pavement. It was a child's way of responding, an effort to distract the listener from what they were being told. "Yeah."

"You're in Vinnie Garvaggio's show?" He'd heard her the first time, but he clearly wanted to make her suffer through telling the truth again.

"It's not his show," I said. "It's Walter Friday's."

He jabbed a pudgy finger in my direction. "You stay out of this, Rosie." He redirected his attention toward Jayne. "What were you doing out with him?"

"It was just drinks, Tony. Rosie was there. Nothing happened. Honest."

"That don't answer my question."

I could see the slippery slope Jayne was about to slide down. Telling Tony the truth, as she wanted to, would involve admitting she fanned Garvaggio's romantic intentions. That wasn't something he would deal well with.

"It was my idea," I said. "All of it. Her taking the job and going out for drinks with him."

"You expect me to believe that?"

"Believe what you want, Tony. Something rotten's going on with Al, and whatever it is, it started in the Bernhardt. That means it probably involved Garvaggio. You might be able to let Al rot in jail for a murder he didn't commit, but I'm not willing to." I expected some sort of response to this revelation, but I didn't get one. "Jayne didn't like the idea of joining the cast any more than she liked the idea of milking Garvaggio for information, but I begged her to help me. Don't be mad at her—it's my fault."

He turned back toward Jayne. "This true?"

"Mostly," she said. She traced a figure eight with her shoe. "She didn't have to beg. I wanted to help Al."

It was hard to know what was upsetting Tony more: the fact that Jayne and I had been snooping behind his back or the knowledge that certain associates of his believed Jayne was stepping out on him.

Tony rapped his knuckles against the Packard's window. "Let's dust," he told his driver. He crushed the still-smoldering cigar with his black-and-white spectator and returned his attention to Jayne. "You call me when you get more sense."

He got into the car and with a squeal the driver pulled away. I watched until the heap had disappeared into the night, then turned, expecting to find Jayne awash in tears. She wasn't. Instead, her pale skin had turned maroon and her tiny hands were curled into even tinier fists.

"Are you all right?" I asked.

"What a hypocrite! *Call me when I get more sense!* Can you believe that?"

"Well, he did tell you to stay away from Garvaggio. It had to burn him good to hear you were out on the town with him."

"First of all, he has no right telling me what jobs I can or cannot take. And second of all, he could've asked me what I was up to. Have I ever stepped out on him before?" There was no reason to answer. Even when estranged, Jayne was as faithful to Tony as Lassie was to Timmy. She lifted her arm above her head. "I've had it up to here with his rules and threats. When is he going to start doing what *I* say, huh?" We started walking toward the subway station. We wouldn't be joining the other girls at the Canteen. Jayne's rage was too combustible for a public place.

The sun was setting, and the tops of the buildings on Fifty-Seventh

Street were slowly starting to disappear into the night. Outside the Canteen the crush of young men would be buzzing with excitement. "I'm going to write him," said Jayne.

"Tony doesn't strike me as the type to be wooed by a letter."

"Not him. Billy."

A group of young women shilling for the Red Cross passed by, asking us to contribute to their fund-raising campaign. I waved them off with a polite smile. "You've lost me."

"The sailor from the other night. His name's Billy DeMille."

"Like the director?"

Jayne nodded. "I need to start expending my efforts on someone who appreciates them."

I couldn't argue with that.

We made it to the subway and boarded our train. Above our heads a sign chided us for chewing too much gum. The soldiers needed it, it said, and like everything else, we were keeping them from getting it.

"Why did Tony want you to stay away from Garvaggio?" I asked.

Jayne shrugged and turned toward the window, fogging up the glass with her breath. "Because he was dangerous, I guess."

Half the men Tony associated with—Al included—had rap sheets, and Jayne had never been forbidden to be around them. Dangerous had to be more specific in this case.

"How involved is Tony with the black market?"

"What do you mean?"

"I mean, what kind of stuff is he selling?"

Jayne turned back to me. "Everything, I guess. You know he doesn't tell me anything."

"So he could be selling meat?"

"I guess." Her face went slack. "Not horses, though—he wouldn't do that."

"I'm not saying he would. That's Vinnie's game, not Tony's. I'm just wondering why those two hate each other, assuming the stream runs both ways. It would make sense if they were competing against each other." If Garvaggio and Tony were rivals, Tony naturally wouldn't want Jayne involved in any rackets that might be benefiting his nemesis. How would it look if word got out that Tony B.'s girl was in the show that was funding the competition?

"I see your point," said Jayne. We got to Christopher Street and headed homeward. As we rounded the corner to the Shaw House, a tall slim figure climbed the stairs and paused before the mailboxes in the foyer.

"What's she doing here?"

Jayne squinted into the distance at the object of my scorn. "Ruby? Maybe she decided she didn't want to go to the Canteen after all." We approached the building cautiously. Rather than climbing the steps and announcing our presence, I pulled Jayne to the other side of the banister and urged her to keep her head low. From where we stood we had a perfect view into the foyer where Ruby remained frozen, reading something she'd removed from her box. She finished it and turned the page over, looking for more. She frowned at the paper and crumpled it into a ball.

"What's that all about?" whispered Jayne.

"Maybe her soldier came to his senses. Come on." I grabbed her arm and pulled her back around to the stairs. I took the steps two at a time and greeted Ruby just as she was about to leave the foyer and enter the lobby. "Hello there, stranger. Got mail?"

The frown was still firmly planted on her face. "I always have mail."

"From your pilot?"

She fumbled with a stack of letters that rested in the crook of her arm. "Of course. He writes me every day."

"I hope it isn't bad news."

"I haven't read it yet, but I'm sure it's not. Thank you for your concern."

She spun on her heel and continued her stomp into the lobby and up the stairs.

"Can't you two call a truce?" asked Jayne.

"I'm not the one who started it."

"Still . . ." My roommate looked exhausted. Her rage had taken the run out and was being replaced by the sad realization that Tony and she might actually be through for good. She was seconds from tears.

"You're right." I gave her a tight, fixed smile. "I can try harder. Let's you and me go upstairs and figure out what to write to Billy DeMille."

An hour later Jayne had a good cry, I had a good drunk, and Billy DeMille had a carefully composed letter ready for posting. Despite the booze, I also had a much clearer head. If Tony wanted Jayne to stay away from Garvaggio and if Al reacted so violently to Garvaggio's name and to the possibility that Jayne believed his guilt, it would follow that Al would be mortified if he found out Jayne and Garvaggio had gone out together. That could be just the news that sent him out of his sulk and into some serious talking.

The trouble was, I couldn't be the one to tell him. He knew I'd been baiting him before, and he'd told me he wouldn't see me if I showed up at Rikers again. It was time to admit to myself that my subtle touch was as deft as a sledgehammer. Jayne, on the other hand, would be a much more welcome sight to him. And if she played things right and made him believe she was leaving Tony for Vinnie, he might be worried enough to squeal about whatever was really going on.

"Jayne?"

"Hmmmm?" Her tears had stopped and she was halfway to falling into an angry, sad sleep. She set her makeup-smeared eyes on me and blew her nose on the last clean handkerchief she could find.

"I think I know how we can find out what's going on with Al, but I'm going to need a favor from you."

"A bigger one than joining a lousy show, going out with a man my boyfriend hates, and losing said boyfriend when he finds out?"

We'd reached the part of the evening where all of her problems were now my fault. Clearly I should've waited to broach the subject until morning. "Sort of." I told her my plan, fully expecting her to collapse into laughter before giving me an out of breath "No!" And laugh she did, until new tears sprouted from her eyes and her face became redder than a freshly spanked bottom. "Am I correct in assuming that's a no?" I asked.

"No."

"So it is."

"No." She fought for breath. "I mean it's not a no."

"Then what's so funny?"

She lay on her back and giggled at the ceiling. "I'm just picturing Tony's face when Al tells him I'm leaving him for Garvaggio. It would serve him right."

"You think he'd tell him?"

"I'm counting on it."

"Take it easy," I said. "You don't want to be Helen of Troy here."

She rolled back onto her side. "Who?"

"The face that launched a thousand ships? The woman who caused the Trojan War?"

"Oh, I know that. I'm going to make it perfectly clear that while my intentions with Garvaggio were initially noble, Tony's stupidity pushed me into his arms. That way, he has only himself to blame."

It wasn't a perfect plan, but far be it from me to criticize a woman scorned.

29 Tell Her the Truth

With opening less than two weeks away, rehearsals had been pushed back to early evening, as though Friday didn't want to just get us accustomed to the play but also to the time of day we'd ultimately be performing it. Jayne and I hoped this delay meant we could catch a little shut-eye, but the city had other plans. During the wee hours of Tuesday morning we were awakened by the whine of the air raid siren. It was only a test, but that didn't mean our hearts didn't leap out of our chests. By the time the all-clear sounded, we were too wired to go back to sleep. We had a whole morning before us and an infinite number of things we could do. Things like going to Rikers Island and getting the truth out of a mob henchman.

On my advice, Jayne dressed to the nines for our visit to Al. She wore a silky red blouse that was surprisingly conservative for something cut to emphasize her cleavage, and a pencil skirt that hugged her hips and showed off her well-toned dancer's calves. While she got ready, I went down to the foyer and checked the morning mail.

"You're not funny."

I turned away from my mailbox and found Ruby behind my left shoulder. "I'm not trying to be. When I'm funny, you'll know it."

"You know what I'm talking about." She was dressed for the day but looked like she'd accomplished that feat in a darkened closet after being blindfolded and spun around. Her blouse was wrinkled and untucked, her skirt bore a grease spot just north of the hem. Ruby was meticulous about her appearance, and seeing her so haphazardly put together made me feel like the earth had tipped the other way on its axis.

"Actually, I don't. It's early and I have yet to plot against you, but give me an hour or two." Even if I hadn't just gotten up, it was doubtful I'd have any idea what she was talking about.

"Jealousy doesn't become you, Rosie."

"I'll keep that in mind next time I go shopping."

"Be glib all you want, but I'm warning you: if you continue this, you'll regret it." With that she left the foyer and entered the street.

I stared after her, trying to figure out how I'd managed to offend her so early. Was it possible this was all because of our conversation the day before? While clearly I'd poked a wound then, it hadn't been one I was aiming for. Something was bothering Ruby, and it was looking more and more like I was getting blamed for it.

I went into the lobby with the intention of going upstairs to retrieve Jayne. Before I could, the dulcet tones of Belle grabbed me by the ear and held me in place.

"Were you raised in a barn?"

"No, but I do enjoy a good roll in the hay."

She bent before the parlor wastebasket and retrieved a wad of paper resting next to it. With a grunt that would've been better suited for a day of pounding railroad ties into the sun-hardened earth, she put the paper where it belonged and once again became upright.

"Watch your aim next time."

"You're barking up the wrong tree."

She shook her head to reinforce that she didn't believe me, then disappeared behind the swinging kitchen door.

"Are you ready?" Jayne appeared on the stairwell. She looked delectable enough to be a Varga girl.

"You might want to go without me. Something tells me this isn't my day."

"What's wrong?"

I listed the offenses that had already been levied against me. As I came to Belle's assault, I approached the wastebasket to illustrate her accusation. Since the offending wad was still there, I picked it up to prove the page and I were unconnected.

"It's Ruby's," I said. "No wonder I got blamed for it." I unfurled the paper to look at the rest of the note. It was brief and to the point: *Ruby, I know what you're doing. Stay away from Donald Montgomery or else.*

Jayne read over my shoulder and squinted at the words. "Who sent it?"

"It doesn't strike me as the kind of note that comes from someone who's willing to identify themselves." There was an envelope in the wastebasket. No return address, though the postmark said it had come from New York the day before.

"You'd think they'd just hand-deliver it and save the postage," said Jayne.

"What would Emily Post say about that?" I tucked the letter into my purse, and Jayne and I left the house. "At least now I know why Ruby's so sore: she thinks I'm behind this. And I'll bet my mother that whatever she was reading yesterday when we walked in on her was kin to this."

"Why would someone threaten her?" asked Jayne.

"Why wouldn't they?"

"You've got to tell her you're innocent."

"And ruin all the fun?" Jayne opened her mouth to protest, but I cut her off with a wave of my hand. "Ruby being mad at me is nothing new. Besides, if she's thinks I'm the one who did it, whoever is really behind these notes might start getting a little careless. Blaming me might be the best thing she could do."

We took three subways and a cross-town bus to the Rikers Island ferry. There we huddled by the railing and watched as Manhattan disappeared into the fog. Our companions were few and kept to themselves, either dreading the return to a place they'd recently left or fearing whomever they had to encounter when they got there. In whispers punctuated by the ferry's whistle, Jayne and I went through what she should say to Al. She had to be emotional and pathetic, keeping up the ruse that she didn't want to tell Al any of this but felt like she didn't have anyone else to turn to.

"Make sure you tell him you and I aren't speaking," I said. "That'll put him on your side out of the gate."

"What if he doesn't take the bait?"

"Then it may be time to confess the feelings you've long harbored for him."

She put out her hand like she was a cop stopping traffic. "You want me to tell Al I'm in love with him?"

"I want you to convince him he has a reason to want to be free. This is our last chance, Jayne. If you can't get him to talk, I doubt he'll be willing to see either of us again. He might spend the rest of his days behind bars."

We arrived at the Island, and I navigated through the gates and guards and took Jayne into the little lobby where other family members and visitors signed in and waited their turn. Al was apparently anxious to see her, since ten minutes after her arrival Jayne was being escorted out of the hall and into the meeting room.

They had added an urn of complimentary coffee to the waiting area. I helped myself to a cup (weak as dishwater but chicory-free) and turned my attention to *Life* magazine and an article on Versailles showgirls who aspired to be army pin-ups. A quarter of an hour passed. It had to be going well; otherwise he would've said his time was up and told the guard he wanted to leave. I'd finally done something right. We were going to get the truth out of Al. We were going to secure his freedom.

I should've known that the minute I started feeling confident was the moment everything went haywire.

"Funny meeting you here." Vinnie Garvaggio lurked near my chair, his enormous girth blocking my view of anything but him. He wore a pin-striped suit, and for a moment I was mesmerized by how much fabric it had taken to construct this single piece of clothing. Was there a shortage of pin-striped wool now? Was he the one to blame for the clothing ration?

"Hiya, Mr. Garvaggio. Sir." I fumbled with the *Life* magazine and rolled it into a tube in case I needed to battle him with it. Clearly, fifty pages of slick paper would fell a man his size.

"Whaddya doing here?" he asked. The cigar was in its usual spot. The teeth around it were the color of summer corn.

"Visiting. A . . . relative."

"You got a friend in the joint?" As I noticed with him previously, his appearance was immaculate. I'm not one to go around smelling men, but I couldn't help but notice a sweet, manly scent hovering around him, obliterating the smell of his cigar.

"As a matter of fact, I do. Not a friend per say, but my pop. He's been on the Island for ten years now."

He frowned. "Ten years? I thought the Island was for short-timers."

"What can I say? He makes friends wherever he goes."

He pulled up the chair beside me. Fortunately, it didn't have arms. "What's he in for?"

I searched the walls for the answer. "Robbery."

"What'd he pinch?" He illustrated the question with one of his giant mitts. His nails had been buffed to a pink sheen. I was dying to ask who his manicurist was.

"Art work. High-end stuff. I'm sure you read about it in the papers."

"Sorry, I don't know art."

So I hoped. "Anyways, I come up here once a month and chat with him. What are you here for?"

"To see a friend."

It was clear I was supposed to accept that answer and move on. While details might be expected of me, they were never expected of Vinnie Garvaggio.

"You know," I said. "I heard Paulette Monroe's murderer is here."

"That so?"

"That's what one of the girls in the show told me. I thought that was kind of strange myself. My pop made it sound like they didn't bring murderers to Rikers."

He removed the cigar from his mouth and wiped his chin. "Not to stay, that's for sure. Sometimes people, like your pop, get special favors."

I looked at my watch: Jayne had been gone twenty-five minutes. She couldn't be in there much longer. Even a guy who could pull strings wasn't likely to get a conference for more than thirty minutes. I was running out of time and conversation. You didn't have to be the secretary of war to figure out that Garvaggio's seeing Jayne here would be bad. When the guard escorted her back, he'd know she'd been to see someone, and claiming we were both visiting relatives at Rikers on the same day wasn't likely to float. Vinnie was swift enough to do the math before you even told him the numbers.

I would have to create a distraction and soon.

I picked up my lukewarm coffee and feigned taking a sip. As soon as it touched my lips, I yelped in pain and jerked the cup away from my body and onto Garvaggio's chest. A puddle of brown formed at the top of his belly before cascading like Niagara Falls down the rest of his once-crisp white shirt.

"Oh my gosh! I am so, so sorry!" I said.

Vinnie stared at the mess pooling beneath him. He didn't so much scowl at his shirt as recoil in horror.

"I bet it'll wash out," I said.

He kept his hands as far from his body as possible, like his shirt wasn't covered in coffee but blood and guts. His horror became panic. Vinnie Garvaggio was not a man who could take looking like a mess, especially when he was about to confront someone.

If he'd killed Paulette—and it was looking less and less like he had—it was doubtful he'd done it himself. Just like with the horses, he had someone else do his dirty work.

There was a bathroom off the waiting area, and he staggered toward it like a poisoned man struggling to reach an antidote. As soon as he was safely behind the door, I approached the gal at the desk and asked in a hushed voice if she knew how much longer Jayne would be.

She glanced at a clock on the wall and looked at the intake time Jayne had scribbled on the clipboard. "She should've been out ten minutes ago. Lemme call down."

It wasn't necessary. With the kind of perfect timing Maureen would've sold out the Bund for, Jayne entered the waiting room with zebra stripes of mascara running down her cheeks. "Sign out," I told her. "We've got to scram."

"What's the rush?"

"Garvaggio's here."

Jayne scribbled her moniker and we breezed out the door. As we rounded the corner to the exit, she took me in for the first time. "What happened? Are you all right?"

"I've been better. Today I witnessed the loss of a man's best dress shirt."

I got the scoop on the ride back to the Bronx. My plan had worked like a charm.

"The minute I told Al I was seeing Garvaggio it was like someone had electrocuted him. Every hair on his body was standing at attention."

I should've been thrilled he reacted as I'd guessed, but instead I felt terribly guilty. Hadn't Al been through enough without having to worry about Jayne too?

"I tell you, Rosie—I'd hate to see what happens when Garvaggio shows his face. I don't think Al is going to take it well."

"I wouldn't worry too much about that—something tells me that Vinnie decided to cancel his appointment after we left. He'd never confront someone wearing a stained shirt. He's obsessed with being spick-and-span. What did Al tell you?"

"Oh, that." She sighed and I could tell that the tears she shed while she was in with Al weren't entirely being used as a persuasion technique. She'd been rattled and good. "Keep in mind that the minute I told him I was involved with Garvaggio, all he wanted to do was keep me from seeing him. At first he was vague, telling me Vinnie was bad news and whatnot. I told him you could say the same about Tony, and look how that stopped me."

I grinned. Jayne could be remarkably self-aware for someone who seemed determined to make poor choices.

"When it became clear he was going to have to give me details if he wanted me to back down, he told me the real reason he was in the joint: Garvaggio put a hit on him."

Even though I'd predicted this very scenario, I still found myself gasping. "For what?"

"Tony asked Al to spy for him. Apparently Garvaggio was undercutting his prices."

So that was it. Tony didn't like Garvaggio, not because the guy was no good but because he was able to sell his black market meat at a greater discount, which meant more business and, ultimately, more profit.

"Garvaggio was getting a big piece of the restaurant pie, and Tony wasn't too happy about it. He told Al to find out how he'd managed to do it, and Al found out what you found out: Garvaggio was able to sell his meat dirt cheap because it wasn't beef. So Al tells Tony, and Tony decides he's going to shut Vinnie down."

My eyes landed on a man across the aisle hiding behind a newspaper. I squinted to make out the headlines. An army plane had crashed into Hofstra College, killing the pilot. And starting April 1, the meat ration would be one and three quarter pounds per week.

There was the missing piece. Garvaggio's urgency to pull out of the Bernhardt wasn't because of something that had already happened but because of something that was going to occur. I tapped Jayne on the knee. "Only Tony doesn't have to shut Garvaggio down because the feds have new regulations that are kicking in on April first and nobody will be able to sell mystery meat as beef anymore. Heck, nobody will be able to sell anything since the new regulations mean the black market meat industry will be finished for good. But why would Garvaggio want to take out Al for that? Even if he found out he was spying on him, he had to know everything was going to change by the end of the month."

"That's the thing," said Jayne. "Vinnie found a way to get around the new regulations: he got his hands on the stamps the USDA is going to make the legal dealers use."

"No!" I felt queasy. As it was, I wasn't sure I was going to be eager to eat meat again, but now there was no way to guarantee that even the stuff the feds approved was what it claimed to be. And what about the soldiers? Who's to say the food we were sending them wasn't pig parts, horse legs, and whatever unfortunate dog wandered into the shop the day the butcher needed to turn over the government's slice?

Jayne barreled ahead with her story. "So not only would Vinnie still be in business come April, he would likely be the only one still making money on meat. Tony couldn't stomach that, so he had Al filch the stamps. Only Garvaggio found out about it. Apparently Vinnie's stamp source dried up. His meat operation's his biggest earner and without those stamps the whole thing was going to be lost come April."

I shook my head. "So naturally he figured if he put the hurt on Al, he could get the stamps back."

Jayne nodded. "It was Tony's bright idea to stick Al behind bars. When Paulette's body was found, he told Al to claim the crime and promised him that as soon as Garvaggio cooled down, he'd see to it that he was released."

"Fat chance that's going to happen. Clearly Garvaggio has been visiting him whenever he can to try and put the squeeze on him." I felt terrible for Al, who was not only in the bing but being subjected to Garvaggio's constant visits and threats. "Here's what I don't understand: if Vinnie still wants Al's head on a platter and Tony's committed to keeping Al safe, why doesn't Tony clear Al's name, get Al out of there, and stash him someplace Vinnie's not likely to find him?"

And why were they letting Garvaggio in anyway? If Al had the clout to say he didn't want to see me, couldn't he tell the guards that he didn't want to see Vinnie either?

Jayne's mouth remained open, but no sound escaped. It was a question without an answer. For now.

I snapped my fingers. "You know who would know? Vinnie Garvaggio."

"And how do you propose getting him to squeal?"

"Same way you got Al to do it: tell him you were Tony's girl but you're finished now. Tell him you couldn't take the way Tony was keeping things from you."

Jayne raised an eyebrow. "You think that's safe?"

"Why wouldn't it be?"

Neither of us could come up with an answer. It wasn't until later that I realized that with Al officially off the hook we still weren't certain who had killed Paulette.

30 A Curious Accident

WE ARRIVED AT REHEARSAL TEN minutes early. While Jayne went to warm up with the other dancers, I attempted to find a quiet place to look over my script. Unfortunately, Izzie had a different idea.

"We missed you last night," she said.

"Sorry about that. Neither of us were in the mood for the Canteen after Jayne's boyfriend got through with us."

She ran a hand through her blond curls. "She told me it's finished."

"She's said that before. Hopefully she means it this time. She actually wrote to one of the boys she met at the Canteen the other night."

"Good for her."

I attempted to return to my script. Izzie was hovering so close she cast a shadow over it.

"And what about you? How are things going with the fellow you met?" she asked.

Zelda was a regular Hedda Hopper. Telling her something was as good as telling it to Izzie. At least I wasn't having to repeat myself. "I'm not sure. I might see him again. He'll be back in a week."

"What do you mean *might*?"

I was getting tired of her giving me the third. I didn't want to think about Peaches. I had bigger things to worry about. "Look, Izzie: I don't think I want this to go where he wants this to go. He's clearly looking for romance, and all I wanted to do was help lift a soldier's spirits."

"Because of your ex?"

Even if Jack never existed, I still wouldn't have felt comfortable plunging into a relationship with a man I'd met twice. I wasn't a woman who fell head over heels or believed in love at first sight; it didn't seem right to take less time choosing a mate than I did ordering a sandwich.

Which reminded me: I was hungry. And I wasn't eating meat.

"You know, Rosie, there's no harm seeing him again. Jack's never going to know about it, and I think the lift you'll give your pilot is worth a little discomfort."

"But what if he's looking for romance, love, and marriage? I can't give him that."

"You're an actress, aren't you?"

Lying about your feelings to make the bills was one thing, but this? This was deception. Sure it made someone in a low spot feel good, but was that fair? Did we really want to convince every soldier, sailor, pilot, and marine that everything at home was A-OK and there was a little woman waiting for each and every one of them? Maybe it would help them get through the night, but what would happen when the war ended and they discovered that the dreams they held in their heads at night were nothing but tin painted to look like silver?

I didn't have time to ask Izzie any of this. Walter arrived and we all went to our respective places backstage. As we huddled waiting for our entrances, I became aware of an acrid odor filling the room. The dim space grew even dimmer and through disjointed, light-headed thoughts I finally recognized what I was smelling: smoke.

I turned to the rear of the stage, where a spiral staircase led to the bowels of the building. The smoke was worse there. "Fire," I yelped, amazed at my own delay. "Fire!"

Everyone ran to the front of the house and pushed out the doors. Thirty seconds hadn't passed before the familiar whine of the NYFD filled the afternoon sky. I counted heads to make sure everyone was out there and was relieved to find no one was missing. We were safe.

The fire, it turned out, looked much worse than it was. Someone had dropped a lit cigar in the costume shop, but rather than spreading, the fire had smoldered, producing a lot more smoke than danger.

The costumes were gray and the building stunk, but otherwise, everything was okay. Had the fire spread and the firemen been forced to delve deeper into the basement, the odds were good that Garvaggio's racket would've been uncovered, a possibility that I'm sure didn't escape his mind when he dropped the cigar to begin with.

"This has got to stop," said Friday. We were given the all clear and the fire truck pulled away. The girls waved at the men who'd allegedly saved us, and they waved back, admonishing us to give up smoking those nasty cigars before someone really did get hurt. Friday left the street and entered the building as the stage manager announced that that was it for the day. No director—not even Walter Friday—could expect us to rehearse in a smoke-filled room.

While everyone else dispersed, Jayne and I crept back into the building in search of Friday. We found him in his office.

I knocked on the doorframe. He was seated at his desk staring into a glass of clear liquid that I was pretty sure wasn't water. "Mr. Friday? Could we have a word?"

He sucked on a tooth and pushed his hand through his hair. "Now's not a good time, doll. Nobody's supposed to be in the building."

Jayne tugged on my sleeve and tried to pull me away from the door. I wasn't ready to give up, though. It was now or never.

"I'm sorry, but this can't wait. Someone could've been killed."

Friday lifted his glass like he was toasting us. "Why do you think I'm drinking?"

"And that's not the half of it. You've had a flood, and so many accidents it seems like we'd be safer overseas than onstage."

He downed the glass and slammed it onto the table. "You think I don't know that?"

"You've got to give this up. Tell Garvaggio you'll shut down the show."

"I can't do that."

"Why not?"

He unsteadily attempted to refill his drink from a crystal decanter. "Because I'll be ruined, that's why."

"With all due respect, it's not that great a show to begin with. I'd think it would be better for you if it never opened than being torn apart by the critics come opening night."

He downed his second drink and tipped himself another tumblerful. "This has nothing to do with the play. You think these guys just lend you money and you pay them the interest? It don't work like that. From the get-go, Vinnie's deal said if the show didn't open, he got back twice his investment. I thought he was doing it to make sure I didn't use the money for something else. It didn't occur to me that he never intended for the show to happen."

And it probably wouldn't have occurred to Vinnie either if the feds hadn't decided to get involved. "Did he kill Paulette too?"

"Why would he?" I had no answer. He wouldn't, clearly, because if he had, then everything he would've done since that point would've been an escalating act of violence to get the show shut down, not these penny-ante annoyances. "Now the press has got hold of what's been going on, and even if I do open, it's unlikely anybody will come see it. I'm damned no matter how you look at it. I'll never earn back the money I owe Vinnie."

I felt for Walter. Sure he was a drunk with wandering hands and bad breath, but he wanted his career back so badly that he'd made a deal with the devil. It had to be devastating to learn that the risk you took was a poor one.

"Any press is good press," I said.

He flashed me *The Times*'s "News of the Stage", which began with the lead, "London may have had its Blitzkrieg, but rumor has it New York is about to be hit by an even bigger bomb: Walter Friday's *Goin' South*."

"I'll never recover from this," said Friday.

"Maybe you could report him," Jayne offered. "Get the feds to raid the joint before we reach the deadline."

"He'd know it was me. He's told me since the get-go that if I breathed one word to the cops I was going to be missing a lot more than money."

"What if someone else did it?" I asked.

"He'd never buy it."

"No, what if it was clear who it was, if that person admitted it and everything. If Garvaggio was in the pen, there's no way he'd be able to pull out his money, right? We've got a week to get the show together, and I'm betting with no more accidents or interruptions it just might have some potential."

He wobbled to his feet. "I guess. But what you're suggesting is suicide. Nobody would cross Garvaggio like that. Any man who did would be dead by Monday."

I gave him a wide grin. "Then it's a good thing it's not a man who's going to do it."

"I know you feel bad for the horses, Rosie, but you're not going to squeal on Garvaggio, are you?" Jayne and I were on the street, a block away from the Shaw House. We'd waited to confer on what the next step was until we were well out of earshot of anyone who might be an interested party.

"Of course not."

She looked relieved for less time than it took for a gnat to blink. "You're not suggesting I do it?"

"Don't get your girdle in a knot—neither of us is going to do the deed." We needed someone who wouldn't have to worry about ret- ribution from Vinnie. There was only one person I could think of who could put the screws to him and walk away unscathed. "I have another person in mind, someone who deserves to see her rat of a boyfriend get his comeuppance."

"Gloria?"

"The one and only. Vinnie used to work for her pop, so he wouldn't dare hurt her. Not only is the guy stepping out on her, but he deliber- ately told her she had talent only to use her to bring down this show. That, to me, deserves revenge."

"But how are you going to get her to do it?"

"That's where you come in handy." We had two goals: set up a scenario where Gloria finds out about her no-good, two-timing boy-friend and get Garvaggio to spill about why Tony hadn't bothered to move Al out of Rikers. I was hoping we could accomplish both activities in one fell swoop.

We entered the Shaw House and crossed the lobby with the intention of heading upstairs to plan out our strategy. Before we made it halfway across the room, Norma Peate called out to us.

"I was starting to think you two didn't live here anymore," she said.

Norma was one of those girls I'd known forever but didn't know at all. She'd lived at the house almost as long as I had, but we'd restricted our conversation to hellos and good-byes, and neither of us seemed to want our relationship to go beyond that.

"You know how it is when you're a week from opening," I said. I thought we were done, so I showed her my back and started up the stairs.

"Did you get my note?"

I paused and turned around. "What note?"

"I left it on your door two days ago."

Jayne shook her head at me. Either someone had filched it or the cat had eaten it.

"Let's assume I didn't," I said.

"You had a phone call," said Norma. "From a Paul something."

"Ascot?"

Norma snapped her fingers. "That's the one."

My heart dropped into my feet. My contact from Jack's unit had called. And I'd missed it. "Did he leave a number?"

"He said there was no point. He was heading out in the next hour. He said he's called before—several times—and was disappointed you hadn't phoned him back."

"And whom do I have to blame for that?"

Norma showed me her palms. "Don't shoot the messenger. This is the first time I've answered that phone in weeks. He said he'd try again the next time he's in town."

"So he's gone?"

"That was how I understood it."

I fought tears. "When did he say his next leave was?"

"He didn't."

I stomped up the stairs and into my room. I did my best to slam the door, but the wood was so flimsy that it didn't provide the satisfactory bang I was looking for. I collapsed onto my bed, and the tears I'd held back came down hot and angry.

"I'm sorry, Rosie." Jayne crept back into the room, closing the door much more gently than I had.

"I hate this place," I said.

She sat beside me and gently combed her fingers through my hair.

"I can't believe I missed him. And what kind of awful, selfish woman wouldn't tell me I had a message?"

"They didn't know how important it was. And we have been pretty scarce."

I sputtered away her excuse. "And who the hell would take a note off our door like that?"

"It could've fallen off and gotten thrown away."

I rolled onto my back and stared at the ceiling. "Paulette had the right idea when she left. Nobody looks out for you but you." I was being melodramatic and I knew it, but I was too upset to care. Someone needed to be blamed for this and for once it wasn't going to be me.

Jayne retrieved a handkerchief from the night table and passed it to me. "You could hire an answering service. Write and give him the new number, that way you won't miss his call next time."

I blew my nose and mopped my eyes. "Assuming I could afford that, how do we know there'll be a next time?"

"Why wouldn't there be?" I glared at her, and she dropped her face to the bed. "Oh."

"Oh is right. I don't think we can depend on anyone making it to their next leave."

31 Caught in the Web

My anger had faded enough by morning that I was prepared to put Operation Gloria and Garvaggio fully in place. We weren't planning on initiating the mission until the lunch hour. Friday had had the stage manager call everyone the night before and tell us to be at the theater that morning to begin rehearsal. We had much to make up for, he said. And, I suspected, by changing the rehearsal time at the last second, he was hoping to foil any other accidents Garvaggio might have planned.

"You look low, Rosie." Zelda joined me in the audience, where I was watching the dancers strut their meager stuff.

"I've been better." I sighed and the night before's tears returned. There was no point in hiding them. "Last night I found out that one of Jack's shipmates called. He was in town and he'd promised he'd get a hold of me and tell me what he knew about Jack's disappearance. Apparently he'd been here for a few days, only nobody bothered to give me the messages, and now he's left again and who knows when he'll be able to reach me."

"Gosh, I'm sorry. I'm sure it wasn't deliberate. Whoever took the calls probably didn't realize how important it was."

"You sound like Jayne. I, on the other hand, think whoever it was probably didn't think at all. I'm really getting tired of paying to live someplace where my every move is monitored and my basic rights curtailed. Sure the rent is cheap, but does that mean I don't deserve to get my phone messages?"

"You could always move into Olive's house."

I hadn't expected the offer. As much as I liked Izzie, Zelda, and Olive, I always assumed the feeling wasn't reciprocated. "Thanks. I appreciate that."

"I'm serious. We have the room."

The Shaw House I could bear to part with, sure, but Jayne? We were two peas in a pod. "I'll think about it. When I calm down. Now's not the time to make drastic decisions."

By the time lunch rolled around I'd put Zelda's offer out of my mind so I could focus on the task at hand. Jayne offered me a wink and a nod from across the room before disappearing into the lobby, where she hoped to find Vinnie Garvaggio. I prayed for patience and approached a cluster of dancers who were pulling sweaters and skirts over their leotards.

"Hiya, Gloria," I said.

She turned to me and smiled. She'd painted a beauty mark to the right of her mouth, and it had begun to grow taller and wider from the dancer's dew that covered her face.

"Hi, yourself. Where's Jayne?"

"I thought you'd know. We were hoping you might want to join us for lunch again. We enjoyed your company so much the last time."

She beamed at the invitation. She may have had plans with the other dancers (or had at least inserted herself into their group whether invited or not), but there was something to be said for palling around with one of the leads and the best hoofer in the show. While we were chopped liver by everyone else's standards, we were royalty by hers.

"Why, I'd just love to," she said in her best Shirley Temple voice. Her ringlets were pulled back in a ribbon, and I was reminded of a friend's grandmother who'd gone so goofy she insisted on dressing in the ornate gowns she'd worn during the Civil War. "I've been thinking you two might be the perfect people to help advise me on my career. I've decided I don't just want to just be a dancer—I want to be an actress and singer too. Where should we go to eat?"

"It's your pick." I started down the aisle and toward the doors.

"Oh, nuts—I forgot. I still don't know where Jayne is. If we leave her behind, she'll never forgive me."

"Maybe she's in the ladies' room."

I made like I was thinking hard about her whereabouts. "You know what? She mentioned that she needed to take something up to Walter's office."

"Oh. So let's wait for her in the lobby."

"I think it may be better if we go up there and get her. The last time she was alone with Walter he chewed her ear off, and I have a feeling she'd appreciate a rescue."

Whether bolstered by her desire to help Jayne or by the chance to see Walter Friday and remind him of her assets, Gloria followed my lead into the lobby and up the stairs. We approached Walter's closed door. Just as I was about to raise my hand to knock, Jayne's laugh rang out two doors down. She was with Garvaggio and her timing, as always, was impeccable.

"That's strange," I told Gloria. "That's Jayne's laugh."

The squeal of delight repeated, followed by "Oh, Vinnie—you're terrible."

I put a finger to my lips and motioned for Gloria to quietly follow me. She slipped off her pumps, but in her heavy-footed, graceless way still managed to make noise. We crept close to his door, which had conveniently been left cracked open. We couldn't see what was happening, but we could hear every word.

Garvaggio's cigar smoke greeted us, and I found myself fighting a sneeze. I squeezed my nose shut as he murmured, "It's the God's honest truth. She couldn't dance her way out of a paper bag. And get this: she wants to be an actress. Can you imagine? I got socks that are more convincing than her. She'll find out soon enough, though. Ain't nobody going to work with her unless she can get someone else to do her a favor."

"If she's so bad, how come you cast her?" asked Jayne.

"At the time, it was because I wanted to make her happy. That's what I do for my girls: they want something—anything—I try to get it for them." I didn't have the courage to look at Gloria. She hadn't made a peep, and I didn't think it was beyond reason that she hadn't figured out who they were talking about yet.

"That's awfully sweet," said Jayne. "But what's the matter—you don't want to make her happy anymore?"

"Gloria and me are two steps from the finish line. It's time I start making another girl happy."

Gloria dropped her shoes to the floor, pushed me out of the way, and entered Vinnie's office like King Kong entered Fifth Avenue. I rushed behind her to make sure she directed her rage at the right person. Vinnie was tapping the ash off a cigar into a souvenir ashtray from the Stork Club. Jayne sat on the edge of his desk, too far away for Vinnie's chubby arms to reach her. Her legs were crossed, her skirt astray, and the show she was putting on was just conservative enough to keep the MPAA away.

"How dare you!" sputtered Gloria. Shirley Temple was gone, and in her place was a girl born and raised in the Bronx. "After all I've done for you!"

Jayne leaped off the desk just as Gloria swept her hand across it and sent the ashtray tumbling to the floor. It broke apart with a thunderous crack as Gloria approached Vinnie and shoved his shoulder. His chair was on wheels, and she sent him into a spin—an amazing feat considering his size.

Vinnie completed one revolution and started another. "Gloria, baby—take it easy. You misunderstood . . ."

She wasn't having any of it, thank God. "No talent. You said I had no talent! Why I oughta . . ." I thought she was going to belt him, and I think she did too. Instead, she stopped his chair mid-spin, plucked his cigar from his hand, and extinguished it on the sleeve of his $500 suit. "We are finished! And let me tell you, Vinnie Garvaggio, I'm gonna make it, and when I do, you're going to hear me laughing all the way from Hollywood."

She stomped out of the room and into the stairwell. A sound like a moose mating began strong and grew increasingly faint as she tramped down the stairs. She was crying.

"We better go to her," I said. Garvaggio was rendered mute by the unsightly gash in his suit sleeve, to say nothing of the angry red boil on his arm. I looked to Jayne, and she shrugged and followed me out the door.

We retrieved Gloria's shoes and found the woman herself in the lobby ladies' room, crying so hard she was choking on her own tears. I freed a roll of toilet paper from the wall and passed it to her, while Jayne huddled beside her and rubbed her back.

"I'm so, so sorry," Jayne whispered. "I went to see Friday and he wasn't in his office. Vinnie called me into his, and the next thing I know he's saying all those awful things. I would never steal another woman's man. Honest."

Gloria noisily blew her nose. "Is it true? Am I an awful dancer?"

Jayne and I looked to each other for help. What did you say in a situation like this? I'd thought Vinnie would make a pass at Jayne and Gloria would hear it, not that he'd mock her dream to another woman. We could lie to her to make ourselves feel better, or . . .

"You're not awful," said Jayne. "You're new, that's all. You should've seen Rosie when she was in the chorus."

I blushed and dropped my head to the floor. It was only fair that my humiliation become an object lesson to make someone I hurt feel better.

"She was awful at first, but the harder she worked, the better she got. You will, too—you'll see. You're out there with dancers who've done twenty, thirty shows before, most of them with years of ballet under their belt. Of course that's going to make you look bad."

Gloria snorted. Or hiccupped. Whatever it was, it wasn't pleasant. "Do you really think I'll get better?"

Jayne bit her lip and tossed me another look. We both knew what had to be said. "Absolutely. And I'll help you."

"We both will," I said. "I mean, I'm not going to help you dance, since clearly it's not my forte, but I'll gladly help you out with the acting thing."

Gloria smiled through splotches of ruined makeup and sighed heavily. "Thank you."

We weren't awful people. We'd turn this around for her or die trying. "You know, Gloria," I said, "I can't get over the way he talked about you in there. If my boyfriend did that—"

"Shhhh . . ." said Jayne.

"No, she needs to hear this. You have to stand up for yourself. If the relationship is over that's fine, but you deserve better than him throwing himself at another woman and telling her those kinds of things about you. I mean who's to say, he hasn't been going all around town doing the same thing since you two met?"

Her tears stopped and her chin rose. "That might be why I hadn't been able to get work until now."

"Absolutely," I said. "Vinnie's a powerful guy, and when you combine that with a big mouth, you've got trouble."

Gloria raised her chin further, giving us full view of her nostrils. "It's not fair. I was always good to him."

"He needs to pay," said Jayne. "He needs to know that he can't treat a woman this way."

Gloria's eyes narrowed and she nodded. "I should call his wife."

That wasn't the answer we were looking for. "Do you really think he'd care?" said Jayne. "Chances are she already knows he steps out on her."

"Then what do I do?"

"Hit him where it hurts," I told her. "Aim for his pocketbook."

Over egg salad sandwiches at Mancuso's, we gave Gloria the lay on the meat trade going on after hours and who she should call to shut it down. Like us, she was mortified at the thought of horse meat being sold as beef. It wasn't the cruelty that bothered her so much as the inconsiderateness of the act. And the frugality.

"He's brought me tons of meat before. I'm sick just thinking about it. I mean, Vinnie won't wear the same shirt twice, yet he has no problem feeding people horse? That's just like him."

We didn't argue. Instead, we told Gloria to call the police as soon as she got home and report what was going on. She was angry enough that she didn't want to wait that long. Instead, she abandoned her sandwich and told Jayne she'd see her later.

"Did Vinnie say anything else useful before Gloria and I arrived?" I asked Jayne. I searched my egg salad sandwich to make sure there was nothing meat-colored lurking inside it. The inspection complete, I placed bread on bread and took a bite.

It may have been meat-free, but that didn't mean it was edible.

"Not a word," said Jayne. "I told him I used to date Tony just like you said, but aside from a few choice words about the remarkable Tony B., he didn't say anything about Al or why he might still be at Rikers."

That wasn't good. Vinnie was the easy way to information, and if he wasn't budging (and he certainly wouldn't be after Gloria's phone call), that left only two equally painful paths to follow: talk to Al again or talk to Tony.

"At least we saved the show," said Jayne.

I fought to swallow a mouthful of surprisingly dry egg salad. "No, we saved the funding. The show may still flop, but our days of random accidents are over."

32 The Awful Truth

EVERYTHING WENT DOWN LATER THAT night. The police raided the theater and caught Vinnie red-handed with a supply of freshly butchered horsemeat being packaged by his lackeys. He was taken in, though it was clear he wouldn't be held for longer than a couple of weeks. Men like Vinnie had good mouthpieces who saw to it they kept their hands clean and their time minimal. That was good enough for us, though. As long as Vinnie was locked up when the show opened, Walter would stand a chance to recoup the money he'd borrowed.

Gloria was jubilant the next day. Having done something to punish Vinnie, and having our promise to help her become a better performer, she was ready for the next stage of her life to begin. We still needed one more favor from her: she had to let Vinnie know she was the stoolie who'd squealed and that she'd be all too ready to testify to that effect if he made one move to hurt Walter Friday in the future. She agreed to do so, and while we weren't there for that conversation (she insisted on doing it face-to-face), it was clear Gloria walked out of the 19th Precinct a changed woman. Vinnie Garvaggio would not be a problem in the future.

While Jayne and I were feeling pretty good about ourselves, nothing we'd done had helped free Al. There were only two ways that was going to happen: convince Tony to spring him or find out who really killed Paulette and let the coppers know they had the wrong man. Two days after Garvaggio was hauled off, I was back at rehearsal trying to figure out how to solve the unsolvable problem. The most logical person to have murdered Paulette was a jealous boyfriend or

fiancé, but I couldn't buy that George Pomeroy was capable of something like that. He was too soft, his pain too palpable to have smashed
a lamp over the head of the woman he loved.

The other possibility was that someone had killed Paulette to
improve her career. As much as I hated to admit it, murder wasn't
Ruby's style. She didn't need to kill someone to get a good role.
Minnie, on the other hand, may have thought she would be bumped
into Paulette's role after she died. When that didn't happen, she may
have sabotaged Ruby in hopes that she could still secure the part.
Perhaps she even caused Olive's accident, hoping for the same. But
Minnie wasn't that motivated. She didn't seem to care much about
the production, and she'd never said anything to indicate she had
high aspirations.

Walter instructed us all to take our places, and I joined Ruby
backstage right, where she was pretending to look over her script.
Since it was obvious she didn't want to speak to me and since the feeling was mutual, I kept my distance from her and tried to concentrate
on my own lines.

It was a surprisingly good rehearsal, until the first musical number. Then, as always, the tight acting, strong characters, and amusing
songs were felled by the still sloppy dance routines. I watched from
the wings, alternating between cringing and laughing. Jayne was
still Jayne, doing her best to make magic from muck, but the rest
of the crew seemed to have abandoned hope that they could elevate
this production from anything more than a farce. As they cleared
the stage to make room for the next scene, I crept behind the scrim
to kvetch with Jayne, leaving Ruby alone to wait for her entrance.
I made it to the rear of the stage when I heard a snapping noise. I
looked upward for the source of the sound and was instantly felled
by the heavy black velvet drape that had been hanging above me. As
I struggled to free myself from the fabric, something landed with a
thud several feet away.

Ruby screamed. An enormous metallic clatter followed her yelp of
distress, and I thrashed about until I found light. I wrestled myself

loose and half-ran, half-stumbled to offstage right. There I found Ruby on her back in a pile of metal folding chairs that had been set up for our use.

"Are you okay?" I asked. The other actors huddled around us, uncertain how to react. Walter Friday made it to my side and offered Ruby his hand. He pulled her to her feet, and we watched in silence as she assessed her injuries. Sore and bruised, perhaps, and mute from the shock of the fall, but otherwise she was fine.

Now that the victim's condition was known, we all hunted for an explanation for what had happened. I searched the fly space for the source of the noise and the reason for the curtain's abrupt fall. As I looked, Jayne grabbed my arm and directed my attention downward. A sandbag lay to the left of the folding chairs, its fabric stamped 120 POUNDS. It had burst on landing, and now the stage was littered with fine white grains.

Jayne took hold of my arm and pulled me down until her lips could meet my ear. "Garvaggio?"

I shook my head. "No way. Gloria put the fear of God in him."

We scanned the crowd, trying to eyeball the culprit. If anybody on the stage was behind this, they didn't tip their hand. They all looked shaken, aware that it easily could've been any one of them standing where Ruby was.

The stage manager appeared with a broom and dustpan and Friday momentarily closed his eyes and rested his fingers on his eyelids. When he'd summoned the courage to move forward from this moment, he clapped his hands and announced that we were going to take a one-hour break.

Ruby rushed out of the auditorium, and I followed behind her. Her usually confident stride grew hunched as she propelled herself onto the rain-soaked street. She hadn't brought her coat or purse with her, and like a wild-eyed dog she searched out a safe place to hide from her invisible pursuer.

"Ruby, wait!" I called out.

She spun toward my voice. "I don't want to talk to you."

"Are you all right?"

"I'm fine." She turned again, determined to move as far as she could from what had just happened in the theater.

"I think we need to talk about what happened."

"It was an accident. Just another accident."

"What about the notes?"

If she was surprised that I knew about them, she didn't show it. Instead, her face lit up with embarrassment as if I'd just revealed that I knew that she had a crush on someone who didn't return it. "It's someone's idea of a joke. That's all. Please—leave me alone." She left the safety of the awning and rushed back into the rain. Before I could follow her, a hand grabbed my wrist and pulled me back to the theater.

"Let her go," said Izzie. "She had a scare. She wants to be alone." She pulled me into the lobby, where Zelda sat reading an issue of *Liberty Magazine*. The cover asked, "How Strong Is Hitler's 1943 Air Force?"

"These accidents have got to stop," Zelda said as I came in. "Someone needs to talk to Friday about it. She could've been killed."

"This isn't Friday's fault," I said. "And this isn't just another accident." I gave them the lay on Vinnie Garvaggio and what we'd done over the last two days.

"Maybe he sent someone else," said Izzie. "It's not like he doesn't have people working for him."

"Believe me—the last thing he wants is Gloria to testify about what was going on here. If she doesn't come forward, he goes free. It's not worth it for him to continue messing with Friday. Besides . . . Ruby's been getting notes."

Zelda and Izzie exchanged a look before they both tipped their heads toward the floor. "What kind of notes?" asked Zelda.

"Threatening notes. About Donald Montgomery. Someone isn't too happy she's engaged, and they made it clear they'd rather she break it off now. *Or else.* I think what we just witnessed was their 'or else.'"

Another look passed between them. It was getting maddening being around them, like I was a foreigner forced to listen to them speak a language I didn't understand.

"Do you two know something?" I asked.

"No," said Izzie.

Zelda put her hand out to stop her. "Maybe—"

Izzie widened her eyes and increased her volume. "No. We have to talk to Olive first."

I was seconds from screaming. "If you guys know who's after Ruby, you owe it to her to tell her. If she ends up hurt or worse, it's on you."

"We don't know who's threatening her," said Izzie.

"Is that true?" I asked Zelda.

She nodded. "We have no idea who it could be. But we've all been getting letters from whoever it is."

Zelda and Izzie agreed to take me to the hospital to see Olive as soon as rehearsal was over. The remaining hours dragged by, their length increased by the sense of doom I suddenly felt. If they'd all been receiving letters, then it was safe to surmise that Olive's accident was no accident. And if that was the case, whoever was threatening them clearly wanted to do more than scare Ruby. Try as I might to focus on the show we were trying to save, my eyes kept wandering upward to where the remaining sandbags hung, waiting for release. Ruby remained skittish, continually searching the air above her to make sure nothing lingered there that might suddenly be set free.

When rehearsal came to an end at seven, we were all still unscathed. I let Jayne know I'd be home later but didn't tell her why. As much as I wanted her with me when I went to see Olive, she wasn't one of their confidantes, and I couldn't depend on them to be open with me with her in the room. Besides, she had plans to rehearse privately with Gloria and Lord knows that was as important as anything I might learn that night.

Zelda, Izzie, and I took a hired hack to East Seventy-eighth Street and filled the ferry trip to Welfare Island with idle chitchat about the show. Upon our arrival, the three of us set aside the casual air we'd tried to maintain and sulked our way into the building and up to Olive's floor.

She had been moved into a private room since our last visit, though how she could afford such accommodations was anyone's guess (her deceased husband, most likely). Her leg was out of traction and she was sitting upright. Dinner had just passed, and the remains of what looked like a pork chop sat glistening on the hospital tray.

"What a lovely surprise!" she said as we entered the room. She took in our solemn faces and toned down her enthusiasm to mildly pleased. "What's with the long pusses?"

"Ruby narrowly escaped ending up here with you today," I said. "She's been getting threatening notes for weeks now, and your pals just told me that all of you have been receiving the same."

Olive frowned and turned toward Zelda and Izzie. Izzie mouthed an apology, but Zelda stepped forward with her head high. "We had to tell her, Olive."

"They're just threats," said Olive. "Someone wants to scare us."

"You could've been killed," said Zelda. "Ruby could've too. That's not someone trying to scare either of you."

"It's a coincidence," said Olive. "I wasn't looking where I was going. I should've known better."

"And what about Paulette?" I asked. "Should she have known better too?"

"Paulette has nothing to do with this," said Olive. "Her killer's in jail."

Zelda put a hand on Olive's leg. "They got the wrong person. The guy in jail didn't kill Paulette."

Olive's mouth opened and closed so quickly that I expected to find she was controlled by marionette wires.

"What do the notes you've been getting say?" I asked.

Izzie and Olive looked away from me as though they feared I

could read the truth in their eyes. Zelda looked like she was about to do the same, then stopped herself. "They're about the men we've been seeing."

"Zelda!" Izzie took a step toward her.

"Honestly, Izzie, it's dumb not to say something. Maybe Rosie can help."

"How?" asked Olive.

"I used to work for a detective," I said. "And earlier this year I got to the bottom of another murder, one the police dismissed as suicide. Here's the crop—either you can put up with me or you can get on the horn and tell the coppers, but one of those two things is going to happen before I leave this room."

"Can we have a minute?" asked Olive.

I agreed and left the three of them alone while I wandered the hospital corridor. Every once in a while a voice rose loudly enough that I could hear it from my roost twenty feet away, but the content of the conversation was unknown to me. My curiosity was approaching boredom when Zelda poked her head out the door. "We're ready."

Izzie was seated beside Olive, holding her hand. Zelda took her place at the foot of the bed. "We want you to help us," said Olive. "We don't think the police would understand."

I pulled up a chair and made myself comfortable. "You've got my ear."

"Will you keep everything we say confidential?"

"Absolutely."

Olive nodded at Zelda and gave her the reins.

"We've been getting the notes since Paulette died," said Zelda.

"And what about Paulette? Was she getting them before she was murdered?"

Zelda left the bed and moved to the window. "Hers started in California. We don't know how long she was getting them before she moved here, but it was at least a few months. That's why she decided to move."

"She was scared?"

"She wanted to make a fresh start," said Olive, "and she thought that by moving she might be able to lose this pen pal as well."

"But she didn't?"

"We didn't know, until after her death . . . and even then, we didn't think . . ." Izzie's voice trailed off. "A few days after she was killed we were cleaning up her room and we found the notes and the envelopes they'd come in. She'd told us about California, but she hadn't mentioned she'd received anything here. There they were, though, with recent New York postmarks."

"And then we started getting them too," said Zelda.

I paced the length of the room, trying to make sense of what they were telling me. "Paulette I can understand. I mean, from what I picked up at the memorial she had two dead husbands, a new fiancé, and probably a boyfriend or two floating around."

"Four dead husbands," whispered Olive.

I raised an eyebrow. "It makes sense that a girl that popular was bound to cross the wrong person at some point, but why would this person come after all of you?"

"There's more," said Zelda.

"I figured there had to be."

She talked to her Ferragamos. "We all have dead husbands."

Something about the way she said it ruffled the hairs on the back of my neck. "That's rotten luck. So let me guess: whoever your pen pal is has been led to believe that you're bad luck. So they tell you to beg off your boyfriends because they think that by doing so they can keep them alive."

"Doesn't make much sense, does it?" said Izzie.

"It certainly doesn't," I said. "I'm as superstitious as the next gal, but it seems to me that if someone is willing to cut down Paulette to keep her out of a relationship, they better have more of a reason to do so than because they think you guys are black widows."

"We live in senseless times." Olive's peepers were wide and innocent, like a porcelain doll's glass marble eyes. "People have killed for much less."

"I'd like to believe you, but I can't. What aren't you telling me?"

Zelda's worried eyes coasted over to Izzie and Olive. Neither of them were willing to speak for her. She was on her own. "Olive married her high school sweetheart right before he shipped out. Two weeks later he was dead."

"His name was Bobby," said Olive.

Zelda took a deep breath before continuing. Even though it wasn't her story, it affected her all the same. "When he died, the air force provided her with his pension and his insurance."

"I didn't want it," said Olive. "All I wanted was for him to be alive."

"Of course," said Zelda. "No one's saying otherwise." She swallowed. "One of Bobby's friends starting writing Olive not long after Bobby died. It started as a condolence thing, but the letters began to get more personal, and she knew he wanted something more than to talk to a dead friend's wife. Olive was torn—"

"No, Zelda—let me." Olive sat up straighter in her bed and released Izzie's hand. "I knew this man would likely die too. There were articles at the beginning of the war about how the pilots had the most dangerous jobs and that the mortality rates were expected to be the highest in the air force. I felt for this man who probably had only a few months left and didn't have someone back home to write to him or to tell him he was missed. He was scared and lonely, and all he wanted was what Bobby had had. Within a few weeks we were talking about getting married. I didn't love him, but I felt responsible for him, so when he came home on leave, I did as he asked and we went to city hall. He was dead a month later."

"And once again," said Zelda, "the money came."

Olive's eyes lost their empty innocence. Her entire face was pleading with me to understand. "I was living with Paulette and Izzie at the time, and I think we all began to realize that we could do the same thing—befriend these men, give them what they needed, including a wife. We started going to the USO dances, the Canteen—wherever we were likely to meet pilots. We offered to write to friends, brothers, and cousins—made it known that we were happy to become pen pals." She paused and licked her lips. "You have to understand how much we were all struggling then. Even Paulette was barely making a living wage. The war had been hard on the theater—nobody knew how long it would last and what people would be willing to see. I was in two shows that closed before they opened. We were living hand to mouth."

I felt sick. They weren't just marrying men for their allotment money; they were banking on their dying so they could get their hard-earned cash. "How did you get involved in this?" I asked Zelda.

She didn't answer me. It wasn't hard to imagine what had happened: a few visits to the Canteen, Izzie's emotional sermon about how much the men needed Zelda, and the next thing she knows she's living in their brownstone, wearing fancy rags, and preaching their gospel.

"And if they hadn't died?" I asked. "What would you have done then?"

"Some of them didn't die," said Izzie. So that's how it was: none of them were capable of predicting who would die, so they married as many men as they could to increase their odds. And I would bet dollars to doughnuts they hadn't anticipated what they would do when some of these men came home.

Lucky for them, it looked like it would be a while before they had to find out.

"What went wrong?" I asked.

"Everything was going well," said Olive, "Until Paulette's Michael died."

"Roger," said Zelda. "His name was Roger."

"She was out in California and had just been tapped for a small part in *The Gang's All Here* when she got the first letter."

"What did it say?" I asked.

Now that Olive had decided to tell me the truth, it came out in a rush of words that moved so fast her mouth became dry and she had to pause for a drink of water. "That she was being watched. That the

writer knew she'd been married before and knew Paulette planned
on doing the same to another man. It was clear this person had been
following her for a while. They threatened to tell the press she was
a bigamist, threatened to ruin her career for accepting money that
wasn't rightfully hers. When neither of those threats caused Paulette
to return the money to Roger's family, the letters changed tone. She
would be hurt if she didn't stop what she was doing. She might even
die."

Olive paused and for a long, quiet moment we took in what
must've happened.

"She moved here to get away from the threats. She was convinced
that everything would stop once she left California. And it did for a
few weeks, but then she discovered another letter."

"And eventually," I said, "whoever was threatening her made good
on their word. How did her killer find out about the rest of you?"

Izzie stepped forward to answer the question. "They probably
followed us to the Canteen. Who knows?"

"So why not just stop? If you're all being threatened, if someone
killed Paulette and ran Olive down, why not give this person what
they want and stop playing this game?"

More silence. Olive picked at her engagement ring. Zelda looked
at her feet, at the expensive shoes that had saved her the day Olive
was hit. Izzie nibbled on a carefully manicured nail, no doubt polished that morning at a Fifth Avenue salon that called her madam
and served her champagne as she waited. Money, they all did it for
money and nothing—not even fear of death—made them willing to
give it up.

"Why bring Ruby into this?" I asked. It was hard to keep the
venom from my voice. I wanted to announce how sick I felt, but I
knew the moment I did, their cooperation would end.

"We work as a group," said Olive. "The more women who partici-
pate, the more men we help."

And the more money they could expect to roll in. They must
all pool their allotment money and any insurance dividends so they

could still receive income even when their pick had the nerve to stay safe and healthy. That's why they lived together.

It was hard to be more disgusted with Ruby than I normally was, but here I was wondering if it was possible for her to sink any lower.

"We're not bad people, Rosie," said Olive.

"Of course not." The venom was there now. I couldn't fight it anymore.

"The men who died were going to die whether we married them or not. They were glad to give us something in return. They were grateful for what we gave them."

"And what about the men you're still married to, the ones who haven't bothered to die yet? What are they getting from you? A few letters? A quick roll in the hay? At least the whores in Hell's Kitchen admit what they are and what their going rate is. Your men don't even know the score until they're six feet under."

"That's not fair!" said Izzie.

"Maybe it's not. I don't know. I think I better go." I picked up my pocketbook and started toward the door.

"Will you help us?" asked Zelda. I turned back to her. Her eyes were wide, and I swore I saw the tiniest bit of regret in them. What would she undo: conning these men or convincing her friends to tell me about it?

"Ask me tomorrow," I said. "Right now I'm tempted to let whoever this is kill the lot of you."

33 Weak Sisters

I TOOK A CAB HOME. I was too numb to board the subway and be part of the evening bustle. And I couldn't stomach the thought of watching enlisted men take their last ride before they were shipped out to God knows where. Once home, I stumbled drunkenly through the lobby and up the stairs. Light was visible beneath Ruby's closed door. I was tempted to bang on it until the entire house filled the hallway to bear witness to what she'd been up to, but I didn't have the strength. It wouldn't matter anyway. Ruby never cared what other people thought, and nothing I could say would change that.

"Hiya, stranger," said Jayne. I lingered in the doorway for a full minute while she watched me. When I couldn't bear the distance anymore, I rushed to her side and collapsed in her arms. The waterworks began the moment I touched her. "Shhhhh . . ." said Jayne. "What's the matter? What's happened?" It took me ten minutes to get under enough control to tell her the story. Jayne listened in silence, punctuating my tear-soaked sentences with a brush of my hair and a squeeze of my hand. "It's horrible," she said when I'd finished. "But it's not your fault. You didn't do anything."

She had hit upon the crux of my misery: I could've been one of them. If I kept listening to them, how far was I from falling down the slippery slope that led to a loveless marriage and insurance dividends?

"All this time I thought they were good people, and here they were taking advantage of these men. What could make them think that was all right?"

This was the side of war none of us wanted to acknowledge, that maybe the country our men were fighting for didn't deserve that degree of sacrifice. We weren't all good people. We sold forged bonds, collected for phony charities, and gave soldiers venereal disease in record numbers. We preyed on the grieving with overpriced funerals and the hungry with black market meat that wasn't what it claimed to be. We could be worse than the enemy, at least as cruel. I certainly wouldn't have risked my life for us.

"What are you going to do?" asked Jayne.

"What I want to do is nothing. But what I need to do is find out who the killer is, for Al's sake."

Jayne left the bed and went to the closet to retrieve our booze bottles. She paused in her activity just long enough to click on the radio: 434 missing were added to the army casualty list; meat shops were reported bare all over the city; and a priest, smuggling $87,000 in cash and an untold amount in valuables, had died on a train. Even our clergy couldn't be depended on to be good people.

"You know. . ." Jayne's voice faded as she focused on finishing mixing our drinks. "It makes sense that it's a family member."

"Who's a what?"

Jayne handed me my drink. "The killer."

We were back there.

She sloshed gin over the rim of her glass and carefully wiped the excess clean with her finger. "Logic wants us to think it's a jealous ex-girlfriend, right? But think about what Paulette actually did. She married a man for his allotment and his benefits, money that should've gone to his family. If they were depending on that cash, it would be pretty difficult to swallow Paulette getting all that dough."

I nodded as quickly as she spoke. "And it would be even worse when they found out she was getting married again."

"Or if they found out she was already married." Jayne took a long swallow of her drink. "You said all this trouble started after one of Paulette's husbands died. Maybe it was someone in his family who snapped."

"Do you think the answer could be that obvious?"

Jayne toasted me with her half-empty glass. "It's about time something was."

It took her a little while, but Zelda was able to come up with a name for me. "His name was Roger Armstrong. He was from Norman, Oklahoma."

I scribbled the name on the pad by the phone. "And it was after he died that Paulette started getting the letters?"

"Yes." Zelda fell silent, and I tried to read in the hiss of the line what she was thinking. "I want you to know: I've been married only once. It wasn't just about the money. I would've been quite happy ending up with him."

"Fortunately, you don't have to find out if that's true."

"If I had just met him, if I'd been through one of those whirlwind courtships without any thought of the outcome, things still would've turned out like this. None of us killed these men. We didn't take anything that they didn't want to give us." Her voice was choked with tears. She needed to convince me as badly as she needed to convince herself.

On the surface, she was right. Just like the contractors who were growing fat from the war, and the black market dealers who would be able to retire on what they made, what Zelda and her friends had done was nothing more than taking advantage of an awful situation. It was the inhumanity of their actions that chilled me, the way they sought out men who were going to find themselves in the most dangerous positions, and instead of waving away the right to their money, they saw it as payment for a job well done. A marriage no matter how tragic wasn't a job, and the only payment they should've wanted to accept when it ended was the memory of the time they'd shared with a man they loved.

That was the problem: love didn't enter the equation.

"You didn't have to take anything," I told her. "Did it ever occur to you where your husband's money would've gone if he hadn't married you?"

She stuttered. "No."

"Well, I bet it occurred to someone. Maybe even whoever it was who bumped off Paulette."

"Are you going to help us then?"

"I'm going to help someone who's been led to believe that they have to do the wrong thing in order to make the right thing see the light, but no—I don't see that there's anything I can do to help you."

Four phone calls and twenty minutes later I had a number for the Armstrong family of Norman, Oklahoma. There was only one of them, thank God.

"Ready?" asked Jayne.

I nodded and asked the operator to connect me. I was going to have a hell of time explaining the long-distance charges to Belle.

"Hello?" An older woman's voice answered the line.

"Is this Mrs. Armstrong?"

"One moment please." The phone was put down, and the voice summoned another. There was a polite distance in the way they spoke to each other, not as relatives talked but the way an employee addressed an employer.

"Yes?"

"Good evening, Mrs. Armstrong. My apologies for calling so late. My name is Rosie Winter and I was a friend of your daughter's some years ago. I was wondering if you might be able to tell me how to reach her. We lost touch and it's very important that I speak to her again."

"I'm afraid you must be mistaken, dear. I don't have a daughter."

I hadn't anticipated that. Perhaps this was a Mrs. Armstrong, Sr. "Are you Roger Armstrong's mother?"

"Yes I am. I was." The wound was still fresh. I could hear it in her voice. "Roger's not with us anymore."

"I know and I'm sorry." My tongue had become too fat for my mouth. "How is his brother?"

"Roger was an only child, dear. What's this all about?"

"I seem to have made a mistake is all. I met someone once who I thought might've been related to him."

"It could've been Paulette," she said. Although the grief remained, her voice became increasingly tender. I could picture her staring at a photograph of the two of them, her fingers gently trailing the outlines of their faces. "That was his wife. Lovely girl. Looked a lot like the family. More than one person said they could've been kin."

"I'll bet that's who it was. I'm sorry for bothering you."

"She's gone now too. It seems like all the young people are."

I couldn't think of a response. I put the blower in the cradle and held it in place just in case the power of her grief forced it up again.

"What happened?" asked Jayne.

"Roger was an only child, and now his mother gets to spend the night confronting his ghost thanks to me."

"I doubt a day goes by that she doesn't have to deal with that, Rosie. You know what it's like. If you hadn't reminded her of him today, a photo might've or a lost sock or who knows what."

I followed Jayne back to our room and slumped onto my bed.

"Maybe it wasn't a brother or sister," said Jayne. "Maybe it was the mother."

"I don't think so. A housekeeper answered the phone. If Mrs. Armstrong has the bees for servants, I doubt she's so desperate for cash that she'd want revenge on someone."

"Maybe it wasn't the money. Maybe it was the principle."

"No, she mentioned Paulette. You can't fake that kind of adoration." I lay on my bed and Churchill joined me, wrapping his body around my arm. "I should've known it couldn't be that easy."

Jayne picked up a copy of *Screenland* with Veronica Lake on the cover and aimlessly flipped through the pages. The cover teased an article called, "Why I Won't Be a Furlough Bride." "So now what?" she asked.

"We could ask Olive and Izzie to tell us the names of every man Paulette ever had contact with."

Veronica shook her head in disagreement. Jayne concurred. "Assuming they know who they were, that could take a lifetime."

Churchill had had enough of my companionship and left my side. "Or we could wait and see what happens. Clearly, whoever this is has their eye on Ruby."

Jayne froze mid–page flip. "Should we tell her what's going on?"

I closed my eyes and wished away the whole awful day. "Why should we tell her? If Ruby was willing to get involved in this scheme to begin with, she deserves to be scared for a while."

34 Good-bye to Love

Naturally, I had no intention of letting Ruby be killed. I wasn't completely heartless. For the next two days I shadowed her, leaving the house whenever she did and making sure I was a step behind her when rehearsal wasn't going on. At the theater I constantly analyzed whatever risks might be present. Friday, unnerved by the sandbag incident, had spent some coin to have the rest of the fly system inspected. Nevertheless, I spent the bulk of rehearsal with an eye set heavenward and an ear constantly listening for the telltale creak of danger.

With Garvaggio in jail and Gloria receiving some much-needed attention from Jayne, the production was finally falling into place. We worked harder than ever before, not because we needed to but because every one of us was starting to believe that the show stood a chance, and we didn't want to be the one person responsible for bringing down *Goin' South*. I did my best to hide my feelings toward Izzie and Zelda during rehearsal and continued spending my breaks with them to ensure that Ruby was safe. I thought I was doing a darn good job of acting like everything was normal, when Minnie cornered me.

"Did you guys have a falling out?"

It was disappointing to learn I wasn't that good an actress. "No. Why do you ask?"

"Everyone's being so polite toward one another. I just assumed that meant something had happened." Although her concern felt sincere, there was a glimmer of hope in her eyes. Maybe she believed that if I was no longer friends with Izzie and Zelda, Ruby might end her association, too, and things could go back to how they had been the month before.

"You know how it is," I said. "If you spend a lot of time together with someone, you're bound to hit a nerve now and again. Is there anything odd you've noticed about this show?"

"You mean like Vinnie Garvaggio's meat business and his attempts to shut things down?"

"Uh, yeah. Exactly like that."

"Well . . ." She looked around the room, cataloging all the information she'd accumulated over the past few weeks. "Debbie Ardo thinks she might be pregnant, which would be awkward considering her boyfriend's been overseas since last June. Judy Reeves is sleeping with the stage manager. And Zelda is looking for a place to live."

Wow. She was good. I hadn't known any of that. "How do you know about Zelda?"

Minnie shrugged. "I heard her talking to one of the dancers, asking them if they knew anyone with a room to let."

Perhaps that was why she was encouraging me to move into Olive's house; she was planning on leaving there. But why? Was she tired of their scheme, or did she want to keep her distance for another reason? "What about what happened to Ruby the other day? Did you see anything that might've led up to that?"

"I thought that was just another accident."

"Definitely not. Garvaggio's in the hoosegow, and that rope was cut."

"But—"

I cut her off. "Can you keep this on the q.t.?"

She nodded.

"Someone's been threatening Ruby."

"Why?" she asked.

I moved closer to her and lowered my voice. "I'm not at liberty to say. Any chance you might've seen or heard something that could help us figure out who it might be?"

The color rose in her cheeks. She was excited by the thought of helping Ruby. "No, but I'll keep my eyes peeled. Is Ruby scared?"

"Like a cat cornered by a bear. Don't say anything to her, all right? I'm not even supposed to know."

She nodded solemnly. "Don't worry—my lips are sealed."

Jayne and I were about to leave the theater that night when Zelda called out my name. No one else was around, so I shed my manufactured joy at seeing her and gave her a stern look that demanded she say what she wanted and quickly.

"Thanks for not saying anything to anyone," she said.

"Who's to say I didn't?"

"I know you, Rosie. You wouldn't have pretended everything was fine the last two days if you wanted to rat out the lot of us."

"I'm not doing it for you; I'm doing it for Ruby. I might hate what she's doing, but I don't want to see her die for it."

"Are you coming with us to the Canteen?" She was dressed to the nines, as always. Her floral silk dress was topped by her black fur coat, and on her feet were a pair of suede Palizzio platforms I hadn't seen before.

I shook my head. "Nope. I'm going home. I think I'm done with the Canteen."

Zelda sighed. "I know we've made an awful mess of things."

"That's the understatement of the year."

She put her hand on my arm. "I agree that it's wrong. I've thought that for a long time. I want to do the right thing."

"Then don't go to the Canteen tonight. And don't let Izzie or Ruby go either."

"It's Saturday. They need us there."

I shrugged off her hand and started toward the doors. "Sure they do, Zelda. Just like you need that mink coat."

•   •   •

Jayne and I exited the subway early and walked the remaining distance home. I needed the cold air to clear my head and quell my rage. "I don't know why I bother," I said. "Whoever killed Paulette had the right idea."

Jayne struggled to keep pace with me. "Zelda's right, though. About the Canteen. It's a good place."

"I'm not arguing with that. It's a great place, but I can't see myself spending one more evening there knowing what they've twisted it into."

We paused in front of a shoe shop and admired the things we couldn't have bought even if we weren't limited by ration coupons. White satin mules strutted beside black platforms adorned with pearls. Just seeing the ridiculous display made me angrier. Men were dying so that Izzie, Olive, and Zelda could wear shoes like these.

Zelda. Something about her didn't sit well with me, and it wasn't just her involvement in Olive and Izzie's scheme. She'd been the one who'd convinced the others to come clean, and she'd hinted to me before that I needed to stand up for myself if Olive and Izzie tried to get me to do anything I wasn't comfortable with. Was she torn by their lifestyle, or was there another reason it was important to her for me to know she wasn't as bad as the others?

"I'm surprised at you," said Jayne.

"How so?"

"I wouldn't have thought you'd give up so quickly."

I started walking again. "Who's giving up? I said I'd keep Ruby safe and I will."

Jayne took my arm and held me in place. "I mean about the Canteen. Why let them ruin it? Why not tell Elaine what's going on?"

"They'll just find another way to meet men."

"But you'll cut off one outlet, right? That has to count for something. At least we'll know the men going to the Canteen are safe. And given how many men go there, odds are the truth of what's going on will spread fast. Who knows how many other people we might save?"

She was right. We owed them that much.

We made it to the Canteen at ten after eight. Glenn Miller and his orchestra filled the tiny stage, knocking elbows as they played "Goodbye, Little Darlin', Goodbye." The dance floor was packed with swaying couples who were trying to convince themselves they would miss each other like "the stars would miss the sky." I searched out Ruby and Zelda and couldn't find either of them. Izzie was there, though, dancing cheek to cheek with a man in a leather bomber jacket.

"Whoa, girls." Elaine blocked our path. "Call time is five o'clock."

"We're not here to work," I told her. "We're here talk to you. In private."

She scanned the room to make sure everything was safely under way. "Let's try outside," she said. "I could use the fresh air."

We went into an alley beside the building. Upon our arrival, couples scattered like mice lest Elaine should catch them doing what the Canteen manual forbid. "Let me guess," said Elaine. "Someone you know is seeing someone outside the club."

"A couple of someone's," I said.

She pulled out a cigarette case and offered us the contents. I shook my head while Jayne plucked free a gasper and accepted a light. "Names?" asked Elaine.

I found an abandoned crate and pulled it over to her. "I think you may want to sit down for this."

We told her everything we knew, and as the details progressed from breaking rules to breaking hearts, Elaine sank down on the crate and smoked down cigarette after cigarette with shaking hands. "Of all the rotten . . ."

"We know," I said.

"They're banned for life, I'll tell you that much." She dropped a cigarette to the ground and extinguished it with her low-heeled abner. "And I'll see to it this story gets circulated faster than a Betty Grable poster. Any idea who they've been targeting lately?"

"Aside from the pilot Izzie's clinging to tonight, not a one," I said.

"I'll find out," said Elaine. "There have got to be other girls who've noticed. The nice thing about staffing the joint with actresses is they're never afraid to stab one another in the back." She stood up and smoothed her apron. "If you'll excuse me, I have some volunteers to kick out."

"Mind if we stay?" I asked. "We'd kind of like to watch this go down."

She looked from Jayne to me and momentarily softened the harsh matron face she'd spent the last year perfecting. "Suit yourselves." The scowl returned. "But next time be here by a quarter to five."

She left and Jayne took her spot on the crate. "Good for you."

"It was your idea."

"Still, you did the right thing."

I tipped my head toward the sky. "Then why do I feel so guilty?"

"Because they were your friends."

"Some friends."

"They weren't all bad, Rosie. Nobody can be." It was a tough thing to accept during a time of war. There was no such thing as pure evil. Maybe even the Germans and the Japs had good in them.

The door swung open and the sound of "Breakin' in a Pair of Shoes" drifted outside.

Jayne couldn't keep her feet still. "I love this song."

"Then go dance to it."

"I just might do that." She started into the building, then paused. "You coming?"

"I'll be in in a few minutes."

She left and I exited the alley and walked the space in front of the building. The couples Elaine had scared away had returned. Some talked. Some held hands and stared into the night. And some kissed, not caring that the blackout didn't provide perfect privacy.

One of those couples looked awfully familiar.

"Zelda?" I said.

She pulled away from her redheaded pilot and looked at me with a start. "I didn't think you were coming tonight."

"Apparently not," I said. "Hello, George."

George Pomeroy tipped his hat and tried very hard not to look like he'd just gotten caught with his pants down.

"He must be quite a hot commodity," I said. "Paulette *and* you? Is there a big inheritance, George, or did you decide to put all of your dough into a nice fat life insurance policy?"

"This isn't what you think," said Zelda.

"Then why don't you tell me what it is?"

She straightened up and tried to wipe the guilt from her face. "We're in love. Really in love. Right, George?"

He nodded.

"And how did that come to pass?" I asked. "Did you turn to each other over your grief for Paulette?"

"It was before that," said Zelda. "That night—the night Paulette was killed—George was with me."

"Is this true?" I asked.

George finally found his voice. "Yes. I . . . I didn't mean for it to happen."

"Neither of us did," said Zelda.

"So that's why you've been sneaking around and why you ended up staying at Olive's house?"

George nodded. "I cared for Paulette, and I thought I wanted to marry her. But the first time I met Zelda . . ." His voice trailed off.

It was all very romantic, but I couldn't let it pass without comment. "Do you know what she's been doing—what they've all been doing?"

I expected a no followed by a demand for an explanation. What I got was another nod. "She told me," said George.

"I'm not doing any of that anymore," said Zelda. "I haven't for some time. Not since Andrew died. I show up and dance, but George is the only man for me."

I hoped that was the case. If it wasn't, I hoped George lived long enough to regret it.

"Your friends can't be too happy about that," I said.

"They don't know. Yet." I raised an eyebrow, and Zelda sheepishly looked away. "They think I'm doing what you think I'm doing—going after George for the money. That's why they let him stay at the house. I figure I'll tell them the truth after the show opens, to keep the peace. I'm trying to find someplace else to live. I don't think they'll want me around if I'm not . . . helping."

The Canteen door opened and "Little Brown Jug" briefly filled the nighttime air. "I'm sorry to say I just ruined your fun. I put Elaine wise to what the four of you have been up to."

"I suppose we deserved that," said Zelda.

"Yes, you did. So, George, am I correct to surmise that you were the one who canceled the date with Paulette?"

"No," he said. "That part was true. I was going to break it off with her that night, but I really did get a message telling me the date was off. I ended up going to the Canteen."

"And you met up with Zelda after Izzie and Olive went home?"

George nodded so rapidly his hat flew off. "Exactly."

"Why did you come to see Paulette's room?" I asked.

As he spoke, Zelda watched him with a glint of jealousy in her eyes. Even though George was hers now, she couldn't stomach the fact that he'd once thought he loved somebody else. "Guilt, I guess. I was relieved when she canceled. In my heart I'm a coward." He took Zelda's hand in his. "If I'd done what I was supposed to—what I told Zel I'd do—than maybe Paulette would still be alive. She always talked about her days at the Shaw House. I thought if I went there, I could be close to her and ask for her forgiveness."

"I don't think that was necessary," I said. "If anyone needed forgiveness, it was Paulette."

"I didn't know that at the time." He looked at Zelda and she looked at him, and their faces were full of such love, such longing, that it was impossible to imagine that either of them had ever been coupled with anyone else.

"If I were you two, I'd scram before Elaine eyeballs you." I started on my way back into the Canteen.

"I have something for you," said Zelda.

I paused with one foot in the door. "What's that?"

She pulled a small packet of letters from her coat pocket and passed it to me. "It's not much, but it might help. These are the letters Paulette was getting."

"Thanks." I palmed the notes and watched as the two of them headed down the block. When they were out of sight, I entered the Canteen stairwell and struggled to read the letters by the dim, bare bulb that lighted the way. No dice. I stepped back outside and searched for a better light source.

"Rosie?"

Minnie was on the walk beside me.

"Funny seeing you here," I said. "Where's the fire?"

"I was wondering if you'd seen Ruby."

"Not a glimpse. Why?"

Minnie worked her fingers into pretzels. "I think I may have done something very stupid."

"I'll be the judge of that."

"Ruby told me this morning that she had a date tonight. Right after I got home from rehearsal she had a call. From a man. She wasn't home, so he asked me to tell her that he'd had a change of plans and he wanted her to meet him tonight at nine at the Bernhardt."

"Was it Donald Montgomery?"

"That's the problem: I don't know. He didn't give me a name, just said Ruby would know who it was. I've never spoken to Captain Montgomery before, so I wouldn't recognize his voice. Anyway, I told her about it, and she left the house a little while ago. I got to thinking about what you said about her being in danger, and it seemed to me that her meeting up with some man at the Bernhardt wasn't exactly the safest thing she could be doing, especially since this was a rather suspicious last-minute change of plans." That was putting it mildly. "I thought I'd better track you down and tell you."

"Good thinking. What time is it?"

She peeled back her glove and squinted at her watch. "A quarter till. We should go there, shouldn't we? Just to make sure she's okay."

"Yeah, I guess we should." I debated whether or not to get Jayne. There was a good chance this was going to be nothing but a trip for biscuits. And after everything that had happened with Tony, Jayne needed a night of fun and frivolity. There was no point in ruining both of our evenings.

We arrived at the Bernhardt and found the main doors locked and the lobby dark. I took Minnie around to the alley, and together we struggled to open the load-in doors. Bingo—they were unlocked and slightly ajar.

We crept into the basement and wound our way through the catacombs. I kept expecting to find Ruby lying in some darkened corner, but aside from ourselves there were no other signs of life. The room that had once served as Vinnie Garvaggio's butcher shop had been cordoned off with police tape. The other doors I hadn't been able to open stood ajar and were also designated as crime scenes. Their contents were finally revealed to us: large, commercial freezers hummed in these small, dank spaces. This was where the meat was stored after the horses were butchered.

We passed through the cross-under and made our way to the stairs that led up to Friday's office. We paused on the first landing—lobby level—and listened for a sign that anyone else was in the building. I put my finger to my lips and gestured for Minnie to stay low. Slowly, I peeked through the window in the stairwell door and searched out the lobby. Nothing.

"If she's coming, she hasn't arrived yet," I said. I pushed open the door and entered the lobby. Minnie clicked on the lights and I settled down for a wait with Paulette's letters.

"What are those?"

"It turns out Ruby wasn't the only one being threatened. The dame that died—Paulette—she was receiving letters too." I rifled through my coat pockets, searching for the letter Ruby had attempted to throw away.

"What are you looking for?"

"I palmed one of Ruby's notes a few days ago. I want to compare the handwriting."

Minnie nodded reverently. My hand landed on a piece of paper in my pocket and pulled it out. It was stuck shut, so I pulled at the seal and forced it open.

"Is it a match?" asked Minnie.

It wasn't even the right letter. I'd just pulled open the V-mail I'd never mailed for Ruby. Curiosity got the better of me, and I scanned the page. What I assumed would be an uncomfortable epistle trying to woo Captain Montgomery into marrying her was something quite different. It was a Dear John that took up less than half the page. She didn't want to see him again and, more to the point, she'd never cared for him to begin with. Their whole relationship was, she confessed, a game.

It would've been a pretty admirable letter if it had been in Ruby's handwriting.

35 Brother Rat

I LOCATED THE LETTER RUBY had thrown out several days before in my pocketbook. I rotated between the three pages. Ruby's threat, Paulette's threat, and Ruby's Dear John were all written in the same handwriting. I turned Ruby's V-mail over and found that it was addressed in a different hand. Clearly, the same person wrote all three of these letters, but someone else addressed the V-mail. That meant the culprit was able to switch Ruby's letter to Captain Montgomery with a note of his or her own and seal it up before Ruby addressed it.

But who would've had access to her mail?

"Is something the matter, Rosie?" asked Minnie.

I shoved the three letters back into my pocket and stood. "Not a thing. I don't think Ruby's going to show up. Maybe we should just call it a night."

"You know Ruby—she's always late."

"True, but Jayne's going to go goofy when she realizes I'm gone."

"I think we should stay."

I started toward the stairwell. "How about you stay, and I'll see if I can intercept Ruby before she's gets here?"

"I don't think that's such a good idea." Minnie pulled a revolver out of her pocket. The iron was so new I could see my reflection in it.

"Fine, have it your way." I grabbed air. "What's this all about, Minnie?"

"You know the answer to that."

"If I did, do you think I would've asked the question?"

The gun shook. It was heavy and she had trouble keeping it elevated. "It's not fair. It's not right to take advantage of them."

"I haven't taken advantage of anyone."

Her eyes glazed over. "These men are being stolen away from us, and instead of honoring them, you're looking for ways to bleed them dry. I won't let you do it."

I backed toward the door. "You're tooting the wrong horn, Minnie. I'm not seeing anyone. I'm not part of this scam. In fact, I'm the one trying to stop it."

She put both of her hands on the butt of the gun and rested a finger perilously close to the trigger. "I thought you were different, but then you went and saw that man at the Canteen again."

"Peaches? I made it clear to him that all I wanted was a few dances. Ask him if you don't believe me."

The barrel of the gun swayed like it was a living, breathing creature. "And then there was that man who kept calling the house, wanting to talk to you."

So that's why I'd missed Paul Ascot's calls and why Ruby had been upset that she hadn't been getting Donald's. Minnie was the one who'd intercepted them and who, presumably, saw to it that I didn't get the message Norma left on our door. "You're misunderstanding, Minnie. None of these men mean anything to me."

Even I knew how bad that sounded.

Minnie's hands shook again, and the revolver refracted the lobby light. "All the while your supposed boyfriend is missing in action. It's probably killing you that he hasn't been declared dead yet. After all, you can't get his money until you have a death certificate."

Things were going from bad to worse. "You're misunderstanding things. I can see how you would, but I'm not like the others. Jack and I weren't married, remember? I'm not waiting for money to come my way. I wouldn't want it if it did."

"Of course you are. You're just like them. It's a game to them. Do you know that? I've heard them talking about their conquests like they were baseball cards they'd collected. And why? So they could get money to buy expensive clothes and afford a nice uptown address. My dead brother paid for those things. And the sad part is if she'd ever really loved him, if he'd come home safe and started a life with her, he would've gladly bought her anything she wanted." So that was the link. Paulette must've been married to Minnie's brother, Mickey.

"She didn't kill him, though. You must understand that, Minnie."

She cocked the gun, and my stomach slid down to my ankles. "Don't you understand the hope she gave them? Each of those men left this earth believing she loved them. Do you think my brother would've taken the risks he did if Paulette hadn't kept telling him to be brave and strong for her? We didn't want him to be brave and strong. We wanted him to come home. We wanted him to live to see another Christmas." She began to cry. "And then to find out that she married again so soon afterward. Just like that, Mickey was forgotten. All of them were forgotten."

The stairwell door banged open. As Minnie turned to the sound, I dove on her and grabbed for the gun. She fired once, and a storm of plaster rained down from the ceiling. I pinned her arms to the floor and pushed all of my weight against her until she lost her grip. She yelped in pain as I tossed the gun toward the figure by the doors. Ruby bent down and picked it up.

"What are you doing here?" I asked.

"I'm going to guess the same thing you're doing here. Minnie told me I was supposed to meet someone here at nine."

It was 9:15. Ruby had, as always, kept us waiting.

Minnie began to sob from her place on the floor. "Someone has to stop them."

I approached her in trepidation. If she attacked me again, would Ruby stop her? Or would she be too busy looking at her reflection in the gun's surface? "Someone will stop them, Minnie. I've already told the Canteen what they're up to, and none of them will be working there anymore. I won't let any of them get away with it again. I promise."

Minnie lifted her tear-stained face to mine. "You can't promise that."

"Sure I can." I fished a handkerchief out of my pocket and passed it to her. "I've got friends who have ways of being persuasive. I imagine they could get those three girls to do just about anything they asked."

Minnie was arrested that night for the murder of Paulette Monroe and the attempted murder of Olive Wright. She also owned up to being behind Ruby's allergic reaction, though she claimed it wasn't to kill her. Like her attempts to intercept our phone calls and the letter she forged to Donald Montgomery, she thought if she could keep Ruby and me from seeing these men, she might be able to save both them and us.

Ruby went home with Jayne and me. While she had to know what could've happened to her if she had been on time for once in her life, she was too wrapped up in playing the heroine to acknowledge that things might've turned out very differently.

"I suppose I owe you a thank you," I said.

"That would be nice."

I dug my nails into my palms. Being grateful to Ruby was a hard state to find yourself in. "And while we're giving each other the things we deserve, how about you give me an explanation: Why have you been so awful to me?"

Ruby sighed and stared into the parlor fireplace. Blackened logs crackled as flames danced around them. "I wanted to keep you out of this. I thought if I made you feel unwelcome, if I planted enough doubts to make you uncomfortable with seeing another man, you might stay home. I guess I was wrong."

I couldn't have been more surprised if she'd lifted her skirt and shown me a wooden leg. "You were protecting me?"

"I suppose you could put it that way." I was strangely touched. I'd never known Ruby to do anything that wasn't for her own gain.

"What happened to your ring?" I asked.

Ruby looked down at her bare left hand. "I gave it back. George and I are through." She put her hand to her neck and massaged her tendons. The necklace George had given her was also gone. The only souvenir of their relationship was the vase of once-yellow roses rotting in the middle of the parlor coffee table. "It was awfully tempting. The money. The gifts."

"So why did you change your mind?" I asked.

"I do have morals, you know." And ambition. Unlike Zelda and company, Ruby had considered what would happen if her soldier came home. She couldn't stomach the thought of giving up her career.

There was no point in telling her that I knew this. Ruby had her own demons to live with.

"I'm glad you changed your mind about George," I said. "But I have to say, I'm a little disappointed that you leaped at the chance to meet another man at the Bernhardt tonight."

She threw her head back and laughed. "Not as disappointed as I am."

"I don't get you."

She fought a smile. "The call Minnie intercepted was from Lawrence Bentley. He's on leave and begged me to see him."

"Oh."

"He may be arrogant, close-minded, and self-absorbed, but he never once told me I couldn't be whatever I wanted to be."

There was a lot to be said for a man like that.

36 Raw Meat

WITH MINNIE'S ARREST, THE COPPERS didn't have a reason to continue holding Al at Rikers. He was released on the day the meat ration coupons went into effect, a fitting date for a guy who'd been locked up because of someone else's violation of the OPA's laws. I accompanied him on the ferry back to the city and let him know that Garvaggio was locked up and Jayne's relationship with him was nothing but fiction. I was expecting gratitude, or at least a return to the Al I knew, but he was as angry and solemn as ever.

"What's it going to take, Al? What do you want from us?"

He put his elbows on the railing and stared at the river. "It's not you—it's Tony. He's not going to be happy about this."

"Garvaggio's locked up. His meat business is kaput. What more could he want?"

"I betrayed him." I raised an eyebrow to express my confusion. "Tony wanted the stamps for himself, and the minute I refused to give them to him, I was dead to him."

So that was why Tony kept Al in the bing. He was hoping to force Al's hand and keep his own illegal meat enterprise running past April 1. "Does it really matter so much?"

He tossed me a sidelong look. "Tony's moving up in the world. He's getting closer to the guys who hold the strings. When someone crosses him, it's all that matters. Just ask Johnny Levane."

Johnny Levane, the body found in the Broadway alley the day after Al was arrested, wasn't just another random death. Tony had killed him or at least facilitated his murder. No wonder Al was scared.

I think he must've seen in my face that I understood his plight.

"Don't tell Jayne," he said.

"I won't."

"She doesn't need to know what's really going down."

"I agree." The river was cold and gray. I'd never seen anything quite so depressing. "She's not seeing Tony anymore."

"You think she means it this time?"

I shrugged. Al lit a cigarette and cupped his hands around it to try to warm them.

"Why didn't you just give Tony the stamps?" I asked.

He was silent for a long while, so long I almost thought he hadn't heard me. "This other stuff we do," he said. "It don't affect anybody except those who know what they're getting into. The meat, though . . . it ain't just charging people too much. You know that."

I thought back to the horses, to the sad resignation I'd seen in their eyes. That was just half the problem. The other half was what might happen to someone if they ended up eating meat that hadn't been taken care of properly to begin with. That was a danger that didn't just plague those of us on the home front. It was another peril that could put our soldiers in jeopardy.

"You've got a conscience," I said.

"I've had too much time to think not to."

I set my hands beside his on the railing. "Maybe though . . . maybe you should just give Tony the stamps. If it would fix everything between you two, if it would keep you safe."

Al took a puff off the ciggie. "I couldn't do that even if I wanted to."

"Why not?"

"The stamps are gone."

"How gone?"

He flicked his ash into the river. "They were in a Grand Central locker. I gave someone the key for safekeeping and they lost it for me."

"Some friend."

Al shrugged. "Maybe they were doing me a favor. Without the

key, I don't know the locker number. There ain't no way I can get 'em back."

I guess it was easier having a difficult choice made for you. "What about you? What can we do to keep you safe?"

He tossed his cigarette into the water. "I got an idea. There's a place I can go that Vinnie and Tony ain't gonna find me."

"When are you going to go there?"

A half smile lingered on his puss. "Soon, but don't worry—I'll let you know before I do."

We were silent for a few minutes, as both of us watched Rikers Island disappear into the distance. I found myself getting emotional at the thought of Al leaving. We'd just gotten him back.

I looped my arm in his and leaned against him. It felt good to stand so close to someone large and warm. Maybe I was wrong about Izzie, Olive, and Zelda. Maybe it wasn't all for the money. Loneliness could make you do the strangest things. "Any chance I can get you to do me a favor before you go?" I asked.

"Depends. What's the favor?"

"I got some friends that could use a little intimidation. They've been doing some things that I'd like them to stop doing before someone gets hurt."

Al cracked his knuckles. "It would be my pleasure."

True to my word, I didn't tell Jayne about what Al feared Tony was going to do. Instead, I told her Al was thinking about going straight. She was thrilled at the idea, though something else was clearly on her mind.

"You sure look distracted," I said. We were in our room killing some time after rehearsal.

"Oh, that." She smiled into her lap. "I got a letter today. From Billy DeMille."

"And what did he have to say?"

She produced the letter from under her pillow. "That he couldn't believe I wrote. He was starting to think the night he met me was all a dream." She blushed a deep pink. "Would you help me write him back?"

"I can't think of a better way to spend the evening."

Jayne started to hunt for a pen and paper and stopped mid-search. "Isn't tonight the night Peaches comes back into town?"

I'd forgotten about that. "I'm not going to meet him."

"Why?"

"It doesn't feel right. If it weren't for Izzie and Zelda, I never would've met him to begin with. After learning what they've really been doing, I'm starting to question my own motives."

Jayne frowned. "So you're just not going to show up?"

"It seems easier."

"For you, sure, but what about him?" I didn't answer. She tapped my knee with her index finger. "Just go, Rosie. Tell him the truth. Tell him about Jack. Let him know you want to be his friend."

"I'm sure friendship is the last thing he has in mind." And I wasn't entirely sure if it was in the cards for me either.

"Even still, you owe it to him to be honest. Isn't that what you wish Izzie, Zelda, and Olive had been?"

Damn she was good. I fell backward on my bed and groaned. "All right, I'll go."

A knock sounded at the door. I bounced to my feet as Jayne shoved Churchill into the closet.

"I got a bone to pick with you." It was Belle, at least I think it was. It was hard to tell for certain since she now whistled when she spoke.

I swung the door open and found her with an ice bag clasped to her face.

"What happened to you?"

She bared her teeth and showed me that one of her fangs was missing. "Your steak is what happened to me." She opened up her hand and showed me a red and white blob and a small gold object.

"What the deuce is that?"

She pointed to the blob first. "That was my tooth and this is the prize I found in the steak's gooey center." She dropped both items onto Jayne's dresser. "Shall I add my dental bill to your rent, or would you prefer to pay for it now?"

"Let's do the installment plan." I fought a grin. "I'm really sorry, Belle."

"You and me both. You had a call by the way. You got a visitor coming over at three."

"Who?"

"Said his name was Paul Ascot."

It was 2:45. She left the room, and I frantically ran a comb through my hair.

"This is it," said Jayne.

"This is it." Everything was working out. Minnie was in jail, Al was free, and now I was finally going to learn what had happened to Jack.

"Do you want me to come with you?"

"No, I think I need to do this on my own."

She plucked the tooth off the dresser and dumped it into the garbage. She was about to do the same with the gold object when I stopped her.

"Can I see that?" It was a brass locker key emblazoned with the number 2194. On the back were the initials G.C. "I think I want to keep this for a while."

"Suit yourself." Jayne took it back and examined it more carefully. "How does a key end up in steak?"

"Who knows? I guess this is why meat inspection is so important."

She dropped it on my dresser with a tinkle. "I bet someone's upset they lost it."

She was wrong about that. Someone was going to be thrilled when they found out I hadn't thrown it away after all.

I pocketed the key and decided to go downstairs to wait for Paul.

I'd made it to the landing when I saw someone was already down there waiting for me. He was early. My last link to Jack was sitting on the parlor sofa, waiting to spill.

As I rushed into the room, he stood and turned to me.

"Peaches? What are you doing here?" A lump rose in my throat. I hadn't resolved everything. I'd left this man hanging, and now here he was, expecting my decision.

"I'm actually here to see someone else." Good. He'd met another gal, someone who could give him what he was looking for.

"Oh." I struggled for something to say. "That's swell. What's her name?"

"Rosie Winter."

My jaw hit the floor. "You're Paul Ascot?"

"The one and only." He looked as confused as I felt. "Did Rosie mention me?"

I exhaled hard enough to muss my hair. "She kind of had to because I'm her."

"Your Jack's . . ."

I nodded. "I'm Jack's."

We let my ownership linger in the air for a moment.

"Why did you tell me your name was Delores?"

I forced a smile I didn't feel. "I wish I could tell you."

"I wish I'd known."

"You're not the only one." The room was suddenly very warm. If I didn't do something soon, my head was going to catch on fire. "Should we go somewhere else, somewhere private?"

"That would be good," he said.

We decided on a coffee shop two blocks away. I hadn't wanted to go someplace familiar. This encounter demanded fresh surroundings.

"I'm sorry," I said. "For the fake name. For not being completely honest with you."

"You don't need to explain." His demeanor had changed. No longer was he the fun, flirty man who'd danced with me at the Canteen.

I felt like we'd already had our relationship and our breakup and now we'd met to divvy up the possessions.

The things I would normally say to right this kind of wrong seemed inappropriate under the circumstances. If I were to claim my feelings for him were genuine, I would be betraying Jack, and if I admitted that I didn't know why I was there or why I was so willing to kiss him good-bye, I would succeed in making myself look like even more of a louse.

Fortunately, Paul felt as awkward as I did and found it unnecessary to prolong either of our misery.

"I suppose I should cut to the chase," he said.

"All right."

The waitress delivered our twin cups of joe and retrieved the menus we were clearly not going to order from. "There was a . . . situation a few months back. Not long after we set out for the Solomons. A boat disappeared with twelve men on it, Jack among them. The ship was eventually recovered, but only two men had survived: Jack and his commanding officer. The story the C.O. told was that the men were lost at sea. Jack seemed to go along with this, but then one day he cracked."

"Cracked?"

"Our C.O. was a tough guy, more so to anyone who didn't fit the mold. If you were black, brown, or yellow, or if there was a chance you were a nance, you became his target from that point on. Things were quiet after the men were lost; the C.O. seemed almost timid. Then one night he started screaming at this Mexican guy. Lopez was his name. Jack was there when it happened and got in the middle of the fight. Next thing you know, he was calling the commander a murderer. The C.O. pulled out his gun and fired a shot at Jack. He hit him in the leg. Jack was taken to the infirmary, and by morning he was missing."

I was finding it hard to breathe. "How do you know all this? Were you there?"

"I wasn't; Charlie was."

"Charlie?"

"Corporal Harrington."

The late Corporal Harrington. So that was how he fit into this whole awful story.

"I thought his first initial was M?"

"He was from Charleston."

"Right." Learning he had a nickname made his loss feel all the more profound. Corporal Harrington had been a real person. "And then Charlie—"

"Committed suicide," said Paul. "At least that's what the official record states. He took a bullet to the head. He lingered for a few days but never regained consciousness."

My lower body began to shake. "And Jack?"

"We don't know. Either the C.O. took care of him later that night, or he had the wherewithal to get out of camp before he could."

I stood up from the table. "We have to tell someone. We have to let everyone in the navy know what's going on. They have to find Jack."

"It's not that easy. Politically, the situation is a little sticky. Our C.O. wasn't just anybody. He's the son of a general."

I wound my scarf around my neck and pulled on my coat. "So? He's also a son of a bitch. Surely the military won't care who his pop is?"

"Unfortunately, they do." He sighed and studied his cup of coffee. "I've been trying to get someone to do something, Rosie. But nobody will. As far they're concerned, Jack snapped, Charlie killed himself, and our C.O. did the right thing. There was no evidence to support Jack's claims that anything untoward happened to the men who were lost at sea."

"So what are you going to do now?"

He looked surprised at the question. "Nothing."

"Tell me I misheard you."

"There's nothing I can do. Before my plane crashed, I was getting a reputation as a trouble boy, and I can't risk losing either my rank or my life."

Up until that moment, I would've admitted to anyone who asked that Paul Ascot was a handsome man. Right then, he became soft and unformed to me. "Then why did you even bother to see me?"

"I thought you should know what happened. I know how important that is. I thought you should know how brave Jack was and how he was trying to do the right thing."

Tears burned my eyes. My lone link to hope was lost. "Was, was, was. So that's it—you've given up."

"We have to, Rosie. There's nothing anyone can do."

So much of the stories of war emphasized how powerful everything was: the men fighting, the equipment they used, the weapons designed by our enemies. It was the powerlessness, though, that really defined war. That was how people became victims, how women became widows, how soldiers became lost. Not because the opposition was so much better than us, but because when you winnowed it all down, we didn't have the strength to change anything. We were impotent.

It didn't have to be that way, did it?

I tied on my hat and picked up my purse. "Maybe you can't do anything, Paul, but I'm not ready to say uncle yet."

I called Tony the next day and asked if I could see him. He agreed to meet me at the Bernhardt before rehearsal.

"Your friend's come around," I said.

"Jayne?"

"Your other friend."

He nodded to tell me he'd caught on. "He told me it was too late for that."

"He was wrong." I held up the key to show him I had it. He reached for it, and I closed my hand tight and slid it into my pocket. "Before I give you what you want, you have to make me a few promises."

"And if I don't?"

"I see this gets lost again."

He was silent for a moment, no doubt debating if he could pin me down and steal the key. "What do you want?"

"First, I want you to promise you'll leave Al alone. Tell me you'll keep him safe."

Tony bowed his head. "Consider it done."

"Second, do right. I don't have any problem with a man trying to make some money, but keep things safe. Our boys abroad are eating that meat. Jayne's eating that meat. Don't be greedy."

I doubt he listened to me on that point, but it had to be said.

He put out his palm for the key. "When do you think Jayne's going to come to her senses?"

"She already has, I'm afraid." I dropped the key into his hand. He slid it into the interior pocket of his suit and started to leave. "I've got more insurance, Tony."

He froze with his back toward me.

I swallowed hard and squeezed my toes together to try to keep myself from shaking. "I know about Johnny Levane. So that means at least two people know your business now, and I'm not afraid to turn canary if I find out you haven't kept your word. Vinnie Garvaggio's in jail and I think you know how he got there."

He slowly turned toward me, and his distended eyes became slits. "I don't like being threatened."

I stepped toward him and held my head up high. "So be it, but I'm not going to back down on this. And if you're interested in testing me, I'll make sure Jayne knows everything too."

He shook his head at me before turning tail and heading toward his car. I didn't exhale until he'd climbed inside and driven away.

Two days later, *Goin' South* debuted. While the reviewers noted the shaky script, they praised the clever choreography, diverse dancers, and universally strong performances. Friday couldn't have been happier. Unfortunately, his joy was short-lived. The same night we opened, a show debuted at the St. James called *Oklahoma!* While you would've thought our tale of a girl turned human radio turned war hero would've aced a sappy love story set among small-town Oakies, two names—Rodgers and Hammerstein—and innovative ballet choreography by Agnes De Mille seemed to give it more credence than our little production. It went on to run for 2,248 performances and had a multimillion-dollar gross. *Goin' South* would close just shy of six weeks. Luckily, that was long enough for Garvaggio to earn back his investment.

On the same day *Goin' South* opened, the USDA and OPA's new meat regulations went into effect. Mayor La Guardia made a public promise to jail anyone found with uninspected meat on their premises. He also urged all private citizens to report any instances they found of people violating the new laws. The American Theater Wing even got involved. They helped sponsor a play depicting the important role of food during the war. Part guide to the ration point system, part lament for American wastefulness and the evils of the black market, the Elia Kazan production was slated to run in 2,100 theaters throughout the United States.

Vinnie Garvaggio's girlfriend Gloria got a bit part in the film version of *Stage Door Canteen.* Two weeks later she was on a plane to Hollywood, where she managed to sign with Louis B. Mayer himself. Zelda moved into Harriet Rosenfeld's old room at the Shaw House and started volunteering her time for the American Theater Wing's other war projects, the ones that didn't require that she spend her time in the company of soldiers. George went back overseas and they wrote each other every day.

Once *Goin' South* closed, I never heard about Olive and Izzie again. For a while I combed the wedding announcements looking for their names, but either they were smart enough not to advertise what they were doing or they decided to find another way to keep themselves in the lifestyles to which they'd become accustomed.

As for me, there was only one thing left to do: write another letter.

Dear Harriet,

I hope all is going well for you in the USO camp shows. I've been thinking a lot about the conversation we had before you left and I think you're right: I should be doing more to help out with the war. You'd mentioned that if I was ever interested in working for the USO you might be able to help me. Jayne and I would love to support our men abroad by joining the ranks of one of the touring shows. We're particularly interested in going to the South Pacific. . . .

—Rosie Winter